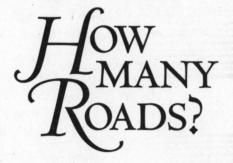

# HOW MANY ROADS?

HEARTS
OF THE
CHILDREN

VOL. 3

# HOW MANY ROADS?

A NOVEL BY

## DEAN HUGHES

DESERET
BOOK

SALT LAKE CITY, UTAH

First printing in hardbound 2003.
First printing in paperbound 2009.

---

**Library of Congress Cataloging-in-Publication Data**

Hughes, Dean, 1943–
  How many roads? / Dean Hughes.
    p.    cm. — (Hearts of the children, v. 3)
  ISBN-10 1-59038-172-6 (hardbound)
  ISBN-13 978-1-59038-172-4 (hardbound)
  ISBN-13 978-1-60641-174-2 (paperbound)
  1. Mormon families—Fiction.  2. Salt Lake City (Utah)—Fiction.   I. Title
II. Series: Hughes, Dean, 1943– . Hearts of the children ; v. 3.
  PS3558.U36H68 2003
  813'.54—dc21                          2003010673

---

Printed in the United States of America
R. R. Donnelley and Sons, Crawfordsville, IN

10  9  8  7  6  5  4  3  2  1

*For Ernestine Adams*
*and in memory of L. Jerold Adams—*
*my friends, "Jerry and Tina"*

## D. Alexander and Beatrice (Bea) Thomas Family
## (1968)

Alexander (Alex) [b. 1916] [m. Anna Stoltz, 1944]
    Eugene (Gene) [b. 1945] [m. Emily Osborne, 1968]
    Joseph (Joey) [b. 1947]
    Sharon [b. 1949]
    Kurt [b. 1951]
    Kenneth (Kenny) [b. 1956]
    Pamela (Pammy) [b. 1958]

Barbara (Bobbi) [b. 1919] [m. Richard Hammond, 1946]
    Diane [b. 1948]
    Margaret (Maggie) [b. 1953]
    Richard, Jr. (Ricky) [b. 1963]

Walter (Wally) [b. 1921] [m. Lorraine Gardner, 1946]
    Kathleen (Kathy) [b. 1946]
    Wayne [b. 1948]
    Douglas [b. 1951]
    Glenda [b. 1955]
    Shauna [b. 1959]

Eugene (Gene) [1925–1944]

LaRue [b. 1929]

Beverly [b. 1931] [m. Roger Larsen, 1953]
    Victoria (Vickie) [b. 1954]
    Julia [b. 1955]
    Alexander (Zan) [b. 1957]
    Suzanne [b. 1959]
    Beatrice [b. 1966]

# CHAPTER 1

Kathy Thomas had planned to sleep in late. She had finished spring semester of her junior year at Smith College and then had stayed with her Aunt LaRue a couple of extra weeks while she worked with a professor on a research project. She was getting paid for the work, but staying was mostly her way of putting off what she knew she had to do: spend most of the summer working for her father at his car dealership. She needed to rebuild her bank account, which was currently down to something like fifteen dollars. At the end of the research project, however, she had purposefully scheduled a couple of "free days" so she could relax a little before she started her bus and airplane trip home to Utah. It was Wednesday, June 5, 1968. Tomorrow she would pack, and Friday she would fly home, but this day was set aside for doing nothing at all.

When Kathy first heard a knocking sound, she told herself that LaRue must be puttering with something out in the kitchen. Kathy had stayed up late the night before; surely LaRue wouldn't be bothering her already. But then she heard LaRue's voice: "Kathy, I'm sorry to wake you, but there's something I have to tell you." Kathy didn't respond; she was still half awake and not thinking straight. "Kathy, it's important."

Kathy sat up, wondering what time it was. She stood and walked to the door, then pulled it open. LaRue was wearing an old robe, and her hair was smashed on one side, but she didn't look tired. She looked upset. "What's the matter?"

"It's bad, Kathy. I'm sorry to tell you."

Kathy thought of her family. "What's happened? Who is it?"

LaRue folded her arms and looked down. She spoke quietly.

"Last night, after Bobby Kennedy won the election in California, someone shot him. He's not dead yet, but people are saying that he's not going to live."

Kathy waited for a reaction inside herself. This didn't seem possible. How could it happen again? "But we saw him waving and smiling."

"It must have been right after we turned the TV off. He was leaving the hall after his victory speech—going out through the kitchen—and some guy stepped up behind him and shot him in the head."

Kathy wasn't sure why she wasn't crying yet. "We should have expected it," she finally said, the words surprising even her. "They're killing everyone."

"Who is?"

"I don't know." The only thing Kathy understood was that all her heroes were ending up dead. Her friend Lester had come over the night before, and he, Kathy, and LaRue had watched the returns. Kathy and LaRue had been hoping for Gene McCarthy to win. They had talked of campaigning for him the way so many college students had done in New Hampshire that spring, but Lester had been pulling for Kennedy, and as his victory had become increasingly clear, Kathy had admitted that he did have a better chance of winning in November. Besides, he had finally begun to speak out against the war. She had promised Lester that she would think about getting involved in his campaign.

So now what?

"The man who shot him was just a young guy. No one knows why he did it."

Kathy hadn't really felt drawn to Bobby, not the way she had to his brother, or Reverend King, but an overwhelming sadness was hitting her. Another assassination. Another Kennedy. She thought of Ethel, Bobby's wife, and all his children. She thought of Rose, his mother, who had now lost three sons. How could the family go through this one more time?

How could the nation? Finally, tears blurred Kathy's vision. "I need to call Lester," she said.

"He probably knows by now."

"Maybe. But I need to talk to him. He's not going to handle this well."

Kathy and Lester had been through so much together. They had held out against the violence their SDS friends were espousing, and finally they had given up on the organization altogether. Since then, they had tried to find an answer—some peaceful way to continue their resistance to the war. The night before, in their excitement over the momentum that seemed to be building for Kennedy, they had told each other that they might be ready to work "through the system," as Kathy's father and grandfather always told her she should do. But Lester would be destroyed by this. He had finally begun to rise from his own ashes after his beloved Martin Luther King had been killed, and who was there for him to believe in now? How could he keep advocating against violence with his own black people when everyone who fought for civil rights seemed to die—violently?

Kathy did call, but Lester had known the night before. He had decided to let her sleep even though he hadn't slept much himself. What worried Kathy most was that Lester wasn't crying, wasn't cursing, wasn't speaking much. "I'll come over," he finally said.

"When?"

"I don't know. I'll see if I can get a ride. Or maybe I'll take a bus."

"Are you okay?"

"No."

"We'll talk, okay?"

"There's nothing to say."

"It doesn't seem like it now, but there will be."

Still, Kathy couldn't find anything to tell herself, and when Lester arrived, almost three hours later, she could only think to say, "Let's walk over to Paradise Pond. We can sit under the trees over there."

So they walked across campus, still saying next to nothing. There were not many people on campus now, mostly just professors, but Kathy saw the gloom in the eyes of everyone who passed by. Bobby Kennedy was loved in this part of the country. "What's wrong with us?" Kathy heard a young woman, a professor, ask another woman. And that did seem to be the right question.

Kathy led Lester to a spot under a giant silver maple, and then she sat down on the grass, but he remained standing, and he looked down the hill toward the pond, where two girls were on the water, sitting in a boat but not rowing. Lester finally said, quietly, "Back in the beginning, the Kennedys didn't care that much about civil rights. Blacks were just a voting block they wanted. But Bobby grew. I believed him this year. I heard that talk he gave on the night Reverend King died. I really think he wanted to do some things."

"But look at the way he waited to jump into the campaign," Kathy said. "He let McCarthy take on Johnson, and then he stepped in and tried to take McCarthy's place." It was not what she felt like saying this morning, but she wanted to remind Lester not to exaggerate the man's greatness. That only made acceptance harder.

"I know. They're all politicians. Still . . ." Lester finally sat down. And then he lay back on the grass. He didn't bother to finish his sentence.

"Don't get me wrong," Kathy said. "I think he meant what he said about the war. And I think he would have followed up on some of the things Johnson did for civil rights. But McCarthy is a good man too. He stands for the same things."

Lester was breathing slowly and deeply, as though relaxation was something he had to work at. He was wearing a white shirt—a dress shirt—with the collar open. He was the only young man Kathy knew who still wore white shirts and ties—except, of course, for Mormon missionaries. He was thin, and he looked especially frail this morning, like a little boy. It was a humid day, getting warm. Kathy could see beads of sweat on his forehead and a misty layer of moisture on his upper lip.

"My father came home from World War II, wounded," Lester said. "He fought with an all-black company in Europe. He got himself shot up, but he thought everything would be different once blacks had shown their loyalty that way—you know, fighting for the same cause along with white people. It broke his heart when he got back to Georgia and found out he was still a 'nigger' in his own country, no matter what he'd done."

Kathy put her hand on Lester's shoulder.

"For a long time after the war, he gave up. He went to work every day—did janitor work in a big office building in Atlanta. He'd come home at the end of the day, read the paper, listen to the news on television, but never say much about it. Then Martin Luther King came along, and my father started to talk. He told me, 'Somethin' gonna happen now. Some heads gonna get broke. Negro heads. But it's time we take a stand.' That's what I've been trying to do ever since. But I had no idea how hard the fight was going to be."

"Lester, it was just some boy who shot Bobby Kennedy—probably for some crazy reason he only understands himself. It had nothing to do with *your* fight."

"Maybe so. But it doesn't matter. The ones who try to change things are always the ones who get shot. This morning, for the first time ever, I said to myself, maybe the Black Panthers are right. Maybe it's time to get me a gun."

"You don't believe that, Lester. I know you don't."

"Kathy, I just want a chance." Lester sat up. "I don't want to wait and keep my mouth shut the way my father had to do. But look what's happening. My people are burning up cities because they don't know what else to do. And your people are screaming for law and order—and all that means is 'stop those niggers before they take our jobs.' Everyone is just looking out for himself and his own kind."

Kathy took hold of Lester's hand. The two were sitting next to each other, both looking out toward the pond and the little island in the center. The girls on the pond were rowing past the island now, but slowly, as though they had no real intention of getting anywhere. "There aren't any *kinds*, Lester. Not to God. We're all his children."

"That's what Reverend King said, and white men killed him."

"Just one man killed him. One crazy man."

"It wasn't just one man, Kathy. You know that. It was everyone who cheered when they heard the news. And everyone who didn't dare cheer but said to himself, 'It's just as well. That man was stirring up too much trouble.' You know as well as I do, a whole lot of white people said that to themselves."

"Sure they did. But it won't do you any good to buy a gun. They're saying that the guy who shot Bobby is a Palestinian. Are you going to go shoot all Palestinians? A lot more people are going to get killed if we don't find a way to calm down and start *talking* to each other."

Lester laughed, surprising Kathy. "I've heard you *talk*, plenty," he said. "I just don't remember you ever being calm."

"I know. I've got to stop acting like I know everything. A lot of people need to do that."

"Are you going to be *calm* about women's rights? Are you going to *talk* to men, tell them they need to be just *a little more fair*—and then be patient while they make up their minds?"

Lester had her now, and Kathy knew it. All this last year, as she had listened to what Gloria Steinem and other women in the new National Organization for Women were saying, her temperature had been rising. Too many women were doing the same jobs as men and getting paid a fraction of a man's salary. Women who wanted to use their education and develop a career were held back at every turn. Men spoke of "lady lawyers" or "lady pilots," as though the very idea was a joke. Things hadn't changed much since the days when her high school counselor had told Kathy that she could only be a nurse, a teacher, or a secretary.

Kathy let go of Lester's hand. "Lester," she said, "black men have come farther, faster than women have. You've got Edward Brooke in the Senate now, Thurgood Marshall on the Supreme Court, and there are black mayors in some of the big cities. You see the injustice in racial prejudice, but you don't care about sexism."

"Is that what it's called now?"

"Yes. That's what it's called." Kathy was half expecting to hear the usual male response—that the women's liberation movement was silly, that women were much better off than men.

But Lester didn't say that. What he did say surprised her. "I'm just giving you a hard time, Kathy. I've been slow coming around to it, but I've been listening and agreeing more all the time with the things women are saying. Men are always the ones who think killing is such a great idea. Maybe women ought to have more control of the world. They might do a better job."

"I'd like to think so. But look down there." She nodded toward a little group of young women standing close to the pond. They looked like high school girls, maybe on campus for some sort of summer program. "They keep looking up this way. And you know very well what they're wondering about: why some white girl is sitting so close to a 'colored boy.' They're liberals—little future Smith girls—but they can't resist staring at us."

"Hey, I noticed them long before you did," Lester said. "But they're just staring. In Georgia, if the wrong white man saw me holding your hand, I could be a dead man. People think that's over with, but it's not."

Kathy took his hand again, pulled it back toward her. "It's good for them to see, Lester. We're friends. Today, there's nothing better than to show that."

"Maybe so. But you know what? I'll never know a time in my life when whites and blacks can just forget what color they are and be *people* together."

"I know. And I'm sure change for women is going to be just as slow."

"We're supposed to be *calm* about that?"

"I'm just saying we have to stop killing each other. But your father was right. We do have to take a stand."

"How? I don't see anything working right now."

Kathy didn't have an answer, and the near future didn't look good. She doubted that McCarthy would be able to win the nomination. Her choice would probably come down to Hubert Humphrey or Richard Nixon. George Wallace was running a renegade third-party campaign and didn't have a chance to win, but his political stance—all redneck stuff as far as Kathy was concerned—was making significant inroads, especially among working-class whites who were frightened by the Black Power movement and upset about crime and drugs and all the unrest on college campuses. Wallace could actually win in some states and change the outcome of the election. But Kathy saw no answer, however the election came out. Humphrey was still talking Johnson's line about winning the war, and she never trusted anything Nixon said.

Kathy looked up to see a man walking along the sidewalk about to pass behind her. Then she realized who it was. "Professor Jennings," she said.

"Oh, hi." He stopped. And then, as though her name had finally come back to him and he was pleased to be able to say it, he announced, "Kathy Thomas."

"Yes." Kathy had taken a sociology class from Jennings the previous fall semester. He was a young man, vaguely attractive, but more for what he thought and said than for anything in his appearance. He was slightly shorter than Kathy but strongly built. His hair was fine and wild and long, down over his collar.

"It's a bad morning, isn't it?" he said. He stepped closer and sat down next to Kathy, but he looked past her at Lester. "A bad day for blacks, I'm afraid."

It was an unexpected thing for him to say. Most people didn't refer to race so easily. "Yes, it is," Lester said.

"If I were you I'd get behind Gene McCarthy. I think he was our best bet even before this happened."

Lester shook his head. "All he talks about is the war. He doesn't say that much about civil rights."

"I disagree with that. He doesn't think in terms of voting blocs, so he doesn't play up to any one group all that much. But that's because he's not a politician—not to the degree most of these guys are. His heart is in the right place on almost every issue—including minority rights."

There was something in Jennings's voice, his confidence, that Kathy liked. "Do you think he has any chance at all?"

"He could have a chance if all the students would stop throwing tantrums, buy themselves a necktie, and go knock on doors all over the country. That's what we need—a real movement to get him elected."

"Are you going to do it?" Kathy asked.

"Yes. I'm getting my hair cut short. In fact, I'm doing it today. And I'm going to work for him all summer. I know some of his people, and they're going to use me on his administrative staff. If he gets nominated, I'm taking fall semester off so I can stay with the campaign."

"What's all this? I remember you talking in class about your days at Columbia. Weren't you one of the campus activists?"

"I was. And I don't regret any of that. But you can't change this nation that way. Finally, you've got to come back to the system. I feel sick this morning about Bobby, but he wasn't my man. 'Clean Gene' is the purest thing to come out of Washington in a long time. You two need to think about working for him. I could put you in touch with the right people. Anyone who wants the war to stop ought to get behind him."

The words rang true to Kathy. She glanced at Lester. "I don't think so," he said.

Kathy nudged him. "Come on. Think about it. You'd be a lousy Black Panther. You look too much like a Sunday School boy."

"I'll get me a *big* gun," he said, but he was smiling.

"Look," Professor Jennings said, "I know McCarthy is a hard sell for a lot of people, and he may not be able to get the old party guys on his side. But the more the other candidates see that this nation wants to end the war, the more they all have to move in that direction."

Lester leaned forward and looked around Kathy. "You must not live in the same country I live in. The man who's picking up momentum is George Wallace. He's the one who's going to pull the other candidates his way. That man loves the war, and he *hates* me."

"But you know what? America is better than that. Wallace will pick up some votes, but the majority of people know he's appealing to their worst impulses. When people get to know McCarthy, they not only like him, they feel good about themselves. In the end, that could carry the day."

Kathy hadn't really looked her professor in the eye up until now. She was self-conscious about his sitting on the grass next to her, talking like a friend. She had always found him exciting, and she loved the way his voice would get raspy when he talked about things he cared about. She heard that sound now, and she looked to see how ardent his green eyes were. She felt better about herself just for liking what he had said. "I think I might be interested," she told him.

He smiled and patted her shoulder. "All right. Great. Are you staying here all summer, or are you going back to Utah at some point?"

Kathy was surprised. How did he know she was from Utah, or how had he remembered? Had he really paid that much attention to her? "I'm going home Friday," she said. "But maybe I could put some time into the campaign somewhere. I'm not sure."

"You've got to do it. Come by my office before you leave. Drop by this afternoon if you have a minute. I'll give you some material, and I'll give you an address where you can get in touch with the campaign management."

"Okay. I need to . . . you know . . . talk to my parents, and . . ."

"Oh, sure. I understand. But Kathy, this is important. You're the kind of person the campaign needs. You know the issues, but you've grown beyond that SDS hate-everything attitude." He looked at Lester again. "And what was your name?"

"Lester Franklin."

"What about you, Lester? We need black people on board. Where are you from?"

"Georgia."

"You could work down there this summer. Julian Bond is mounting a movement for an alternative delegation to be seated at the Democratic convention. He's the most exciting black leader since King. You need to get to know him."

"I've met him."

"Well, then, stop licking your wounds. This fight isn't over."

"McCarthy has no chance in the south," Lester said. "The Republicans will get the votes that don't go to Wallace."

Kathy thought that was true, but she liked what she saw. Lester was coming back to life.

"Of course," Professor Jennings said. "But if you can get the Democrats to seat at least some of your people at the convention, you could help Gene get nominated. Then, after the convention, you could work up here in a state where McCarthy can win."

Lester nodded, but he didn't commit himself. And Kathy knew he was thinking what she was: that this was all pipe dreams. McCarthy had no real chance. Still, she had always fought for causes that seemed impossible, and this one felt good to her. She looked at Professor Jennings's eyes again, how intense they were. If she was going to take a stand, he was the kind of person she wanted to work with.

∼⁀∽

Kathy did stop by Professor Jennings's office that afternoon. He was busy reading papers, but he was also eating a Fudgsicle and listening to "Mrs. Robinson" on the radio. He had been to the barber. He looked surprisingly different with the hair off his neck, but he looked good. Kathy had never gotten over her preference for guys who appeared "clean cut."

"Hey, do you want a Fudgsicle?" he asked. "I have my own refrigerator." He pointed to a white enamel box, about three feet high, in the corner of his office. Books were stacked on top of it.

"No thanks."

He grinned and asked, "Do you like Simon and Garfunkel?" Then he reached over and turned his radio down to about half the volume it had been set on.

"Sure." Kathy was a little surprised that he seemed in such a good mood on a day when most people were depressed. But she rather liked his playfulness. She knew that she was way too serious herself.

He found the materials he wanted to give her, but he had to search through a lot of papers on his desk. He handed the sheets to her, but he said, "Sit down. You don't need to run off so fast, do you?"

"No. I just don't want to take your time. You've probably got a lot of things to do."

"I do," he said. "But I need a good excuse not to do them. Tell me a little about yourself. I always thought you were the smartest student in my class. There were some others who could write a good test, but you really *got* what I was talking about."

Kathy sat on a straight-backed chair that was crowded rather close to his desk in the little office. He was sitting in a swivel chair. He leaned back and clasped his hands behind his head. "That was the first semester

I started to study seriously," Kathy said. "Before that, I spent so much time working for SDS that I let my schoolwork slide."

"Hey, that's what college is for. It's a time to find out who you are. That's why I don't regret my radical years at Columbia. But how did you end up in SDS, coming out of Utah?"

"I'm not really sure. My Aunt LaRue—you know, LaRue Thomas, the professor—she took me down to Mississippi during Freedom Summer. That's where I got my first taste of activism."

"I know LaRue fairly well. You're both Mormons, aren't you?"

Kathy nodded but then glanced away from his gaze. She didn't tell him that she hadn't been going to church lately. He had an amazingly messy office, with too many books for his shelves. She wondered how that was possible. This was only his second year of teaching.

"I was religious, growing up," he said. "My parents took me to church almost every Sunday. I used to go to youth retreat in the summers—all that stuff. I don't regret any of that either, but I don't believe in God now. I don't think about heaven; I think about earth. I've vowed that I'll never spend more than a subsistence amount on myself. The rest of what I make will go to people who need help. The same with my time. I'd love to curl up with my books and just give my life over to *thinking*. But that's not right either. I want to *act*."

"That's how I feel, too, Professor Jennings. I—"

"Don't call me that. It makes me feel like an old man. Just call me Gary."

"I don't think I could." Kathy laughed.

"Why not?"

"I don't know." She looked at him straight on again, saw that he was smiling rather more slyly than she would expect. Was he flirting with her?

"You're a professor. That's what I've always called you."

"So how old do you think I am?"

"I have no idea." But that wasn't true. She thought he must be in his early thirties.

"I'm twenty-nine. I won't be over the hill until next January."

Kathy nodded and smiled, but she had no idea what to say.

"So you're, what? Twenty-one?"

"Yes."

"Well . . . we're both adults."

Kathy ducked her head for a moment, and then, on impulse, she stood up. "I guess I'd better—"

"Hey, I was just kidding. I didn't mean anything by that."

"That's okay." But she knew how red her face had to be. Her ears were hot, her throat.

"No, really." He stood up. "I wasn't coming on to you. I just meant that we're both in our twenties—barely. On either end of the decade. It came out wrong."

"It's okay. Honest. I blush really easy."

"I'll remember that. And I'll always be *proper* from now on. You can even call me Professor Jennings. I won't complain."

Kathy thanked him again for his time, felt her face burn all over again—because it seemed such a stupid thing to say—and then stepped out the door. As she did, Professor Jennings turned the radio back up. Kathy heard the song "Young Girl." She heard him laugh. Was he making fun of her? She couldn't believe how stupid she had acted.

❧

Kathy waited until after eight o'clock to phone her parents that night—six o'clock in Utah. She wanted to call during the time when her dad was home from work but before he went off to a stake presidency meeting or some such thing.

Glenda answered the telephone. "Hey, thanks for the birthday present," she told Kathy. "I didn't care that it was late. That just gave me another birthday." Glenda had turned thirteen in May. Before Kathy could ask to speak to Dad, Glenda said, "Hey, Douglas wants to talk to you, but don't talk too long, okay? My friend is going to call me any minute now. We've got Mutual tonight, and we have to . . . well, anyway, I need to talk to her. Are you upset about Robert Kennedy?"

Kathy took a breath, since Glenda hadn't. "Yes. I am."

"Me too. It seems like every Kennedy gets shot. Jackie's going to feel so bad. Bobby always took care of her after Jack died. That's what they said on the news just now."

"I've heard that," Kathy said. "Could I talk to Dad after I talk to Douglas?"

"If he's here. I'll see. I'm not sure if he got home yet."

Kathy was about to respond when she heard Douglas. "Kathy, when are you coming home?"

"In two days. Not tomorrow, but the day after that."

"Good. I'm coming to the airplane with Mom."

"That's great, Douglas. I can't wait to see you. I'm going to give you lots of hugs and kisses."

"Nuh-uh. I'm too big."

"No way. I'm going to put smackers all over you. With lipstick."

"You'd better not," he said, but he was laughing. Douglas was seventeen now, but he would always be a little boy.

"Is Dad there, Douglas?"

"Yes. He's telling me to give him the phone."

"Do it then, okay? And I'll see you in just *two* days, and then we'll talk a lot."

"Why don't you come in *one* day?"

"I can't. I have a ticket for the airplane. It's too late to change it."

"Okay."

And then Kathy heard her father. "Hi, honey," he said. "How are you doing? It's been a tough day, hasn't it?"

Kathy didn't know whether it had really been tough for him. Maybe it had been. "I just can't believe this has happened again," she said. "Have you heard anything new? Do you think he has any chance at all to live?"

"They say he's breathing, but that's all. They operated and took the bullet out of his brain, but he's got massive damage. He's not going to make it." He hesitated and then added, "I respected Bobby more than I did his brother. I think he had higher principles."

Kathy wasn't sure, but she knew her dad was trying to say the right thing—so they wouldn't start off the summer on a bad foot—and she did appreciate that. "Dad, I know I told you I wanted to stay home and work all summer, but this thing with Bobby has gotten me thinking about something else today."

There was only silence on the line.

"I think you know I've given up on SDS, but I'm still against the war." She had thought about this little preamble. She knew that nothing pleased her dad more than to hear that she was no longer active with the Students for a Democratic Society. "If you want to talk about high principles, I just don't think there's a better person running for president than Gene McCarthy. I was thinking today, I might want to spend part of the summer campaigning for him. I know it costs you a lot to have me back here and everything, but I—"

"Kathy, I think that's a great idea."

"Do you really?"

"I do. And I'll tell you why. I'm no fan of McCarthy's. You can guess what I think of anyone as liberal as he is. But he's trying to do something through the system. He's running for president, and he's telling people exactly what he believes. I think he's going to lose. I even hope he loses, but honey, I like the idea that you would get out there and talk to regular people, hear what they have to say, and try to sell your candidate. It's one thing to get up before an SDS rally and say what everyone there already believes, but you're going to learn a whole lot when you have to make your case to people who are trying to feed a family and make a mortgage payment."

Kathy liked the general sentiment but maybe not the little speech. Still, she was learning better these days what to say to him. "That's how I feel too, Dad. I *do* want to hear what people have to say—you know, not just about the war, but everything."

"You may be a Republican before the summer is over."

Kathy laughed. "Dad, I'm not even a Democrat. I don't believe in most of these guys. But I do believe in McCarthy."

"You are coming home for a while, aren't you?"

"Oh, sure. I just wanted to call McCarthy's campaign office and get an application, but I didn't want to do it if you felt I was backing out on you, after promising to work in your office."

"Well, that's one thing you're not very good at. Your typing stinks, and you argue with all the other secretaries. So if you take off part of the summer, that may not be all bad."

He was laughing, and Kathy did too, but she said, quite seriously, "I'm not doing that so much anymore, Dad. Really. I don't want to argue with people."

Wally laughed, softly. "You never have *wanted* to, Kath. You just can't help yourself. I was sort of worried that you might organize the secretaries and stage a strike."

"I should. You don't pay them enough."

"Oh, oh. Here we go again."

"No. Not really. I am getting better."

"And what about settling on a major? Have you done that? I'd really like to see you graduate next year."

The words came out before she thought much about them. "I've decided to major in sociology. I've got about half the hours I need already, so I think I can finish up next year."

"Why sociology?"

"It's not the theory I'm interested in. It's social work. I want to help people—you know, not just talk about it."

"Well, at least you've finally picked something."

Kathy was feeling a bit the same. She was also thinking that she would like to take another class or two from Professor Jennings.

∾

Robert Kennedy died during the night. On Friday, while his body lay in St. Patrick's Cathedral and thousands lined up to walk past his coffin, Kathy flew home to Utah. On Saturday morning the funeral was held. Kathy read about it the next morning in the Sunday paper. She loved Ted Kennedy's tribute. He said that his brother was "a decent man who saw wrong and tried to right it, saw suffering and tried to heal it, saw war and tried to stop it." After the mass, his body was transported on a train to Washington. All through New Jersey, Pennsylvania, Delaware, and Maryland, people lined the railroad tracks to watch his casket, in a glass-sided railway car, pass by. He was buried that night, at Arlington Cemetery, not far from his brother.

Hans Stoltz sat down on his bunk, then decided to stretch out for a minute or two. He was so weary that he wanted to sleep, but if he dozed off now he would lose the precious hour or two of evening he looked forward to, and with the morning would come another day of hard labor. It was June now, 1968, and he had spent almost six months in a prison work camp. He no longer despaired at his routine—the rigorous workday in the uranium mine and the absence of change—but it occurred to him sometimes that he had become like an old workhorse. He merely plodded through his days and responded to instructions. The worst thing he could do was think about his future or try to imagine a day when he would be free. Far better to take his meals, do his work, get his sleep, and hang on to those few personal hours when he could read his Bible, write a letter, or occasionally receive mail that he could read and savor. His term of imprisonment was three years, but he had reason to hope that it might be cut shorter than that. Still, when he thought of the time that stretched ahead, it all seemed never-ending. So he tried to find small pleasures in his life and to view his existence in the perspective of eternity. He told himself that mortality was a time to learn, and this prison experience had its worth.

He was drifting toward sleep in spite of his vow not to do that, and then he heard heavy-booted footsteps. He didn't open his eyes until the sound stopped at his bunk. He saw Spitzmann, a brutal guard, standing near Hans's feet and looking down on him. "Be ready in the morning," Spitzmann said. "Eight o'clock. You're being moved."

"Where?" Hans asked.

"I don't know. Just be ready."

"Ready? What do I have to do to be ready?"

"Wait, that's all. Wear your prison clothes. Someone will transport you. But don't go to the mine in the morning."

"Am I going to another work camp?"

"I told you, I don't know." Spitzmann tromped on through the barracks.

Hans glanced around to see that others were looking at him. He noticed no sign of envy, or for that matter, dread. Everyone was as tired as he was. But Hans had to wonder: would he be going someplace better, worse? He found himself struggling not to get excited. Eight o'clock seemed the middle of the day. Would he be allowed to sleep past five? And would there be no work at all tomorrow? Even if the work was terrible, wherever he was going, he would have a day off, a ride in a car perhaps, outside where he could see. It all sounded like a holiday.

But Hans knew better than to build up hope. It was wiser to accept what came, enjoy the bit of change he might experience for a few hours, and expect nothing very good. Some of the men had spoken of worse jobs. One man had worked in a chemical plant where he had breathed fumes that had burned his eyes and lungs. Others had worked on road construction crews where the labor was perhaps no worse than mining but the weather conditions had been fierce. Most of the men thought the uranium mine was a good assignment.

Still, Hans could hardly contain his curiosity. He got up and walked to the far end of the barracks, where Gustav slept. Gustav was a hardcore dissident, and not someone Hans normally wanted the guards to see him with, but tonight that was probably nothing to worry about. He found Gustav lying on his bunk. He was the oldest of the prisoners, a weathered man with deep wrinkles in his gray skin, and a stubble of white beard. Hans's first thought was not to disturb him. But Gustav's eyes opened into yellow slits. "What is it, Stoltz?" he asked.

"Spitzmann says they're moving me in the morning. Where do you think they'll take me?"

Gustav considered for a moment, but then he said, "There's no telling. I've given up predicting what these people will do."

"Is this the best work camp? Will I go to something worse?"

"It could happen. There are worse. We eat better here than in most places." Gustav rolled to one side, then lowered his feet to the floor and sat up. He rested his elbows on his knees and didn't look at Hans.

Hans wondered now why he had asked. If he worried about all this, maybe he would have a restless night and lose the one sure benefit he was receiving—a longer night to sleep.

"How long were you interrogated before you came here?" Gustav asked.

"I was at *Hohenschönhausen* for almost six weeks. But after the first couple of weeks, they didn't call me in much. They just left me in my cell."

"Did you tell them what they wanted to hear?"

"No. They wanted to know who else was involved in the escape. But I didn't know. I only knew my friend's name—the one who was killed. I saw another man, but he was killed too, so there was nothing I could give them."

"I'm sure they didn't believe that. They never do. My guess is, they wanted to break your spirit a little, let you find out how long three years is. It would fit their pattern to call you back to *Hohenschönhausen* now and question you again."

"I hated that place."

"The food is bad. But it's the best of the prisons. I've seen much worse."

"There's nothing to do. They keep you secluded."

"Yes. Of course. The work camps are always best for the young men. But this place is wearing me out. I would welcome some interrogation, some rest, but they don't question me now. What they hope, I'm certain, is that the work will kill me. I suppose they'll get their wish before too much longer."

"You're too tough for that," Hans said, but he didn't believe it. He saw how depleted Gustav was. "So you think that's where I'm probably going?"

Gustav looked up at Hans. "I don't know. I only know *Stasi* agents never give up. It's like a madness with them. If they think you know *anything* that you haven't told them, they'll keep working on you until they get it."

"But there's nothing I can tell them."

"It doesn't matter. They'll work on you until you say *something*, even if it's information they already have."

"Will they torture me?"

Gustav looked back at the floor, down toward his bare feet. Hans could see the thin, brittle bones, gnarled toes. "No. They usually don't beat up on people now. They think of themselves as good socialists—practitioners, not monsters. They'll warn you about terrible consequences for not talking. They'll give you special favors, then take them away, or they'll look for ways to gain your confidence. But just remember, they don't care about you. Keep your balance. Don't let them scare you. And give them nothing. You'll be tempted to feed them some bit of information in hopes they'll be satisfied. But they're like sharks. A bit of blood in the water only gets them excited. In the end, it's not the information they care about. It's your compliance. What they want you to do is submit to them so you'll leave the prison system without your self-respect—ready to serve the state, no questions asked."

Hans didn't want to go through all that. He didn't want to be questioned, but even more, he didn't want to go back to a cell. "But maybe I'm going to another work camp," he said.

"Yes. Of course. That may be what it is."

"Thanks, Gustav. You've helped me get by so far."

Gustav stood up and shook Hans's hand. "You're a nice boy," he said. "Just do your best to survive all this—and salvage some sort of life."

"Will they let me do that?"

"Not the way you might like. They'll keep an eye on you always. You were 'hostile to the state,' and in their eyes, you always will be. But in time, if you cause them no trouble, they might give you a little more room to live. They'll keep you from getting more education and from advancing in your trade, but they might eventually leave you alone."

Hans was sorry he had asked. However much he told himself not to expect much from his life, he sometimes hoped that in time things might change.

Hans walked back to his bunk and sat down again, and he read in his Bible. He had been studying Israel's ancient kings: Saul and David and Solomon. They were wise men, good men, and yet they had all made mistakes. He told himself that successful men—ones with status and riches—were often the ones who grew proud. They did things that would limit their chances to grow in the next life. It was consoling to tell himself that his mistakes had come early in life, and they had brought him low, but if he could learn from them, and overcome the pride he had sometimes been guilty of, this prison life might be his greatest blessing.

He had hoped for a long night's sleep, but his curiosity kept him awake longer than he expected, and in the morning he awakened early. He lay in bed after the others were up and moving, willed himself to enjoy this luxury, but he was much too nervous. So he finally dressed in his prison clothes, packed a little satchel with his few belongings, and waited. Eight o'clock came and went, and by then Hans was pacing, actually longing to be with the other men. The uncertainty was worse than labor. It was almost 9:30 when a guard walked into the barracks and said, "Someone is here for you. Come with me." And then, just as Hans reached the door, the guard handed him two envelopes. "These came for you," he said.

Hans took the letters, read the return addresses. One was from his mother, the other from Elli. He wished the letters had come sooner, not on this day of worry, but he tucked them into his pants pocket and followed the guard outside. An old Barkass van—a kind of panel truck—was parked inside the barracks compound. A man smoking a cigarette was standing by the van. When he saw Hans, he walked to the back, stuck the cigarette in his mouth, and opened the double doors.

"Where am I going? Can you tell me?" Hans asked.

The man hesitated, inhaled, then grasped the cigarette with two fingers. "You'll find out soon enough," he said. "Step in. Get in that first container."

Hans saw a double row of boxes, but they didn't seem large enough to get into. He looked at the driver.

"Go on. Get in." The man took Hans's satchel from him.

Hans stepped into the van, then realized that he could back into the box and sit, that it was barely big enough. But as soon as he sat down, the driver shut the door on the box and locked it. It was dark inside, with only some cracks to emit a bit of light. But it was not the dark that bothered Hans. It was the closeness, the confinement. He had hoped to see the countryside.

Hans couldn't understand. Why was this necessary? What did the driver—or the *Stasi*—fear? Supposing he did manage to break out and leap from the van? Where would he go? The whole country was a prison. The *Stasi* had thousands of informants who watched for anything suspicious, and every citizen had to be registered in the town or city where he lived. No one could wander around without identification—especially in prison clothes.

Time passed. Hans supposed that there were papers to process. He had hoped to read the letters along the way, but there was not enough light for that. So he sat and waited, aware that his body would soon ache from sitting in this cramped position. He wished the van would start moving.

When the cab door finally slammed and the engine started, Hans was surprised by the noise. These Barkass vans had two-stroke engines and only three cylinders. The sound was choppy, like the putting of a boat motor. The van moved ahead, then stopped, probably at the gate, and then chugged ahead again. When Hans felt himself pressed to the left, he knew the driver was making a right turn—north. Maybe they were heading for *Hohenschönhausen*. But they could also be going to one of the factories or steel plants east of Berlin.

It was pointless to speculate. He decided to sleep, if he could, and for a time he may have actually drifted off a little, but his discomfort mounted as time passed. He thought maybe a couple of hours had gone by when he began to hear the noise of traffic outside. That might mean that he *was* in Berlin.

When the van stopped, there was another wait. Finally the back doors opened, and then the door on his little cubicle swung wide. Hans managed to unbend himself from the box and step out of the van into the light. For a few moments he couldn't see much of anything, but he recognized the big U-shaped building. It was *Hohenschönhausen*, as Gustav had predicted, and all the memories came back. It was in these cells that Hans had first realized what "alone" meant.

A neat little man in a green uniform stood at a side door in the courtyard. He nodded to the Barkass driver. Some papers passed between them, and then the guard said to Hans, "This way." He turned a switch, and bright red lights illuminated a long hallway. Hans had not understood this the first time he had been here, but he did now. The lights were a warning that a prisoner was in the hall. No two prisoners were ever allowed out of their cells at the same time. It was one of the ways to keep the men constantly segregated. Hans followed the guard down the hallway. On each side were cells with heavy metal doors, clad with wood. Hans remembered the peepholes with metal covers. About every ten minutes someone would look through the hole to see what he was doing—which, of course, was nothing at all. Even at night, almost as often, the lights came on in the cell as a guard peeked through the hole. Last time around, Hans had never gotten used to that. He had awakened over and over, all night.

The guard used a key to open cell number 30, then motioned for Hans to walk inside. The cell was not all that bad, about like his last. The walls were painted in ugly shades of brown and yellow, but the building was relatively new. There was a decent toilet in the corner, a sink, a little table, and a stool. That was all acceptable—not the real horror of this place. The vicious requirement was that every morning his bed had to be folded up against the wall, and the only place to sit was on the little stool. A prisoner could move around a little, or stand, but he could only lie down at night, from nine until five. Hans remembered the backaches, the long evenings waiting until the bell rang that signaled he could fold down his bed, place a cushion on it, and spread out his two blankets.

The guard stood in front of Hans and recited a speech he had obviously given many times. "You will receive meals three times a day, issued through the slot you see in the door. When you're finished, push the tray back through the same opening. You will not attempt to communicate with other prisoners—not by speaking, calling out, tapping, or any other means. You must not cover the peephole in any way, or stand in such a way as to block the guard's view inside your cell. You may not cover your face or hands during the night, while in bed."

On and on he went, but not once did he look Hans in the eyes. He gave the sleeping rules, rules about defacing property, about throwing items in the toilet—and lots of other things. After a time, Hans wasn't listening. The guard ended by saying that all these rules were posted on the door and Hans should review them often.

"Do you have any questions?" the guard asked finally, with surprising politeness.

"I haven't eaten today. Will I receive a meal before evening?"

"Our midday meal has been served. An evening meal will be delivered at six o'clock," he said, almost as though he were conveying good news. But Hans remembered the thin soup served at noon, and the dinner consisting of four slices of black bread, spread with lard, or on good days, margarine, and always coffee to drink. It was just as well to be plenty hungry when he had to eat his bread, which he would have to wash down with the foul-tasting water from the sink, since he wouldn't drink the coffee.

When the guard left, Hans stood and looked about. At one end of the room was a window, but the glass was muted, so he couldn't see out, and the shadow of bars shone through. Still, he had decent light in the day, for reading, and he had his Bible. It was in the evening, especially in the winter, when reading would be difficult. There was a lightbulb in the room, but it could be turned on only from outside the cell, and that was done only when the guards wanted to look inside. Still, this time of year he would be able to read for many hours. That would be his salvation. And he would be allowed about a quarter of an hour each day for "free time"—the chance to go outside, into a little enclosed area in the courtyard, and exercise in the open air. He could also walk back and forth as long as he didn't draw attention to himself. That would help his back some, and it would give him more exercise. But he was remembering how immensely long a day could be, alone in this space. What he hoped was that he would be questioned every day until his interrogator was satisfied, and then sent back to the mine.

But it was a disheartening thought: his brightest hope was only to return to hard labor. And what he also knew was that the interrogation was not likely to end quickly, not unless he thought of something to "reveal"—and Gustav had warned him not to start inventing things. If he didn't tell them anything, would they keep him here the rest of his term? It hardly seemed possible, and yet, standing in the closeness of the cell, it was hard to imagine anything but evil ahead for him.

He felt some panic and decided he had to do something. He got his Bible and sat down at the table. He was about to start reading when he remembered the letters tucked away in his pocket. The thought of them was an immense relief: the best of pleasures in his life.

He pulled the letters from his uniform pocket and looked at the postmarks. They had been sent almost three weeks earlier. Why did the guards always do things like that? Why hold back the one thing the prisoners wanted most? Was it merely to be cruel?

He read his mother's letter first. He loved the tone of what she always said to him, but in truth, she had little that was new to tell him. Life didn't change much for her or for Papa, or even for Inga. His parents worked, and Inga went to school, and they all went to church on Sunday. She did mention that Inga, now fourteen, was planning to go to Youth Conference for the first time. Hans thought of those experiences, his times with Greta, and the memories were not easy for him. For so long he had put most of his hope for happiness in Greta, and now she was married, and he was here. But he felt his mother's warmth, and he was reminded that the world was still actually going on without him.

Hans pulled the other letter from its envelope. Both letters had been opened before. What Hans couldn't see was any sign of censoring. Most people who wrote to him seemed to have a sense of what they could and couldn't say, but sometimes whole sections of a letter would be blacked out. Elli had written:

> Dear Hans:
>
> I greet you. I'm sorry that I haven't written often lately. Since I started working, my days are full. But I should take more time to write. I know you like to receive letters.

Hans always noticed a careful neutrality in her letters, and he wondered whether that came from her concern about censors, or whether she wanted, now, not to give him the impression that she was waiting for his return. Perhaps she knew that he was not someone she should think of as a prospective husband. Maybe her parents had told her that.

Elli had recently completed her schooling and was working as a secretary in the office of a clothing store in Magdeburg. She never said so, but Hans had the feeling that it wasn't a job she found much satisfaction in. But there was usually a lightness about her style, and he loved to imagine her voice.

> All is well with my family and in our branch. Everyone sends greetings to you. We all pray for your well-being. It's my hope that your re-education will be successful and that you will someday visit us again here in Magdeburg. You may be interested to know that your friend sometimes visits us, and he also sends his greeting.

Hans understood her using the language of the government, but he wondered what friend she was speaking of. He could only think that she was referring to Rainer. Did she mean that he visited *her*, at home, or that he was showing up at church sometimes? That hardly seemed likely, and so Hans had to wonder. Was Rainer interested in Elli? He had always thought she was pretty. Maybe now that she was growing up, he was pursuing her. But didn't he still have a girlfriend back home?

Hans felt a pang of jealousy, and even more, frustration, that so many questions couldn't be answered. He had told himself over and over that he needed to forget about Elli. He couldn't think about marriage, not for many years to come. He had no right to subject a woman to the troubles he would have to face when he was finally released.

> As you know, your friend doesn't say very much. He hasn't changed. He wants you to know that.

What? Was this really about Rainer? Rainer talked more than anyone else Hans knew. And then Hans realized: she was telling him something in the only way she could. Rainer was reassuring him, through Elli, that he hadn't revealed anything to the *Stasi* agents who had surely interrogated him since Hans had been imprisoned. Hans wanted to believe that Rainer was telling the truth, but he wondered. Hans had admitted to *Stasi* agents his participation in Berndt's attempted escape, but he had done so only because the agents interrogating him already knew every detail. They had insisted that Hans would receive an easier sentence if he admitted to what he had done. What Hans had never known was whether those agents had gotten that information from Rainer. It was possible that others who had planned to escape with Berndt had been arrested, and that these people knew Hans's identity. On the other hand, the one person who knew the story for certain was Rainer, and Rainer was a committed socialist. Now Rainer was coming to church, or at least visiting Elli. Was this another act of a spy? If so, what did he have to learn from her? What Hans wanted to believe was that Rainer's declaration was honest, that he hadn't reported on Hans. At the same time, he struggled to think of Rainer and Elli together. It was hard to imagine that that was good for her. She was only seventeen. Hans hoped that Rainer wouldn't lead Elli away from the things she believed.

The rest of Elli's letter was chatter, showing that she still was young, still happy, still living in a world so foreign to Hans that he hardly knew how to think about it. He read his mother's letter one more time, and Elli's, and then he put both of them away. They hadn't been as satisfying as he had hoped, and now there was only the cell. He knew instinctively that he was starting to lose a battle with his emotions, so he positioned himself at the table where he could get the most light, and he opened his Bible. He turned to 1 Kings, but he couldn't bear to read any more about the corruption of Israel. He turned instead to Matthew. He decided that he would read the New Testament one more time, and he would try to comprehend every word.

He concentrated hard and tried to push other thoughts away, but as he read about the events that led to the birth of Christ, what came to mind was Christmas, and that brought thoughts of missing Christmas at home the year before, and of being forced to miss it again this year and perhaps the year after that. He stood up, walked the length of the cell a few times, then thought of exercising, maybe running in place, but that was against the rules. Remembering that rule—remembering that every second of his life was under someone else's control—pushed him from frustration to raw emotion. He tried not to cry, made fists of his hands and pressed them against his temples, then resorted to slamming them against his head, but tears were coming all the same. How could he do this—live in this tiny cell without one thing to look forward to?

But he got himself under control rather quickly. He knew that he had to. He knew that God was still with him, just as he had been with the Prophet Joseph in the Liberty jail, just as he had been with Joseph of old. Jail was nothing new for those who loved God. He could do this. He would be all right. He sat at the table and began again to read his Bible.

# CHAPTER 3

Gene Thomas's wedding, on June 12, 1968, was performed in the Salt Lake Temple. He and Emily Osborne held their reception outdoors at the Garden Park Ward in Gene's stake. It was the perfect spot for a summer reception, with a stream running through the gardens, a romantic little bridge, a pond—and, as it turned out, ideal weather. Everyone from the entire valley seemed to be there, with plenty of people from Bountiful as well. The guest line extended all the way around the church and on out front. That morning, after the wedding, there had been a wedding breakfast at Log Haven in Mill Creek Canyon. Kathy had gone to the luncheon—she didn't know why they called it a "breakfast"—but she had only had a chance to talk to Gene for a minute or so, and now, as she sat at a remote table, she wished that she could spend more time with him, just to find out how he was feeling about everything. And yet, she knew. He was clearly happy, and in truth, he wasn't likely to say anything very interesting. Kathy had wondered at times whether she had a best friend. Her cousin Gene was the only person she had ever been able to name to herself—and yet, the only thing they really shared was their mutual love. They had never agreed, not since they were kids, on much of anything.

Kathy had arrived at the reception rather late. Her parents had brought the other kids for the final pictures, taken just before the reception had begun, but Kathy hadn't felt like being there for that. Still, she had put on a fancy dress that she hadn't worn in years—a blue sheath that took advantage of her height and made her look, she thought, quite elegant. She had had her hair cut that week too. She was tired of so much hair, especially in the summer heat, but she also knew that bringing her hair closer to shoulder length made her look more like her cousins.

She had waited in the long reception line, seen a great many people she knew, and tried to make conversation the way people "back home" did: "Yes, I'm still going to school in the east. I hope to graduate next year, but I'm afraid I've changed my major too many times." What Kathy knew was that most of these people still believed the "domino theory," that somehow winning in Vietnam was protecting the shores of California. She was annoyed when she listened to them talk that way, and yet, she liked them—felt at home with their kindly interest in her, felt something familiar and appealing in the satisfaction they found in life. She was so weary of bickering and shouting. There was something lovely in the touch of these elderly women who patted her arm and called her "Sister Thomas," and in the greetings of cousins who loved her even though she was the strange member of the family. So she avoided all the subjects that would separate her from people and found herself pretending without exactly meaning to that she was "normal."

Kathy had finally reached Emily and Gene, hugged them and wished them well, but had had to move on, and all the wait had been for only that—those few seconds. Now she wasn't sure whether there was any reason to stay. But just as she had stepped away, Gene had called, "Stick around, Kathy. I want to talk to you. I'll sneak out of line when I get a chance."

Kathy doubted that Gene could actually do that, but she decided she'd better not leave, at least for a while. She hugged Aunt Anna and Uncle Alex and then introduced herself to the first bridesmaids—Emily's sister and two of Emily's friends. Of course, she knew Gene's sisters, her cousins Sharon and Pam. All the girls were wearing long, peach-toned dresses. Little Pammy was ten now, and certainly still a kid, but she was wearing a bit of lipstick, and her hair was wound high on her head with a pretty bow worked in. She looked cute. She told Kathy, "I'm glad you're home. I miss you when you're gone." Kathy was surprised but touched.

Kathy moved from the reception line to the buffet table, where everything was first class. She knew that Uncle Alex had taken on some of the cost of the event, since he and Anna wanted to hire a caterer to do something special, and the price was a little out of the Osborne's range. The buffet was a grand spread of delicacies: salmon in a creamy sauce, boiled shrimp with lemon and red sauce, garnished new potatoes, cold asparagus spears, several kinds of salad (none made with Jell-O), and at the end of the table a waiter slicing and serving hot roast beef. Kathy wasn't hungry, but she took some green salad, a dab of potato salad, and a few of the shrimp. And then, when she looked at the pastries and desserts, couldn't resist a rich, dark brownie, with walnuts, and one of the assortment of truffles.

She had spotted her parents across the lawn, with Douglas and the girls, but Bobbi and Richard were at the same table, with Maggie and Ricky. Kathy hadn't wanted to drag another chair to the crowded table, and she hadn't been sure she wanted to enter all the small talk that was surely going on. She was actually feeling sad, or maybe nostalgic, and her reclusive tendencies had begun to take over. So she found a distant table that was just clearing.

She had only just begun to eat when she heard a voice calling her name. She looked up to see Diane Hammond walking between the round tables, making her way through the people, dragging along Greg, her fiancé, and a middle-aged couple. She guessed that the older ones were Greg's parents. Kathy had met Greg only once—didn't really like him much—and now she wished she hadn't stayed.

"Kathy, I was hoping I would find you," Diane said. Greg stepped up next to her and smiled, and then Diane made the introductions. "We've already eaten," Diane told Kathy. "Greg and his parents have to leave, but I want to hang around for a little while. Can you give me a ride home?"

"Sure. But I wasn't going to stay too long."

"That's okay. But we need to talk. This might be our last chance for a while. Things are going crazy with our wedding coming up in . . . what?" She looked at Greg. "Eight weeks?"

"Fifty-eight days," he said. He put his arm around Diane's shoulders and pulled her close to him. He was wearing an expensive suit—wool, glen plaid—but Kathy wondered why, on such a warm evening. Without looking, Kathy already knew that he was wearing black wing tips and that he had another pair at home, in brown. And there was his father next to him, an older twin, with slick gray hair and a gleaming blue suit that had probably set him back a hundred and fifty dollars. He was smiling, looking remarkably pleased. His wife was plump and sophisticated in rose-colored organdy. She was smiling but not really looking at Kathy. Instead, she was scanning the crowd. From what Kathy had heard, the Lymans knew *everyone* in Salt Lake.

"Right after our honeymoon we're heading for Seattle to get settled in before school starts," Diane said.

"Law school. Right?" Kathy said. She looked at Greg.

"Yes," he said. "The University of Washington has a really fine school. I'm excited."

"Let's see now," Brother Lyman said, "you're Wally's daughter, aren't you?"

"Yes. Do you know my father?" She motioned to the table. "Sit down. Please."

"No, no. We have to run along. But yes, I've known your father for many years. And of course, Alex too. I call him up every now and then and tell him to stop voting with the Democrats so often. But he won't listen to me."

"I think he *does* listen, Dad," Greg said. "He knows where his support is back here in Utah."

——— 35 ———

Brother Lyman shook his head, as though to deny, but he said to Kathy, "I understand you go to college in the east."

"Yes. Smith College."

"Your father's a brave man to send you to a place like that."

Kathy wasn't going to say a word in response, but Diane apparently saw the danger. "Kathy's thinking about law school too," she said, quickly. "Have you decided about that?"

Kathy couldn't bring herself to admit to social work, not to Greg and his father, so she simply said, "No. But I've got to make up my mind soon."

"I think that's great," Greg said. "I want this little doll of mine to go back to school sooner or later. I've promised Richard and Bobbi that she will. She won't need to work, but I still think it's great to have a good education."

Kathy looked away. She wouldn't have known where to start if she had tried to tell Greg how annoying he was. But telling him to lay off the "Richard and Bobbi stuff" might have been a possibility.

"Listen, gals, you have your little gab session, and I'll run along with my parents. Di, I'll call you tonight as soon as I get home."

"Okay, sweetheart. I'll stay up, so call me even if you get in late."

Sister Lyman was saying to her husband by then, "I do need to say hello to the Fergusons. I haven't seen Edna in such a long time. And I saw the Roylances somewhere. Do you see them now?" The Lymans said good-bye and moved off toward the Ferguson table. Kathy knew one of the daughters, knew that the family was well-off.

Greg tightened his grip on Diane, and when she looked up, he kissed her, made a smacking noise on purpose, and they both laughed. Then he wiped the lipstick from his mouth. The stuff was much too pink for Kathy's taste, but Kathy rarely wore lipstick. Diane also had way too much eye makeup on: liquid eyeliner with a little line at the end—like cat eyes—and emphatic blue eye shadow. She was wearing a little paisley dress that seemed rather short for a BYU girl, and tall white "go-go" boots. To Kathy, she looked like the girls on "Laugh-In," a crazy new show on television.

"I'd better say hello to the Fergusons too," Greg said. "I love you." He kissed her again.

Greg walked away. "Isn't Emily *beautiful?*" Diane said as she sat down next to Kathy. "I love dark hair against a wedding dress. Hair like yours. I almost want to dye mine."

Emily did look pretty. Kathy liked the clean lines of her dress, but the veil was enormous, almost down to her feet in back, and that seemed excessive. Kathy always wondered how girls knew what was "in" at any given time. "Oh, come on, Diane," she said. "You'll be stunning. You'll be Greg's *little doll.*"

Diane rolled her eyes. "I *knew* you'd pick up on that."

Kathy laughed. "I just don't like the image," she said.

"I know. I agree. I've told him about twenty times not to call me that."

"You used to say that you wanted someone *dangerous*. I don't see that in Greg."

Diane laughed. "I know. He's like the Rock of Gibraltar. You can set your watch by his daily schedule."

"Is that okay?"

"It's probably what I need. He'll do everything right, and I won't ever have to worry. I can give full-time attention to my kids, and that's what I've always wanted."

Kathy couldn't think of anything she would hate more: a husband who "took care of everything." But she didn't mind that Diane felt otherwise. In fact, there was something nice about seeing things work out for her. When Kathy looked around at the other tables, so many of the people seemed to have the same things. The men looked solid in their business suits, or "dressed down" in blue blazers. The women, the kids, seemed appendages: "retainers" who followed their princes. She wasn't quite sure when she had begun to feel there was something wrong with that, but tonight she at least felt some comfort in the stability.

A little gust of wind came up, and Kathy saw women patting their hair, smoothing their collars. Someone had to grab a vase of flowers that had tottered. But the crisis passed in seconds, and everyone, if slightly more vigilant, settled back to their chatter. Kathy smiled and looked at Diane, but Diane hadn't seemed to notice. So Kathy decided to unsettle her just a bit. "What about Kent?" she asked. "What happened to him?"

"Oh, Kathy, I think I broke his heart. He was such a sweet boy, and he really did love me. It took a lot of prayer before I knew for sure that I loved Kent for being a nice boy, but that he wasn't ever going to be the family leader that Greg will be."

"So you sent Kent a 'Dear John'?"

"Don't call it that, okay? I just hate to think of it that way."

"What did he say when he wrote back?"

Kathy could hear in Diane's voice that this wasn't easy for her. "Kathy, he was so kind to me. He wrote the nicest letter. He said he would always love me. He hoped he could find someone he would love just as much, but that it was hard for him to imagine. I just cried and cried for him. I hope he does find someone really perfect. I think he will. He'll be back at the Y this fall, and there are *so many* cute girls down there—a lot cuter than me, that's for sure."

Kathy let that one go. Two couples were heading toward the table, carrying their plates. "Let's make some room for these people," she said.

"Okay. I have a couple of things I want to ask you—and not with a bunch of people around." So they slipped away from the table to some folding chairs that had been set in the shade, under a cottonwood tree. Diane took hold of Kathy's hand when they were seated, and then she said, "Kathy, are you okay? I feel so bad that Gene and I are both so happy, and you seem kind of lost."

"Being lost is not all bad," Kathy said. "How can you find yourself if you're never lost?" Kathy wasn't exactly sure what that meant, but she had some sense that Diane had never really challenged herself or asked herself questions that would force her to make any self-discoveries. Maybe she really ought to do that before getting married so young.

"I wish you had come down to BYU instead of going away to school, Kathy. I think, there, it's a lot easier to stay with things that are tried and true."

"Like what?" Kathy was suddenly irritated, and she didn't want to be. The best thing was not to express her own feelings at all.

"Well, you know. The Church. Meeting a nice guy, settling down."

"Does everyone in the family talk about my not going to church?" Kathy pulled her hand loose from Diane's grip.

"I don't know. But my mom knew. She told me."

"Just because I don't go to church doesn't mean I'm evil. On Sunday mornings I read the scriptures. I've been reading the New Testament lately. I'm trying to understand what Christ tried to teach. I think a lot of so-called religious people miss the point."

"You're better than me. I've never read the New Testament all the way through. I was supposed to in my religion class, but I didn't keep up like I should have."

Kathy didn't know how to talk to Diane, but she decided to ask a real question. "Diane, tell me what you want out of life."

"I guess I don't know what you mean."

"You ought to. I don't think it's a hard question."

Diane wouldn't look at Kathy. She took her time before she answered. "I just want love. I want Greg to love me every minute of every day. I want him to call me from his office to tell me he misses me, and I want him to bring me flowers sometimes, for no reason. And I want children I love, who also love me. I want to give them everything I can. I want them to discover what their talents are, and really develop themselves fully—

but not feel like they have to do that to satisfy me. I don't want them ever to feel like I'm disappointed in them. I just want to support them in whatever they do—as long as it's something righteous."

It was a pretty thing to say, and Kathy knew she ought to let it go. She watched a little boy who was wearing a bow tie, his white shirt hanging out on one side. He was teasing his sister, an older girl, maybe ten. He kept skipping around her, pulling at her frilly skirt. She slapped at him and told him to stop. Finally the mother stepped in. She grabbed the little guy by the arm and pulled him next to her, but she continued to talk to the people at her table.

"I wish it could be that simple, Diane," Kathy said. "But I don't think life is like that. Greg won't be falling all over you all his life, and your kids will mess up sometimes. So will you. If you go into marriage thinking it's all going to be sweet and pretty every minute, you can't help but be disappointed."

"I know what you mean. I'm realistic about that. But at least I know what I'm striving for—and I'll do everything I can to make it happen."

"Okay." Kathy decided to let it go. Diane would have to learn the hard way. Or maybe not. Maybe she would have such a simple, lovely attitude that she would create a family that was the image of her sweetness.

"What do you mean, 'okay'?"

"I don't know, Diane. You and I never have seen life the same way."

"But that's what I wanted to tell you, Kathy. Look how happy I am. I think if you would come back to the Church, maybe move back here and meet a really good man—the way I did—maybe you could find the happiness you've always been searching for. I know that you want to change the world and everything, but all that does is get you frustrated. Isn't it better to just live a good life and be the best example you can to others?"

Kathy took another look around her: so many well-dressed people, all so polite and friendly. Who could fault them? On the other side of the world bombs were dropping, but fortunately the unpleasant sounds didn't carry this far. The banquet could continue. Never mind that no one had invited the hungry to the table. Kathy had to wonder how Diane could be so certain that she was setting a good example.

And yet, Diane was right about one thing. She was happy and Kathy was not. Sometimes Kathy wanted to take Diane's advice—come back to this protected place, pull it over herself like a big comforter and never peek out. But that's not what she said. "Don't worry about me, Diane. I'll be okay. I just have to sort some things out. But I'll tell you the truth. I'm just as worried about you as you are about me."

"Me? Why?"

"Don't let him make you into a doll, Diane. I've always told you that you're more than that."

Diane still wouldn't look at Kathy. "I know," she finally said. "I know what you mean."

"Be careful, okay?"

"Okay."

For a long time after that the two merely sat next to one another, saying nothing. Kathy saw Grandma Bea across the way, watched as she laughed and chatted with friends. And that was the other side of all this. Maybe Grandma didn't think enough about the war or about the problems in the world, but she *was* an example. If everyone would live the way she did, wars wouldn't happen. Grandma did understand Christ—or more than that, her instincts told her what was right, without much philosophizing. Maybe most of these people were that way, and it was Kathy's growing cynicism that was clouding reality.

To Kathy's surprise, Gene finally did leave the line and walk to the distant chairs where she and Diane were sitting. "I saw you two back here," he said. "I've been dying to sit down and talk for a while."

"Oh, Gene, you can't," Diane said.

"I know. But I at least wanted to tell you that I'd really rather be over here." And then he looked at Kathy. "Are you okay?" he asked.

Kathy smiled. "That's what Diane wanted to know. Why is everyone worried about me?"

"Kathy, I don't have any time, but I just wanted to tell you one thing. Being in the temple today, getting married for time and all eternity, that's the most beautiful thing I've ever experienced. Don't give that up."

Kathy was losing air—like a balloon with a leak. She nodded, but she didn't say anything.

"I just think the Church is still the answer, Kathy."

Kathy wasn't going to talk about that. "Thanks for worrying about me, Gene," she said.

He waited for a moment, clearly not sure what else to say, and then he added, "This thing with Bobby Kennedy—I'm sure that was hard on you. I hope you aren't letting that get you down."

"I'm not," Kathy said. "I'm leaving on Friday to work on the McCarthy campaign."

"Are you serious? You just got home."

"I know. But I called one of the head guys in the campaign organization, and he said they could use me right now."

"And you're going to work for *McCarthy*?"

"Why does that surprise you?"

"I don't know. He's just so . . ."

"Liberal?"

"Well, sure. But he's not very realistic, is he?"

Kathy laughed. "You're the guy who spent two years trying to convince Germans to believe in Mormonism. Don't talk to me about *realism*."

Gene looked confused. He obviously saw no parallel.

Kathy stood up. "You'd better get back to your line." She wrapped her arms around Gene. "I love you," she said. "I hope you'll always be as happy as you are today."

"We need to talk," Gene said. "Will you be home at all this summer?"

"Yes. I'll be back for a while before school starts again."

"Maybe Em and I can line you up with someone, or . . . hey, whatever happened to Marshall?"

"He'll be home from his mission in the fall. I guess he'll go back to the U."

"Have you written to him?"

"No."

"You ought to look him up when he gets back. I like him."

"I do too. But . . . you know."

"Anyway, we'll get together. You'll be gone before we get back from Hawaii, but—"

"*Hawaii?*"

"Yeah. That's where we're going for our honeymoon." Gene had begun to blush. "To Maui. It's my parents' wedding gift to us."

"Well, I'll see you sometime. Enjoy yourselves."

"Okay." He was still blushing.

◈

Maui was everything Gene had hoped it would be, and so was Emily. There were moments when his happiness was almost too exquisite. It set off a fear that some required balance in the universe would demand the other end of the extreme. Emily was so pretty, so much in love with him, so unabashed in her desire to make him happy. Or at least, that's how the week had gone—until now. She had just raised up from bending over and was saying, almost harshly, over the top of their rental car, "Stay there. Don't come around here."

"I just want to—"

"Just leave me alone. I'm not finished." She ducked again, and Gene heard the sound of gagging, the splat on the ground, and then more coughing and spitting.

"Did that help?" Gene called. "Are you feeling any better?"

"No. Leave me alone." She was leaning against the car now, her head against her arms. A minute or so passed and she didn't vomit again.

"Is the nausea passing away?"

But that seemed the wrong thing to say. Suddenly she bent again, and he heard all the same sounds. This time he left her alone, but after another minute or two, she said, "I can't get back in the car—not for a while."

"But you're feeling a little better?"

"Yes. A little. But you'd better not ever tell anyone about this."

"About what?"

"That I got carsick on my honeymoon—and *puked,* right in front of you."

"Hey, it's no big deal."

"Oh, yeah? Do you want to come over here and kiss me?"

"Yes, I do. I always do."

She managed to laugh. "Well, you're not going to do it."

"Let's walk up this trail. There's supposed to be a waterfall up ahead. You can wash your mouth out." Gene had been driving Emily over the famous "Road to Hana." It was a spectacular drive, with amazing views of blue water and crashing white waves against black rock. But it was also a narrow road, with switchbacks like U-turns. Emily had told Gene that she sometimes got carsick, but he kept telling her how slowly he would drive, and how often they could stop if she started to feel queasy. But going slow hadn't helped enough, and places to stop weren't plentiful. By the time Gene had pulled into this little parking lot, near a trailhead that led to one of the many waterfalls, it had been too late.

"Let's turn around and go back after we look at the waterfall, okay? I don't want to go all the way to Hana."

"No problem. We've seen the pretty views."

"Yeah. Like the one of me hunching over, tossing up that bisque I had for lunch?" She walked around the car.

"I didn't see a thing."

"I'm not kidding, Gene. I don't want this to become one of those family stories you tell to our children and grandchildren."

"I promise. It won't happen. I'll only tell them how passionate you are, and how you wouldn't leave me alone the whole time we were here."

She punched him in the ribs. "You'd better watch that too or I might start getting lots of headaches."

He took her in his arms. She was wearing white pants and a brown shirt that looked great with her dark tan and made her blue eyes stand out. "Are you okay now?" he asked. "I feel so bad I talked you into coming over here."

"I'm doing better. Just don't kiss me."

"Not ever?"

She laughed. "Not until we get back to the hotel and I can brush my teeth and gargle with mouthwash for about an hour."

He kept his arm around her and started up the trail. No one else was around, and the path, which worked its way through a stand of bamboo, was almost like a tunnel. But up ahead they found plumeria growing wild, and before long they began to hear the rush of the waterfall. It turned out to be a high, thin column of water that dropped, white as foam, into a dark pool. It was an ideal spot where they could sit alone on a little outcrop of rock.

For a time, they just watched the water and listened to the sound, but eventually Gene said, "This has been so perfect over here. I don't want to go home."

He was still holding her close to him, his arm around her shoulders, and now she wrapped her arms around his middle and rested her head across his chest. "Let's not go home. Let's turn into hippies and just live off the land, right here."

"We might get tired of trying to live on guava and love after a while."

"Not me." She gripped him tighter. "Gene," she said, "we need to talk about some things."

"What?"

"For one thing, it might be 'the pill' that's making me sick—not just the car. I've felt kind of funny all week, especially on the airplane. The doctor told me that could happen."

"Maybe you shouldn't take those things."

"Oh, sure. And then, how long before I get pregnant?"

"That's okay with me. I've told you already, I don't mind if we have a baby right away." But the two of them had discussed that already. Emily had talked to her mother and to some of her married friends. Everyone thought they needed some time together, just the two of them, before their first pregnancy.

"Gene, we have different opinions about things, and you never want to talk about that."

"Like what?"

"You always say you want a big family and I'm not so sure I do."

She had mentioned some feelings of that sort lately, but Gene didn't think it was anything to worry about. He figured it was a matter they could work out as they went along. "So how many kids do you want?" he asked.

"I don't know. Not eight or ten, like some people have. I don't think it's responsible."

"Responsible?"

"The world is getting full, Gene. There are too many hungry people already."

"Our kids won't go hungry."

"That's not the point." She sat up straight and pulled out from under his arm. "Dr. Pierson talked a lot last year about the way population is exploding in the world. He thinks a couple should do nothing more than replace themselves—just have two kids."

"And did this liberal professor of yours ask God what he thinks about that?"

Emily glanced at him quickly, and Gene saw a hint of anger in her eyes. He had seen that little spark turn into flame a couple of times during their engagement. He didn't want to quarrel with her now, not on his honeymoon. "Listen, Em," he said, "I didn't mean that the way it sounded. But I do think we need to consider *everything* before we make our decision."

"My bishop told me that every couple has to make its own decision," Emily said. "There's no right answer that fits every family."

"That's right. But we don't need to let a history professor decide for us."

"I know. I didn't mean to sound like that. But *you* can't make the decision by yourself, okay? It's my body we're talking about."

Gene laughed. "Let's see. I think we're hearing Dr. Eberhard's words now."

"Maybe so. But she's right about a lot of things. Men have been making decisions for women for a long time. And that's not fair. Even my institute professor agrees with that."

"Hey, I do too. I'm not one of those guys who tries to be the *boss* around his house. You'll never get that kind of stuff from me."

Emily got up. She stood in front of Gene, but when he tried to take hold of her and pull her close again, she held back. "Then listen to my opinion about one more thing. I've said it before, but you won't even take me seriously."

"What?" He dropped his hands and crossed his arms over his chest.

"Gene, this whole week I keep thinking about you getting drafted next year. Now that we're married, I don't see how I can ever let you go. It's just too terrible to think about." She stepped toward him and enclosed him in her arms.

"Emily, what can I do about it? I have no choice."

"Your dad could do something. He could get you into the Reserves. A couple of phone calls and you'd be in."

"Maybe. Maybe not. But I'm not going to do that."

"Why?"

"I've told you why, Emily." He pulled his head back so he could look at her. "I'm not going to use my dad's influence."

"You want to go, don't you?"

"I have no *desire* to go to Vietnam. But I do think it's the honorable thing to do. I've been saying for years that we need to fight this war. How can I say, 'But let someone else do it'? I feel guilty, as it is, just to use college and my mission as a way of staying out so long."

"Gene, it's a stupid war. It isn't accomplishing anything. America shouldn't even be there."

"Emily, that's more stuff you're hearing from your professors. There *are* reasons. Maybe, in time, we need to turn the war over to the Vietnamese themselves, but for now, we're still trying to stop that whole part of the world from going over to Communism."

"I can't do it, Gene. I can't let you go. Really. I just can't. If you graduate after spring quarter, you could be gone in less than a year."

"You've known that all along, Em. We've talked about it since we first met."

"But I didn't really know. Not until this week."

And that much Gene did understand. It had all been an idea until now, but this was real. He stood and took Emily back into his arms. She had started to cry, and he could feel her shake.

CHAPTER 4

Kathy had not expected to be quite so nervous about going from door to door. It had never occurred to her that at each house she would feel frightened all over again. It was only her second day on the front lines of the Eugene McCarthy campaign, but several bad experiences had led her to wonder whether the next person she faced might shout at her, or perhaps, coolly, tell her to get lost.

She had arrived in New York on Friday, June 14, and had received some hasty training that evening. The next morning she had been sent by bus, upstate, to Syracuse, and from there driven by a volunteer to a town called Fulton. She was part of a last-minute statewide blitz before the primary election on Tuesday. This was an attempt to solidify an apparent solid showing by McCarthy. What made the campaign complicated was that voters didn't choose presidential candidates; they voted for representatives to the state Democratic delegation. The goal was to promote McCarthy and let voters know which potential delegate was a McCarthy supporter. What Kathy learned quickly, however, was that in spite of McCarthy's popularity in New York City, he was viewed with suspicion by many people in the smaller towns.

Kathy had the feeling that she was fighting a losing battle here in Fulton, but New York's was the last of the primaries, and the rest of the summer wouldn't be like this. She had agreed to join an organizational team and do advance work in the cities where McCarthy would be making appearances. Professor Jennings had put her in touch with a top aide who had been happy to know that she could make herself free for the summer. Or maybe he was most impressed that she would work without pay—as long as her meals and expenses were covered. Kathy's dad had been somewhat less than excited about that arrangement, but when he heard what Kathy would be doing—making housing arrangements, organizing local campaigns, checking out facilities—he decided the experience would be a great practical addition to her education.

Kathy felt the same, but canvassing—although a good chance to see how grassroots politics really worked—was not something she ever wanted to do again. She was staying in a shoddy little motel and sharing a room with another girl, even sharing a double bed. Most of the campaigners were students, and many had been activists on their campuses, but they were "McCarthy Kids" now, "clean for Gene." The women wore skirts, and the guys wore dress shirts and ties, trimmed hair, and no beards. They were taught to answer questions politely, not to argue, and certainly not to say anything unpatriotic.

Kathy liked most of the campaigners she had met so far, but she was surprised at how much they drank and how late they stayed up. What bothered her more, however, was how quickly some of the men started making advances. There seemed to be a lot of room swapping going on, and Kathy realized, once again, that she would have to establish what she would and wouldn't do. It wasn't so hard for her to do that, but it was tiring. She was weary of being the outsider, the person who went off to her own room early, who had to lie in bed and listen to the noise—and not complain. After all, she didn't want to seem prudish.

But this morning Kathy was tired, and her roommate and canvassing partner—a girl named Virginia Downs, from Delaware—seemed half-asleep. They had trudged up and down the streets of the hilly little town of Fulton, passing out literature, advocating for their candidate, and for the most part, feeling anything but encouraged by their reception. Virginia had recently graduated from Williams College. She was tall—almost as tall as Kathy—and she was bright. But she was quiet, and she had become something of a veteran after a month on the campaign. To

Kathy, she seemed a little too careful, and not as enthusiastic as she might have been.

The two were working their way along a street filled with charming old frame homes, mostly two-story, with big chestnut trees and maples in the yards. The trees created a canopy over the sidewalk, which was pretty, but the heat was coming on, and the air was sticky under those trees. There was a Nestlé Cocoa plant in town, and the smell of chocolate was always in the air. Kathy had liked that at first, but now it seemed too sweet, mixed with the heavy air. The two stopped at a gate in front of a house that was set higher than the sidewalk, with a flight of steps climbing to the front porch. "Do you think they have a dog?" Virginia asked.

Kathy scanned the yard. "I don't see one," she said. She laughed. "Or any *signs* of one."

"They hide in back and then charge around as soon as they hear the gate swing open."

Kathy shrugged, then gave the gate a try. It came open. She waited, but nothing else happened, so she walked up the steps with Virginia right behind her. They stepped onto the porch and Kathy knocked. In a moment she heard a scrape, as though a chair were sliding on a hardwood floor, then a pair of thumps. But nothing else happened. "I heard some-one in there," she said. She waited a few more seconds and then knocked again, harder this time.

"Just a minute," someone called, a man.

Kathy heard thumps again, but this time rhythmically, coming closer. Finally the door opened, and through a battered, dark screen, she saw a man standing back, shaded. She could see that he had a beard and long hair and a red bandana around his head. He was hunched forward a little, resting his weight on a pair of metal crutches.

He didn't speak, so Kathy said, "Hello. We're supporters of Eugene McCarthy. We have some materials we'd like to give you that explain his stand on important issues."

"No, thanks," he said, quietly.

"Have you made up your mind which delegate you plan to vote for?"

"I won't be voting. Thanks, but—"

"You sound like you might be disillusioned with 'politics as usual.' I feel exactly the same way. But I'm excited about McCarthy. He *is* a 'peace candidate'—as everyone calls him—but he's much more than that. He wants to lead this country toward some important changes."

"Look . . . I said thanks. Now leave me alone. If I did vote, the last guy I'd choose is McCarthy."

He took hold of the door and began to push it shut, but it was awkward to do so, with the crutches, and Kathy took the chance to say, "Why do you say that? Are you in favor of the war?"

He pulled the door open again and swung his legs forward, then pulled his crutches into a position that would hold him up. "Look, sweetie," he said, "you need to go learn something about the world before you try to tell other people how to vote." He cursed. "I left my legs in Vietnam, and the war did *this* to my face. So tell me, just what does it mean to be in *favor* of the war?"

"I *respect* you, sir. I know what you've been through, and I—"

"No, you don't. You don't know anything about me, and don't tell me you *care* about me. That's just something to say. I know exactly who you are. You're a couple of college girls who've been spending more time marching in the streets than studying. You cheer for Ho Chi Minh—and rag on *our* country."

Kathy had lost a little momentum, and her hesitation made him laugh. But it was that laughter that brought her back, hard. "I have marched. I *am* opposed to the war. I hate what it's done to men like you. And I hate what it's doing to the Vietnamese people. But I've never—"

"Get off my porch. Move to some Communist country where you'll be happy."

"I'm no Communist. Don't start that. That's the problem with guys like you. You may have fought in the war, but you don't know the first thing about it. And you don't know anything about me either, so lay off the stereotypes."

She felt Virginia take hold of her arm. "Let's not do this," she whispered. "Let's just go."

Kathy nodded. She knew she had gone too far. "Well, anyway, thanks for your time," she said. "We all have different opinions. But we encourage you to vote for the candidate you think will do the best for America."

"Wait a minute. What do you mean I don't *know* anything about the war?"

"Really, there's no point in arguing."

"I don't want to argue. I want to be educated. You two little sweethearts come in and enlighten me. And then I'll tell you a few things I know that maybe you don't."

Virginia was stepping away, but Kathy said, "I think we *can* talk, sir. We don't have to get angry. I'd be happy to tell you a little about the history of our involvement in Vietnam—and some of the politics behind it."

"Hey, great," he said, with false enthusiasm. "You come in and make your little speech, and when you're finished, I'll give mine."

Kathy feared what was coming, but she couldn't walk away now. She pulled open his screen door and looked back at Virginia. "I won't argue," she whispered. "I'll just explain our point of view."

"Kathy, no. It won't do any good."

But the man used his crutches to turn, and then to swing his way across the room, in three strides. Kathy stepped in and held the door for Virginia, who followed. The man took both crutches in one hand, and he let himself sink into a chair that seemed specially built—higher than most living-room chairs. Now she could see his face. A white scar—a patch of scooped-out flesh—ran from his left eye across his cheek, below his ear, forming an inch-wide gash where his beard didn't grow.

"Sit down," he said. Kathy looked for a seat and decided that a shabby couch with an old plaid blanket over it was the only choice. The room smelled of something fried, maybe eggs, and of stale cigarette smoke. Kathy glanced at the lamp table next to her and saw that dust had been collecting for a long time.

"I appreciate the two of you being so concerned about me," the man said. "Never mind that you encourage the North Vietnamese. After all, you mean so well."

"I understand that argument," Kathy said. She was careful to sound calm, respectful. "I don't agree with it, of course, but it helps me understand where you're coming from."

"Hey, it's easy to have an opinion when you don't have to worry about getting called up yourself."

Kathy decided to ignore that one. "My name is Kathy," she said. "And this is Virginia. We're here, along with other volunteers, because we believe this campaign is important. Do you mind if I ask your name?"

"Not at all. Everybody around here calls me T. D. It stands for 'touchdown.' I was a pretty good football player in my day. But I'm not much into sports anymore. I suppose you may have guessed that already."

Kathy could see that she had made a mistake. She never should have come in. All he wanted to do was make fun of her. Still, she had to say something and then get out. "What I love about democracy is that people have the right to speak up. The citizens *are* the government. So if our political leaders do something we disagree with, we not only have the right but the responsibility to voice our opinions."

"Let's skip that garbage, okay? Just tell me all the things I don't know about Vietnam. Because I thought I knew quite a bit." T. D. had wooden prostheses in place of his legs. Kathy could see his metal joints that served as "ankles." She could also see that he held one arm stiff across his body. She wondered what he must have gone through, how long he must have suffered during his recovery.

"Maybe you know," Kathy began, "that the French tried to defeat the Vietnamese for—"

"I know all about the French involvement. I know about the defeat at Dien Bien Phu. And I know how the U.S. got involved after that. I know about Kennedy sending in advisors, promising never to send ground troops. And I know all about Johnson's big ego. He made up his mind he couldn't be the first American to lose a war, so he kept building the numbers up, but it did no good. And I know the reason we haven't won the war is that the North Vietnamese are willing to give up all the lives it takes to keep it going—until we wear out. He can lose ten times as many as we do and never stop. And I'll tell you something else. The gooks are evil little creeps, but they're also brave warriors. I've got plenty of respect for the way they fight."

Kathy was stopped. She had no idea what else to say. But he was waiting, smiling, obviously pleased that he had taken the wind out of her sails. "It's a civil war," she said. "We have no right—"

"I know that argument too. But you don't know what it's like over there. The people in the *villes* don't care about politics. They just survive. When we take over, they go along with us, and then they do the same with the Vietcong. You can't really say what the people want."

"Maybe not. But our leaders have it in their heads that we're doing the people a favor—supposedly stopping the spread of Communism. The Johnson administration has lied over and over about the so-called progress of the war, but all we're doing is destroying the whole nation, both North and South. We've dropped almost as many bombs on Vietnam as we dropped in all of World War II."

"Those are facts. But you still don't know what you're talking about." T. D. cursed again, his tone harsh and cynical. "At our camp we had this little gook who—"

"Please don't use that word."

"All right, fine. We had this little Vietnamese guy who came to our post and cut our hair all the time. Nice guy. Laughed with us. Knew a little English. We called him Benny. One night one of our guys shot a sapper, trying to come through our wire—you, know, get into our post. Guess who it was? Good old Benny. Stuff like that happens all the time. No one knows who the enemy is. These people smile at you by day and try to kill you at night."

"But that's my point. We're not helping the South Vietnamese. They don't even want us over there."

"Some do. More of them don't. But that's *my* point. Nothing about this war makes any sense."

"Well, then . . ." But Kathy couldn't think what to say. Wasn't he agreeing with her?

"Look. Here's what I know. When you get called up, you go. You fight for your country. And you don't have to be ashamed of that. You don't have to listen to college girls tell you that what you did was wrong."

Kathy nodded. "I understand that. And I do respect you for what you did." She glanced toward Virginia and nodded again, as if to say, "See. We can talk." Then she said, "We aren't so far apart, T. D. For one thing, it sounds as though we both agree that this war can't be won."

"Don't start that. We're a million miles apart. If I vote, it'll be for Wallace."

"*Wallace?*"

"Why does that surprise you?"

"He's a racist. He—"

"Who isn't? At least he's honest about it. And he wants to bring some law and order to this country. He doesn't live in a fantasyland like your beloved Gene McCarthy."

Kathy had heard enough. This guy wasn't even consistent. He wasn't worth her time. "I guess we are pretty far apart. You admit the war is fruitless, but you won't vote for the one man who wants to stop it."

T. D. smiled. Kathy hated to see the way the scar distorted his face.

"Fruitless," he said. "What a word. You say that like you know what it means."

"I just meant that it—"

"Hey, it's a good word. You plant a tree, and it doesn't give off fruit. There's a lot of that kind of stuff in the Bible, as I recall."

Kathy didn't know where this was going. She sat back and tried to think what to say. "In any case," she finally said, "you understand our position. Gene McCarthy is an honest man. He wants to do what's right for our country. He's convinced that we should negotiate a treaty and turn the war over, through a series of steps, to the South Vietnamese. He isn't talking about—"

T. D. had begun to laugh. When Kathy stopped, he asked, "Are you finished now?"

"Yes. Except that we have some material you could read, and we do encourage you to vote on Tuesday." She slid forward and Virginia stood up.

"Wait a minute. That wasn't the deal. You made your speech and now it's my turn."

"I thought you made your point."

"No. Not at all. Sit down, Virginia. The show isn't over."

Kathy heard the sarcasm in the way he intoned the name, but Virginia did sit down. T. D. clutched his prostheses and moved them out a little so he could lean forward. "You don't have any idea what it's like over there. Soldiers in Vietnam don't fight for their country. They fight to stay alive. No one talks about politics. It's all about 365 days—getting your year behind you and getting out of there."

Kathy nodded, but she didn't see the point.

"You fight in the jungle most of the time. You hump up and down hills, sweat like dogs. You try to find Charlie, and you try to kill him. It's a body-count war because no one ever holds any territory. So you kill a few if you're lucky, maybe lose some, and you go back to your post. All the time that you're outside the wire—outside your post—you're so scared that your bowels won't work, and you're miserable. So when you get back inside, you hunker down and hope you won't be going back out the next day. That's all there is to life."

"But that's what I'm saying. McCarthy—"

"Shut up, okay. I gave you your turn."

He hadn't. Not really. But Kathy sat back and listened. She felt a little frightened, and she wasn't sure why.

"You gotta understand—it's all kids over there. Eighteen- and nineteen-year-old kids. And some dumb lieutenant right out of college, maybe twenty-two or three, trying to act like he's your leader. Some of those young kids think they're playing cowboys and Indians—never had so much fun—but most guys don't really care about anything. After a while you just figure you're going to get it one day, and you sort of wish you would—because it's all so bad. You don't shower for weeks, live out there in the mud all through the rainy season, get swarmed by mosquitoes, don't sleep for days at a time, catch all kinds of diseases. I had immersion foot so bad my flesh would come off with my socks when I finally got to change them. The only thing you know is that you have to kill Charlie because he's the one waiting for a chance to kill you. But you don't care about 'the war.' You just want to go home."

Kathy had known all that. Or at least she thought she had. But it wasn't quite the same, coming from him.

"One day I was walking point—that's going first in line. I was moving down a little path through the jungle. Out there, you watch everything. The point guy has to watch for booby traps. And Charlie is a master at booby traps. He'll run a little wire across the path, hide it in the vegetation so good that you have to know exactly what you're looking for, ever to notice. Or he'll dig a hole and cover it with sod. You're out there in this half-light, under a double or even triple canopy of trees, and it's hard to see the little changes in the footing. You take one step too many

and you fall into that hole. And what do you suppose is in there, girls?"
He waited, his eyes locked on Kathy's. "Pointed stakes—*punji* sticks—all
erect and waiting. And what do you suppose they put on the tips of those
stakes?" He laughed. "I won't say the word. It's a bad word, and girls like
you wouldn't want to hear a bad word. I'll say that they put 'human feces'
on the points of those stakes. So you don't just get stabbed; you get sick,
too. And the illnesses they got over there, you don't want."

"I know it's terrible, T. D. I understand that."

"No, you don't. Don't claim that. Because you don't know the first
thing about it. You could never know. Only guys who have been over
there know."

"And they're the ones we want to bring home, so they can escape that
nightmare."

"Please. Just shut up. You're a nice girl, but you're stupid, and the
worst thing is, you don't even know it."

Kathy didn't need this. She decided to say nothing more. She would
let him have his say, and then she would leave.

"So I'm walking point, and I'm watching *everything*. It's tempting to
watch only the path because you're so scared you're going to hit a wire or
step on a land mine. But you've got to watch the trees, too, and all the
undergrowth. These little guys can hide anywhere. They'll wait in a tree
for days, sit up there, covered, in their little black pajamas, and they'll let
you walk under them before they start picking you off, one at a time. They
usually die, but not before they get some of our guys, and that's good
enough for them. That's the kind of soldiers they are.

"So anyway, I'm walking point one day, and I'm hearing little
noises—birds maybe, animals, I don't know—but I think every sound is
Charlie. I think every flicker of movement is Charlie. My mouth is all cotton inside, and my breath won't come right. I'm sweating so bad, I've
soaked through my fatigues—almost everywhere. And that's when I make
a mistake—maybe because I'm so tired. I step on a mine, and when it goes

up, it throws me about ten feet backward. I come down on my back, and I feel pain everywhere—so much I can't even tell where it's coming from. I want to yell for help, but nothing will come out. I pass out a few times, and each time I come around, I can't think straight. I don't know what's happening. But two of my buddies . . . and by the way, you have no idea what a buddy is. You never will know anything about friendship because you've never faced death with a bunch of guys. You also don't know the first thing about fear, nor even a hint of what courage is. You know books. That's what you two know. You know 'the *history* of the American involvement in Vietnam.'"

Kathy had always hated the argument that only those who had been there really understood the war, but she didn't say that. She was beginning to feel that he had a point, that he was saying something she needed to hear.

"My friend Hunch—that's what we called him because he always thought he knew what was going to happen. He shoots some morphine in my leg, and I go out, halfway sort of, and then two guys, Hunch and another guy named Lard—a man I cared about in a way you'll never care for anyone—they start running with me. My company commander had called in a medevac—a helicopter—to get me out, and Hunch and Lard took off to get me to a landing zone. I can't remember much about that. I just remember all the bouncing, and the jungle up above, the light filtering down through, and a lot of pain, even with the morphine.

"So we get to this clearing and we wait, except I don't remember any of that. What I remember is that I'm bouncing again, and I wake up. I can hear the medevac, and then I see it coming down, and my buddies are running into the clearing. Then one disappears. Hunch just disappears, and I'm on the ground, on my back. So Lard picks me up—big old Lard. He's about six-five and two-forty, and he picks me up, and I'm spinning as he turns, and then we go down again. When I hit this time, I sort of understand that Lard is under me, but nothing is very clear. Then some other guy, off the helicopter, grabs me and pulls me across the ground. It hurts so bad, I lose consciousness again. I don't remember anything after that. When I wake up I'm in a hospital."

Kathy waited for the rest. She knew he was going to hit her one more time, but there was no way to protect herself.

"Hunch died. So did Lard. And by the way, Lard was black."

Kathy knew better than to say anything. She nodded, tried to say with her eyes that he was right. She didn't know what he knew.

"So look at me. I'm the lucky one. I'm alive. Alive and kicking—with two wooden legs. And two guys died so I can have this great life I've got."

Kathy wanted to tell him she was sorry, but she didn't know quite what she meant.

"I used to like to hunt," T. D. said. "This last year my two brothers wanted me to go again, so I went with them. They mostly had to carry me, but they put me in a good spot and told me they would try to scare up a buck and drive it toward me. They handed me my old deer rifle and walked off, and they pushed a couple of little bucks my way. But I didn't shoot. My brothers came back to see what was wrong, and they found me shaking and crying and going to pieces. My big brother just said, 'Come on. We'd better get you out of here.' They carried me back to my brother's truck and drove me home. So I don't think I'll be doing any more hunting. It kind of ruins the whole thing for my brothers. Maybe you can understand that."

Kathy was nodding.

"You don't know what I'm saying. You think you do, but you don't. You're upset now because I told you some hard things. But that doesn't mean you understand. I'll just say this. Don't come in here and talk to me about 'fruitless.' There may be something wrong with me, but I don't happen to like being told that what I did was *fruitless*."

"I'm sorry," Kathy said. "I really am."

"Hey, go ahead and say it. This is where you're supposed to tell me, 'But Gene McCarthy will save other boys from a fate like yours.'"

"No. I wasn't thinking that. I'm just sorry. I wish I could do something to change . . . what happened."

"That's just the trouble with you noble little girls. You think you can make things right. But this world is a place where all kinds of *fruitless* things keep happening. So I'd just rather say, I did what my country asked me to do. I gotta keep it that simple—that, or go crazy. Maybe you don't appreciate what we did over there, but there are a whole lot of guys in this country who know exactly what I'm talking about. And those are the only people I care about. I guess that's the wrong attitude, but it's how I feel."

Virginia stood up again. Then Kathy did too. "Thank you for telling us," Kathy said. "I know it's hard to talk about."

"Not at all. It's my big show. This is the most entertaining thing I've done in weeks. I'm the one who ought to thank you. It's just that I *hate* you too much to give you the satisfaction."

"No, you don't," Kathy said. "You don't hate us."

T. D. shrugged, but he didn't speak. She saw the change in his face. So she walked to him and put out her hand. He reached out after a moment, and they shook hands. But then, without knowing why, she touched his face, ran her fingers along his scar. "I really am sorry," she said. He stared at her, looking startled, and then his chest began to shake.

So the girls left, but they didn't go on to the next house. They didn't say anything to each other; they just walked down the street to their car, and they drove back to the motel, where they had lunch a little early. When they went back out canvassing, Kathy didn't argue with anyone.

# CHAPTER 5

Diane Hammond was stomping off to her bedroom when Bobbi, her mother, said, "Diane, stop right there. I'm not putting up with one of your tantrums. We can talk about this."

Diane stopped and turned around. "No. We obviously *can't* talk about it. You were *yelling*."

"I was not." But Diane saw her mother take a breath. "Let's both back off a little and lower our voices. Come and sit down."

Diane walked back to the living room, and then she dropped onto the floor and leaned against the couch. She actually had wanted to talk—before this little blowup. She had wanted to tell her mother what she was really worried about, but she wasn't sure she dared.

Bobbi sat down in Richard's big chair. "Listen, Diane, I'm only saying that the *bride* and her parents normally make the decisions about the reception. If *you* want to hold it in Salt Lake, that's one thing, but I don't like the Lymans making the decision."

"I thought this was all about money."

"That is part of it, Diane. Greg keeps talking about the Hotel Utah or the Salt Lake Country Club. Those are very expensive places. And we were thinking about cake and punch—maybe some little sandwiches or something—but Greg's got it in his head that we ought to serve a whole dinner. Do you have any idea what that costs?"

"He said his family would help."

Bobbi crossed her arms. Diane could see her jaw muscles tighten. "Is that what you want—to ask them to help us pay for it?"

"No. Of course I don't. But you keep making us sound like we're poor. What do you expect Greg to say?"

"I'll tell you exactly what I expect from Greg. I expect him to be patronizing and manipulative. That's how he operates."

Diane felt as though her mother had smacked her in the forehead. How could she say such a thing?

"I'm sorry," Bobbi was already saying.

But it was too late for that. Diane got up. "As I said before, we can't talk about this."

Bobbi stood too. She took a hesitating step toward Diane. "I really am sorry."

"You hate him, don't you?"

"No, I don't. But he does expect to get what he wants. I guess he's used to it."

"It's his parents who want to have the reception in Salt Lake. Greg doesn't care."

"They *also* know how to get what they want."

Diane didn't care anymore. She was tired of being caught in the middle. A month earlier her mom had paid a reservation fee at the "White House," in Ogden—with Diane's approval—but ever since, the tension had been building. What embarrassed Diane most was Mom's talk about the expense. She wondered what sort of family the Lymans must think they were getting involved with. "Fine. You don't like the Lymans and you don't—"

"Don't do that, Diane. If you're old enough to get married, you're old enough to discuss this like an adult." Bobbi let her eyes drift upward, as though she caught the irony in her own words, and she added, "But I guess you could say the same about me." She took one more step toward Diane. "Honey, listen to me. We can afford a fancy reception, if that's important to you. But I never have liked showing off. Most of the people we'll invite are folks in our ward and people from the college. They don't do extravagant wedding parties. If it were up to me, we'd hold it in the cultural hall at the church. I understand that you don't want that, but it just seems to me that the White House is plenty nice enough, and since we're the ones putting it on, I don't see why the people from Salt Lake can't drive here—instead of the other way around."

"I don't care, Mom. *You* talk to the Lymans. Have it wherever you want."

"No. You're not getting off that way. I want you to look Greg in the eye and tell him what *you* prefer. No pouting, no crying in your room. Just make a decision for yourself."

Diane knew what all this was about. Her mother still thought she was a little girl. She had told Diane more than once what she feared: that Greg would dominate her all their married life. "Fine," Diane said. "We'll have it here in—"

"Diane, stop it. This is your little martyr act. I don't want you to decide right now. I want you to think about it, and then I want you to tell Greg what you've decided."

"He's too mad to talk right now. We had a big fight last night, and it was all about this stupid reception."

Bobbi took hold of Diane's shoulders. She didn't speak until Diane looked back at her. "But that's exactly the point," she said. "You two need to have a good fight before you get married just so you'll find out how to work things out. It sounds to me like he's the one doing the pouting— because he hasn't gotten his way. I'd bet good money that you spent the whole time saying to him, 'Mom wants this' and 'Mom says we have to do that.' No wonder he's frustrated. If you tell him what you want, I think he'll respect that. Marriage lasts a long time, Diane, and you need to let him know, early, that you can compromise, or even give in sometimes, but that he has to be willing to do the same thing."

Diane had heard enough of this. It was the same old thing. "Mom, I think *he* respects me more than you do. You're the one who's convinced I can't think."

"No! I'm convinced you *don't* think. That's very different from *can't*."

Diane tried to turn away, but Mom was still holding her shoulders.

"I love you, Diane. And I believe in you. I also believe you're too pretty for your own good. It's always been enough for you, but it won't be any longer. He's going to treat you like his little beauty queen all his life if you don't force him to think of you as a real person."

That wasn't fair. Mom didn't know how much she and Greg had talked about things, how many times he had been willing to compromise. "You've made your point, Mom. Many times."

"Maybe so. But, Di, I'm not trying to put you down. I love you and I—"

"I know." Bobbi finally let go, and Diane used the chance to turn and head for her room.

Behind her, she heard her mother say, "Make a decision by tomorrow. If we're canceling the White House, I need to call."

Diane didn't reply. She stepped into her room and shut the door, and then she cried—whether her mother thought that was a bad idea or not. The truth was, Diane did know what she wanted. She wanted a beautiful reception in an elegant hall—like the Empire Room at the Hotel Utah. But how could she demand that if her parents thought it was too expensive?

Diane had been working all summer at L. R. Samuels, in Ogden. It was a beautiful women's store; all the well-off ladies from Ogden shopped there. One of the things she loved about those people was that they rarely asked the price of a dress or pair of shoes. The ones who did ask usually ended up saying that they needed to shop around, and probably ended up buying something at J. C. Penney or the Bon Marché. Mom took such a dim view of wealthy people, but Greg had made a good point about that. When it came to charities, or donations to universities and symphonies and zoos—all the things that made life nice—it was the well-off people who shelled out their money. Brother Lyman was always getting hit up by fund-raisers, and he rarely turned anyone down. Sister Lyman served on several boards of charitable organizations. Diane's parents did a lot too, but they were always more worried about someone starving in Africa than they were about local needs. All Diane knew was that she didn't want to feel guilty every time she did something for her family or herself. How could a nice reception be such a terrible thing? It only happened once in life.

The day—a Monday in July—was already hot. Diane had the day off, and she had planned to sort through her things. Her wedding was more than a month away, but she wanted to start choosing what she would take with her when she left for Seattle, and what things could go to Deseret Industries or her little sister. Now, however, she really didn't care. Greg was mad at her and so was her mom, and there was really no way to satisfy both of them.

But that wasn't her biggest worry. Diane had stayed up late after her spat with Greg. She had even asked herself whether she wanted to marry him. Behind the question was the almost certain awareness that she didn't have the courage to back out at this point, but she wondered why she kept thinking about Kent Wade. He would be home soon, and she remembered how simple her feelings for him had been, how pure his love for her. She was never sure that Greg knew how to give over to a love that had no requirements, no expectations.

Still, Diane wanted to think the best of Greg. Mom didn't really know him; she didn't give him credit for how kind he could be. He was like a little boy in some ways, so intent on making his way in the world, and whether he knew it or not, a little afraid that he wouldn't do as well as he wanted to. She loved him most when she saw those doubts. She wanted to be his support, the one person who believed in him absolutely. The only problem was, she liked him most when they were alone. She was embarrassed by his neediness around others. His style, his apparent self-importance, came out when he tried to impress people, and at times his insincerity was as obvious to Diane as it must have been to everyone else.

Diane sat up after a time and dabbed at her eyes with a tissue she pulled from a box by her bed. Then she picked up a scrapbook she had set on her bed—another project she had thought of working on today. She turned the pages, looking through some of the loose items she had stuck in, but she didn't try to choose what she wanted to keep. What she felt was nostalgia for her childhood and for her high school years. She had never thought of her life as simple then, but now it seemed as though it had been. What she wanted, more than anything, was to go back to BYU for another couple of years. She wondered whether she was ready for the seriousness of working out a relationship, day in and day out. What sounded better was a year of dating Kent—and a dozen other guys—and fun with her roommates and the girls in her social unit. As much as anything, although she hated to admit it, she knew she would always regret that she had left BYU before she had had a chance to compete for Belle of the Y. It was a dream she had taken with her as a freshman—seeing her initials in lights on the mountain, announcing her victory. A couple more years in college seemed preferable to three years in Seattle with her husband gone long hours to law school.

Still, what could she do? She did love Greg, and she was almost sure that she would choose him over Kent, even if the two were around at the same time. Waiting a year or two would probably only complicate things. Besides, backing out of the wedding would be unthinkably embarrassing.

Diane actually didn't think much about the reception, but she reached a decision: the inevitable one. She would tell Greg that she wanted to have it in Ogden. She had been feeling lately that her mother was right about one thing: Greg needed to be told once in a while, "I'm sorry, but this is important to me." She could be strong when she had to be. She had taken a stand with Scott, long ago, and now was the time to make a statement to Greg. She had thought many times lately about the things her great-grandmother Thomas had told her. A woman should walk alongside her husband, not behind him.

Diane did finally get herself going, but she put off her decisions about clothes and began to sort through her old records—a big stack of forty-fives. She even got out her portable record player and listened to her old favorites: "I Get Around," by the Beach Boys; "Walk on By," by Dionne Warwick; and the Lettermen singing, "When I Fall in Love." She sang with them, "When I fall in love, it will be forever, or I'll never fall in love." It was how she had always thought of love, and it bothered her to admit that reality was so much more complicated. When she heard the doorbell ring, she didn't think much about it until she heard her mom say, through the bedroom door, "Diane, Greg is here to see you."

Greg was supposed to be at work on a Monday morning. What was he doing here? She felt some trepidation. She thought she knew why he was here, how he would handle this, and she wasn't sure she wanted to deal with him right now. She hurried to her mirror, ran a brush through her hair a few times, checked her eyes to make sure they weren't red, and made a couple of quick, light strokes with a tube of lipstick. She was wearing a pair of faded cutoff jeans and a short-sleeved cotton shirt. She thought of changing, quickly, but decided that was silly.

She walked down the hall and found Greg standing in the living room, alone. He was holding a big box with a pink bow and a bouquet of red roses. He was dressed in a gray suit. "Hi," he said, and he smiled, rather shyly.

Diane stopped several steps away. This was exactly what she had feared.

"I'm sorry about last night," he said. "I brought you some peace offerings. I'm really sorry I lost my temper. The decision about the reception should be completely between you and your parents. I'm not going to say another word about it."

He finally walked toward her and reached out with the roses. She took them and said, "They're beautiful, Greg. Thank you. Aren't you supposed to be at work?"

"Yeah. That's where I'm going. But I told Dad I had to take care of a little matter first and I'd be coming in late."

"Was he okay with that?"

Greg grinned. "The truth is, I'm no help at all around that office. I can't even type very well. He just gives me the job so he can overpay me and not call it charity."

"You'll be a big help after you get a year of law school behind you."

"I hope so."

Diane wanted to thank him and send him on his way. She wasn't ready to talk about the reception. But now he was handing her the gift box. "I ran down to Castleton's as soon as they opened this morning. I wanted to get you something nice."

Diane found that strangely annoying. The flowers seemed more than enough. But she sat down on the couch and opened the box. What she found inside was a violet-colored dress with a vest-like top and an A-line skirt. It was pretty and the right size, but probably not the color she would have chosen. "It's *really* cute, Greg. Thank you."

Greg sat down on the couch next to her. "Don't I get a little kiss for that?"

Diane had no idea why that bothered her so much, but she ignored the request and said, "Greg, I don't think this is the right way for us to deal with things. If we have a disagreement, we should talk it out. You don't need to 'pay me off.'"

"I know. But I wanted to do something nice for you. I should have done it some time when everything was going great. I thought about it, but I didn't do it. I'm sorry."

"It's okay. In fact, it's very sweet." She finally bent toward him and gave him a peck on the lips.

"I love you," he said. "And as far as I'm concerned, this whole matter is ended. I'll just tell my parents that we're having the reception in Ogden. I think they've got it in their heads that it's farther to drive from Salt Lake to Ogden than it is to drive the other way."

This was a change. "Last night, I got the impression *you* were the one who felt that way."

"No. That wasn't my point. I just have a feeling, knowing my parents, that they'll invite more people than your parents will. So it was just the idea that fewer people would be driving to Salt Lake than the other way around."

"Why don't we allow the same number of invitations to both families? That's what some of my friends have done."

"Hey, that's perfect. That's exactly how it should be. My parents can do a little slashing and get their list down to a reasonable number. I told them already that they're inviting too many. I haven't seen the White House, but it's quite nice, isn't it? And I guess it has enough room."

Diane felt the loss. It was her mother who had won this fight. "Greg, I really would rather have it at the Hotel Utah. It's so pretty, and there's more room. But I'm kind of caught in the middle on this whole thing."

Diane knew that her mother would say she was being weak, but for once she had actually said what she was feeling. Greg nodded, and then he slipped his arm around Diane's shoulders. "I understand," he said. "I guess your mother really has her mind made up about this."

Diane wondered where her mother was, whether she could hear anything. She said quietly, "Not exactly. She told me it's my decision. She'll call the White House and cancel if that's what I want. But it's pretty obvious what she thinks we ought to do."

"What about your dad? What's he saying?"

"Dad probably doesn't care. He just thinks we shouldn't pay out a ton of money. My dad can't eat at a restaurant without wondering how many hungry people in Africa he could have fed. We do have money, Greg, but my parents just have their own ideas about how they spend it."

"I know. And I guess I said the wrong thing last night. To me, it seems like there's nothing wrong with both families sharing the cost of a reception. My parents only have the one daughter, so my brothers and I are putting the bite on all the families we marry into."

"It's just the tradition, I guess."

"Yeah. I know." Greg leaned back and stretched out his legs. She was glad to feel some ease again, but she wondered whether she was handling this right. It hadn't been ten minutes since she had decided to take her stand. And yet, what was all the fuss about? She wished that her mom had stuck around to hear what Greg had said. He wasn't trying to pressure her at all.

"So your mom is leaving the decision up to you?"

"Sort of."

"What do you mean, 'sort of'?"

"She told me to decide for myself. But if I tell her we're going to have it in Salt Lake she'll think you pressured me into it."

"It sounds to me like she's the one doing the pressuring."

It's what Diane had been thinking, but she felt a little defensive that Greg would say it.

"Well, I'd better head back to Salt Lake. You give it some thought today, and then let me know. I really think you might want to talk it over with your dad."

"Why?"

"I don't know. It just sounds like you want it at the Hotel Utah, and you're giving in to please your mother. Maybe your dad would be a little more neutral about it. And maybe he wouldn't take offense if you mentioned that my parents don't mind paying for the catering. They're the ones who want to have a dinner, so it only seems right that they should spring for it."

"Greg, what are you saying, that we ought to—"

"No, no, no. Not at all. I'm just saying that I want you to decide, and it looks a little as though your mother is the one who's keeping you from making your own choice. Maybe you need to talk it over with your dad." He pulled his suit coat off and draped it over his arm.

Diane was trying to think what to do. She wasn't entirely happy with Greg. She thought she understood what he was doing. And yet, he had a point. Diane did want to have the reception in Salt Lake, and Mom had been the one making a point that Diane ought to choose. It was facing her mom with the decision that was hard. Maybe Dad would be easier to talk to.

Richard was not teaching this summer, but he spent his days at his office at the college, researching and writing. Diane decided not to say anything to her mother about Greg's visit. She would wait and talk to her dad, and then she would make her decision. So she stayed in her room much of the day, and later on she borrowed her mother's car to run to the grocery store to find some boxes she could use to pack some things in. She took Maggy with her, and after they stopped at the store, Diane drove all the way downtown and bought snow cones. More than anything, she didn't want to be drawn into another conversation with her mother.

After dinner that night, Diane asked to talk to her dad, and the two walked downstairs to his little office. Richard had added a little couch to the room this last year, so the two sat on that, next to each other, and Diane said the words she had been planning all day. "Dad, Mom says she wants me to make my own decision about my reception, but she's going to be upset with me unless I do what she wants—which is to hold it here in Ogden."

Richard laughed, but he turned so he was facing Diane. He put his arm over the backrest of the couch, behind her. "Actually, she called me today and told me about your conversation. She's worried that you're getting railroaded. She wants you to stand up for yourself and do what you want to do."

"Right. But if I do what the Lymans want, she'll say I'm giving in to them, and if I do what she wants, she'll think I'm brilliant and independent."

"It's interesting you say that, because I told her that was the trap she had put you into."

Diane turned, slid back to the end of the couch, and looked at her dad. Why was he always so much easier to talk to? He was like looking into a mirror, with his crystal blue eyes, but he also seemed to understand her better. "What did she say to that?"

"Well . . . your mom is worried, and I think I understand why. Greg is a young man with clear notions about what he wants, and you've never liked to confront people. You—"

"The way Mom does?"

"Well, yes. Your mother is formidable. She has strong opinions, and she's not afraid to express them. But honey, she also has a good heart. She's a very caring person. It's not impossible to be nice and strong at the same time."

"Do men want their wives to be strong?"

Diane watched her dad. He never seemed to rush into anything. He took his time before he said, "I wish I could tell you that all men like strong women. I'm afraid the majority don't. But that's why a woman ought to avoid the majority. If you can't be yourself, and you have to tip-toe around your partner, life could be *very* tedious."

"Don't you have to tiptoe around Mom sometimes?"

"No. I don't think I do. I can disagree with Bobbi and she doesn't mind. We usually go down different paths to reach a conclusion, but in the end, we decide things together. There are some things that don't matter to me, and so, if it matters to Bobbi, I go with her opinion."

"That happens a lot, I think."

"Yeah. I guess. I'm a little easier going about most things. But when something really matters, we take a lot of time and we sort it all out. It's never even occurred to me to try to dominate her, but she doesn't take charge either. To me, that's what marriage is about: two people sharing a life, figuring it out as they go along. I think it's better to make a bad decision *together* than it is to make the right decision the wrong way."

Diane liked that, but she wondered about herself. "Dad, I don't have many opinions. Maybe Greg will always decide everything for me."

"Not if his heart is right. He'll want you to think with him, maybe even *need* you to do it. He'll assume you have a brain—and a spirit—and he'll want to know what both are telling you."

"He calls me his 'little doll' sometimes. Kathy told me to watch out about that."

"Does he make you feel like that's all you are?"

"Sometimes."

"So what are you going to do about it?"

Diane gripped her hands together and looked down at them. "Sometimes—like today—I get thinking that I don't want to get married yet. Or even that I shouldn't marry Greg. I love him, but I'm not sure I know how to deal with him. He's sweet to me, but sometimes I feel like I'm trying to stand up against a hurricane. He just carries me along, and my feet aren't even touching the ground."

"Wow." Richard bent forward and put his hand—the one with the deepest scars—on top of Diane's two hands. "Honey, that's hard. I didn't know you were having doubts about Greg."

"Doesn't everyone have doubts when they get married?"

"I don't know." He thought about that for a time. "I never doubted Bobbi, but I doubted myself. I went through a bad time when I first came home from the war."

"Maybe that's what I'm doing—just doubting myself."

"Diane, you're young, and you're taking that giant step that forces a person to grow up. It's only natural to have some fears. But I would say this: If you're not sure about Greg, don't marry him. It would be better to back out now than to wait a year or two and file for divorce."

The idea struck Diane hard. She couldn't imagine a failed marriage. She had always wanted a good husband and family. If she failed at that, she had nothing.

"So if I'm hearing you right, maybe this isn't just about a reception," Richard said. "Maybe this is about your relationship with Greg."

For a few seconds Diane tried out the idea. She asked herself, could she call the wedding off? But her response was instant fear. She couldn't do it. What followed was a sense of alarm. She didn't want her parents—especially her mom—to think she was making a mistake. "Dad, I'm just a little down today. I think it's this fuss about the reception. Greg came over this morning and told me he wants me to make the decision. He didn't pressure me at all. He's strong, but I don't think he'll ever try to rule over me. He loves me too much for that."

"Maybe. All I would say is that you'd better be sure."

"I am sure. I just have to remember to put the brakes on sometimes—you know, stick my heels in the ground when the hurricane gets blowing too hard." She tried to laugh.

But Richard looked worried. "Can you do it? *Will* you do it?"

"Yes. But Mom wants me to tell him we're having the reception in Ogden, and I think I would rather have it in Salt Lake."

"You *think* you would?"

"I'm almost sure. I just need to think about it a little more."

"Honey, if I were you, I'd do this. Before you worry about the reception, I'd start a fast tonight, and I'd pray about Greg. That's the real decision. If you're having some doubts, you need to go inside yourself, and even more, you need to get some help from the Lord. Just be really sure you're doing the right thing."

"I shouldn't have made you think that I—"

"Honey, it can't hurt to take twenty-four hours and ask the question all over again. You need to start your marriage confident you did the right thing."

"Okay."

"The reception is pretty simple by comparison. Just ask yourself what would make you happiest on your wedding day. Decide what you want and then ask Greg what he wants. I don't want him to railroad you into anything, but I don't see why it's entirely your decision either. Your mom wants you to speak up for yourself, and I agree—but that doesn't mean you have to veto everything Greg wants. This is your first experience with learning how to work together. The reception isn't very important, but the process is."

"Okay. That's good advice." She kissed her dad on the cheek, and then she walked back upstairs to the kitchen. She drank a glass of water, and then she went to her room to start her fast. But when she knelt down to pray, she felt the fear return. Dad was asking her to consider throwing away the decision she had made last spring. If she had wanted to back out, she should have done it then, not now. The Lord had answered her once. Why did she have to reconsider everything? She relaxed when she thought of that, and she told herself that was her answer. She didn't need to fast.

She also knew what she wanted for a reception. So in the morning Diane called Greg before he went to work. "I've made a decision," she said. "I think we should try to get the Empire Room at the Hotel Utah, if it's available. And I do want more than punch and cookies—but maybe not a full meal. A lot of people do something like that. And I'm sure my dad will pay for it. Your parents won't have to."

"That all sounds great, honey. But really, my parents don't mind paying some of it. I already talked to them about that."

"Well . . . we'll have to work that out. But let's do have it in Salt Lake."

"Okay. I'll run down to the hotel this morning and see which rooms might be available. And I want you to know, I'm proud of you for making your own decision."

Diane felt just a little bothered by Greg's enthusiasm, even his choice of words, but she was glad the matter was settled. The hard part now was facing her mother.

## CHAPTER 6

"A re you cold?" Gene asked. Emily nodded, and the question seemed to make her shudder. Gene got up from his chair and stepped to the examination table, where the doctor had left Emily sitting. She was wearing a flimsy paper robe. He put his arm around her and held her next to him. She rested her head against him and whispered, "Thanks."

"Are you feeling sick now?"

"Kind of. I wish the doctor would come back. I want to know what's wrong with me."

Emily had been sick, off and on, all summer, and it was the middle of August now. The doctor had told her when she started taking "the pill" that it might cause her some troubles for a while, but this had been going on way too long.

"You got such a dud when you married me, Gene. I've never been sick in my life, and now everything makes me throw up."

"You're allergic to me. That's what I keep telling you."

She put both her arms around his waist and hugged him. "Don't say that, okay? This isn't very funny to me right now."

So Gene held her with both arms and they waited that way. He could feel her body, even slimmer than when they had married a couple of months before, quivering against him. There was something wonderfully tender about her need for him, but he was nervous, too. He didn't want her to be sick. He hoped the problem really was the pill. Then she could just stop taking it.

When Dr. Hancock finally showed up, he was looking at his

clipboard, reading a report, but even before he looked up, Gene could see that he was smiling. Gene stepped away from Emily and said, "She was getting cold." He was a little embarrassed. He didn't want the doctor to think they couldn't keep their hands off each other, even for a few minutes.

But Dr. Hancock was smiling broadly by now, showing his big teeth. He was a lumpy man with unruly hair and a certain unkempt quality, his white coat wrinkled, his horn-rimmed glasses balancing crookedly on the bridge of his nose. "Everything looks very good," he said. "Your blood is fine. You're very healthy. You do have one little medical problem, but I think it will work itself out in time." He chuckled. "From what you told me before, I'd give it another thirty-six weeks or so, and then see if you don't start feeling better."

Gene didn't get this at all, but he saw Emily sit up straight. "Doctor, that can't be. I was taking the pill."

"Well, yes. But those things don't always work. You're definitely pregnant."

"Oh!" Gene said. And then he tried to let the idea settle in. "Hey, that's *great*," he added.

He looked at Emily, but she wasn't speaking. She looked ready to cry.

"Everything is fine," the doctor was saying. "This morning sickness usually lets up after the first trimester, and—"

"It's not just in the morning," Emily said. "That's why I thought it was something else."

"'Morning sickness' is actually a misleading name." Dr. Hancock pushed his glasses up with his index finger, but they slid down almost immediately. "Different women react different ways. Morning is a common time to get nauseated, but it can happen any time of the day."

Gene had his arms around Emily again. "I'm going to be a dad!" he said. "Honey, this is really cool. I know it's a little sooner than . . ."

But Emily *was* crying now. She pressed her head to his middle.

"Emily," Dr. Hancock said. He stepped closer and gave her shoulder a pat. "I shouldn't have broken the news to you that way. It's difficult to find out something like this so suddenly. But be thankful nothing is wrong. This is a blessed thing, having a baby."

Gene knew that Dr. Hancock was also a former bishop and now a member of a stake presidency. That had something to do with his perspective. "Actually, we're very happy about it," Gene said. "I think it's just kind of shocking right now. We wanted to wait a little while before we had a baby. I think Emily talked to you about that."

"She did." He patted her shoulder again. "I certainly understand. I'll leave you alone now, and Emily can go ahead and get dressed." He walked toward the door, then stopped. "By the way, congratulations. I'll tell you who's going to be happy. Alex and Anna."

"Oh, yes. Definitely. Mom will start buying up baby clothes as soon as I call her."

"Well, it's a great time in life. You kids are in for an adventure, I promise you that."

He stepped out and closed the door.

"Don't tell them yet," Emily said instantly.

"What?"

"Don't tell your parents yet. I don't want to tell anyone."

"Why?"

Emily pulled back and looked up at him. Tears were still on her face, but she wasn't crying now. "Just don't say anything yet. It's too soon."

"Okay. But they're going to be here a lot, with this campaign going on. It might be kind of obvious if you're still sick a lot."

"We'll tell them. But not for a while, okay?"

"Sure." But Gene had no idea why. "Are you all right, honey?"

"I don't know. Could you go out?"

"What?"

"I just want to get dressed."

"You can do that with me here, can't you?"

"Not right now. Please. I just want a few minutes alone."

Gene suddenly felt awful. "Em, this isn't a bad thing. Not at all. Some couples have trouble getting pregnant. We're really lucky."

"I know. You don't have to tell me. I'm fine. But go out to the waiting room and I'll be out in a minute." She slid down from the table. She looked tiny and frail standing there in that paper robe, her feet bare, her face so thin.

"Okay. But are you still feeling sick?"

"Not bad. Go ahead. I don't need your help."

Gene smiled. "I guess I did my *helping* already."

But she didn't smile. She gave him a little nudge toward the door. So Gene walked out, but he felt a little embarrassed when he passed a nurse, since he was coming out without his wife. But he sat down in the waiting room, and by then his worries were mounting. He had never seen Emily like this. He had no idea what she was thinking. Did she really not want to have a baby? How could she not be at least a little excited? And then an image came to his mind: a little boy, big enough to get his first baseball glove. Gene saw himself in the backyard, making his first toss, underhand, the little guy trying to make the catch. Gene had a feeling this boy was going to be a fantastic athlete, and beautiful, with his mother's dark hair and blue eyes. His child. His boy.

But actually, he didn't mind if it was a girl. He thought of a little girl as pretty as Emily, sitting on his lap, kissing him on the cheek. He saw her in pigtails, going off to kindergarten.

Emily was taking a long time, longer than seemed necessary, just to get dressed. He hoped she wasn't vomiting again. Or crying. He wondered whether he needed to go back to her. But in another minute or two she appeared, looking composed, pretty. He could tell she had washed her face. She smiled at Gene, but he still didn't see the joy he was hoping for.

He got up and walked to her. "Be careful now," he said, smiling. "You're in a delicate condition."

She didn't answer, and she didn't smile. She walked toward the door without stopping to say anything at the desk. Gene didn't know whether they needed to make an appointment with a gynecologist, or pay for this visit, but he hurried after Emily, and the two walked outside. In the parking lot Emily didn't wait for Gene to open the door. She opened it herself and got in. Gene hurried around to the other side, sat down in the hot car, and rolled down his window. Then he started the engine. He looked over at Emily and was about to say something when she said, "Gene, I'm fine. But you have to admit, it's a lot to get used to. We just got married."

"I know. But think about—"

"Could we get going—so we can get some air in this car?" She rolled down her own window. Gene had bought a newer car this summer. Uncle Wally had given him a great deal on a 1964 Chevy Impala. It had come in on a trade, really clean, with only about thirty thousand miles on it. Gene knew he couldn't afford it, but Wally had told him he would discount it below low book. Then he had said, "Pay me back as you can. No interest." That had been almost too good to be true. Gene's Ford was falling apart, and this gave him and Emily a nice car they could drive for several years.

Gene started the car and then backed out from the parking place. On the car radio, the Doors were singing "Light My Fire," but as soon as Gene shifted and started forward, he turned down the sound, and then he said, "Hon, I'm getting excited about this. I think I'll go out and buy a baseball glove. I can't wait to teach my son how to catch. Or throw a football."

"So it has to be boy?"

"No, no. Not at all. I was thinking about a little girl, too—one who looks exactly like you and wears little pigtails. I'll buy dresses for her. And by the way, I want to be in on all this. I want to change diapers and give baths and take my turn getting up at night. Really. I'm going to help with everything. I know it's going to be a big adjustment, but it'll be great, too. Boy or girl, it's going to be a great kid. I don't see how it could be anything else."

But Emily didn't answer. She was leaning toward the window, apparently trying to catch some air.

"Emily, tell me what you're thinking. Don't you want to be pregnant?"

"Not *by accident*, I don't. I wanted a year alone—just the two of us. Everyone told me that was really important."

"Okay. I understand that. But now that it's happened, it's okay, isn't it? We can deal with it."

"That's easy for *you* to say."

"I know. I don't have to be the one to get sick and be all uncomfortable and everything."

"*Uncomfortable?* Is that what you think being pregnant is? A little uncomfortable?"

"No. I know it's hard. And I know that giving birth is one of the hardest things a woman ever has to do. But if it didn't happen now, it would happen next year. It's not *that* much of a change."

Again, Emily didn't speak. What Gene hated was how solemn she looked, as though she had received horrible news. That kind of attitude couldn't possibly be good for the baby. All Gene wanted was to help Emily feel better, but he had learned something new in the past couple of months. There were times to shut up and let Emily have her time. She wasn't going to be persuaded right now.

So Gene drove and didn't say anything, but he felt terrible. It shouldn't be like this. This was supposed to be a happy time.

Emily said nothing all the way home. When they reached Gene's parents' home on Harvard Avenue—where they were living while his family was in Washington—she walked directly to the bathroom and was gone for such a long time that Gene thought of knocking on the door to ask whether she was all right. But he knew better. He went to the living room, sat down, and waited. He had to get to the dealership as soon as he could, but he didn't dare leave yet, not until he was sure Emily was going to be all right.

When she finally came out, Gene could see that she had been crying, but he could also see that some of the stoicism was gone from her face. She sat down next to him on the couch and said, "Gene, I'm sorry. I'll be happy about this as soon as I start thinking right. I kind of knew what the doctor was going to tell us, but I didn't want to believe it."

"It's a big adjustment. I understand."

"It's something I've always been afraid of. I watched what my mom went through each time with my little brothers and sisters. I can remember the babies coming home from the hospital, and how much work they are at first. I just wanted to put all that off for a while, I guess, and now it's coming before I have myself ready."

"Okay. I see what you're saying. I guess I was kind of playing up the good side too much."

"No. It's what we have to do. I've got to get my head on straight, and then I'll be happy too."

"Well . . . okay. I've got to get to work. We can talk a lot more about this tonight."

But as Gene began to slide forward, Emily reached for his arm and held him back. "Wait a sec. I need to tell you a couple of things."

"Oh, sure." He slid back, then turned to look at her.

"I want to finish school this year, no matter how hard it is. If I don't finish college now, I don't know if I ever will."

"Are you sure that's a good idea when you're so sick?"

"I'll probably get over that. Most women do. And it's better than sitting home or going to a job."

"But when will the baby come?"

"He said about thirty-six weeks, and I've been counting up. That's in April—like about the twentieth."

"But you can't be finished with school until June, can you?"

"I could maybe carry some extra hours fall and winter quarter, and then take a light load in the spring. Something like that. I need to think it through. But I don't want to get this close and then stop."

"What if you went back when the baby is a little older, or—"

"By then you'll want another one, and I'll never get back."

"Hey, I don't decide these things. We'll decide together."

"But you want a lot of kids."

"Honey, I told you already, we'll work that out as we go along. I'm not going to tell you we have to have a lot of kids if that's not what you want."

"Everyone expects it, Gene. Your family, my family, everyone in our ward. They think you're not a good Mormon if you don't have at least half a dozen kids."

"That's not true at all. My parents had six, but Bobbi and Richard only have three."

"Come on, Gene. You know very well that Bobbi had trouble getting pregnant. They would have had more if they could. Your other two aunts have five each. And look at my family. It's like we're trying to populate Davis County all by ourselves."

"Every situation is different, Em. I keep telling you, I'm not going to press you about this. Your health is the most important thing. If you're going to be sick every time, that can't be good."

Emily released his arm and leaned back. "I just wish Mormons would let each other decide for themselves about things like this. I want to finish school, and I want to do some things with my life. I don't want to spend twenty years having kids, and still have children at home when I'm in my fifties. Mormon women do nothing but produce offspring—that's the whole story of their lives."

"But it's a pretty good story, isn't it? My mom is really smart, and really talented, and she's used her skills to raise a good family, but she also finds time to do a lot of community work, church work, things like that. In some ways, I envy women. What's the big joy of going to some office every day of your life and missing out on being around the kids?"

"Oh, come on, Gene. You sound just like my dad."

"But it's true, isn't it?"

"There's *some* truth in it, but you know what? It also makes a wonderful excuse. Men should be doing a lot more in their own homes. Men are *parents*, the same as their wives, and way too often they spend sixteen hours a day at work, building up their own little kingdom, and they leave their wives home to wash diapers and make peanut butter sandwiches. Men ought to be home a lot more than most of them are, and women ought to be heard a whole lot more, out in the world."

Gene could usually understand when Emily expressed her personal needs, but it was this kind of talk that frightened him. She was sounding like these women's lib types. Gene had always thought that a woman *should* be home, and that was a place of honor. President McKay had made that very clear. Still, he knew better than to say something like that right now. "Emily, the only thing I know is that women can have babies and men can't. They can nurse babies and men can't. So when children are little, I think a mom needs to be home. Later, that's where the balance comes in. And I'll tell you right now, I want to be just as involved in my kids' lives as I possibly can. I look forward to it."

"But what if I want a career at some point in my life?"

Gene laughed. "My Grandma Bea started working during the war, and she worked for a long time after."

"That's fine. But what about my going to school? I want to do that now."

"That's up to you. I can't decide something like that for you." He got up. "Let's talk some more about this tonight. I've got to get to work."

"Okay." But she stood up and took hold of his arm again. This time she pulled him to her and kissed him. "I'm sorry," she said. "I'll try to be in a better mood by the time you get home tonight."

Gene felt reassured by that, but he found himself thinking about Emily all day. He wanted to call his parents and tell them about the baby, but he didn't dare—not until Emily said it was all right. Still, he was excited, and it was hard not to tell anyone why. At the same time, he worried about some of the things he had told Emily. Maybe if he were the right sort of leader in his home—the patriarch—he should have told her that women's lib was making women think a career was important, when in fact, that just wasn't so. But he wanted her to be happy, wanted to give her a life that would satisfy her. He wasn't sure how he was supposed to do that. He didn't think his dad had ever had to face these questions.

He was trying to close the sale on a car about the time he usually tried to leave the dealership for the day, so he stayed just a little longer than he had intended. Still, when the man kept dickering, Gene pushed the matter to a conclusion, offered his final price, and let the man walk away. Gene had a notion that the guy was only trying to save a couple hundred bucks and that the walkout was a bluff, but he let the man go and gambled that he would be back the next day, not quite so confident. Mostly, though, he didn't care. Sale or no sale, this was not a night to come home late.

When he got home, he found Emily curled up on the couch in the living room. The TV was on, but she was sound asleep. It was almost eight o'clock. He kneeled down next to her and brushed his hand over her hair. Her eyes came open with a start. "Oh!" she said. "What time is it?"

"I'm a little late."

"But I was going to have dinner ready for you. I was just going to lie down for a few minutes."

"It's okay. How are you feeling?"

"Not so bad right now." She sat up.

He was still on his knees. He leaned forward and rested his head in her lap. She ran her lovely, smooth hands over his hair, his cheek. "Gene, I've been thinking all day. I'm really sorry how I acted this morning. I'm getting excited about our baby. He's going to be so handsome, just like his dad."

"I'm thinking more and more about a little girl. I can just see her holding my finger when she's learning to walk. All day, I could feel that little hand, grabbing onto my pointer finger."

Emily laughed. "You're such a sweet boy. Who invented you?"

"I don't know. But you're doing some serious reconstruction work. I know that."

"I don't mean to do that, Gene. I know some of the things I said this morning aren't exactly right. I was exaggerating to make my point."

He raised his head. "Em, I'm just not sure what a husband is supposed to be anymore. It seems like everything is changing—all the ways we think about everything."

"Well, one thing hasn't changed. You need some dinner. Do you mind if I just make some tuna fish sandwiches and maybe open up a can of tomato soup?"

"That's my favorite choice from your menu."

"That's only because I mess anything up that I actually have to cook." She stood up and then pulled on his elbow. He stood too. But he made no comment. He had teased her at times—and she really wasn't much of a cook—but he was pretty sure this was no day to toy with her emotions.

They walked into the kitchen, and Gene flipped the light on. He looked in one of the cabinets and found some Campbell's Chicken Noodle. "I don't see any tomato," he said. "Chicken noodle okay?"

"Sure." She reached into the same cupboard and got a can of tuna, and then she waited while he used the can opener on the soup. When he was finished, he handed her the opener and walked to the cupboard where the saucepans were. He was pouring the soup into the pan when he heard Emily gasp and say, "Oh, no." She dropped the tuna can on the cabinet and dashed from the room.

"What's the matter? Did you cut yourself?" Gene chased after her, but she ran to the bathroom and slammed the door behind her. In a moment he heard the sound he had gotten used to. She was vomiting again.

Gene walked back to the kitchen and finished opening the can. Then he dumped the tuna into a little bowl and mixed in some mayonnaise. He liked some pickle in his tuna, so he got out a bottle of dills and was dicing a pickle when Emily returned. "I'm sorry," she said. "The smell of that tuna was just too much for me."

"I figured that's what did it."

"In fact. . . ." Emily was retreating into the hallway. "I can smell it from here, Gene. I've got to get out of here." And she was gone.

"Should I bring you some soup?"

"No. I don't want anything."

So Gene finished preparing his gourmet meal, sat down at the kitchen table and ate it, and then covered the extra tuna and put it in the refrigerator. He wondered whether he shouldn't just take it outside and dump it in the garbage can so she wouldn't have to face the stuff again. But he decided he could make a sandwich in the morning and take it to work with him. He rinsed off the utensils he had used, along with the saucepan, stuck them in the dishwasher, and then walked to the living room. Emily was curled up on the couch again. She still looked pale.

"How are you feeling?" he asked.

"Steady as she goes, for the moment."

"Doctor Hancock said we had an adventure ahead of us."

"Yeah." She laughed softly, and Gene smiled.

She looked so beautiful lying there, and she was going to be a mother. The idea of it brought tears to his eyes. He knelt next to her. "Wow. Something really strange just happened to me."

She opened her eyes and looked at him. "What?"

"I just felt my love click up one full notch. It just hit eleven on my love meter, and the thing only goes to ten."

She looked up. "What are you talking about?"

"I didn't think I could love you more. But all of a sudden, I do. You know, because of what's happening inside you—what you're making for us."

"Oh, Gene, I'm such a poor excuse for a wife. I can't cook at all, and now I can't even make tuna fish sandwiches."

Tears had come into her eyes, but Gene started to laugh, and after a moment, she did too. He kissed her face, her eyes, and then he stroked her pretty hair. "We have a lot of stuff to figure out," he said.

"I know. I'm sorry I ruined this day."

"You didn't. It's one of the best days of my life. I'm going to be a *dad*. Can you believe that?"

"Gene, don't you know what's bothering me the most? You haven't mentioned it. It's like you don't want to think about it."

"What?"

"You won't be home when the baby starts to walk. You won't be able to hold her hand."

Gene *had* thought of it—and *had* pushed the thought aside. It was too terrible to consider. "Maybe I won't have to go—for some reason."

"Gene, you will."

"Well, we'll just have to deal with that when it comes, too. We can only take one step at a time."

But Emily was crying hard again now, and Gene felt an old hollowness return. But he didn't want reality right now. He just wanted to think about tossing that baseball or holding that little girl in pigtails.

# CHAPTER 7

Hans had sat in his cell for more than two months—seventy-one days, actually, by his own count. It was now August 20, 1968, a Tuesday. He never saw anyone except the men who came by three times a day with his meals. The food seemed hardly enough to sustain life, especially to provide enough nutritional variety for good health, and yet he felt little hunger. He had to force himself to eat the same black bread and thin soups every day. The bread was dry and hard, difficult to get down. He sat all day in this lonely section of the prison where he had been placed that first day. He knew there were men in other cells. There was one who cried at night—wailed, really—but with solid walls and doors, only a voice that loud could be heard, and to call out to others was absolutely forbidden. He sometimes tried to talk to the guard who brought the food, but the man would hardly respond.

Hans would like to have slept a great deal more than he did—simply to kill the time—but he had to sit on his stool, or stand, and leave the bed folded. If he walked too much, the guards who looked through his peephole five or six times an hour would tell him to stop. He had no idea why. He needed to feel alive, so sometimes, soon after a guard left the cell block, he would run in place, hard, for a few minutes. Most of the rest of the time, for as long as his eyes would hold out, he read his Bible. It was that, more than anything, that kept him going. The small print was a strain in the afternoon, once the light was no longer on the muted window glass, so he tried to use the late afternoons and evenings to think about the things he had read—and to connect, in his mind, one passage to another. He would read one of Christ's parables, and then he would spend hours thinking about it—what it meant generally and what it meant to him, or what it might mean to him once his life actually had significance again. The nothingness in his life, the stasis, had so little to do with the rest of the world that it was hard to be human, hard to know how he related to anyone or anything else. He did pray a great deal, and that was his other way of surviving, of reaching outside himself. He told the Lord—often, out loud—what he felt, how thankful he was for what he was learning, but he almost never asked for anything. He had learned, by now, that nothing was coming, not for a long time, and maybe not ever. So it was better not to think of joy but only to find little pleasures in subtle ways, and most of the pleasure now was in his recognitions—what he discovered in Christ's teachings. He wondered at himself that at one time he had found so little to believe. Now, life was almost all belief.

And then one day after breakfast he heard a key in the lock of his cell door. The door opened, and a man walked in. "Stoltz, come with me," the man said.

Hans followed without asking questions. In the outer hallway he had to squint to adjust to the bright red lights. He tromped along behind the man, aware that he hadn't taken full, long strides for such a long time that his legs felt stiff. He was led up two flights of stairs and down another hall, and then the man opened a door and ushered him into an office—a rather nice office, with a carpet on the floor and a wooden desk, stained in dark chestnut. "Sit down," the man said. "Here." Hans took his seat in a wooden chair in front of the desk, and then the man left. Hans assumed that someone else would be coming in, but he didn't mind waiting. In fact, he was surprised at the joy he felt in looking around, having new objects before his eyes. The room was sparse, but there was a picture on the wall, just a simple mountain scene. Hans studied it and thought of the mountains he had seen in his life, how much he would like to see them again. A little sign behind the desk, on the wall, read, "The people's state: where freedom includes all."

Hans wondered what it meant, why it was here. He told himself that these were new words to run through his head, to consider later, during the long hours alone. He had thought a great deal about socialism lately. He had always resisted the propaganda he received at school, but now, he knew he would have fewer choices. He would have to live in this country, and he might as well take what was best from the system and give what he could both to the "state" and to his fellow landsmen. What would Christ do, living here? he sometimes wondered.

The door opened, and Hans turned in his chair to see a man in a dark suit and black tie. He was a hefty man with heavy cheeks and big, puffy hands, but he was shorter than Hans. He looked rather pleasant, with fleshy lips that seemed curved into something close to a smile. He sat down, and then he did smile, almost playfully, showing teeth that were stained like an old porcelain sink. "Hans Stoltz. I've been reading about you. It's very nice to meet you, finally." He stood again, reached across the desk, and stuck out his hand. Hans took hold of it, felt the flabbiness, but gave it a firm shake.

"I know you've been lonely with us here. I meant to meet with you sooner, but I'm busier than I would like to be." He smiled. "Our little hotel is almost fully occupied these days. This seems to be a popular place to stay. It must be our scenery." He laughed, the sound coming mostly from his nose. "Is everything going all right for you so far?"

"I'm not complaining."

"*Ach*. Nicely put. One does learn that sort of thing, in time. I don't know whether you have given it much thought, but so much of a prison term is exactly that: learning to be satisfied with things. And learning to appreciate the normal freedoms we miss when we lose them. It can be— what? Quite educational. It's part of the rebuilding process we put you through. And if one accepts the situation with goodwill and some trust in higher socialist ideals, it can enhance one's commitment. At least that's what we tell you. Not true?"

He was laughing again. Hans had no idea how to take this man. No one in the prison system had ever used an ironic tone with him.

The man leaned back in his chair and looked at Hans for a time, seeming to study his face. And then, with a bit of surprise in his voice, he said, "Oh, my goodness, I haven't told you my name. We're going to spend a good deal of time together. You should at least know who I am. My name is Felscher. You can call me *Herr* Felscher."

Hans nodded, surprised a little at the informality. He had expected a title.

"Now, Hans, where should we start? Could you tell me, perhaps, how you feel about your experience in prison so far? All in all, I'm certain you would rather be home, but how has it been? Can you tell me anything you've learned?"

"I worked hard in the mine," Hans said. "There's value in that, I think, and I liked some of the men I worked with."

"Yes. Isn't it remarkable what good men end up in prison sometimes? It's what gives me hope. They want to do right, I think. They want to be contributors to our state. I never give up on the idea of reform. I have seen dissidents—actual enemies of our government—become good citizens, devoted to socialist ideals, and all because they had some time to think, to reconsider their own role in society. Is that happening to you, Hans?"

Hans knew already that Felscher was dangerous. He wanted to play games. Hans knew he would have to choose his words carefully. "I *have* thought a great deal. More than at any time in my life. I feel more desire to serve my countrymen than I ever have before."

"Now that's interesting, how you say that. You express a desire to help, as an individual, other individuals. There are few things more inspiring than that. But you managed to avoid the use of those collective words we love so much in a socialist country. Ultimately, we all must find our way together and give up some of this individualism, don't you think?"

Hans nodded, and he calculated his response. "I think there is nothing more important than to forget oneself and to serve others."

"Others? But not the state?"

"The state is made up of all the people."

"Hans, Hans, you are a clever boy. It's what I notice in your file. These are all Christian ways of speaking, not so? I ask you for socialist language and you give me the words of Jesus Christ. Is that what you mean to do? Aren't you finding a clever way to voice your own independence and perhaps nettle me a bit?" He laughed, pleasantly, as though he admired Hans.

"I'm only saying what I believe," Hans said. "I *am* a Christian. That's allowed in this free country."

"You're a Mormon. Not true?"

"Yes."

"And that's very important to you, I assume?"

"Yes. It is."

"It's your right. As you say, we do nothing to inhibit religion in the GDR. It must always be the hope of a true socialist that such thinking will become archaic in time, a kind of stepping-stone to a higher plain, but I will say this: I admire Mormons. I've known a few. They don't disrupt our government. They may not embrace it as fully as one might like, but they accept realities, and they are, for the most part, good citizens. Why was it that you acted as an enemy of the state, Hans? I don't think that's anything your parents or your church encouraged, is it?"

"No, it isn't. But I'm not an enemy of the state. I was only trying to help a friend."

"One individual serving another, just as you think people ought to do—even if the man you chose to help was a traitor. Is that what it was, Hans?" Felscher had a way of rubbing his thick hands together, as though molding some lump between them, his lips still making that smile, but all the while his eyes, deep behind his heavy cheeks, remained unmoved, severe.

"I didn't think of it that way."

"How did you think about it?" Felscher leaned forward and stared more directly into Hans's eyes, as though he were trying to send a signal: *be sure to say the right thing this time, if you know what's good for you.*

"Berndt was unhappy. He thought he would be happier in another country. He asked me to help him."

"Wait. Wait. That's not the truth. Your action could not have helped Berndt. If you had done what you intended to do—cover up the exit from that basement—you would only have helped others to escape once Berndt Kerner was gone." He hesitated and kept his focus intently on Hans. "Be careful around me, Hans. I don't like rationalizing. And I don't like lies. If that's what you want to do, plan to stay in prison for a long time."

Felscher, of course, had a good point about whom Hans had meant to help. He knew better than to deny it. "I only mean that it was Berndt who asked me. It was out of friendship that I agreed."

"But you know there is no logic in that. You're an intelligent young man. Everyone knows that about you. So speak the truth this time. You must believe that people have the *right* to leave this country. Many people believe that. They say that our nation can only have freedom when citizens are given the opportunity to move to the capitalist West."

"I've never expressed any such belief."

"Oh, no? You tried to leave once yourself. What were you saying then?"

"There is no proof I did that. The *Stasi* reached that conclusion, but Berndt and I always said we were only taking a day off from school. We took a little trip to the sea."

"Oh, Hans. This is not good. This is, in fact, very bad. We thought, after some months in work camp and some time with us here—ample time to think—that you might reconsider your place in our system. You're the sort of young man this country needs. But when you find clever ways to deny what you have done—and show no remorse—what choice have we but to hold you here for your entire term? Or perhaps even longer. We can extend your term if we determine that you have learned no remorse."

Hans thought of three years in these prisons. The work camp had been bad enough, but if he were kept in his little cell all those months, he didn't think he could last. Still, he said nothing; he knew better than to give the man weapons.

Without warning, Felscher smiled, his big lips stretching. "So. How is the food here? Do you like what you've received so far?"

"It's adequate."

"Now I know you're not trying to tell the truth. We don't want to make things so nice here that you'll want to stay. You can understand that. But I would like to express my goodwill toward you so that we can make some progress. What would you like for your midday meal? Name anything you like. A nice veal cutlet?"

Hans hesitated. He didn't know what Felscher was up to.

"Or is there something you like better?"

"A cutlet would be fine."

"Good. Good. *Schnitzel* it is, then. I will order it. You sit here and think a little, and then have a nice meal. When you're finished, we'll talk a little more. How does that sound?"

"Good."

Felscher got up and walked out. He left Hans to sit for the better part of an hour, and all that time Hans wondered how he should deal with the man. Maybe he should have turned the food down—but something decent to eat sounded much too inviting. He knew the food was supposed to win him over, but Hans would never give in to this brute with his all-knowing manner and constant smirk.

Still, when the food came, it was even better than Hans had hoped. It was not only *Schnitzel*, but there was everything to go with it: red cabbage, buttered potatoes, and a green salad. And with it, a mug of beer. He didn't drink the beer, of course, and he wished he had some *Apfelsaft*, but the food was so wonderful that he ate slowly, savored all of it. He was eventually uncomfortably full, but he couldn't resist eating every bit of it.

He was close to finishing when Felscher returned. "What?" he asked. "You aren't going to drink your beer? I thought that would please you the most."

"I don't drink beer."

"Not any? Not at all?"

"No." Hans had been sitting at the front of Felscher's desk, using it as a table. He slid his chair back now.

"I suppose this has something to do with your religion."

"Yes."

"My goodness. Such a religion. It takes away all pleasures. I was about to offer you a cigarette, but I suppose you don't smoke either."

"No, I don't."

Felscher laughed, pleasantly, but even his joviality seemed a stance, another calculation in the process of feeling Hans out. "You won't be an easy one to reach," he said. "Many men will do almost anything for a cigarette. But what do I do with you? Have you no bad habits?"

"No. At least nothing of that sort."

"Tell me about this—I'm curious. What does smoking have to do with religious faith?"

"We take good care of our bodies. That's all."

"I see." He stared at Hans for some time. Hans tried to return his gaze, but he found it difficult. "And can a Mormon believe in the Marxist idea of the dialectic? Can he accept that sort of inevitability? Can he help his people work toward a Communist state?"

This was tricky. Hans had to be careful. "Mormons can believe what they want about political matters."

"Yes, yes. But aren't they told in church that the GDR is a godless state?"

"We never say such things in church. Our bishop tells us to support our government."

"Well, then, what do *you* believe? Tell me honestly. It's all right to do that here. We don't punish people for their beliefs."

Hans didn't believe that. Indirectly, Felscher had already told him the opposite. Still, Hans was not going to deny his faith. "I don't believe in inevitability, as Communists do," he said. "I believe in a Father in Heaven. I believe in his commandments. I believe in the virtues that Jesus Christ taught: loving and serving others, living a clean life."

"I see. So naturally, you would like to leave our country and go somewhere with less socialist influence. I can understand that."

"I didn't say that."

"But it's only logical."

"The GDR promises me I can live my religion. I can serve here and be a good citizen—as much here as anywhere."

Felscher sat for a time, chuckling to himself, rubbing his hands again, and then he said, "I rather like you, Hans. You're smart. You're good at this. But I'll warn you—I'm better. I have to be. And finally, it all comes down to this. I have control over your life. I can keep you here as long as I choose. So you see, cleverness, in the end, is not wise. I can be your excellent friend, and I will be, but there's only one way out of here. You must tell me the names of all those who left our country or planned to do so. I especially need to know those who remain and may be plotting at this moment to effect another breakout. Without those names, I can make your whole life—not just your years in prison—entirely miserable. So now is the time to speak. I will get the names sooner or later, so make this easy. Simply tell me now—and then we'll start planning a way for you to have the life you want. If there's one thing I know about you it's that you worked hard in school. You wanted a career. I can't give you everything you once thought you could have, but I can keep you from ending up stuck in the deepest mud. I would give some serious thought to that."

"*Herr* Felscher, I don't know any of those people. Berndt didn't want me to know their names, and I didn't want to know. I only met one man other than Berndt, and I only knew his first name. But he is the man who died with Berndt. I saw some other men cross the street, in the dark, but they were only shadows. As to any who planned to go later, I know nothing about them. That's the whole truth. I will never be able to tell you anything else but that. I could invent some names, but what good would that do? You would soon know I was lying."

Again, Felscher laughed. "You sound so very sincere, Hans. It's amazing to me how you religious people can be such excellent liars. But here's something I've learned. There will be a way to reach you. I don't know what it is yet, but there will be some vulnerability in you that you don't even know yourself. I will find it, and when I do, you will tell me everything. It would be so much better for you to tell me now, but I can do this the other way. You go sit in that cell of yours for a time—perhaps a long time—and then we'll talk again."

Felscher stood and Hans did too. He was tempted to plead with Felscher, vow that he really knew no more, but he was certain that would make no difference. What he had to do was keep himself strong. When he was led back to the cell block, however, he felt the dampness, heard the echo of the emptiness, and he sensed the loneliness that would only multiply with the coming days. He wished that he did have something he could tell Felscher.

When the jailer locked the door, Hans stood in the middle of the cell for a time, partly to let his eyes adjust, and partly because he dreaded the hours ahead. Once he sat down, he would be back to the tedium he had escaped for a few hours. He wondered how soon he would be interrogated again and whether he would receive another good meal when that day came. But he doubted that would happen, and he suspected he might be left for many days, maybe months, before he got out of the cell again. The thought of that—all the long hours and days ahead—sent him into a bit of a panic. He felt his breathing begin to labor, felt tears come to his eyes.

Hans knew he had to do the things that kept him going, so he stepped to his table and decided that he would read his Bible while he still had a little light. But the Bible wasn't on the table where he knew he had left it. He looked around the room, the floor, even broke the rules and opened his bunk. But he knew the truth already. Felscher had had it taken. He was searching for Hans's vulnerability, and maybe he had found it. Hans sat down at the table, rested his head on his arms, and cried. He couldn't think what he would do now. How could he possibly live without *anything*?

He cried for a long time, and he prayed, kept praying until he had said everything too many times to repeat again. He received his dinner but gave it back, still full from his meal and glad not to eat the hard bread for one night. But then he had to wait for bedtime, and the minutes ticked away with painful slowness. When the bell finally rang and he was able to make his bed, he tried to plunge into the blankness of sleep, but he awakened after a few hours. He tried to sleep again and couldn't, but some words came into his mind, and he knew immediately that they were a gift. He was remembering the words he had been reading. Christ's words. He searched for more, and he realized that whole passages had remained in his head. He could think of the Sermon on the Mount, and he could call back large parts of it.

He felt better, comforted, and he was able to sleep again. Then, in the morning after his breakfast, he tried to use the words that were stored in his brain. He found that he could recite a verse or two, and then he could dwell on the meaning. He could mull the words over carefully and try to think of their implications. He could compare them to other ideas, other words that came to him, from Christ or from the Old Testament. He could link them to things his father had said, or his branch presidents. He could apply them to things that had happened in his life. He could even develop the idea into a little sermon.

That afternoon he worked for hours on a talk he would like to give in church someday. Over the next few days, he developed his ideas into a full speech, and he gave it many times, adding examples and illustrations, quoting scriptures, until he thought he had a clear message. After that, he delivered the talk a couple of times each day, always trying to improve it. He embellished certain ideas, and then decided to cut in places. He eventually told himself the sermon was ready, and he delivered it officially, out loud, and cried as he bore his testimony at the end. He told himself he would hold the talk in his head, deliver it from time to time, but now he needed to find more verses, more thoughts, and start another talk. It was the bread of life he was finding, and all of it resided within himself.

At least that's how he felt on the best days, at the best moments. There were also times when he grew weary of so much concentrating. He would exercise then, try to work himself to exhaustion, but that was difficult with so little food and with exercise possible only in short bursts. And so there were times when he would give way to his discouragement, and he would stare into the dimness and think of life outside. What seemed true at such times was that there would be no end to this endlessness, that he couldn't survive.

Still, days passed. He had promised himself that he would keep track of every day, but sometimes he lost confidence in whether he had already made his mark for the day. He would ask the guards what day it was, but they wouldn't answer, as though they understood that part of the punishment was the loss of time, the numbing effect of a continuous run of days.

One morning he awakened with a start, as he often did, suddenly aware of where he was. He was longing for light, feeling the dread of another day, when he heard a tapping sound. At first it seemed nothing more than the eerie sounds of the old building, but it became apparent that a pattern was repeating itself, that the taps were controlled, apparently with a purpose. They were coming from a pipe that led from the ceiling and probably passed through another cell above him. The pattern of taps was one, one-two, one-two-three, a hesitation, and then the same pattern repeated. He didn't know what it meant. What he did know was that prisoners sometimes communicated this way. He had heard about it in work camp. He now wished that he had asked for at least the rudiments of the code.

He went to the pipe, and after one of the repetitions, he imitated the pattern. The same beats came back to him. What was the point?

What followed, however, was a long, steady flow of taps. He didn't think to count the first time, so he didn't repeat, but when the taps began again, he did count. Fourteen. Then one. Then another long run, this time thirteen. Then five. He had answered each time by mimicking the pattern, but he still didn't understand. So once again the other prisoner tapped, one, one-two, one-two-three.

And then Hans knew. The man was setting up the alphabet. One was A; two was B. Hans counted on his fingers. Fourteen was N. One was A. Thirteen was M. Five was E. NAME."

Hans started tapping. Eight, one, fourteen, nineteen. HANS. And now the conversation could begin. "*Guten Morgen,*" the man tapped. Good morning.

"*Danke.*" Thanks.

The day that followed turned out to seem shorter than usual, much more interesting. Hans was almost breathless with fascination as he deciphered letters, put them together, retained them long enough to find a word. Some of it made no sense, and he knew he wasn't counting right, or not remembering. It was tedious business and would take a while to learn proficiency, but Hans wasn't alone.

By the end of the day, Hans was catching on better all the time, understanding quite well, and he knew the name of the tapper, even a little about him. He was a man named Stefan Hart. He was a West German. He had crossed into East Germany, legally, but then had tried to help a friend escape, hidden in his car. Stefan had been caught and had now served almost four years. He told Hans to find a metal object, if possible, and to tap sharply but softly, but to stop before mealtimes and to listen for the guards in the cell block. He even suggested a warning tap, so the other knew when to stop.

Hans told Stefan that he had been in prison less than a year, but he told him little else. He didn't want to say something that might be used against him. Maybe this was a guard or a *Stasi* agent doing this tapping, maybe even Felscher himself. And maybe the goal was to get Hans's confidence and then trick him into revealing things about himself.

And yet, it was hard to think that way. In truth, Hans had little to hide, and the joy of having someone to communicate with, however awkward the process was, was something that could keep him alive on those days when recalling scriptures felt like too much work. He told himself he could spend part of each day tapping, getting better at it, part of his time exercising, and still, a good deal with his scriptures, his sermons. This gave him a kind of schedule along with meals and sleep. He still longed to walk down a street, or to spend some time with his family, but this tapping was something new, and it felt like blood flowing, warming his body, exciting his mind. He actually had a friend.

After a few days, his proficiency with the code seemed to take a sudden jump forward, and Stefan taught him to replace some of the letters higher in the alphabet, such as "c" for "s" and "d" for "t," and reduce the number of taps. Hans also found a little pebble in a corner of the floor. It wasn't quite what he needed, but it made a sharper sound on the pipe than his knuckle did, and he got so he could use it pretty well.

Stefan told him about his life. He had grown up in East Berlin and had left with his family in 1960, before the wall went up. He had kept in touch with his East Berliner friend, and he had eventually been allowed to cross the border on business. By then, he was working as a sales representative for a West German company, and he had come to the annual commercial fair in Leipzig. It was there that he arranged to meet his friend, and they had planned the escape.

Stefan and Hans talked about various interests, but the captivating subject for Hans was any information he could get about life in West Germany. A person could travel about freely, he said, and choose his own career. He described all the things people could get on the other side of the wall: the cars, the food, the vacations they could take. Sometimes, when Hans awakened and it was too early to begin tapping, he would picture himself in the West somewhere—maybe even living in America, as he had once dreamed of doing—and having a nice home, not fearing that he was being watched all the time. He still wished that he could go back to his university studies and be able to pursue the interests he had once had. But thinking of those things wasn't helpful. He told himself he should converse with Stefan, to pass the time but not to discuss with him the things that he would never have.

## CHAPTER 8

Kathy's hotel room was on the fifteenth floor of the Conrad Hilton in Chicago. All the McCarthy aides were staying on the same floor, near their campaign headquarters. It was now Wednesday afternoon, August 28, and the 1968 Democratic National Convention was underway, but Kathy had arrived the previous week, and she had been working hard the whole time. Until this morning she had held out a bit of hope that the delegates would decide Humphrey couldn't win in November and would turn to McCarthy, who, according to polls, was more popular with voters across the country. But the morning papers had carried a story that McCarthy had already admitted he couldn't win the nomination and that he was now fighting only for a compromise peace plan that was being offered as a minority plank in the platform. His admission was hard for his staff members to understand, and they were deflated, even a little angry with their candidate—after all the work they had done for him.

At the moment Kathy was looking out the open window, through the screen, watching the demonstrators in Grant Park as she had done off and on all day. The antiwar people had gathered in front of the band shell, and they had been listening to speeches by various counterculture leaders. She could hear the amplified voices, the intermittent roar of response. She was also listening to television reports on the peace-plank vote at the convention, and she knew that the people in the park, with transistor radios in their pockets, were listening too. That was obvious from the moans she could hear as the votes were announced. As it became clear that Johnson's hawkish proposal was going to win, someone in the park tried to lower the American flag, and the police reacted. Police had been staying on the edges of the demonstration, standing guard in lines on three sides, but one large group of officers, maybe a hundred or so, had moved in close. When the flag started to come down, some of the policemen ran north along the west side of the crowd and waded into a group of demonstrators who had collected around the flagpole. Kathy cringed when she saw nightsticks flash, saw people falling, and then, when rocks and other debris began to fly at the police. The skirmish lasted only a few minutes while one of the rally leaders pleaded on the microphone for everyone to be calm and not to throw things. The police moved back, but in another few minutes, someone tried to raise something else in the place of the American flag. Kathy saw a flash of red, didn't know whether it was actually a National Liberation Front flag—the banner of the Vietcong—but understood the implication. The police were back in more force this time, and the confrontation was uglier, longer, wilder.

Kathy could hardly breathe. She hated the idea of desecrating the flag, but she couldn't see why beatings had to be the response. She continued to watch, hoping that someone would pull the plug on all this anger, but the police had now gathered in a large group, west of the crowd. They were dressed in light blue shirts and blue helmets, and she could see that their black nightsticks were out and ready. She could also see, even hear to some degree, the young people taunting them.

And then everything broke loose. The police charged the crowd in a group, plowed through, swinging their sticks, battering anyone in their way. The crowd fled, broke in half, but debris was flying again, coming in on the police. It was all so inane and pointless. Someone on the microphone was screaming, "Sit down! Sit down!" But it was quite some time before people began to listen and the police withdrew. By then, Kathy could see that a lot of the demonstrators were injured. They lay on the grass after the police moved back, and then other demonstrators ran to help them. In another few minutes Kathy heard sirens. She was sick. It was such a perfect day, the sky and Lake Michigan almost the same shade of blue, the air warm, not sticky hot, and into that beauty had intruded this hatred and violence.

It was all so disappointing and disillusioning—the lost vote, this pointless violence, and really everything she had seen at the convention. President Johnson, even though he had dropped out of the race, was still pulling the strings in the party, and the old-line Democrats were bent on nominating Johnson's choice, Hubert Humphrey. Meanwhile, Humphrey was doing everything to keep that support. He was vowing to continue the fight in Vietnam, to negotiate "from strength." What bothered Kathy was that in many states, such as New York where she had campaigned, McCarthy had won a huge percentage of the popular vote but hadn't received a commensurate number of delegates. In other states, such as Texas, the majority—according to a "unit rule"—took every vote, and that meant that those who preferred McCarthy had no voice. In Georgia, where delegates were appointed by the governor, a mostly white delegation had been chosen. Young Julian Bond had led a "challenge delegation" to the convention, and according to the guidelines of the party, should have been the only acceptable group, but the credentials committee had compromised, seated both delegations, and given each member half a vote.

Most members of the California and New York delegations had come to Chicago ready for a fight, hoping not only to pass a peace plank but perhaps also to find another candidate. There had been a lot of talk about uniting antiwar delegates behind a peace advocate. What few people seemed to believe, even before McCarthy's concession statement, was that he was the one who could gain enough votes. One rumor was that young Senator Ted Kennedy might carry enough "Kennedy mystique" to excite a disillusioned nation. But it was all talk, and Kathy could see that nothing like that was actually going to happen.

Kathy, by now, was disgusted with the whole political process. She was an office worker, not a power broker, but she was in the middle of the action, and she liked little of what she had observed. McCarthy himself had remained strangely withdrawn, so it was his campaign leaders who seemed frantic to cut a deal, to come away with *something* from all their effort. They argued violently, screaming so loudly that she could hear them through closed doors, and they said things around the office that made her wonder whether politicians really believed in anything they said. Everything was about wordsmithing, making claims, gaining votes from one constituency or another. She had always seen McCarthy as pure, an idealist, fighting for change—and maybe he was all of that—but "his people" certainly knew how to assert what leverage they thought they had, and they were willing to make backroom deals in desperate attempts to line up votes.

Kathy had also been following television news all week, watching to see what the antiwar groups were doing. Before the convention even started, there had been clashes between demonstrators and police, and then on Sunday, Monday, and Tuesday nights, as the convention got underway, thousands of demonstrators had gathered at Lincoln Park on the Lake Michigan shoreline north of the Loop. Each night the police had cleared the park, using nightsticks and tear gas, and had made hundreds of arrests. There had been a lot of accusations back and forth about who was creating the trouble. Mayor Richard Daley had vowed to keep the city under control, and he was not afraid to use massive force against the conglomeration of counterculture groups who were supposedly ready to disrupt the convention and bring Chicago to a standstill. Kathy knew some of the people being quoted, however, and she knew that the rhetoric was more put-on than real. Abbie Hoffman and Jerry Rubin had been getting most of the press. They were a couple of freewheeling antiestablishment leaders of a group they called "Yippies." They had given various explanations for the meaning of that title, including "Youth International Party," but essentially Hoffman and Rubin were young guys who hated middle-class earnestness and wanted to encourage a more communal, free-spirited lifestyle. They had been behind the attempt to "levitate" the Pentagon the previous fall, a tongue-in-cheek event that had brought a National Guard response. It was there that hippie girls, with flowers in their hair, had stuck daisies into soldiers' rifle barrels. Kathy had seen the pictures in all the newspapers.

Now Hoffman and Rubin were making new claims every day, pushing Mayor Daley's temperature higher and higher. They had started by holding their own little "convention," where they nominated a pig they had named Pigasus. They promised to lace the Chicago water supply with LSD; to float nude, with all their friends, on Lake Michigan; to burn draft cards in a giant display that would spell out "Beat Army." It was impossible to imagine that anyone could take such stuff seriously, and in Kathy's opinion, Richard Daley had overreacted. He had placed an eleven o'clock curfew on city parks, refused to issue demonstration permits, and ringed the International Amphitheatre—where the convention was being held—with barbed wire.

Meanwhile, a group called "the Mobe," short for National Mobilization Committee to End the War in Vietnam, and led by Tom Hayden, Rennie Davis, and other SDS and "movement" leaders, was calling for nonviolence but encouraging thousands of antiwar demonstrators to meet in Chicago and show that the convention did not represent the will of the people. A lot of McCarthy supporters, some of whom had been movement people themselves, were also gathering in Chicago even though McCarthy had warned against doing so. He feared violence and didn't want things to get out of hand.

The demonstrations in Lincoln Park had gotten more intense each night, and the police kept cracking down harder. Today, however, the focus of the hostility had moved to Grant Park, across from the Hilton on the lakeshore. Mobe leaders had been promising a peaceful march down Michigan Avenue from the park, whether Daley granted a permit or not.

But now, after the skirmish at the flagpole—with so many demonstrators injured—Kathy wasn't sure what to expect. That night Humphrey would be nominated, and no one out there in the park was happy about that. "Dump the Hump" had been the demonstrators' war cry all week. Chicago could explode before the day was over, and Kathy was depressed to think that her attempt to work through the system had come to nothing.

She left the window and walked down the hallway to the McCarthy headquarters. A lot of the aides were there, but no one was doing much. Most were standing in little groups, talking quietly. She looked for Professor Jennings but didn't see him. He had been in Chicago even longer than she, but he was working mostly at the convention itself, and she had hardly seen him. One of Kathy's three roommates, a girl named Louise Bowen, was sitting at her typewriter, staring ahead. Kathy could see that she had been crying. "Are you okay?" Kathy asked.

"No," Louise said. "I still thought we had a chance on the peace plank—but the vote wasn't even close. We've worked all these months, and what good did it do?"

Kathy didn't try to answer. There was really nothing to say. "I think I'm going to walk over to the park," she said.

"Don't. It's getting bad down there."

"I know." But Kathy wanted to go. She didn't want to be part of any violence, but if the Mobe was still going to hold its peaceful march, she wanted to be part of it. It was the only way she could express what she was feeling.

So Kathy took an elevator down to the elegant, vaulted hotel lobby with its fancy double staircases, and then she walked on outside. She used the Balbo Street bridge to cross the railroad tracks and enter the park. She passed through a double line of National Guard soldiers, who glanced at her but didn't try to stop her. What she knew, however, was that if she tried to go back the same way, she would have to show her McCarthy staff credentials, and even that might not be enough. Still, she headed south to the band shell area. She saw a long line of police along Columbus Avenue, on the west side of the demonstrators. They were watching, ready, apparently intending to keep the demonstration contained in the park. The scene reminded her of some of her experiences with SDS. A speaker at the band shell was using the sound system like a musical instrument, whining, yelling, whispering, always receiving an intense response. And yet, the sound was not very different from the voices she had heard from the convention platform. People with huge egos were at work in both places, and the followers usually knew nothing of the deals being made behind the scenes. There were always so many beautiful abstractions to express at such rallies, but behind it all, the private needs of the leaders were being met, and those needs seemed always to involve power. Kathy felt physically weak; a weariness that had been building up for years, not hours, seemed to be taking the strength from her legs as she walked. Still, almost all these people opposed the war, and down at the Amphitheatre, the majority wanted to keep bombing the Vietnamese people. She felt more at home here.

Kathy kept walking—and watching. She wasn't certain she would march. That depended on whether the demonstrators seemed under control—and how the police were responding. But she did want to drink in some of the passion she felt coming from people who shared her disgust with what the police had been doing. That did seem the clearest of the evils this week.

A lot of the demonstrators looked straight—students with button-down collars and horn-rimmed glasses. Others looked wild, in their hippie garb. And some were obviously local teenagers, there primarily to get in on the action. She smelled marijuana, saw a few people with glazed, drugged eyes, but the majority were just hanging out in the park, laughing, talking, not paying much attention to the speakers or even the police. Music was everywhere, on radios and sung by guys with guitars. Kathy heard a young man with a sort of Bob Dylan voice who was saying, as much as singing, "Come on people now, smile on your brother. Everybody get together, try to love one another, right now." It was a Youngbloods song, and apparently meant sincerely, but it struck Kathy as ironic at the moment.

As she walked closer to the band shell, she could hear one of the Mobe leaders giving instructions. "When we move out, we carry no sticks or anything that could be considered a weapon. If you want to throw rocks or get into a fight, that's up to you—but stay out of our march. This is strictly nonviolent."

All the same, shouts were going up, vows. She heard someone say, "Okay, this is it. We march, no matter what the pigs say"—except that he used more modifiers, variations on the word everyone seemed to love out here.

Kathy kept moving through the people, watching. There was little sign of organization so far, but people were edging west toward Columbus Avenue, where the police were bulking up the line. She heard a few shouted taunts at the police, but no one was making a move to charge the line. Kathy was almost sure that something was going to erupt soon, however, and she began working her way east, away from the greatest concentration of people.

She heard a voice boom over the speakers: "We're trying to work something out. The police are saying the march might be allowed if it's peaceful. But the sergeant here has to get permission from his commander. Sit tight. Don't force the issue."

Many in the crowd shouted their satisfaction, as though they sensed a kind of capitulation from the police. But others were angry. They yelled insults at the "pigs" and at the Mobe leaders. "We don't need permission. Let's go."

All the same, a tension that had built over the past few hours seemed, rather suddenly, to pass away, and a party atmosphere took over. There were kids running around, teenagers, yelling, "Kill the pigs," and cavorting as though they were excited about a fistfight after a high school football game. She saw lots more men than women, and not many blacks; maybe that's why she happened to spot Dee Dee, her friend from Massachusetts.

Kathy pushed through the crowd toward Dee Dee and called out her name. Dee Dee looked at Kathy and laughed. "So what are you all dressed up for?" she asked.

Actually, Kathy was wearing a simple skirt and blouse—not anything fancy—but she knew that she did look out of place. Most of the women were wearing frayed jeans and army boots, or wrinkled shirts they had slept in a night or two. "I just came outside to have a look around, maybe join the march."

"*Outside?* What does that mean?"

Someone bumped against Kathy from behind and pushed her up against Dee Dee. Dee Dee rolled her eyes and then pointed east, and the two worked their way out of the crowd. "I'm staying in the Hilton," Kathy shouted. "I've been working for McCarthy this summer. Here at the convention I've been helping out the staff at campaign headquarters. Lester has been working for the campaign too. But he's not here. I guess you know that."

"I don't talk to Lester these days. I have no idea what group he decided to sell out to. He's an Oreo. I have no use for his kind."

"Oreo" was a term Kathy had heard. It meant "black on the outside, white on the inside." She wasn't going to quarrel with Dee Dee about that, but Lester had spent most of his summer in the South, campaigning for McCarthy in places where he actually had no hope. That seemed enough to prove his grit. "Have you seen anyone else from UMass or Amherst?" Kathy asked.

"Sure. Some are here. I saw Robby and some of his people just a few minutes ago—over by the band shell."

"I guess I'll look for them."

"If I were you, I'd get out of here before this thing blows up—unless you want to get blood on your cute little blouse."

"What if the police give us permission?"

"That's a stall. They won't do it."

"Okay. I appreciate the advice. And I want you to know I love you, Dee Dee. I honestly do." She patted Dee Dee on the shoulder and then headed back into the crowd, in the direction Dee Dee had pointed. As she neared the band shell, she tried to see whether she knew anyone. It was maybe ten minutes before she spotted Robby's friend Stu Yates and some of the others from the SDS group she had once been part of. As she moved closer, she saw Robby. He was walking toward her. For a moment she thought he had spotted her, but she realized he was looking past her. Something in his eyes also said that he had been taking something, or at least smoking grass. "Robby," she said, and he stopped.

Robby smiled, then shook his head and swore. "So what are *you*, of all people, doing here?"

She leaned close and yelled, "I'm working for McCarthy. Aren't you proud of me?"

He understood her irony. He shook his head and laughed, and then he said, "Hey, I like the guy. He's just stupid. He thinks he can move a mountain, and he's got no dynamite. That's the only real way to get attention these days, little girl—TNT."

She wasn't going to be baited into that conversation again. "I still believe in nonviolence," was all she said. But she had lost some confidence in her old beliefs. Maybe Gandhi's principled nonviolence or Martin Luther King's sit-ins could lead to something, but the chaos down here, the adolescent posturing, made her wonder whether demonstrations like this accomplished much of anything, violent or not.

Robby was looking over the heads of the people, toward Columbus Avenue. "I've got to find someone," he said. "We're going to march whether the cops say we can or not."

"Who's in charge?"

"No one is. It's the biggest mess I've ever seen. Sid Peck, one of the Mobe leaders, went to talk things out with the cops. But they're just blowing smoke. Who's supposed to control all this? Half these people don't even know what's going on. They just think it's fun to call out the pigs. Tom Hayden keeps trying to take over, but one minute he's playing cozy with the liberals down at the convention center and the next minute he's talking like he's a new-left guerilla. Then there's Hoffman and Rubin. They've never had so much fun in their lives."

"So what's the point?"

"The point is, most of this crowd is still like you. They're still hanging on to the idea of nonviolence. But watch what happens. We're going to push and the cops are going to shove. And these Chicago cops are stupid. They're going to bust heads all over the place, and all these idealists in this park are going to be *radicalized*. I see nothing but good coming from that."

"A lot of people will get hurt," Kathy said. "How can that be good?"

"It's the *greater* good we're looking for," he said. But he laughed at himself, and Kathy had the clear impression that Robby believed nothing anymore, that he was only going through the motions. But then he added, "I won't feel righteous unless I get bloody myself. I'm going up front. See yuh." He pushed past her.

"Robby."

He turned back. "Yeah?"

"Just get arrested. Don't get hurt."

"You've still got the hots for me. You just don't know it."

"No. But I love you. I love what we all tried to do. I don't know where it's going now, but it was pure, in the beginning. Wasn't it?"

"No, my dear. It wasn't. But you were. That's why you never did belong."

He shoved against a guy's shoulder, made some room, and slipped away. Kathy watched him walk north, skirting the crowd for a time, and then work his way through the crowd, west, toward Columbus Avenue and the line of police. She tried to think what she should do, but she could hear the taunts becoming more heated as the delay continued. Robby and Dee Dee were both right. This would never stay nonviolent. So Kathy headed back to the north. She wanted to get back to the Balbo Street bridge and cross west, back to Michigan Avenue, where the hotel was. But as she walked that way, she saw that police were still at the base of the bridge, blocking the way. And now someone was on the loud-speakers again. "The pigs have gone back on what they promised. They say we can't march. What do you have to say about that?" There was an enormous response, and Kathy looked back to see the crowd surge west, toward the street.

Kathy was not sure how long before things were going to break loose, but she knew she wanted to be in the hotel before they did. She hurried toward the bridge, away from the major mass of people. She had creden-tials, and she wasn't dressed like most of the crowd; she hoped she might be able to talk her way through the police line.

Suddenly the volume of noise leaped to a new level, and Kathy looked back. The crowd had pushed too close to the police, and night-sticks were flying again. The confrontation lasted only seconds before the retreat began. The police were pushing back hard, swinging their clubs with every step. Then Kathy heard a strange sound. "Whomp, whomp." In a few seconds she could see the smoke. Tear gas canisters were being fired into the crowd.

Kathy heard a rolling sound, the distant screams and shouts coming in waves, and she saw the panicked faces as people charged in her direc-tion. She hurried north, but the rush caught up to her, was all around her. She was angling toward the bridge, and most people were heading north-east, up through the park but away from the bridges, where the police were blocking the way. Kathy still thought her best shot was to go for

Balbo Street, as she had planned. She took some jostling, but she broke away from the others, and then, once she approached the police, she slowed to a walk. Police and guardsmen were standing almost shoulder to shoulder at the base of the bridge. "I'm staying in the Hilton. I have credentials," she shouted from some distance away. She didn't want to admit that she was working for McCarthy; one night the police at Lincoln Park had slashed the tires of cars with McCarthy stickers. Still, it was her McCarthy staff identification she waved in front of her. She kept walking toward the line, but she saw no one make room for her to come through or even motion to come close to show her I. D. She walked straight at a young, husky policeman, and said again, "I'm not part of the demonstration. I'm staying in the Hilton. Could I please pass through?"

She was almost face to face with him when his stick suddenly shot up. He gripped it with both hands and held it like a gate in front of her. "No one goes out this way!" he shouted.

"But I'm not—"

He shoved the stick at her and caught her across the chest, causing her to stumble backward and fall. He hadn't hit her all that hard—she wasn't hurt—but she was furious. "I don't understand. I'm an American citizen. I haven't done anything to anyone. I just want to go back to my hotel."

But that seemed the wrong thing to say. As she was getting up, an older policeman stepped forward and used the end of his stick to stab at her. He struck her shoulder as she turned and she fell again. He called her a filthy name. "It's you people from the press who want it both ways," he yelled. "You call us pigs in the paper, and then you want our help when the tear gas starts blowing in." He jabbed at her again as she was trying to get up.

Kathy made it to her feet and ran a few steps back. "I'm not with the press. I'm part of this convention. I have credentials. I want your badge number."

But he exploded at that. He rushed at her again, this time swinging the club. He caught her in the side as she tried to spin away. She dropped to the grass and rolled up, waiting for the next blow. But it didn't come. "Get going, right now," he screamed. "You're not coming this way. No one is."

Kathy couldn't breathe, but when he yelled at her again, she struggled to her feet. She knew better than to say anything more, but she tried to memorize the man's face. She wanted to report him. For now, however, she walked north, angling east with the others, holding her side. She wondered whether any of her ribs were broken.

When her eyes began to sting, she realized that she wasn't far enough away from the tear gas. A lot of the crowd was still walking or running north, and that seemed the only way the police were letting people escape. So she kept going, but her throat began to close and then to burn. She cupped her hands over her face, started to run again, but her nose and throat kept hurting worse, as though she had breathed in steel wool. She could hardly see, her eyes were running so badly. "Keep blinking," someone yelled. "Don't shut your eyes." That made sense, but it wasn't easy to do.

She was getting farther away from the trouble, away from the gas, so she kept going. What she had to do was get out of the trap somehow. She saw, finally, that there were no police on the bridge by the Art Institute. People were crossing over the railroad tracks there, streaming over to Michigan Avenue. She followed, kept blinking, and was gradually doing better. When she made it across the bridge, she turned back to the south, to get to her hotel, but that meant she was heading into the gas, which was blowing all through the area. Some people had soaked handkerchiefs and were breathing through the cloth, but she had no handkerchief with her. She decided she just had to hurry, survive the stuff, and get into the hotel. Her ribs were still hurting badly, and it wasn't easy to run, but she began to trot again.

As she neared the Hilton, she could see that things were crazy. Some demonstrators had found ways out of the park, and they were shouting, still taunting the police. Cops were grabbing the ones they could, pounding them with their sticks. Kathy tried to get through it all. There was no blockade, not like the one she had faced before, but police were watching all the entrances to the hotel. She couldn't see well enough to know what to do, but she knew she had to get inside.

She ran toward a policeman and stopped. "I got caught in this crowd," she shouted. "I'm not a demonstrator. Please help me." She fumbled in her skirt pocket for her identification.

"Show me a key," the cop demanded.

"A key? I didn't take one with me. I have three roommates, and we—"

"Move back," he yelled in her face, and he shoved her.

"What's wrong with you?" she screamed. "I have I. D. I'm staying in the hotel."

She saw the stick coming, and she managed to turn and throw out her arm. She took a hard blow across her forearm, and the pain sent her spinning away, falling, but before she seemed to hit the pavement, someone had hold of her other arm, was hoisting her back to her feet. She thought she was being arrested, but she didn't care. She only felt the pain in her arm, the agony in her throat and eyes. And then she was being shoved through the door by the same cop who had hit her. "Don't come out here again," he said. "It's stupid to come out here."

But what did that mean? Why had he knocked her down and then let her in? It made about as much sense as anything else Kathy had seen that night, that week. She couldn't breathe yet, but she sat on the floor and tried to deal with the pain while she hoped for her lungs to clear.

Eventually, Kathy was able to get up and take the elevator to her room. Her arm didn't seem to be broken, only bruised so badly that she could hardly move it, and her ribs were much the same. But her tears gradually went away. Later that night she sat in the window, bending as little as possible, but looking up Michigan Avenue when the demonstrators regrouped and tried another march. The police let them go a few blocks this time, then cut them off, and there was more tear gas, more clubbing. Kathy couldn't see any of that from her window. She only heard it on the news, later. What she did see was the crowd streaming back, and then the chaos below, at her corner of Balbo and Michigan. She couldn't see everything that was happening, but she learned later that one group of demonstrators had been pushed by police against a plate-glass window of a Hilton restaurant. When the glass broke and the kids fell through, the police followed them inside, chased them down, and clubbed them.

But someone filmed all the beatings—seventeen minutes of brutality, with the police pounding the demonstrators unmercifully—and that night, and again the next day, the film was on the news, everywhere. On the following evening everything started again, and this time the demonstrators chanted, "The whole world is watching. The whole world is watching." But it was the seventeen minutes filmed the night before that made the greatest impact, that shocked even middle-class Americans.

On Thursday night, the McCarthy people held a party, not to celebrate but to say good-bye, after a long, hard campaign. It started late and lasted almost until morning. Kathy had long since gone to bed by then. Around five o'clock she heard a terrible banging at her door. One of her roommates opened the door to face a policeman demanding to know who had been throwing things out the window: bottles, cans, and feces, he claimed, although that wasn't the word he used. The girls were ushered out to the offices, where the party had been going on, and then everyone was taken down to the lobby. By then, ten of the McCarthy staffers had been beaten. Four had to be hospitalized, and yet no one ever knew of anyone throwing anything out the window. Gene McCarthy was finally brought to the lobby from the twenty-third floor where he was staying, and he denounced the police with more vehemence than anyone had ever heard from him. The police, rather surprisingly, responded to his anger and relented. The McCarthy staff members were finally allowed to go back to their rooms.

That was the final straw for Kathy. She saw no reason for the extreme measures the police had taken in the streets, and this last action seemed nothing more than an attempt to attack a group whose politics they didn't like. But she had seen the worst of so many people, she wasn't certain who had disappointed her most. She had once believed that she could help change the world. Now she knew, without ever expressing the idea to herself, that people needed to change; hearts needed to change. What she didn't feel at the moment was any hope that would ever happen.

At the International Amphitheatre, the delegates watched television reports and learned what had been going on outside. Some of the chaos moved inside at that point. Liberals screamed about police brutality, and Richard Daley cursed the liberals in rank profanity that was easily read from his lips on home television sets. But nothing changed. Humphrey was nominated for president, with Edmund Muskie for vice-president, and the nation was divided about who had caused the trouble in Chicago, the demonstrators or the police. In spite of the belief by the demonstrators that "the whole world was watching" and that that would change minds, a majority of the general public sided with the police. Kathy had no way to explain that.

## CHAPTER 9

Diane and Greg were renting an apartment not too far from the University of Washington. They had arranged for it without seeing it, on the recommendation of a "friend of a friend" of Greg's father. Greg's parents had also given them some furniture to get started with, and had even had it shipped. So Greg and Diane had stuffed what clothes and personal belongings they could get into Greg's Ford Mustang, and they had driven to Seattle. They had spent a honeymoon week before that in Palm Springs, where Greg's father had part-ownership in a resort. Now, with a cute apartment to decorate and a kitchen of her own, Diane really felt married. She and Greg had had a nice time together in California, and they had laughed and talked during their day-and-a-half drive to Seattle. Everything seemed perfect, and Diane felt sure she had made the right decision, no matter how often she had questioned herself those last weeks before her wedding.

The wedding itself had been elegant, and before the reception, the wedding party had gathered for lots of pictures. Diane had seen the proofs when she got back from Palm Springs, and she was impressed by the way everyone looked, especially Greg in his tailored tuxedo. The luncheon, the reception that night at the Hotel Utah—everything had been exquisite. Greg was so much better at details than she was, and even though she had chosen the flowers, the bridesmaids' dresses and the table decorations, Greg had discussed everything with her, made suggestions, and often thought of little things she would have forgotten: silver bracelets for the bridesmaids, for favors; a prettier veil than the first one she had chosen—one that had a tiara built in; and a perfect backdrop for the wedding line. When they had arrived in Palm Springs, a dozen fresh red roses had been waiting in the room. And Greg had brought along a wedding gift for Diane: a lush, red negligee. It was a little more daring than the powder blue one that Diane had chosen—but still, beautiful.

Now, in Seattle, Diane wanted to get to work unpacking and arranging things, but Greg was too excited to do that first. "Let's go walk around campus. I want you to see what it's like."

"I at least need to get the bed made and find our cooking utensils so we can—"

"We'll do that when we get back. I'll help you. But let's go take a look around first."

"Okay." She kissed him. "This is fun, isn't it?"

"It's more than fun. But don't kiss me again or we may not get out of this house."

"Boy, you never get your fill, do you?"

"I don't know. Let's keep trying and see if I do."

He pulled her toward him, but she laughed and twisted away. "No, no. Not now. Let's get you some fresh, cool air."

So they drove to the university and found a parking spot on University Avenue, in the "U District"—the business area close to campus. "They call this street 'the Ave,'" Greg told Diane.

She was astounded by what she was seeing outside the car. She had seen hippies on the news, had even seen a few kids around Ogden and Salt Lake wearing long hair and hip-hugger pants, but these people were the real thing. It was as though she had arrived in Haight-Ashbury. All up and down the street were people in psychedelic clothes and peace beads, their hair wild. To Diane it was a freak show, and it actually frightened her a little. "Do we have to park here?" she asked Greg.

"Why? What's wrong?"

"Look at those people."

"Hey, they're gentle. They've got flowers in their hair."

"But they're *so* weird. Don't you think some of them are on drugs?"

Greg laughed. "Yeah. Maybe. But I don't know what they're going to do to you."

Diane supposed that was true, but she wondered what people like this would think of her capri pants and Keds. She didn't want anyone to make fun of her. Or worse, she had heard about druggies on bad LSD trips, how they could go crazy. "I just feel funny to be around people like that," she told Greg.

"Me too, in a way, but we'll just walk to the corner and then head over to campus."

When they got out of the car, Diane realized that either direction they walked, they had to pass through pockets of street people. But Greg took hold of her hand, and they hurried up the street. They did hear a few comments. There was some panhandling going on, which Greg ignored, but one guy in a fringed vest and a wide red beard tried to joke with them. "Hey, what's your hurry? Stick around and feel the groove." Somewhere a radio was playing a new Beatles song, "Revolution." It seemed the right choice.

Greg laughed at all this, but Diane walked a little faster, on ahead. When Greg caught up with her, he said, "Just be cool. We're okay." They turned the corner and walked a block to the edge of campus. When they stopped at the corner, Greg said, "Look up that way." To the north was a green area filled with tall trees. But it was also full of hippies, who were lounging on the lawn or playing with Frisbees. "They call that Hippie Hill. A guy told me about it when I made my campus visit up here. I guess they smoke a lot of marijuana and take drugs, but the university doesn't worry too much about it. If they don't bother anyone, no one bothers them."

"If they're taking drugs, they ought to be arrested. Maybe people laugh at BYU, but at least there, they didn't let us ruin our lives that way."

Greg was laughing again. "You're not at the Y anymore, sweetheart. You're going to have to get used to that."

Diane knew that was true. She didn't want to be a prude. She even thought it was exciting to see some of the things she had only heard about. But as she and Greg crossed the street, they passed a couple coming the other way, and Diane was shocked by what was going on. The guy was dreadful looking, with stringy hair and a fuzzy attempt at a beard, and he was wrapped all over the girl. Diane had to look away, she was so embarrassed—and disgusted.

What Diane did love was the campus. Greg took her first to see "Frosh Pond." "The mountain is out today," he told her. He pointed down through an open, grassy area of the campus beyond the pond. In the distance, in the afternoon light, Diane could see snowcapped Mount Rainier, with the sky behind it so blue it hardly seemed real. "They call this area Rainier Vista," Greg told her. "The university doesn't build anything in here. They keep it clear so you can see the mountain. Most days it's clouded over, I guess, but the guy who showed me around told me that everyone says, 'The mountain is out,' whenever the clouds clear off."

"It's a good day to be here, then. Maybe it's a good omen."

"Yeah, in a way. But you should have seen this place in the spring. Those trees over there are dogwoods, and all those shrubs are rhododendrons. You just can't believe how beautiful the campus is when everything's in bloom."

They walked past the library, which was a Gothic structure on one end and a modern building on the other, and they went on to the law school, an old brick building surrounded with tall chestnut trees. It all looked the way a university was supposed to look, and Diane was excited for Greg to be here. She only wondered about her own life. While Greg was busy and maybe even stressed, what would she be doing? She knew one girl from BYU whose husband was now here in grad school, but she and Diane hadn't really been close, and beyond that, Diane didn't know a single person. Images had been popping into her mind all day as they had approached Seattle. She kept seeing her apartment at the Y, her friends, the Wilkinson Center, the library. Or she saw her home in Ogden, her room, and her Mom and Dad at the dinner table. She wanted something familiar. She had been homesick when she had first gone to BYU, but she could always run home for a weekend there. Here, she really did feel on her own.

"Greg, I've been thinking. I know you say I don't need to, but I want to get a job."

"Why?"

"I just need to do something, and I need to meet some people."

"They have a married student ward here. I talked to Brother Holland, the Institute director, and he said you could take classes. He also said the student ward was really active. You'll have all the friends you want."

"I know. But I don't want to sit home all day."

"As far as I'm concerned, we should start our family right away, and then—"

"Greg, the last I heard, you can't order a baby and get it tomorrow. What am I going to do this whole year?"

"If I were you, I'd use the time to read. You keep telling me that you want to go back to school someday. Maybe for right now you can use the time to improve your mind."

They had walked into the Union Building, which wasn't nearly as nice as the Wilkinson Center. As they strolled through the mostly empty hallway, Diane asked, "Why don't you want me to work?"

"It's not that. If you really want to, I guess it's okay. But I just don't see why you think you need to. We might as well start out, right from the beginning, following the prophet's advice. Women should be home and men should provide."

"Greg, every girl I know works while her husband is in school—at least until the first baby comes. How can that be bad? Why take so much money from your dad if we can manage for ourselves?"

"I'm not saying it's *wrong* for you to work. I just want to give you a great life, right from the beginning, and I hate to see you going off to some stupid job every day." He put his arm around her shoulders, leaned over, and kissed her ear. "I want you all rested up when I get home at the end of the day, not worn out from working."

Diane pulled away. She wondered about Greg sometimes. There were moments when he made her feel like that hippie girl she had seen crossing the street—with the guy hanging all over her. "Life isn't *all* about that, Greg. You'll be in school the whole day, and you'll be studying lots in the evenings. That's what you always tell me. I just need to do something other than sit around. If I stay home, I'll start watching too much daytime TV. That's what I always do."

They had come to the glass doors at the end of the building. Greg opened the door for her, and they walked outside, then crossed the quad area, back toward the library. Greg didn't say anything for a few minutes, and Diane hoped he wasn't going to pout, but finally he said, "Well, it's okay with me. Why don't you start looking around for a job, if that's what you want. But don't get in a hurry, and don't take something you'll hate. Above all, be ready to quit if you're pregnant and it's just too hard to go to work every day. In fact, you might look for something part-time."

Diane took hold of his hand. "Thanks," she said. "I know you just want me to be happy." She *was* touched by the way he tried to look out for her, but she also liked the idea that she had taken her stand about working and he had relented. Her mom would be proud of her.

When they got back to the apartment, Diane started shuffling boxes, trying to find all the ones marked "kitchen" and "bedroom." Their reception had been enormous, with more than a thousand invited. On top of that, presents from ZCMI, where they had registered, had continued to arrive at the Lymans' house all during their honeymoon. Diane had decided to leave her china, silver, and crystal in storage for now, but most everything else had been shipped—with more coming—and she could already see that she would never get everything into the small kitchen. She had gotten more than one of a lot of things: toasters, blenders, waffle irons, even electric can openers. She had wanted to make trades at some of the stores around Utah, but Greg had said he was embarrassed to trot around doing that, and they didn't really have time. "We'll need another toaster once the first one wears out," he had told her. "Just leave the extra ones here."

"But everyone trades things after their wedding," Diane had said. "That's part of the fun. We could trade for some more place settings of our china, and—"

"You don't need to. Mom likes to give place settings for Christmas presents. We'll probably have more settings than we know what to do with. And someday I'll buy you all the sets of dishes you want. If you're like my mom, you'll never meet a dish you don't like."

That was sort of true, but Diane didn't like the idea that everything could be quite that easy. She had always romanticized these early years of marriage when "getting by" was supposed to be a struggle. What would be the fun of getting the things she wanted if she and Greg never had to work hard—and wait?

But she wasn't worrying about that now. She was trying to figure out where she was going to put everything. She and Greg had rented a two-bedroom apartment with the idea that one bedroom might be a nursery before Greg finished school. That way, they wouldn't have to move. But she didn't want one of the bedrooms all cluttered for now, like a mere storage room. She wanted everything to look nice.

Greg helped her sort through the boxes, which she appreciated, but then he started opening them and finding places to put things. "Honey, don't just stick things away like that," Diane told him. "I need to think this all through and figure out where I want everything."

"I know. It's up to you. But I just thought that Crockpot would fit in the cabinet under the sink, and I don't know where else it would go."

"Okay. Leave it there for now. That probably is where I'll want it."

"Whatever you say. I don't care. I'll just open boxes and bring things to you."

But that was not what Diane wanted either. She would prefer to bring things a few at a time, wash them, and then move them into the right spots. What he was soon doing was cluttering her cabinet tops and creating confusion. She finally told him to slow down, and he did, but he stood and watched. "Let me make a suggestion," he said. "It seems like the knives and forks ought to be on the right side of the dishwasher, not the left."

"Why?"

"We're both right-handed."

"I'm going to use the drawer on the right for the bigger utensils: serving spoons and pancake turners—all that kind of stuff."

"Yeah. I can see that. But there's nothing we use more than knives and forks."

"I know, Greg, but I don't see what difference it makes whether we're right-handed or not. It's one step from the dishwasher, either way."

"Okay. Good point." But still he watched, and after a time, he said, "It's not just a matter of being right-handed. It's also closer to the table. You'll have to walk farther this way."

Diane gave him a long look. She felt some strain in her voice when she said, "I'll be using serving spoons all the time too, Greg, and they'll be more convenient where I have them."

"Hey, okay. I was just trying to help. Can't a man have an opinion about the kitchen?"

"A man can have an opinion about *everything*, and you do."

He shrugged, and Diane could see immediately that she had hurt his feelings. "Sorry," he said. "I didn't mean to enter *your* domain." He walked into the living room.

"Come on, Greg. Don't do that."

"Hey, I'm serious. You worry about the kitchen and I'll worry about paying the bills." He began opening a box that Diane knew was full of books.

"What does that mean—that you won't help me with the dishes?" She tried to make her voice light, to show him she hadn't been angry.

"Do you *want* me to help with the dishes? I'll do whatever you tell me." But his voice was full of irony.

"Greg, I'll put the knives and forks in the other drawer if it means that much to you."

"What are you talking about? I don't care. It was just a thought." He was pulling out books, stacking them on the floor, probably sorting them by subject. He always knew exactly where to find his things. His apartment at college had always looked perfect.

"Don't you think we need to help each other, Greg? Of course I'd like help with the dishes. My dad always helped my mom."

"And mine never did."

"But isn't that how it should be? Can't we work together? I don't want you to pay all the bills. I want to understand where our money is going. My parents planned their budget together. They talked about things like that all the time."

"And mine never did."

"So what are you saying?"

"I'm saying that you want it both ways. I was trying to get involved in a way my dad never would have, but it turns out I'm trying to tell you what to do in the kitchen. So I guess I'll leave the kitchen to you, and I'll look after the money. I'll do things the way *my* parents did. But I never thought we'd be that kind of couple."

Diane didn't know how this had happened. That hadn't been the point at all. She was pulling drinking glasses from a box, getting ready to wash them, but now she set them down and walked to the living room. "Greg, I'm sorry," she said. "I don't know why I made such a fuss. We are both right-handed. It probably does make more sense to put them the other way."

Greg stood up and faced her. He smiled, and then he stepped to her and took her in his arms. "I'm not even sure what we're arguing about," he said. "None of this is important. The only thing I care about is how much I love you. But I do want to do dishes with you—and steal a kiss after every dish I dry."

"Honey, I don't know the first thing about money. I can't even make a checkbook balance. But I do want us to make decisions together."

"And that's what we'll do."

He loosened his embrace, looked into her eyes for a moment, and then kissed her. "I have an idea," he said. "Why don't we let this kitchen wait until we're fresh in the morning? Let's go to bed early, if you get my drift, and make sure we've made up properly after this *huge* argument we've just had."

"Greg, it's not even dark. Just let me—"

"Is that the rule, that it has to be dark?"

"No. But just let me work a little at this. Go read a little of that stuff you were supposed to read before the first day of school. I'll putter at this for a while, and then I'll come in and we'll make up our bed together. Okay?"

"More than okay. Just don't *putter* too long."

"Okay."

He kissed her again, this time with some fervor, and then he went off to the bedroom. But Diane was still out of sorts, and she wasn't sure why. She decided that she would pull the knives and forks back out and reverse them with the other utensils, but she wondered why she was doing it. She thought he was probably right, that it *was* a better arrangement, but still, it was irritating to make the concession. Even more, she didn't feel like going to bed so early. She had loved her honeymoon, and loved this new intimacy with Greg, but there was something about his single-mindedness that was becoming annoying.

Still, Diane didn't want to think ill of him. It was nice, really, that he loved her so much. Mom and Dad always said that a couple had to talk things out, and Diane simply needed to teach Greg what she responded to.

∽∾

Three weeks later Greg was in school and Diane was taking a bus to her new job. She had found a sales position at Frederick and Nelson's department store in downtown Seattle. Even though Diane had never traveled by city bus in her life, she thought doing that made the most sense, with parking difficult downtown and Greg sometimes needing the car. But she had found the ride this first day rather stressful. She had known black students at Ogden High, but not very well, and suddenly she was riding a bus that was filled with many more blacks than whites. She told herself she didn't mind that, and in theory she didn't, but she was uncomfortable when she saw some teenaged black guys checking her out. She was used to that kind of attention, of course, and she couldn't think what difference the boys' color made, but she still felt nervous. Her mom had talked to her a thousand times about not stereotyping people, but a notion was stuck away in her head somewhere that black guys were dangerous. One of the boys had a radio with the sound turned up loud. The Doors were singing "Hello, I Love You," and he was singing along, with his head bobbing to the beat, and he kept smiling at Diane. She tried not to look at him.

But the boys didn't say anything to her, and when she got off the bus she felt silly that she had been frightened. She had arrived downtown early, so she went for a little walk. As she crossed Pike Street, she saw two women with long straps on their purses and very short skirts. She was sure they were prostitutes. It was the middle of the day, and they were hanging around on the street, eyeing the men who walked by, sometimes even speaking to them. She heard one say, "Hey, looking for a date?" How was that possible? Weren't the police supposed to arrest them for that?

When she arrived at the store, she reported to her supervisor in the young women's and petite clothing section, and within a few minutes she created something of a sensation. Her supervisor, a woman named Shelly Gustofferson, was the only other clerk working in their section at that time of day, but there were other women who worked in ladies' wear, and they all came around, apparently to have a look at her. A tall and rather classy-looking young woman with red hair, along with a somewhat older woman with dark hair and an extremely short skirt, stood back a little and made no attempt to hide the fact that they were watching her. "I'm sorry," the red-haired woman finally said, "but you won't do. You're fired."

Diane smiled and walked over to them. "Hi. My name's Diane," she said.

"My name is Cherie, but don't stick around long enough to remember. We don't need young and *gorgeous* girls around here. I'm feeling old enough as it is." She seemed to be thirty, at most.

"And I'm suddenly *elderly*," the other woman said. But she stuck out her hand. "I'm Suzanne. The word is going around the floor like an ill wind: Miss America has just joined the staff."

"Then they must be talking about someone else. I'm just a hick from Utah. I don't know anything about Miss America."

"You could win."

"I don't think so, since I'm not a miss."

"You're *married?*" Cherie said. "How old are you?"

"Twenty."

"Oh, honey, you could have used those looks to reel in anyone you wanted. I hope you didn't take the first offer."

"I think I did all right," Diane said, and she winked.

"But think of all the men you could have played around with before you decided to get serious."

Diane wasn't quite sure what "played around with" meant, but the way Cherie had rolled her eyes to one side, she thought she had a pretty good idea—and she was suddenly at a loss for words. She didn't think she had ever heard a woman say anything quite like that.

Shelly walked over. "Leave her alone. I've got to show her the ropes," she said.

"Just dress her up in anything you want to sell," Suzanne said. "The young girls will all want to look like her."

Diane thought she had heard enough now, but she actually did like the attention.

Shelly spent some time with Diane, explaining the layout of the department, and she showed her how to take payment with credit cards. It was something that didn't happen all that often in the young women's department, she said, but sometimes mothers came along and flashed a card at them. Shelly also talked about store policy on allowing girls to try things on. "We've had a lot of shoplifting lately," she said. "Girls will put a shirt or a sweater on in the dressing room, slip their own top on over ours, and walk out that way. In the winter, you have to watch the coats that women wear. We've had women come in with big satchels inside their coats, or even sewn-in pockets, and they fill them up. Watch girls who are looking at earrings, or any of the jewelry—especially Negro girls. You just can't take your eyes off them for a minute. They'll walk away with the whole store."

Diane thought again of her mother's little talks about attitudes toward people. She was suddenly upset with herself for the things she had been thinking on the bus. She could tell she was going to learn a lot by being away from Utah, by facing realities she had never dealt with before. It was as though she were putting in the first day of her "adult" life.

Diane was scheduled to work five hours, from one until six, four days a week. As the Christmas season came on, she would work more. What pleased her this first afternoon was how much she was able to sell. Later in the afternoon a lot of girls came in. It was early enough in the school year that school shopping was still going on. Diane stayed busy—even more than Shelly, who had some paperwork to take care of. Since part of Diane's pay was based on commission, she was excited to do so well.

Some of the customers fussed over Diane. "I like this dress," one girl told her. "But you're the one who ought to wear it. You'd look fantastic."

At one point, when there was a lull, Cherie walked over again. "Wow. You've really been selling, haven't you?" she said.

"Yeah. It's been busy."

"You're getting more business than we are right now. Back-to-school is great in your department."

"Does it die down pretty soon now?"

"Some. But we're not all that far from Christmas shopping now. The only trouble then is that you start dealing more with the mothers than the girls—or worse yet, girls *with* their mothers."

Diane didn't really think she would mind that. She liked the idea of being here through the Christmas rush. She had always loved to do her own Christmas shopping. What she was thinking was that this would be more fun than college—or at least the studying part of college.

"So how long have you been married?"

"Well . . . only. . . ." Diane could feel herself begin to blush. "About a month and a half." The truth was, it had been five weeks.

"You poor thing. Your husband's probably still got only one thing on his mind. Do you ever get a night off?"

Diane was mortified. How could she ask such a thing? She looked away, tried to think of something she could say.

"I've got you blushing bright red. But I'm forgetting. You're so young, you've probably only got one thing on your mind too. Maybe he's the one getting headaches."

This was even worse. Diane didn't know people ever said things like that. She glanced at a rack of dresses. "Aren't these cute?" she said.

"Okay, okay. I won't tease you anymore." But Cherie did look at the dresses. "I couldn't get into any of these now. In fact, I probably never could have. But you ought to use your first check to buy this little number." She pulled it off the rack. It was a party dress: very short, black, with no sleeves. Diane thought that it actually would fit her, but she would never wear anything like that. "It *is* pretty," she said.

"Do you go out a lot?"

"Well, not really. My husband is a law student, just starting out, and we're not much for nightlife." She had heard that term, but she wasn't even exactly sure what it meant.

"Maybe not, but when your husband gets that law degree and you're socializing with the jet set—you know, the senior partners and their wives—you could just blow those old geezers away in that little dress."

"I don't really wear dresses that short. I used to sometimes—maybe almost that short—when I was in high school, but I wouldn't feel comfortable in it anymore."

"Why? Because you're married?"

"No. It's just that . . . I don't know . . . I went to Brigham Young University, and they had rules there about things like that. I've gotten used to their standards. I don't even wear sleeveless things."

"What?"

"Sleeveless. I don't—"

"Why? You don't want to show your smallpox vaccination? What's that all about?"

"No. It's just . . . actually, I don't even know." But Diane did know, and there was no way she was going to try to explain it to Cherie.

"Well, my dear, it all seems a waste. If I had the equipment you've got,

I'd dump my husband, wear the sexiest clothes I could find, and get some rich boy to show me a *very* good time."

"Well . . . I'm happy with the husband I've got."

"Let me tell you something, sweetie." Cherie leaned forward and whispered. "A lot of women are running around today saying they want equal pay for equal work. What I want is no work. And that's never going to happen with the guy I married. If I had it to do over again, I'd look for the richest guy I could find." She was laughing. Maybe she wasn't really serious. All Diane knew was that she had never heard this kind of talk before.

Diane could see some girls looking at blouses not far away. She was relieved. "Well, I'd better go help those girls," she said.

"You do that. But I'd think about that black dress. It was created with you in mind."

Diane laughed. But the truth was, she was a little worried about working here. She wondered how many times she would have to explain herself to these women. She had always liked to think of herself as fairly aware of what was going on in the world. At the Y, she had been the Ogden girl, much more up on things than so many of the girls from little towns. But she was suddenly feeling as though she had jumped into the deep end of a pool without her water wings.

# CHAPTER 10

Kathy was walking across campus on her way to the library. When she had returned to her house after classes earlier that afternoon, she had planned to study in her room, but she had started to read *Middlemarch* for her Nineteenth Century British Lit class and had fallen asleep. She decided the hike back to the library would wake her up. It was one of those New England early-autumn days she loved, with grand old horse chestnut trees dropping their prickly pods on the sidewalk and the light working its way toward that wintertime "certain angle" that Emily Dickinson wrote about. The air seemed unusually clear and mild, and the oak trees were shading to red, up high. She loved the campus, and she knew she would miss it when she graduated, probably miss it all her life, and at the same time she also wished it were already spring and she were finished with school. She had passed through a long process of change in her first three years at Smith, and she wasn't sure she liked the result. Looking back, she had been almost too focused when she had arrived, too sure she could fix the things she saw wrong in the world. But that had been better than what she was feeling now—this empty sense of having no clear direction. She hadn't recovered from what she had experienced in Chicago, and she didn't know how she ever could.

When she saw a chestnut lying loose from its cracked husk, she couldn't resist stopping to pick it up. She looked at the wood-grain pattern in its rich brown skin, and memories came back to her. She thought of the little girl she had been, the one who had gathered up chestnuts in the fall and stored them in a shoebox under her bed. Was there any remnant of that kid left in who she was now? It was as though a child had once lived, and now, another person had taken her place, but she couldn't find the path back to that little girl. And yet she longed to know her— the one who had played hopscotch behind her elementary school, who had bragged to her dad about getting 100 percent on her spelling test, who had once told Lamar Shumway she would knock him "into outer space" if he ever tried to kiss her again. In a way, she wished she could have one more go at life and make a few choices along the way that wouldn't leave her feeling so estranged from others and so uncomfortable with herself. She would still want this experience here at Smith, but she wished she could do her college years over too, and this time study harder in the beginning, be more a part of everything.

"Don't eat it. It's poison."

Kathy turned to see Professor Jennings approaching. He was looking relaxed, with his tie off and his collar open. Kathy always thought it was funny that he identified himself with the "movement" and seemed to consider himself a free spirit, and yet he always wore ties to class, often bow ties, and natty tweed jackets. "I know they're poison," Kathy said. "I was once a collector of horse chestnuts—and something of an expert."

"Collector?" He stopped in front of her. He stood an inch or two closer than Kathy would normally expect.

"That's right—a collector. There were some chestnut trees not far from my elementary school, back in Salt Lake. All the kids, walking home, would try to get to the trees first and pick up the new-fallen chestnuts. I could run fast—faster than most of the boys—and I'd try to get there ahead of everyone. I wanted the perfect ones that hadn't broken when they fell."

"But what for? They're not any good for anything, are they?"

"Professor Jennings, how can you say such a thing? They're *beautiful*."

She held the chestnut out to him. He took it and looked closely. "It really is. I don't think I've ever paid much attention. We had them in our yard when I was growing up, and they were just a nuisance when I wanted to play football with my friends."

"You played *football?*"

"Hey, I played *serious* football. Not just as a kid, either. I played at my prep school. I was a halfback, and pretty good, too."

"Well, well, we do have interesting pasts, don't we?"

He laughed. "If you ask me, we both wasted our time. Football ruined my right knee, and the time I gave to it probably kept me from getting into Harvard. I suspect your chestnut collection is also gone."

"Oh, yes. They do dry up after a while."

Professor Jennings nodded, as if he saw something sad in that. "Are you okay?" he asked.

She took the chestnut back from him and slipped it into her pants pocket. "Sure. I'm all right," she said. "At least my ribs have stopped hurting." She tried to smile.

"But don't you still feel some ache, *underneath* your ribs?"

"I'll tell you what I really feel. It's like there's nothing there—like my heart stopped beating and I'm running on batteries."

"Yeah. I've felt some of that myself this fall. I'm having a hard time giving the students what they deserve."

"I'll bet it's not just you. It's the students, too. Suddenly everyone in my house is a radical. About the time I gave up my hippie outfits, they all started to wear them. But no one believes in 'the revolution' the way I did a few years ago. Everyone's turning cynical."

"Yeah, I know. The girls—I mean, *women*—all curse in class, like that shows they've joined the counterculture." He was carrying a leather briefcase, which he now set on the sidewalk. "I also love the way every singer is suddenly doing protest songs. It's like their agents tell them, 'Hey, there's good money in this antiwar stuff. Why don't you knock out a little something about peace and love?'"

"'People Got to Be Free,'" Kathy said. It was the new Rascals song.

"That's right." He laughed. "Did you see what happened at the Olympics last night?"

"No. I haven't really watched much."

"Tommie Smith set a new world record in the 200 meters, and John Carlos took third. But when they got up on the podium, they each had a black glove on. When 'The Star-Spangled Banner' started to play, they held their fists up—you know, in the black power salute—and they bowed their heads. There's talk today that they might get kicked off the team."

"Why?"

"Everyone's saying that the Olympics aren't supposed to be about politics—which is kind of funny, since Russia and the U.S. use it as a propaganda war every four years."

"What were they protesting?"

"I don't know if you follow sports enough to know, but this summer a lot of black athletes said they didn't feel like they could represent the country, given the way blacks are treated. Everyone begged them to stay on the team—since we have no track and field team without them—but I guess Smith and Carlos still wanted to make a statement. I don't blame them, in a way. It embarrassed the country—which I'm sure we deserve—but I still wish it hadn't happened. It just seems like everyone is protesting something now. It all starts to wear me out. I just wanted to watch the Olympics." He smiled. "And see ol' Fosbury do his flop."

Kathy did know what that was. Fosbury was the guy who was jumping backward and winning all the high jump events these days. But she shared Professor Jennings's feeling that protesting had become too much the "thing to do." She had hoped for so long that the nation would turn against the war, and now that was actually happening—but nothing had changed. Nixon and Humphrey were both talking about "peace with honor" as the bombs continued to fall. Most Americans now said, according to polls, that the United States never should have gotten involved in Vietnam, but that same majority still wanted to "win" the war. Spiro

Agnew—the Republican vice-presidential candidate—was talking about the "silent majority," the people who didn't protest. Those were the people he and Nixon were supposedly representing. She wondered, though, whether the silent people weren't actually the people who simply didn't care.

"So what are you going to do?"

Kathy was still holding the chestnut inside her pocket. She ran her thumb over the hard, smooth surface. "I don't know, Professor Jennings. I—"

"I would think by now, you could call me Gary."

"I don't think so."

"Try."

"Okay. But anyway, I don't know what I'm going to do. Grad school, I guess, but I'm not very excited about that. I feel like I've been kicked out of every 'club' I've tried to join in my life: my church, SDS, and now the Democratic Party. I'm not sure what's left."

"In a way, that's not such a bad thing." He shoved his hands into his pockets. He was wearing gray flannels with black penny loafers. Kathy suspected, on a cool day like this, that he had started out his morning with a blue blazer. She also noticed how flat his stomach was. She was seeing him a little differently after his comment about playing football. "I think it's healthy to break away from all the groups that tell us how to think," he said. "It's actually quite refreshing to cast off everything you've learned and start over."

"If it's so *refreshing*, why don't you sound refreshed?"

He laughed, making almost no sound but looking delighted with her summary of him. "I guess I'm still just very disappointed. I really believed in McCarthy. I've always been annoyed with people who say they don't vote, but right now I'm not sure whether I'll flip a coin in the voter's booth or just not show up. What difference does it make which candidate wins?"

"I know what you mean. I've been telling myself I'm just discouraged, but I'm also frightened to think what's coming—no matter who wins."

"I might take some time off from teaching and join the Peace Corps."

"Really? I've been saying for years that I might do that. But I can't seem to get up the courage. I'm not sure I want to sleep in a mud hut and eat locusts for breakfast—or whatever it is they do."

"It's not that bad, Kathy. I've been looking into it."

"Really? I'd love to get some information about it."

"I've got some stuff right in here." He picked up his briefcase again. "Do you want to walk over to the student center? Maybe we could get a cup of coffee and I could tell you what I've learned so far."

"Yeah. Sure." But Kathy felt strange about this. For one thing, she had the nagging feeling that she was behind in her reading and really needed to put in a good, full evening of study. But she also felt awkward about the idea of sitting down with a professor in such an informal way. She liked the man and really respected him for his views and his skills as a teacher, but he also made her feel self-conscious. She had planned to sign up for one of his classes this fall, and then, at the last minute, hadn't done it. She had felt for some time that he was "interested" in her. She had seen it in the way he looked at her, and in the familiar way he spoke to her, especially in Chicago, even though they hadn't seen each other very often there. He was clearly being careful now that they were back on campus, but she wondered whether he had in mind to ask her out—maybe after she graduated. She actually liked to think that he would, but she also wondered whether it was wise to think of him that way. He wasn't someone she could be serious about. Her family would never comprehend someone like him. She knew that if she were to marry out of the Church, she would burn the final bridge behind her, and yet, she also doubted she could marry anyone in the Church, given the way she felt about so many things.

Still, she walked with him to the student center, and she talked again about growing up in Utah, about being the strange girl in her high school who had decided to stand up for civil rights. Clearly, he liked that. He told her he had never been serious about much of anything until college. He was walking close enough that his arm was brushing hers when he said, "I wish I'd known you then."

"No. I was so intense and obnoxious. I fought with *everyone*. And I may look bad now, but you should have seen me when I was *nothing* but bones. The boys in my high school thought I was some sort of pillar, just part of the building. They never gave me a second look."

"They would certainly give you lots of looks now."

Kathy drew in her breath. She knew she had actually intended to elicit that kind of response, but now that she had gotten it she had no idea what to do with it. She made up her mind never to call him Gary. And yet, she felt lighter, better than she had in weeks.

When they reached the snack area in the student center, Professor Jennings bought himself a cup of coffee and a 7-Up for Kathy. She tried to pay for her own drink, but he set it on a tray with his coffee and went first to the cashier. "I'll get it," he said, and Kathy only protested a little. Still, she didn't want to do anything like this again.

They sat down at a distant table in a nearly empty room, and he got out some materials from his briefcase. He explained a little about the application process and what he knew about the training, and then he gave her a brochure that described the Peace Corps programs.

"I'll tell you what I'm feeling," he told her. "This stuff sounds meaningful. Sometimes, in class, I start to think that I'm all talk, that I don't do anything but *philosophize*. I get thinking, if I could make one little village in Africa or South America a better place to live—improve conditions for the people just a little—I would always know I had performed one worthwhile act in my life. And I have a feeling I might return to the classroom with some of that ivory tower point of view expunged from my system. I think I'd be a better teacher."

Kathy couldn't help but think of Gene and of all the other missionaries she had known in her life. They went out for two years to take the gospel to people, but when they came home they often said they had benefited even more than the people they taught. Kathy liked the idea that she could serve her own mission on terms that worked for her. "I can't think of anything more important, Professor Jennings."

"Gary."

She laughed. "Sorry."

"Just try it once. Just call me Gary."

"Okay, *Gary*. But you know what I'm talking about: one person helping one other person. Maybe that's the answer for me. I've tried to influence a whole ocean. Maybe I'd be better off to bless one raindrop."

She knew she was blushing from the whole first-name business, and because of the way he was smiling at her. But he seemed to make a decision not to push the matter. "That's right," he said. "My family believes, absolutely, that life is all about 'being comfortable,' having a summer home at the Cape and vacationing in Europe. They give generous donations to CARE every year and tell themselves they're 'giving back' a little, since they've been so blessed, but they're really just buying off their consciences. They never have to touch a starving child. They just see the pictures and send a check."

Kathy had thought the same thing about her own family. Her parents were generous with their money, and Mom was active in charity organizations around town, but she never crossed the valley to meet anyone on the west side and never asked herself what she could learn by doing so.

Professor Jennings—Gary—went back to his Peace Corps literature, explained a little more about procedures and time commitments, and praised the leadership of Sargent Shriver. Kennedy had hardly announced the program, back in 1961, before thousands of volunteers had been heading out across the world, and the organization had grown rapidly from there. "Maybe a little too fast," Gary said. "They're doing a little soul-searching and changing right now. But that's good too. Shriver never did set anything in stone. He called every program an 'interim' approach because he didn't want ideas to harden. One change is that they're sending more technical people these days. We liberal arts types don't always have the skills they want. We might not even get in if we apply."

Kathy had the strange impression that the 'we' was meant more collectively than she had in mind. It was almost as though he wanted the two of them to go together. Did he have some notion in his head that they might marry and then join the Corps as a couple? Kathy didn't think so, but she was titillated by the thought. She did think it would be satisfying to marry someone who shared her interests and commitments, and then to live their lives together with devotion to good works, not merely to lining their own pockets.

In the background, Kathy could hear the faint music of the Fifth Dimension, singing "Stoned Soul Picnic." It was such a strange world now, where things that had seemed so wrong a couple of years before were suddenly the norm. Kathy hated what drugs were doing to so many movement people, and yet music was often romanticizing the drug culture. It was exciting to talk to a man who was willing to check out of this confused society and go off to do something he thought was right.

"Kathy, let me ask you about something you've said a couple of times. You say you've dropped out of all your clubs, and the first one you mentioned was your church. I knew you'd become disillusioned with SDS, and you and I had pretty much the same reaction in Chicago, but I didn't know you had dropped your membership with the Mormon Church."

"I actually said I'd been kicked out. But that isn't true. I just haven't gone to meetings for a long time. Not very often anyway."

"So where are you with that?" He set his elbows on the table and then rested his chin on his hands. It seemed a way of showing interest, but something in his voice, his manner, made him seem hesitant to bring up the subject. She wondered why he wanted to know.

"I'm not sure. I love my family, and I always want to be part of them, so it's hard to go some other way, but when I go to church, I usually get upset, not inspired, so it's easier for me to stay away."

"But do you believe in God?"

Kathy had often thought about that question lately, but she didn't want to voice her concerns and somehow make them her "new position." "I think I do. But it's something that's just part of me. I pray at times, and it gives me comfort, but I don't know much of anything for sure. I like to think that there is a God. Life seems so pointless if there isn't."

"That's the question all bright people ask, sooner or later: If there isn't a God, what does the world mean?"

"What do you believe?"

"I told you before, I grew up going to church every Sunday. My parents sort of shopped around for ministers they liked, but they were always members of one congregation or another. I notice they don't go as much now that their kids are grown up, and I'm not so sure they didn't go back then primarily because they thought it was good for children to have a religion. But I did believe in God when I was growing up. Now, though, I've given up the mythology part of religion. What I'm trying to cling to are some of the teachings of people like Jesus."

"I guess I don't understand what you're saying."

"Well, if you pressed me, I'd have to say the only belief system I can buy into is existentialism."

"I keep hearing about Sartre and Camus, but I don't think I understand existentialism."

"You need to read Camus's *The Myth of Sisyphus*. That's the only concept of 'meaning' that rings true to me."

"Isn't Sisyphus the one who had to push a rock up a mountain over and over?"

"That's right. And what Camus did with that was to put aside all the creation myths that various religions are based on and focus on the meaning of an existence that doesn't come from outside oneself. If there's no God, what can life mean? It means you have a rock. And that rock has no meaning until you find your own meaning in it."

"But what if I decide that the best thing in life is self-indulgence? Let's say I want what someone else has, so I kill him and take it? Why can't I conclude that's a perfectly good thing to do?"

"That is the problem, of course. But Sartre says you also have to ask yourself what the implications of your choice would be if everyone acted the same way. Too many so-called Christians don't seem to care about others. They only want an eternal reward."

"That's a superficial kind of Christianity. I realized a long time ago that God doesn't want us to do good so we can win some sort of contest. He wants us to do good so we can become more like him, and it's the goodness itself that brings the joy."

"Now that, I would say, is a kind of Christian existentialism. It reminds me of things that Kierkegaard talked about clear back in the nineteenth century."

"I guess I don't understand the difference. What is it you get from existentialism?"

"I simply don't find meaning in the myths I grew up with. But I can say to myself that it's good for the family of man to care for one another. There's something very pure about that."

"But maybe from pure logic you could conclude that too many people exist, given our resources, and we ought to let hungry people die—so others can have a better existence."

"But see, that's the thing about existentialism. It's more than logic. Camus and Sartre advocate a subjective search for truth. Is it right to kill a man who wants to kill you? Who's to say? You find the answer when the event occurs. You respond to the deepest kind of morality: your honest response at the moment of truth."

"But maybe it's God who tells us what's right—not our insides, which are just a bunch of organs."

Professor Jennings laughed, again without sound. And his look was full of fondness. "You're very bright, Kathy. I love entwining our minds this way. It's sexy stuff."

Kathy looked at the table. She had not expected him to say such a thing.

"I'm sorry. That was an expression—not a come-on."

"I know." She tried to look natural, but suddenly she could hardly think what they had been talking about.

He cleared his throat, looking a little embarrassed himself. "Anyway, my point is, I can't believe in the voice of God, but I want meaning in my life, and existentialism speaks to that. I have questions too, and that's why I only said I would call myself an existentialist *if you pressed me*. But I do want to do good, and I want to be true to what seems *large* inside me. I want to look at life through the widest possible lens and act the way I wish everyone else would act. People say the golden rule is in the Bible, but it isn't, at least not in those words. It's just something that rings true to all of us."

"Mormons believe in the *light* of Christ. It's a spirit of truth that everyone can feel when they're open to it. That's where goodness comes from. It comes from God and emanates through the universe."

"Do you believe that?"

"I think so."

"It's a very nice idea. You find the truth within yourself, but it's God who issues it to you by speaking to your spirit."

"That's right. Could you believe that?"

He thought for a time. "No. I don't think so. Everything still goes back to God creating the world in seven days and placing Adam and Eve on the earth. It's a story I can't buy. But let me ask you this: Could you live without this idea of the light of Christ? Could you take one more step and allow the truth to be something you discover in your own actions—not your *guts*—and more about internal consistency than *eternal* reward?"

"I told you—the reward is not the main thing."

"Okay. Could you believe in goodness without believing in a life after death?"

"I believe in goodness, no matter what. I'm just not sure I would ever deny some of the feelings I've had: you know, feelings that God does hear me and does speak to me."

She had the impression that Professor Jennings had actually intended a much more specific question than the one he had voiced. Maybe he was asking, "Could you and I ever believe something similar enough that we could accept each other?"

She didn't know the answer to that question, but she was struck with the idea that the light of Christ had rung true to her at the moment she had described it.

Alex and Anna and the kids were home for Christmas. That meant that the house, which Gene and Emily normally had to themselves, was full of people. Gene loved having everyone around, especially during the holidays. Alex had been home often during the campaign that fall, but Anna and the kids had usually not come along. They had flown out for the victory celebration when Alex had won reelection, but they had had to return the next morning. Gene liked playing board games and doing a big jigsaw puzzle; he liked to see his mom come home with the trunk of her car full of groceries; and he *loved* the smells when she began to bake. She always made *Weihnachtsstollen*, the Christmas cake he had grown up with and had learned to love even more in Germany, and she filled the house with the sweet smell of gingerbread. Gene and Emily couldn't really afford snack foods, but with the family home, Gene would discover caches of mixed nuts, chips and dips, black licorice—his father's favorite indulgence—and always, quality chocolate, which Mom loved. She bought Cummings Chocolates and knew where to find wonderful European candies.

Joey had returned from his mission. He was going to the University of Utah and living in an apartment with some guys he knew from high school. Sharon was at BYU. But both, along with Kurt and Kenny and Pam, were home now, and everyone was busy, shopping, running around, getting ready for Christmas. Gene was glad to have finals over. Business at the dealership was usually slow this time of year, so he wasn't working all that many hours, and he was really enjoying the extra time at home.

One night a couple of days before Christmas, everyone but Kurt was home for dinner. Gene had something he wanted to say to his whole family together, but he decided this might be as close as he was going to come. He waited until Pammy had said the blessing and everyone was passing plates around the table before he said, "There's something Emily and I want to announce." He plopped some mashed potatoes on his plate and handed the bowl to Kenny. When he glanced at his mother, she was already beaming, so Gene said, "Emily dropped a piece of Mom's Dresden china and broke it."

"Oh, I did not," Emily said. She looked at Anna. "He's just trying to be funny. We don't use your nice china—not at all."

Anna was still smiling. Gene wondered whether Emily had already broken the news. "Well, okay, that's true," Gene said. "That was my clever way of trying to throw you off."

"I'll bet Emily's pregnant," Sharon said.

"No. That isn't it," Gene said, disappointed that Sharon had stolen his thunder. "Or is it? Oh, yeah. That *is* it. I'm going to be a dad. And Emily is going to do everything she can to help me."

Alex seemed taken by surprise. He stood abruptly, sliding his chair across the hardwood floor. "Oh, Gene, that's great news," he said. He came around the table, not to Gene but to Emily. She stood to meet him, and he grasped her in his arms. Then he looked at Anna, and Gene saw that his dad had tears in his eyes. "Just call me Grandpa," he said.

Anna got up too. She also went to Emily. By then, Alex had Gene in his arms. "This is such great news," he was saying. "You're not going to believe what a change this is going to bring to your lives."

When Anna embraced Gene, he said to her, "You knew, didn't you? Could you tell from all the loose blouses she's been wearing?"

"I knew it the minute I saw her at the airport."

"She's not showing *that* much."

"Oh, she's showing all right. It's in her face, in her eyes. I even saw it in her skin." She turned and hugged Emily again.

Joey didn't get up from the table, but he said, "I'll tell you who's going to be excited: Grandma Bea. She can't wait to see this next generation get started."

"My father too," Anna said. "I just hope he lives that long." Grandpa Stoltz had taken a bad turn lately. His heart was beginning to fail.

"When are you going to tell everyone?" Alex asked. He was walking back to his place at the big dining room table.

"We thought we'd tell all the Thomases on Christmas day. We were going to break the news to you that day, too, but I couldn't stand to wait any longer. And Emily was afraid it was getting sort of obvious anyway."

"I think you're a skunk for waiting as long as you did," Anna said.

"We didn't want to say anything *too* early." What Gene didn't want to mention was Emily's initial reaction. He was glad that she seemed happier about the baby now, even though she was still sick at times.

"When's the baby due?"

"April 24, around the time I finish school," Gene said. "I'll be finished after winter quarter."

"How have you been feeling?" Anna asked Emily.

"I was really sick at first," she said. "School was hard this fall, but I want to keep going. I want to graduate in June if I possibly can. I'm taking some extra hours this next term so I can take a light load spring quarter."

"Can you get through that last quarter with a new baby?" Alex asked.

"I don't know. If I had to, I could take some 'Incompletes' and maybe finish up in the summer. I just want to graduate, since I'm so close."

Food was being passed again. Anna had cooked stuffed pork chops, which she always served with applesauce, and there was corn and a Jell-O salad—the kind with whipped cream and marshmallows—and hot rolls, still warm from the oven. Gene had also smelled the spiciness of Mom's apple pie. He knew that would come with ice cream. It really was good to have his mother home.

"I don't blame you for wanting to finish," Sharon said. "Maybe I can come up from Provo and help out a little when the baby comes."

"*Grandma* is going to be here," Anna said. "I wouldn't miss this for anything." Gene saw her take a look at Dad and exchange a little nod of satisfaction. It touched Gene to see how much this meant to them. He had already thought about standing in a circle with Grandpa and Dad and his uncles, blessing this little baby. Grandpa had always talked about the trials the family had gone through in the early days of the Church, and then during the depression and World War II. He seemed to measure family prosperity now by the growth of a righteous progeny. The beginning of a new generation was sure to bring on one of his orations. Gene loved to think of it, and loved to think of those fine old hands caressing this baby while Gene tried to say the things Grandpa might say.

"Gene," Alex said, "when Kurt gets here, could you tell him about this yourself? And maybe express some thoughts about what it means to you?"

"Sure. But he gets tired of hearing what I have to say."

"No, I don't think so," Anna said. "In fact, I hope you'll talk to him all you can while he's here, and maybe do some things with him."

"I've noticed," Gene said, "that since you got home, no one wants to talk about Kurt. Is he still having troubles?"

"It upsets Kurt when we talk to you about him," Alex said. "So we try to avoid the subject."

"So what does that mean—that he's still having problems?"

The table was suddenly quiet. The sun was down, early this time of year, and here in the dining room Gene had felt a lovely sense of seclusion, as though his family were isolated from everything outside. But that feeling was gone now.

Alex glanced at Anna, and then he set down his utensils. "Kurt didn't want us to say anything, but maybe it's just as well that you know."

"I won't say anything."

"Kurt got picked up for possession of marijuana at school. And then, when they checked his locker, they found some amphetamines. He claimed that those belonged to a friend of his, but he admitted to me, later, that he had taken several different drugs, and he's been smoking marijuana for quite a while. We had suspected something like that, but he had always denied it."

"What's going to happen to him?"

"He didn't get detention. But I'm not sure that it wouldn't have been better if he had. He's on probation now, but I don't see a lot of regret. We try to monitor him and keep him away from the crowd he's been running around with, but it's almost impossible. He's not honest with us, Gene."

"He stole some of my money," Kenny said, and again there was silence.

After a few moments Alex said, "Kenny had been saving up to buy a skateboard, and the money disappeared. Kurt never has owned up to that one, but I don't know of any other explanation. Anna's had money come up missing from her purse, too."

"Isn't there some kind of program he could get into?" Emily asked.

"Yes, there are some. And maybe we should have looked into that. Kurt made lots of promises and talked us out of it, but I don't know whether we can trust him."

"He's not *bad*," Pammy said. "He's nice to me."

"That's true," Anna said. "He's so likeable, so sweet when he wants to be. We just keep thinking that it's some rebellious thing he has to pass through. He graduates next spring if he can make up for a couple of failing grades. We'd actually like to send him out here to college—just to get him away from his friends—but I don't know whether we could let him get that far away from home. And I'm not sure he'll study if he does go to college."

"I'm not very popular with him right now, since I've tried to crack down," Alex said. "So any influence you can have on him would help."

"What if you sent him out here? He could live with us and finish high school here."

"We've thought of that," Anna said. "But he'd be too much for you. I hate to say it, but he knows how to manipulate people. It would be hard for you to keep control of him."

"Won't you be going into the service this spring?" Dad asked.

Gene looked down at his plate, remembering that he had stopped eating. "Maybe. But I'm not sure how soon after I graduate they'll draft me."

"Well . . . we're not sure what to do. But try to think of any way you can to help him. He looks up to you. He doesn't admit that, but I know he does."

"Okay." Gene went back to eating, but not with the same pleasure as before. The trouble in Kurt's life was disturbing, and the reminder that he might not be around to help was even worse. "Dad," he said, after a time, "do you think there's any chance that Nixon can get the war over fairly soon?"

"I don't know. Don't say it outside this house, but I'm not sure I trust this whole 'secret plan' promise Nixon made during the elections. I'm not hearing anything that gives me faith that he knows how to do anything more than Johnson to get North Vietnam to negotiate a peace."

"They can't even decide on the shape of a table," Emily said.

Alex nodded. "That's right. But Thieu may be stalling, waiting for Nixon to take over."

All through the fall Gene had followed the news and hoped that peace talks would begin in Paris. Johnson had halted the bombing of North Vietnam on October 31 in hopes of enticing the North Vietnamese to agree to the talks. Some people thought the halt was only a political move to help Humphrey, with the elections only a few days away, but Humphrey had lost all the same in a close election. Now the South Vietnamese were refusing to cooperate in the proposed talks because seating at the table might suggest that the National Liberation Front—the

Communist insurgent troops fighting in the south—should be recognized as a legitimate power. How could peace be negotiated if the shape of the table couldn't be agreed upon—or the participants in the talk? Gene wanted to believe that Nixon would announce, soon after he was inaugurated, some new approach that would change things. It wasn't encouraging to hear his Republican father suggest that wasn't likely.

But Gene, as always, told himself not to think about that. What he had to do was trust that the Lord would guide his life. If he wasn't supposed to leave his family, a way would be opened for him to stay at home. So he ate his meal, enjoyed the pie and ice cream, helped with the dishes, and then tried to be cheery when everyone moved into the family room and he and Emily and Sharon sat down at the puzzle.

It was after eight o'clock when Kurt finally came in, even though he had promised to be home for dinner. Gene heard him say to his mother, "Is any of that food left? I'm starved."

She went with him to the kitchen, and after a time, she returned to the family room. "He's in there alone," she told Gene. "Go tell him about your baby, and maybe just chat with him."

Gene got up and strolled into the kitchen. "Oh, hi, Kurt," he said, trying to sound surprised. He got out a bottle of Squirt from the refrigerator and then took out a tray of ice cubes. "Hey, I made a little announcement at dinner. You missed it."

"What's that?" Kurt asked, with no apparent interest. He was eating fast, and Gene worried that he was planning to go out again. Gene didn't think Kurt's old friends in Salt Lake were taking drugs, or drinking, but it was hard to say what sort of people Kurt had met up with last summer when he was home. Certainly, there were plenty of kids around town getting into that stuff these days.

Gene poured some Squirt over the ice, let the fizz die down, and poured a little more. Then he sat down across from Kurt.

"We're going to have a baby. In April."

"Oh, yeah? That's nice." His tone seemed purposefully neutral, as though he wanted to demonstrate no sign of interest and stop the conversation before it started.

"So you'll be Uncle Kurt. How does that sound?"

"Dad and Mom will warn the kid to avoid me—so I won't pollute him."

Gene tried to laugh. "I doubt that," he said.

"When did you start wearing glasses?" Kurt asked.

"I got them during my mission, but I don't wear them much—except to read. We're working on a puzzle in the other room. I need them for things like that. Why don't you come in and help us with it?"

"I don't think I could stand the excitement." For the first time, Kurt smiled. Gene smiled too, but he didn't know what to say. He was trying to come up with something when Kurt asked, "So what are you going to name the kid? Alexander? Do we get one more?"

"I don't know. If it's a girl, definitely not."

"What's wrong with Alexandria? Any kid would want to be named after the great *congressman,* girl or boy."

"They didn't name *me* after Dad."

"He wasn't a *congressman* back then. They stuck you with the name of some dead uncle."

Gene felt a flash of anger. How could Kurt not know what that name meant to the family? But it was better not to react. "It's hard to know what to do about names—whether to pick something from the family or just choose one we like."

"I don't think I'll have to worry about it. My plan is never to get married. You got all the good genes in the family. I got the bad ones. No use passing them along. I'll save Dad the embarrassment."

"Come on, Kurt. Why do you say things like that?"

But Kurt wouldn't look up. He had cut his whole pork chop into bite-sized pieces—even though Mom had taught the kids all their lives that it wasn't good etiquette to do that—and he had scraped all the stuffing away. Now he was gobbling down the chunks, never finishing his chewing before he stuffed in another piece. Clearly, he wanted to finish and then escape—if not the house, at least Gene. It was pointless to talk to him tonight.

"If you want," Gene said, "I can get us into the church in the morning. We could go over and shoot some baskets."

"I don't play basketball anymore. I stink at the game."

"No, you don't. I couldn't believe how quick you were when we—"

"Look, Gene. Maybe I'm no big brain, like you, but I'm not stupid either. I know what this is all about. Mom and Dad have been telling you to 'do some things' with me. Get close to me. Have some nice little chats, and see if you can't straighten me out."

Gene wasn't going to deny that, but that left him with nothing to say.

"Look at it this way, Gene. Mom and Dad have you and they have Joey. And Kenny's going to be another *fine son*. Why don't you all just let me be the black sheep of the family and leave it at that? It's a tough job, but somebody's got to do it."

"Kurt, we don't think of you that way."

Suddenly Kurt's finger was pointing at Gene. "Don't give me that." He swore—said a word Gene never thought he would hear from anyone in the family. "Pretend that you really care about me if you want to, but don't tell outright lies. I can tell you every word of what Dad has told you about me. I'm on drugs, according to him. I'm on a slippery path, heading directly down to hell."

"Kurt, come on. He's worried about you. Why shouldn't he be? He's your dad. Just wait until you have kids some day, and then you'll know why he worries. As long as you want honesty, why don't you try a little yourself. You've given him some good reasons to be worried."

Kurt set his knife down carefully, and then his fork. He looked into Gene's eyes. "Do you have any idea how much I hate you, Gene? Do you have any idea how *long* I've hated you? Do you have any idea how much I've tried to be *nothing* like you? You're Dad's show horse. He trots you out in front of all his friends, and he says, 'See what I produced? He's another *me*. A future *congressman*.' Then he looks at me and says to himself, 'So what went wrong with that one? He must have come to me *defective*. I certainly wouldn't produce a kid like that.'"

"Oh, get off it, Kurt. I'm so sick of this line of bull you throw at me every time I try to talk to you. You've got all the talent that any of us have. You just make stupid choices, and then you blame Dad for worrying about it. If you would do something with your brain and your God-given skills, you wouldn't resent me and Joey—or anyone else."

"Turn around. Let me look. Does Dad have his hand in your back? Isn't that *his* voice I hear?"

"Lay off."

"Dad used to take me to your football and basketball games, and everyone would come up to us and tell him how great you were, how much like *him* you were. But the first time I tried out for basketball, the coach told me, 'You'll have to work hard to be as good as your brother. The game doesn't come as easy for you.' And then he cut me—first cut."

Gene was trying to calm down. "Look, I see what you're saying. I don't blame you for hating stuff like that. Coaches shouldn't compare kids. They ought to take them for what they are and—"

"Shut up, okay? Just shut up. I'm not one of your *customers*—looking for a used Rambler. You're a *phony*, and I'm not sure you even know it. The only thing you know is, act like Dad, and maybe you can be a big shot too."

"Kurt, you're the one who needs to figure yourself out. To you, everything's *Dad's* fault. Or it's *my* fault because I was good at sports. Or it's the big, bad coach who cut you from the basketball team. Do you have any idea how hard I worked at my game before I ever tried out in junior high?

What you are is lazy, Kurt. And if you don't figure that out right away you're going to be messed up all your life."

Kurt stood up. He was smiling again. "Hey, you guessed my goal. When I grow up, I want to be all messed up. And I plan to work *hard* at it. In fact, I think I know some things I can do right now. See you later."

"Don't, Kurt. Come back here." Gene jumped up and hurried around the kitchen table. He met Kurt heading for the door and grabbed his arm. "Don't run away. Let's have it out. Let's say what we've got to say. Maybe we can—"

"I've said all I want to. Let go of me." Kurt tried to pull loose from Gene's grip, but Gene grabbed his shirt with his other hand. Kurt tried to twist away, and then, suddenly, he drove a fist at Gene's face. Gene felt his glasses snap in half, felt the plastic cut into the sides of his nose. He let go, stepped back, and grabbed his face. The kitchen door swung open, and he knew Kurt was gone. When he pulled his hands away, he saw blood on both his palms, but what scared him more was that he was looking through blood in his eyes.

"Emily," Gene called, and he walked quickly to the family room, his hands cupped over his nose. "I need some help," he said. He could feel blood dripping from his fingers. He leaned his head back to make sure it fell on his shirt, not on the carpet.

"What happened?" Mom was suddenly next to him. She took hold of his arm.

"I said some stupid things to Kurt. He took off."

"He *hit* you?" Alex asked.

"Yes. But I don't blame him. I said some things I shouldn't have."

"Come with me to the bathroom," Anna was saying, and now Emily was there, holding his other arm.

They led him down the hallway, with Alex following. "Are your eyes all right?" he asked. "Maybe we'd better take you to a hospital."

"I think it's just my nose," Gene said, but he wasn't sure of that. His eyes were burning. When he reached the bathroom and bent over the sink, he pulled his hands away. What he realized then was that most of the blood was coming not from the cuts but from a bloody nose. His vision began to clear, once he washed his eyes with cold water.

"Where did Kurt go?" Anna asked.

"I don't know," Gene said. "But he was really mad. I should have kept my mouth shut."

"It's not your fault," Alex said. "We can't keep making excuses for him. The kid has to be stopped."

But what did that mean? Gene didn't want his dad to do anything that would make things worse.

Anna placed a square of gauze over the scrapes on his nose and taped it in place. Then she went to the kitchen and came back with some cubes of ice wrapped in a hand towel. She led him back to the family room and had him lie down and hold the ice to his nose. Alex had walked outside. When he came back, he said, "He took Mom's car. I told him he could have it this afternoon, but he had no permission to run off with it tonight."

"Dad, he was furious," Gene said. "He just wanted out of here."

"He's always furious. I've never met a kid with such a chip on his shoulder. He does these incredibly dangerous, stupid things, and then he directs all his anger at anyone who tries to stop him. He needs to start living with the consequences of his actions."

If Dad laid the law down, Kurt would say that Dad was siding with Gene. But if Gene hadn't lost his temper, this never would have happened. What Gene wanted was to head Kurt off somehow before this got worse. He waited ten minutes or so, and then he sat up. "I need to find Kurt and talk to him," he said. "Emily, do you want to come with me?"

"Sure," she said. "But are you sure the bleeding has stopped?"

"Yeah. I'm fine."

But Alex was saying, "Gene, I don't think talking will do any good.

I'm thinking that I'll call the police and tell them he stole our car. Maybe he needs to spend some time behind bars so he starts to understand how easy he's had things all his life. I keep trying to keep my name out of the papers, but I don't care if I'm reelected; I've got to deal with this boy."

"Just let me look for him. I need to talk to him when I'm not so mad."

Alex didn't say anything, and Gene took that as agreement, so he stood up. He waited for a moment, just to be sure he wasn't dizzy. He was all right, but the pain was setting in, spreading through his forehead and cheekbones. All the same, he walked to the hall, grabbed his coat, and zipped it up over the dried blood on his shirt. He waited until he and Emily were in the car, however, before he said, "Kurt told me he hated me. He said he's hated me for a *long* time."

"Gene, he's seventeen. He's not mature enough to admit what's really going on."

Gene wanted to believe that was true, but he kept thinking about the things Kurt had said. He worried sometimes that he *was* too much the slick salesman, too much the fair-haired boy in the family. He did try to please people—to live up to the family image—and maybe there was something phony about that.

Gene drove to the Wilson's house, the home of Kurt's best friend from junior high days. Anna's car wasn't there, however, and when Gene went to the door, John—the boy Kurt always called Bucky—wasn't home. Sister Wilson hadn't seen Kurt, but she reminded Gene of some of their other friends and even looked up some addresses for him. She also asked about his nose. Gene said as little as he could, but she seemed to guess the rest. She said she had heard that Kurt had had "a few problems" in the east.

Gene checked out the other friends' addresses and had no luck. But he picked up several new names from one friend who was home. He and Emily checked out those too and came up with nothing. Then they drove past some of the hangouts Gene remembered from his own days, and some

Emily knew of. But by then they had been searching for almost two hours, and they were starting to realize how remote the chance was they could find him. They were actually on their way home when Gene remembered a guy who had stopped by the dealership to talk with Kurt a couple of times during the summer. He was a year younger than Kurt, but he had seemed exactly the sort Kurt needed to avoid. Gene couldn't remember his first name, but what he did remember was that he had an older sister who had gone to East High. He thought he knew the area where she lived, or at least *had* lived back then. It seemed an unlikely hope, but Gene had been praying all evening, and he wanted to think this might be a bit of inspiration.

He drove to the girl's neighborhood, which was west of 1300 East, and tried a couple of the streets. He was cruising along slowly when Emily said, "I think that's your mother's car up there, isn't it?"

They drove closer, and by then Gene could see that it was. But now he was frightened.

"What are you going to do?" Emily asked.

"Go in. See if he'll talk to me. I want to be straight with him."

"Should I come in with you?"

Gene thought about that. He didn't want this to be awkward. "Yeah," he finally said. "I think so. I get the feeling he likes you better than me. And you're better at this kind of stuff. You can at least stop me if I start saying something stupid again."

"He might not be here. He might have left the car and gone with his friend."

"I know."

But they walked to the door and Gene rang the doorbell. In a few minutes the friend opened the door. "Hi," Gene said. "I'm Kurt Thomas's brother. I'm looking for Kurt. Is he here?"

"Well, it's hard to say." The guy leaned against the door frame and laughed, and it was not hard to tell that he was drunk, or maybe stoned.

"I just want to talk to him."

"Someone did a job on your nose, I see. Maybe you want to go for round two."

"Look, I just—"

But from inside the house, he heard Kurt's voice. "If Mom is worried about her car, I'll give you the keys. But leave me alone."

Gene heard the same slurring in Kurt's voice. "Kurt, I'm sorry about what happened. We need to talk."

In a moment Kurt was at the door. He pulled on his friend's shoulder, and the boy stumbled backward. "Hey," Kurt said, "we're cool. That was all just *talk* before. You know how it is. But I'm over it. I'm doing fine now."

"Kurt, you're drunk."

"No, no. No way. If you saw me *drunk*, you'd know it. I'm just feeling good." He had begun to laugh, and so had his friend, from inside the dark living room. Gene wondered where the boy's family was and where the boys had gotten the alcohol.

"I love you, Kurt."

"Let's not get into all that. I'm sorry I hit you, okay? And I'm sorry I broke your glasses."

"I love you."

"I love you, too," Emily said.

Kurt looked at Emily, as though noticing her for the first time. He stared at her for a few seconds, but then he looked back at Gene and said, "I was mad. I was just trying to get to you. Let's not make a big deal out of it."

"I love you, Kurt," Gene said again.

Kurt stuck his hands into the back pockets of his jeans. He tried to stand straight, but he was swaying, ever so slightly. Gene saw tears in his eyes. "I'm sorry, but I don't believe that," Kurt said. "I really don't." He stood for a time, obviously trying to keep control, but tears were slipping from the corners of his eyes. "I wouldn't love me, if I was you. But then, I don't even *like* me."

"You're my little brother," Gene said. "I remember all the stuff we did together. Do you remember that time you and Joey and I took the wheels off Sharon's baby buggy and tried to make a go-cart out of it?" Gene tried to laugh, but he felt his own voice break.

"I hate you because I don't know how to *be* you," Kurt said. He bent forward with his hands on his knees, and he began to sob.

Gene stepped to him, raised him up, and then wrapped his arms around him. "Let's start over. Two grown-up guys. Let's figure all this out."

"I can't, Gene. I don't know why. I just can't."

"Come home, okay?"

"Mom and Dad will know I've been drinking. Dad will throw the book at me."

"We'll take you to your room and you can sleep, and then tomorrow we can talk."

Kurt didn't say anything for a long time. But eventually he pulled away and wiped his eyes. Then he turned and said, "Mike, I'd better go. I'll see you again before I go back."

"Hey. It's cool. Gotta do what you gotta do."

So Kurt came with his brother, and he gave his keys to Emily, who drove Anna's car home. When they got to the house, Gene walked with Kurt upstairs, and afterward, he came down and said to his parents, "I found him. He's okay. He's going to bed."

"What was he doing?" Dad asked.

"He was just hanging out with a friend. He told me he was sorry he hit me. I told him we'd talk tomorrow. I think maybe it was good he threw that punch. Maybe we got some things out in the open, and now we can talk."

"I hope so, Gene," Alex said. "I love that kid. But be careful. He tells you what you want to hear, and then he's right back where he was before."

"I know. But I do think he meant what he said tonight."

"He does," Anna said. "He really does want to change. He just can't figure out how to do it."

"That's the same thing he told us," Emily said.

"Well, thanks to both of you," Alex said. "I appreciate you looking for him. I'm going to bed now."

So Alex left, and Anna stayed a little longer, and the three worked on the puzzle. But after Anna went to bed, Gene told Emily what he had been thinking about all evening. "Earlier, before Kurt hit me, he told me what a phony I am."

"Gene, you search your own soul as much as anyone I know. You're always second-guessing your own motives and trying to be a better person."

"But he's got a point. I do try to live up to what everyone expects of me. And I do imitate Dad."

"Do you know anyone better to model your life after?"

"No. But I wanted to be student body president at East because he was, and be the very best athlete because he was. And on my mission, I kept worrying that I wasn't accomplishing as much as he had."

"I think it's okay, as long as he's just a positive image for you—a role model. But I do worry sometimes how hard you strive for things. It's like you think you have to prove something all the time."

"I just feel like I have to achieve something in my life. I always feel that."

"Why? Can't you be satisfied to be a good husband and a good dad? What's more important than that?"

"Nothing. That's what I want to be. But people expect a lot more of me than that. They always have."

"What people?"

"I don't know. My family. Everyone. It started with sports, I guess."

"You don't have to prove anything, Gene. You're a good person. That's what matters."

But Gene wasn't sure he was nearly so good as Emily thought he was. He tried hard to be good—but he feared that he tried even harder to *look* good. In some ways he did understand Kurt, who had decided to drop out of the race, not live up to the family name. But Gene couldn't do that, and he knew it. He was the first son, the first grandson. He had always understood what that meant.

# CHAPTER 12

Diane and Greg were in Utah for the holidays. Diane would actually have preferred to stay with her own parents but hadn't wanted to be selfish about that, so she had allowed Greg to persuade her that they would have more fun in Salt Lake. They stopped in Ogden first, however, and Greg agreed they could spend a couple of days there before they moved on. Greg actually spent most of that time in Salt Lake. He still needed to do his Christmas shopping, he said, and he knew the stores in Salt Lake much better than the ones in Ogden.

Diane enjoyed the chance to be with her mother. They did some shopping, some baking and gift wrapping, and they spent lots of hours talking. Diane thought she felt closer to her mom than she ever had before. She had been trying to do some reading lately, and she asked about Bobbi's favorite writers. They ended up having a long talk about Jane Austen, whom Diane had hated in high school but had started to enjoy this fall. Diane liked the love stories and the feisty heroines, so she was embarrassed when her mom talked about Austen's view of English society. Diane told herself she would have to notice more of those things. Still, she could tell that her mother was pleased that she was reading. It gave them a connection they had never had before.

They talked about marriage, too, and Diane admitted to her mother that she worried that Greg seemed disappointed with her at times. He was rather frank about saying that she wasn't much of a cook, and he implied sometimes that she wasn't as smart as the women in his classes at law school. What Diane didn't dare mention to her mother was that Greg hinted rather often that he found her too inhibited.

"I've never been a great cook. You know that," Bobbi told Diane. "But Dad never says a word about that. I don't even get that 'my mother cooked it some other way' stuff I hear women talk about."

Diane had thought many times lately about her father's kindness and the good heart he showed toward Mom. Diane had always assumed that was how men treated their wives. But she told her mother, "Greg's been under a lot of pressure this fall. He's really sweet to me most of the time. I think he gets a little cranky at times, especially after he's up so late studying."

"Diane, there's always pressure," Bobbi said. "Just wait until he's practicing law. You need to talk to him, let him know—without getting angry—that some of his words hurt you. If you take those jabs and don't say anything, he'll never learn."

When Diane and Greg moved on to Salt Lake, Diane had a chance to spend an afternoon with Grandma Bea. Christmas was only two days away, and Grandma was baking. Diane loved the smell of sugar cookies, still hot, and the lingering aroma of fudge. And she liked the chance to ask about all her cousins. The shocking family news was that Hans Stoltz, Aunt Anna's nephew, was in prison in East Germany—had apparently been there for a long time. No one knew the whole story, but Anna was guessing it had to be something he had done to offend the government. She knew for certain that he wasn't a criminal.

Then there was Kurt, the family worry. Grandma Bea told Diane, "I know he's got problems, but he's a lovely boy. Since he was little, he's always been so cute to me. I think he would rather sit in this kitchen and talk to me than do anything else in the world."

"Grandma, we all would. This is the center of the universe as far as I'm concerned. All the stars orbit around it. Or really, around *you*."

"Oh, now, don't say that. I get to be more of an old fuddy-duddy all the time. I used to tease Al about being old fashioned, but I'm a little more like him every year." She smiled, her deep dimples showing.

Grandma was well over seventy now, but she looked at least ten years younger.

"That's interesting you say that," Diane said. "Does it take a long time until a couple gets that way, so you think the same about things?"

"Oh, goodness, I hope *that* never happens. Al is still wrong about a whole lot of stuff. If I ever got him trained to think exactly like me, I don't know what my next project would be."

"But did the two of you have to make adjustments when you got married?"

Grandma laughed. "Back in those days all the adjusting was done by the woman. But I've gotten spunkier over the years. I'm like a sheepdog now. I don't bite, but I nip at his heels and he pays attention. You can't imagine how much he's changed. He's set in his ways when it comes to the things he likes to talk about—politics, mostly—but on all the questions that come up between us, he's very willing to listen."

"Are there that many things to work out? How long have you been married?"

"Fifty-four years, and yes, I guess so. Different things come up at different times in your life. It's been a big change for me to have Al around the house so much lately. At first, I didn't like it. But we manage to work around each other, and I think I'd miss the sound of him now."

"That's nice, Grandma. Really nice. You two are a great example to the rest of us."

Grandma was getting cookies out of the oven. She brought them to the table and scooped them off the sheet onto a wire cooling rack. "We're just old," she said. "Old people always *seem* to know more than they really do."

"But you've experienced a lot of things I'm still trying to figure out."

"Like what?"

Diane looked at the cookies, not at her grandmother. "Grandma, sometimes Greg is sarcastic, and critical, and I don't know how to make him stop."

Diane glanced up to see the concern in Grandma Bea's face. "Diane, I think it's important to respect your husband. He's a holy man, a holder of the priesthood. At the same time—and this is the tricky part—don't settle for anything less from him. You're holy too."

"But what should I do?"

"I don't think it's easy, Di. It's hard to know whether you're protecting yourself or just being too sensitive. But a woman doesn't have to sit still for it when a man gets abusive."

"I wouldn't call it that. He just . . . I don't know . . . gets irritated with me. Or he compares me to other people."

"What other people?

"His mother, for one. And he brings up this student at the law school. Sondra Gould. I guess she's really brilliant."

Grandma walked back to the table. She sat down and took hold of Diane's hand. "As your aged grandmother, let me give you one warning. I've seen women make the mistake of thinking it's best to subject their will to their husband's, mostly to avoid trouble, and maybe because that's what they think the Church demands. They think they're being generous when they do that, but gradually they lose their sense of self. It can look like the right thing, but in the end, it isn't. Our ultimate goals are too great for that. In the eternities, we have to be two people, both strong, both good—and united."

"Thank you, Grandma. I know that's true. Great-Grandma Thomas told me once to walk beside my husband, not behind him. I think, in a way, that's what you're saying, too."

"I am. But my mother, in certain moods, liked a good fight just for the fun of it, and I don't think anything good comes of that."

"I don't do that, Grandma. In fact, I'm always scared I'll start a fight. That's one reason I hold back."

"Talk to Greg. Tell him what you're feeling. You can't just assume that he knows. One of the great mistakes women make is to drop little hints, pout or whatever, and then wonder why their husbands don't understand them."

It was what Mom had said. Talk to him. Diane knew she had to do that. But she found the idea more frightening than she wanted it to be, and she hated feeling that way.

&#8734;

Kathy always felt mixed emotions about her trip home for the holidays, but this year she was frightened. She had made an important decision in the past few weeks and she felt she needed to let her parents know. She procrastinated doing it, however, until a couple of days after Christmas. Her dad and Douglas had been watching the splashdown of *Apollo 8*, after its moon orbit, but when that was over, Kathy said, "Dad, do you think you and Mom could come into the living room for a few minutes? There are some things I need to talk to you about."

She saw the look of concern in her father's face. She watched her mother, too, who was always harder to read, more controlled, no matter what happened. "What's on your mind?" Wally asked, and he and Lorraine sat down on the new couch they had recently bought. It was crushed velvet in a dark shade of gold. Kathy hated it.

Kathy sat in a matching chair on the opposite side of the glass coffee table. "Well, for one thing, you've been asking me for a long time what I'm going to do when I graduate, and I've made a decision." Then she thought to say, "Or at least I wanted to see what you think about it."

Kathy saw her father relax a little. "Sure. What are you thinking?" he said.

"I've talked off and on for years about going into the Peace Corps. I finally decided that's what I want to do. I've sent in my application, and I haven't heard back yet, but if I get an appointment, I think I'd like to accept."

"That's good," Wally said. "Peace Corps will be a sort of mission for you. You're going to learn a lot, and you're going to *give*. The only thing that worries me is that you won't be around many Mormons. I keep hoping you'll meet a young man in the Church. That's been hard in the East, and it's going to be even worse overseas somewhere."

"And by the time I get back I'll be *twenty-four*—an old maid." She had spoken with a little more bite than she had intended. But at least her parents smiled.

"I'm not saying that," Wally said. "But you know what can happen. I've seen *great* girls, *beautiful* girls, miss their chance. Look what happened to your Aunt LaRue."

Kathy decided to let the subject go. She had enough bombshells coming without making Dad angry. "Actually," she said, "that's something else I wanted to talk to you about. I have met someone—maybe."

"Who is it?" Lorraine asked.

"It's actually one of my professors—one I had last year. Gary Jennings." Kathy thought she saw her parents stiffen. "He's never told me that he's interested in me, but we love to talk, and we've gradually realized that we see life pretty much the same way."

"How old is he?" Wally asked.

"He's *very* old. He'll be thirty next month." She smiled, but her parents didn't. "You have to understand, we just get together and talk. He's very proper about everything. We started talking about Peace Corps, and we both decided to join. That's been our main connection. What I feel, though, is that once I graduate—and he *has* dropped a few hints about this—he does plan to ask me out."

There was a rather long pause. Her dad folded his arms, and Kathy could hear him trying to seem casual when he said, "I don't suppose he's LDS."

"No."

The new pause was much longer. But it was Lorraine who saw the safety valve. "But you're both going off this summer, and you won't see each other for two years?"

"Right. So nothing is likely to come of all this. I just . . . you know . . . wanted to tell you about him. I suppose it's conceivable that we would end up in some whirlwind romance, get married quickly, and then go *together* into the Peace Corps, but I really can't picture that."

Kathy actually heard the air coming out of her father. But he waited for a time before he said, "But Kathy, would you consider marrying someone who's not in the Church?"

"Dad, I haven't been to church in a long time. You know that."

"But you always tell me you aren't that far away."

Now Kathy was the one to let some time pass. "Dad, that's the other thing I need to talk to you about," she finally said. "This thing with Professor Jennings may never go anywhere. In fact, it probably won't. But as we've talked this fall, I've finally been able to sort out my feelings about religion. I think, for a long time, I was mainly just mad at our members for not believing the same things I do—you know, about Vietnam and things like that. But I've gotten past all that. People have different beliefs, and it's important to respect that."

"We've said that to you many times, Kathy."

"I know. And I think I've finally let it penetrate my thick skull. But that's just the point, Dad. One culture believes that God is part of nature—a life force—and another one believes in a myth about gods rising up out of the ocean. I think I can now accept the idea that each myth or explanation, or whatever you want to call it, is helpful for those who accept it, but it doesn't mean that I have to choose one over another."

"So what are you saying? There are no truths?"

"I guess I am saying that, at least in the sense that—"

"Oh, come on, Kathy. What is this guy? An anthropologist? I know how those people talk. *Everything* is true, which only means that *nothing* is true."

"Dad, don't do this."

"Don't do what? Defend the gospel of Jesus Christ?"

But Lorraine was quick to say, "Don't get mad, honey. Let's just talk about this."

"I'm not mad at Kathy," Wally said. "But I am bothered by a thirty-year-old guy who thinks he can fill my young daughter's head with a bunch of mumbo jumbo."

"Dad, I wanted to explain, but I guess I can't. I'll just go ahead with my life, and you don't have to approve of my choices."

"So is that what all this is leading to: an announcement that you've found a higher understanding of the world and you don't believe in the Church any longer?"

"I would never have said it that way, Dad, but I'll let you use your own terminology."

"So you're an atheist now?"

"I don't know, Dad. I'd say I'm more of an agnostic. I don't know whether there's a God, and I'm not going to pretend that I do. Have you ever read anything about existentialism?"

"Oh, brother. I knew this was coming."

"Dad, stop it. I won't talk to you if you're going to react that way."

"Don't ask me not to get upset, Kathy. I *love* you." Tears had filled his eyes. "You're the little girl we raised. And now, some all-knowing professor from Smith College is feeding you lies straight out of Satan's mouth."

Kathy hated what her father was saying, but she loved him for his tears. "Dad, just hear me out. You and Mom are as good and moral as anyone I know. And Grandma and Grandpa are the same way. That's what religion has given you, and I have no problem with that. I love the way I was raised. I love the Mormon pioneer stories and the way we bless babies and gather as a family for baptisms—all those things. But you need to know, Gary Jennings is just as true and good as you are. He tries to determine what's right and wrong, what his duty is, what he owes to the family of man, and he acts on those beliefs. That's what I want to do, and I think you ought to be proud of me for that."

"It's not that easy, Kathy."

Lorraine touched Wally's leg, as if to say, "Don't explode. This is too important." Then she looked at Kathy. "We've always been proud of you, Kathy. And you need to know, you can't do *anything* to lose our love. But please, don't make a decision like this after a couple of months of consideration. Can't you keep praying and keep an open mind? I really believe that if you'll—"

Wally had been leaning farther forward all the time, and words finally burst from him. "That's right, honey. All we ask of you is that you not give up on everything we've taught you—not just like that. Give me some equal time. Let's kneel down and pray together, and let's look at the scriptures together." He stopped for a moment, his voice cutting off. Tears were on his cheeks now. "Please," he said. "Please. Don't make a decision like this yet. That's all we ask. Keep asking God for guidance."

"Dad, that's the great thing about existentialism. It's never finished. It's almost more about asking than it is answering. You keep yourself open to whatever truths you find. You go inside yourself and search for what honestly means most to you. I may come back to *everything* you've taught me. There are Christian existentialists. Why couldn't there be *Mormon* existentialists?"

Wally had lowered his head while Kathy was talking, but he raised it now. "I'll tell you why. Because we're not philosophers. We're children of our Heavenly Father. We're humble enough to listen to him and to follow. We don't 'go inside ourselves,' as you put it, and make up truth as we go along."

"Okay, fine." Kathy was finished. "I've told you what I'm thinking. If you can't respect it, that's okay. I want to be able to come home, all my life, but if you refuse to understand me and my beliefs, maybe that won't be possible."

"Don't say that, Kathy," Lorraine said. "Of course you can—"

"Kathy, do you have any idea how arrogant you are?" Wally stood up. "Since you were fifteen you've been telling me how stupid I am. How wrong I am. Your problem is, you listen so carefully to *yourself*, there's no room in your heart for God."

Kathy stood too. "Maybe you're right—at least about part of that. I have been arrogant for long time. I thought, when I finally found some humility, you'd notice, and you'd be happy to see it. But if it's not your version of humility—not 'Church approved'—you don't have enough humility of your own to listen. Maybe arrogance is a Thomas trait."

"You're talking to your father, Kathy." He pointed to his chest. "I'm not your enemy. There's no one in this world who loves you more than I do."

"Oh, is that right? Is that *love* I hear in your voice? If I were to tell you that *you're* right and *I'm* wrong, I would be your lovely daughter, after all. But as soon as I disagree, I'm a daughter of Satan."

"I'd be *overjoyed* if you told me I was right—then I'd know you were hearing the voice of the Lord."

"Oh, excuse me. Is that who you are? I didn't know."

"*Kathy!*" It was her mom. But Kathy had heard enough. She stomped away, heading for her bedroom, but then she realized that she didn't want to stay in the house. She changed directions and marched through the front hall, stepped outside, and slammed the door behind her. But she hadn't grabbed a coat, and it was cold outside. Her response was to run. She wanted to get away; she wanted to get warm; and as much as anything, she wanted to run until she hurt, just to feel something other than frustration.

She only reached the corner before she slowed to a fast walk, but she kept heading down Country Club Drive, with no idea where she was going. Her thoughts were coming in a rush. She kept making little speeches, saying the things she could have told Dad, things she *wished* she had told him. It was almost impossible to believe he could be so narrow.

She kept going, kept reciting her arguments, but what she sensed, as she calmed, was that she had now made a break that changed everything about her life. She had hoped to make a transition, agree to disagree, always feel close to her family and still go her own way. Now, all of that was impossible, and she wondered what her future would look like.

She eventually cut north to 2100 South, and then west again. She thought of going to Grandma and Grandpa's house and asking whether she could stay there, but Grandpa would be just as bad as Dad—probably worse. When she reached Highland High, she was flushed from walking and, at the same time, cold. She had never returned to her school since she had graduated, and she suddenly wanted to look inside—partly to warm up for a few minutes. She tried a couple of locked doors and was about to give up the idea when she saw, through the glass doors, a young man walking down the hallway. She knocked and he walked over. He opened the door enough to say, "Yeah?"

"Could I come in?"

"I'm not supposed to let anyone in," he said. "We're cleaning the floors."

"I just wanted to look around for a minute. I graduated from here a few years ago."

He hesitated, then pulled the door farther open. "You can walk down that way," he said. He pointed to the south end of the building. "But stay out of this wing up here."

"Okay. Thanks." She stepped inside and he walked away.

Kathy watched him for a moment, and then she turned and strolled slowly down the hall. She was surprised by the familiarity she felt, the sameness in the floor tiles, the color of the walls. It was as though she had never left, and yet it was strange to think that only three and a half years had gone by. She felt a century older. Nothing had turned out quite the way she had expected, and as she tried to think what she had done with her life so far, every aspect of it was disappointing. She was thinking now that the Peace Corps was her answer, and existentialism, but how would she feel about those things in another few years? Would all her latest certitude be gone? How could she know things with such confidence at one point, only to be so shaken in her beliefs a few months later? How many times could that happen to her?

She came to the end of the hallway, then stood at another set of doors. She remembered going out these doors one day and running to a car, where her mother was waiting for her. Mom had been driving a new Rambler that Dad had brought home to her. But it was an ugly shade of green that he admitted hadn't been selling well. Mom had driven the car for two years, and the kids had teased her about how ugly it was. But Mom had said, "Lots of people would love to have a brand new car. I don't think I'll complain too much about the color."

Kathy had hurried to the car that day, a winter day like this, and Mom had driven her to her piano lesson, then picked her up when it was over. It was a simple thing, but Kathy felt it now in a way that she never could have then. There was such a cost in raising a child, such devotion. Music had always meant a lot to her mother, but clearly, Kathy herself had meant much more. So what was Mom feeling right now? What had she just done to her parents?

But what could she do? Should she try to fake belief just to make them happy? Wasn't it better to make this break all at once rather than tear their hearts a little at a time? She loved her parents so much, and all her family. Why couldn't she be the kind of person who simply accepted what they believed, loved what they loved, and acted the way they did? It would be so much easier.

Kathy stood and looked out the glass doors, and she wondered what she would do once she stepped back outside. She would have to walk home. There was nowhere else to go. But what would she say to her parents when she got there? She told herself she would be kinder this time, but there was no way to make things easier. So she pushed the door handle and stepped back into the cold, and she walked fast, with her arms wrapped close around her body. But as she reached the sidewalk she saw a car slowing to a stop, just in front of her. It was as though Mom had arrived to pick her up again, but Kathy knew the car—a big maroon Buick—and she saw who was driving. It was probably the last person in the world she wanted to see at this moment: Grandpa Thomas.

He reached across the front seat and opened the front door. "Jump in. I'll drive you home," he said.

She stood on the sidewalk for a moment, thought of telling him that she wanted to walk, but she did want the ride. Maybe he had only spotted her by accident and didn't know what was going on. "Hi, Grandpa," she said, and she slid into the wide front seat.

"We've been looking for you," he said.

"Who has?"

"Lorraine called your Grandma and told her about your little spat, and then she called back after a while and said you hadn't come back. So Bea told me to drive up toward your house and take a look around. I guess Wally is doing the same thing."

"You didn't need to that. I just wanted to walk a little and clear my head."

"Or freeze your tail off."

"It is a little cold," she said, and she laughed.

Grandpa hadn't shifted the car into gear. He turned in his seat and looked at Kathy. She didn't want to look back. "I got this all second hand," Grandpa said, "but your mom told Grandma you've been listening to some professor. As I understand it, he's been filling you with some of these modern philosophies."

Kathy was not going to do this again. Her dad could be narrow, but

Grandpa was just plain bullheaded. "No one has filled me with anything, Grandpa. I do believe that existentialism explains some things I've never understood before, but I'm still trying to decide what I believe. You know me. I've been doing that for years."

"But Lorraine had the feeling this was pretty serious—that you're breaking away from the Church—and that you might be interested in this professor besides."

"Grandpa, I haven't gone to church for a long time. You know that. I'm sorry, but it doesn't seem the right answer for me. I love all of you and respect what you believe—and I *really* don't want to argue about this— but I do think you should respect my beliefs too."

"Kathy, in every age, from Old Testament times down to now, there have been false prophets who replace true doctrines with the philosophies of men. I know more about existentialism than you might think. It's not a philosophy; it's a rationalization. It's just a fancier way of saying what these hippies say: 'If it feels good, do it.' You're way too smart to be taken in by something like that."

Kathy looked out the window, back toward the school. She had always loved her grandfather, but when he was like this, it was all she could do not to lose her temper. "Maybe so, Grandpa. It's just something I've been thinking about. But we ought to head home. I didn't know Mom and Dad were so worried about me."

"Look at me."

Kathy turned toward him, and she prepared herself for a lecture. But she vowed as she never had before that no matter what he said, she wasn't going to get mad, and she wasn't going to fight with him. He was an old man, set in his ways, and she would let him have his say.

What she saw, however, was not what she expected. There was quiet in his eyes, softness. "When you were born," he said, "Bea and I hurried to the hospital. When we got there, they had cleaned you up and put you in your mother's arms. Bea wanted to count your fingers and toes, so she took the blanket from around you, and there you were, not much bigger than a frog, and Bea handed you over to me. There was nothing on you but a little diaper. I took hold of you, and you were barely enough to fill these big old hands of mine." He held his hands out before her, as though he were holding her now. Tears had begun to drip onto his cheeks. "I loved you right then, Kathy. I don't know whether you'll understand that until you have a child—or a grandchild—of your own. But it happens in an instant."

Kathy had been struggling to contain her emotions all afternoon, but now everything seemed to give way. She too began to cry.

"I still love you the same way, little girl, and I almost wish you were that baby again so I could just hold you in my arms and keep all the evil in this world away from you."

"I know, Grandpa. But I have to make up my own mind."

"No. No. That's not true at all. That's the last thing you need to do. You need to get down on your knees, sweetheart, and you need to plead with the Lord for *his* answers. I don't want to get you mad at me, Kathy, but you don't *listen* enough. You try to figure everything out for yourself. Remember, you've got your parents, and you've got me and your grandma. You should ask us sometimes. And read the scriptures. But most of all, you just need to pray and pray and pray—and listen for the Spirit."

"I do read the scriptures, Grandpa—more than most people. And maybe I haven't prayed lately, but I did for a long time."

"Honey, don't tell me that. You haven't even *lived* a long time. Learning to know the Spirit can take a lifetime."

"I can't wait a lifetime, Grandpa. I have to decide some things now."

"I know. But watch for a glimmer and then work from there."

It was all so easy to say, but Kathy had tried and tried, and she felt none of the "burning in the bosom," or any of those things Mormons always talked about. How could she deny what made sense to her, all in the name of a "glimmer"?

"Look at me."

She looked into his eyes again.

"I got in this car and I told myself I would drive up toward your house and look for you. Then I heard some words inside my head: 'Go look for her at the high school.' So I drove over here, and there you were, walking out the door."

Kathy felt a vibration pass through her. It was powerful, breathtaking, but she fought it. Those things happened. The high school was one of the places she might have decided to walk to. It was a reasonable surmise, just his mind at work, whether he knew it or not.

"Please look at me," he said again. "I want to say something to you." He hesitated, and she watched those dark eyes, under big, tangled eyebrows. She saw the mottled, wrinkled skin, gathered in pain, the tears seeping into the creases. "You do have a Father in Heaven. And he loves you. I know that. I know it for certain. Four generations of our family have known it. They put up with ten times more than we've had to face— because they *knew*. You've got to trust me a little for now. You've got to say to yourself, 'Maybe old Grandpa Thomas drives me nuts sometimes, and I think he's all wrong in his politics, but he doesn't lie. And he wouldn't tell me he *knows* unless he really does.' Can you do that?"

"I don't know, Grandpa. I think I have to get my own answer."

"Of course you do. But you don't have to do it alone. During the war your father was pressed to the absolute limit of human agony, and it was the gospel that got him through. If he gets upset with you when you want to throw aside what he gained through so much pain, then try to understand him a little. Trust him just enough not to throw all this aside. All I ask of you is that you keep asking."

Kathy wanted to say yes, that she would, but she wouldn't say it unless she meant it, and she wasn't sure.

"I know you're talking about going into the Peace Corps, and that's fine. I hope you do that. But honey, you're a member of an organization that has the power to do more good than any other. I don't think you have any idea what the Church is doing and will continue to do as it grows larger and more influential in the world. You may not think the Relief Society has much power compared to the Peace Corps, but it's one of the great forces for good in this world. Why do you think the National Council of Women elected Belle Spafford, our president, to lead their organization this year? Those women felt something from her. They recognized her inspiration. As the Church grows in numbers, and spreads to more lands, the power in women reaching out to each other, changing lives, teaching spirituality, raising families to a higher level—it's all what Joseph prophesied, and it's going to put the Peace Corps to shame. You may come home from your experience and find out the most powerful work you can do in this world has been sitting right before your eyes all along."

Kathy thought of the sisters in her ward, quilting and sharing their love, and she did like all that, but Grandpa got carried away sometimes. She couldn't imagine the Relief Society ever mattering as much as he wanted to believe.

"Kathy, I'm not as good a man as I ought to be. But I want you to think of your Grandma Bea. And then I want you to think about your mother. Are there any two women on this earth you would rather model your life after?"

"No, Grandpa. I know that. I've always known that." Everything broke loose in Kathy when she said the words. Grandpa reached for her, and she let him take her in his arms. His goodness seemed to wrap around her with his arms, and she felt a kind of "rightness" inside her that she hadn't felt in a very long time.

"Please just try some more. Ask. Just ask."

"Okay." She was sobbing.

"Honestly? Will you get down on your knees and plead with the Lord to know the truth?"

"Yes. I promise. I will."

CHAPTER 13

Hans had spent the entire fall in *Hohenschönhausen* prison. He had been left to sit in his cell more than six weeks after his visit with *Herr* Felscher in August, but since then he had been called in many times. Sometimes a week or two would go by and he would be left alone, but then he would be brought in on three or four consecutive days. But always, the questions, the pattern of the interrogation, was much the same. For hours, Felscher would ask Hans every detail of his life, his growing-up experience, his school days. Hans found in that a certain pleasure. It was diverting to have someone to talk to, or at least someone to listen to him. Back at his cell he had a better friend, but Stefan was only a pattern of taps, someone Hans had never seen. Felscher, on the other hand, was there, and although he never expressed any attachment, Hans had the feeling that the man liked him, that he found their conversations rather interesting. He never revealed anything about his own life, but he sometimes compared attitudes or opinions. Hans was wary about trusting any of that, since Felscher had ulterior motives, but it was hard to imagine that he didn't mean some of the things he said.

In the end, however, every conversation came back to the same issue. Felscher continued to insist that Hans must reveal the names of those who were involved in the breakout. There was nothing he could do, he claimed, to get Hans out early—unless he got the names. So they would talk about Hans's first contact with Berndt, about the escape, the tunnel, and go over every detail of Hans's involvement. And always, the game was to probe for a revelation that might show that Hans knew more than he was admitting. But, of course, that never happened because Hans had already told the man everything he knew.

It was winter now, and the cell was not well heated, but Felscher had ordered an extra blanket for Hans, and the blanket had come. Again, Hans suspected that Felscher was trying to win him over; it was what Gustav had warned him about. All the same, he did appreciate the kindness, and sometimes Felscher saw to it that Hans got a special meal, one with a little meat or some vegetables. It was hard not to think of the man as his only ally in this dismal place.

One morning in early January 1969, Hans was led to Felscher's office, and he felt some pleasure at the thought of doing something different, even of seeing Felscher, whom he hadn't seen since before Christmas. But Felscher didn't look at all congenial this morning. He sat with his arms folded and waited for Hans to sit down. He didn't greet Hans in his usual offhanded way, didn't begin with any small talk. "I have received a report that concerns me," he said. "You have broken a serious rule, and now, I'm afraid, you have lost all hope of an early release."

Hans was learning not to respond to such threats, but this one sent a chill through him. He had been telling himself all along to plan on the full three years, and then, perhaps, to see his term extended. There was no expectation of fairness in this system, and if Felscher believed he could get something out of Hans by keeping him an extra year or two, Hans didn't doubt for a moment that the man would do it.

"What rule?" Hans asked.

"You have been tapping on the pipes in your cell, communicating with the man in the cell above you."

Hans wasn't about to deny the accusation, but he also knew better than to admit to anything. He said nothing.

"I'm certain you see no reason for such a rule as this, but it is our rule, and you knew it. You have defied our orders and now you must pay for that."

Hans continued to stare at Felscher, but he remained silent.

"We bring men to prison when they break our laws. We hope to help them reform and change their behavior. It is our great wish that you will someday leave our institution ready to be a contributing citizen, but we see no promise of that when you come here and continue your rebellion. When you communicate this way, back and forth between prisoners, you surely breed discontent. You complain and encourage each other to be hostile to the state. How can we make any progress when you persist in clinging to your antisocialist attitudes?"

Hans wanted to laugh. He knew very well that the guards knew all about this form of communicating, had known that he was tapping for a long time. It was one of the few little pleasures that prisoners could use to pass the time. He and Stefan had been tapping out messages for many weeks now, and even though Hans was careful to desist whenever it was time for a meal to be delivered, or when a guard came near, it was highly unlikely that the guards had never heard any of their signals. Most of the guards seemed to care very little about anything, and certainly their jobs were easier when the prisoners found a bit of contentment. As far as any negative attitudes being shared, Stefan and Hans had never been daring enough even to say anything about conditions in the prison. Occasionally they had mentioned the poor quality of the food, or the cold in the cells, but nothing more. What they had done, primarily, was share one another's history. They had both become proficient at the code, but still, it was a slow process, spelling out every word. Nonetheless, they had told about their homes, their schools, the things they liked to do. Hans had revealed little about his beliefs, but he had shared a great deal about his outings with the Church, youth conferences and the like. Stefan, as it had turned out, had actually been active in Free German Youth as a boy, before leaving with his family for West Germany. He had said once that he liked the West much better, but he hadn't explained why. What neither wanted to do, clearly, was tap out a message that could be picked up by some listener and then used against them.

Hans's suspicion was that Felscher had known for a long time about Hans and Stefan's messages, had probably had them listened to, hoping for information he could use, but now, realizing that the conversations were of no value, was finally using them for leverage of another kind. But again, Hans didn't answer.

"You will stop this behavior this instant. We are seeing to that. Your partner in this surreptitious activity is being moved from his cell today. Don't ever attempt such an act again or we can send you back to the judge who sentenced you, and we can have more years added to your sentence. Do you understand that?"

"Yes. Of course."

"This is bad for you, Stoltz. I'm most disappointed. I was hoping to see you released before the end of the year. That would appear impossible now. But you have a chance to rectify this wrong. You can tell me the names I have been asking for—or give me descriptions of men you might have met with. I need something from you that shows your commitment to this nation and this people. The names themselves are not so important as is your change of attitude. So I'm sending you back now. When you have more to tell me, let a guard know. Otherwise, you may sit in that same cell for the rest of your term. Or longer."

"*Herr* Felscher, I have told you many times, I only knew Berndt. I only met one other man, and that man died with Berndt. I can't change my testimony. I've told you everything I know."

"That's what you always say, but answer me truthfully—if you did know names, would you give them to me?"

Hans had come to take a certain pride in his inner consistency. He didn't like to lie. And so he said, "I think not."

Felscher laughed. "I had a feeling you would say that. But that's your little game, isn't it? It's your way of telling me that you do know, and yet will not say. Now I'm going to give you some time to think that over." He called out for the guard.

Hans knew he had made a mistake by answering honestly, but he didn't really regret it. It was satisfying to hold a certain power over this man. Felscher was getting desperate to tell his superiors that he was getting somewhere with Hans—there seemed no doubt about that—and at least Hans wasn't giving him anything he could use. What he worried about, however, was what Felscher might think of next. He had heard that it was not beyond these interrogators to bring in *Stasi* agents and to resort to beatings and torture.

But within a few days Hans would almost have welcomed a beating. He was back to empty days in the cell. He still missed his Bible, and now he had no one he could communicate with. He had nothing. He exercised as much as he could, but the food he ate provided little energy, and the water in his cell had a disgusting taste. He hated to build his thirst, through exercise, since that only meant he had to drink more of the water. His prison clothes had become loose on him; he guessed that he had lost at least twenty pounds. But there was really nothing he could do about any of that.

Day after day he had only the appearance of the silent guards to look forward to. He sometimes spoke to them, just to hear his own voice, or in the hope of hearing a word or two in return. But these men apparently had their instructions too. At times in the past he had received a short response, but now the men acted as though they hadn't heard Hans speak.

So Hans was forced to find his entertainment inside his head. He would think of the ancient kings of Israel or of Christ's apostles, tell himself the story of David, for instance, or of Peter, and then he would try to remember every aspect of the man's life. What was there to learn from him? Then he would go back to his practice of preparing sermons. Each time he developed a new talk, he would learn it by heart, and recite it. He would practice the older ones, too, the ones from months back.

Sometimes a sentence would get away from him, or he would add an example or a verse of scripture, and then he would relearn the talk in its new form.

It was "his work," he told himself, but there were times when it became dangerously tedious. When he lost interest in the talks, the stories, he had nothing, and it was easy to slip into memories, which only caused him pain. Worse, he would sometimes fall into the doldrums. He would find himself sitting, staring, thinking of nothing, merely waiting for another day to pass. It all felt a little like madness at times, all this life of the mind, this wrestling with his own thoughts, and no one to respond. Still, on his best days, when he used his mind well, he liked what was happening to him. He didn't know whether he would ever deliver his sermons, but he felt the power of the scriptures he was probing, and he felt as though he were conquering those walls around him, making himself free.

A month passed and nothing happened. Felscher really was waiting for Hans to break, it seemed. But Hans had begun to think about the Sermon on the Mount. He was trying to remember the beatitudes, the parables, the principles Christ had taught. As he did, new ideas came. He thought he was beginning to comprehend the meaning of humility in a way that changed the whole doctrine in his mind, made it the centerpiece of all doctrine.

And then one day, not long after breakfast, a guard opened his cell door and motioned for him to follow. They walked, of course, to Felscher's office.

"*Wie geht's?*" Felscher greeted him. "I haven't seen you for a long time. I thought it was about time we talked again." Hans had expected a direct approach this time: a simple demand for the names or a return to the cell. But he could never outguess this man. "I know you haven't had a really fine meal for a long time. Would you like us to bring something in today? Perhaps a cutlet. I know you like a nice *Schnitzel*."

"I have no information. The food won't make a difference."

"That's fine. I suspect you would like a nice meal all the same."

Hans nodded.

"Sit down."

Hans took his seat.

"Tell me something. It's something I often wonder about, and it never seems the same for any two of our inmates. How do you occupy your time, there in your cell, with so little to do?"

"I had a Bible once, but you took it away. All the same, I remember many of the teachings and stories. I try to recall those now and consider their meanings." He was not about to tell him about the sermons.

"My goodness, I've never heard that one before. Is it something you actually enjoy?"

"Yes. Very much."

"I believe you, Hans. You seem well balanced, mentally. You're holding up better than I thought you might—especially for such a young man. But can you keep doing that for—let's see, how long have you been in prison?"

"Fifteen months."

"So . . . it *is* well over a year now. But can you do this for almost two more years, maybe longer? I've seen some men hold up for quite some time and then collapse, almost without warning. I would think there's a lot of strain in all this . . . how should I call it? . . . this *nothingness*. Surely, you must hate this life."

"Of course I do," Hans said. "But it's taught me more than I thought it would." He loved to show strength to Felscher even though he might do better by breaking down and promising to be a noble socialist.

"What is it you are learning? Give me an example."

"When Joseph was cast into an Egyptian prison—even though he was guilty of nothing—he became a better man, a great help to the pharaoh."

Felscher exploded with laughter, the sound a roar from his heavy chest. He slapped the desk and said, "You are amazing to me, Hans. You always have a clever answer ready. You must try to imagine ahead of time what I'll ask you, and prepare these answers. There's no other way."

"No. That's not so. I try *not* to think of you when I'm in my cell." And that was true.

Again Felscher laughed. "But this religion of yours, it must consume your thinking. I don't think I ever met a young man so interested in the Bible, of all things. What was it your parents did to ingrain these beliefs in you so deeply?"

"It wasn't what they taught, verbally. It was the way they lived. I was a skeptic about religion at one time, but my parents are very good people. I saw what our religion has done for them. I began to feel my father's power, in his priesthood."

"Priesthood? He's a priest?" Felscher rubbed his fat hands together, as always—a gesture Hans had never understood.

"We have a lay priesthood. But yes, he's a leader in our congregation."

"Has he been limited in his career because of this?"

"Yes. Somewhat."

"Doesn't he resent that?"

"He doesn't worry about it."

"But surely, he must hate our government. He must have taught you that socialism is an enemy to religion. I'm sure you were raised with negative attitudes of this sort. No wonder you wanted to escape."

"My father is loyal to our country. At one time he may have resented certain practices, but he's come to care more about living the gospel of Jesus Christ than anything else. And when a man believes in Christ there is no room in his heart for hatred of anyone."

"But there might be room for hatred of a system or a philosophy. No?" Felscher was leaning back, his arms folded over his white shirt, which stretched at the buttons. He had returned to the chatty style Hans had experienced many times before.

"Our members are taught to honor their governments and to be good citizens, no matter what the philosophy."

"Very nice answer again, Hans." Felscher got up and stretched, and for a moment Hans thought the interview was ending. "But you did try to escape once."

"I did. But I was very young."

"*Ach.* Now this is interesting. You've never admitted before that you tried to escape, even though you knew that I knew. Why the change?" Felscher came around and sat on the edge of the desk so that he was looking down on Hans.

"There's no reason to hide it."

"But that tells me that you choose what you will say to me. You don't ask yourself what is true and then answer honestly. You calculate what you ought to say to me."

Hans thought about that, knew it was true to a certain degree, and yet wondered whether he should admit it. But he was tired of the game they had been playing so many months. "What else can I do?" he asked.

Felscher smiled. He got up and walked back around his desk. He grunted as he sat down. "What you can do is put some trust in me. I have your future in my hands. When you tell me that you don't always answer honestly, what am I supposed to do? You told me that you wouldn't give up the names even if you did know them. So how can I ever trust you?"

"I don't believe in reporting on people. That's all I'm saying. But I don't know who the others were. That's an honest answer."

"Still . . . if you did know, you wouldn't tell me, so what am I supposed to believe?"

"I don't know. It's a dilemma for me—and for you."

"It's only a dilemma because you have a negative attitude toward the GDR. If you believed in a future Communist state, you would understand the need to purify this people. How can we make any progress if dissidents are among us, trying to undermine our purposes? It would be nice, in an abstract way, to let people believe what they wish, but when they want to destroy everything our government and most of our people are working toward, we have to flush them out and stop their underground activities. You tell me that you don't like to report on people, and I understand that. It is an unsavory business. But I can't allow enemies of the state to destroy us, and that is my dilemma. So how do we solve this problem?"

"I don't know."

"Do I dare let you out of this prison—ever?"

"I'll be a good citizen, like my father. You need not worry about that."

"No, no, Hans. You have it wrong. Until you give me those names, you can never be a decent citizen."

"I know no names."

"And so the circle is complete. Once again we are back where we always start. Are you ready to go back to your empty cell and sit there for years to come? A prison term can be extended, as I keep telling you. I can report your communications, your tapping on our pipes, and that will extend your term, I can assure you."

"*Herr* Felscher, what can I do? I know no names."

"But I do. I have a list." He took a sheet of paper from off his desk, and he handed it to Hans. "We have worked hard on this," he said. "We may not have all the names, but as you see, we have several. Merely tell me whether you ever heard of any—or perhaps all—of these people. Cooperate. Help me on this, and then I can make a recommendation that you be released in three months, when you reach your halfway mark."

"I would be condemning these people."

"They are condemned. You would only be giving me something I can take to my supervisors. I can tell them you cooperated. Your life would get better immediately."

"I don't recognize these names."

"You don't seem to understand, Hans. Simply tell me that you recognize them—even one of them. You wouldn't be hurting anyone. We have arrested these people. They are going to jail whether you say anything or not."

"Then you don't need my statement."

"Think, Hans. Listen to what I'm telling you. Merely show me that you wish to help our state. Say the words, and you can begin to hope for better days."

"I don't believe you, *Herr* Felscher. I think you would use my testimony against them and put them in prison whether they were involved or not."

"Hans, it's up to you. I've told you the truth. You can trust me, or you can go back to your cell. And stay."

"I've never heard of any of these people. I swear it."

"And you wouldn't tell me if you had."

Hans didn't answer, but they both knew it was true. So Hans stood up. "I'll return to my cell now," he said.

"And miss the meal I ordered for you?"

"Yes." That was more of a sacrifice than Felscher could possibly know, but Hans, above all, wanted to show no weakness. Whenever he did depart from this prison, he knew he had to leave with his integrity or he could never respect himself. Once he claimed to recognize one of the names, he was destroyed, and Felscher understood that.

"Wait. Let's think about one other possibility."

Hans waited.

"Let me ask you this. How would you like to have your parents come for a visit?"

Hans took a breath. This was a greater test. He would give almost anything to see his family. "Of course I would like to see them." He told himself not to hope. This was only one more of Felscher's machinations.

"Tell me one thing that you've never revealed before—one thing that you think I would like to know—and I'll arrange a visit."

"I told you one thing already today. I told you that I tried to escape the country, with Berndt."

"No, no. We knew that. You paddled out on the North Sea on air mattresses. That's all in your report. I need something new."

"There's nothing else."

Felscher came around the desk again, stood close to Hans. "Tell me about Rainer Kuntze, your roommate. How much did you confide in him about your involvement with Berndt Kerner?"

Hans saw what Felscher was up to. Rainer had been asked by the *Stasi* to report on Hans. Now they wanted to know whether Rainer had held back information. It could be Rainer, next, who could be in jeopardy. But Rainer might have been the one who reported on Hans and caused him to be here. Hans's impulse was to protect Rainer, to keep his promise, but he had to ask himself, what if he was being loyal to the very man who had betrayed him?

Hans had no time to consider all the ramifications. He merely said, "No. I told him nothing. We were roommates, but we weren't close friends."

"And what if I told you that we had a written report from Rainer? What if I can show you that he reported on you?"

"He couldn't have done that—not unless he lied."

"If I show it to you, you'll know I'm telling you the truth. But there's a problem with that. Once I show it to you, how can I tell my supervisors that you've begun to cooperate? Just admit this much: that you told Rainer the same thing you've told me—that you helped Berndt Kerner with his escape."

"Why? What do you want to do to Rainer?"

"Do to him? Why would we do anything to him? He told us what you had done. I'm only asking you to admit to that. It won't hurt Rainer, but it would be *one* thing I could put down in your report—one sign that you want to be honest with us."

"I said nothing to Rainer. If he says that I did, you must have pressured him into saying so."

"Think about it, Hans. Why are you here? Rainer was reporting on you the whole time you roomed together. You may think that's a bad thing to do, but he was a good member of Free German Youth, and a good young citizen. He thought it was important to reveal these things to us. I'm only giving you an opportunity to look good in my report. When a man hands you an opportunity like that, you're a fool to turn it down."

"You're lying, *Herr* Felscher. I told Rainer nothing. You're only asking me because you want to destroy another man."

Felscher smiled, his thick lips stretching, folding back a little. "But you would lie for this man, wouldn't you—to protect him?"

Hans looked into Felscher's eyes for a long time before he said, "Yes. I would."

"So. Nothing has changed. And nothing will. It's a pity too. I'm sure you would like to see your family. But I will offer you this much. I won't report anything immediately. I'll give you time to think. Let a guard know if you want to talk to me."

Hans didn't respond. He merely walked to the door and waited for Felscher to call for the guard. But back in his cell, he wondered. Rainer probably had betrayed him. It made sense that he had. And now Rainer had apparently befriended Elli. What did Rainer think he might learn from doing that? Was he spying on the branch of the Church in Magdeburg? That seemed a likely possibility. Hans had vowed not to reveal their conversations, but maybe he had made a promise to a Judas. Hans couldn't help thinking how much he would like to see his parents. It was the one opportunity in the world he would most like to have, short of being released.

And so all evening he thought about his options, considered whether he should merely go to Felscher and admit the truth. Maybe he shouldn't be telling lies anyway. Maybe if he admitted this one truth, Felscher would trust that he really didn't know anything that would identify the others who had planned to escape. So was it better to lie and protect a friend, who might well be, in truth, an enemy, or to lie, and break his vow?

But all that was merely something to think about. Hans knew he couldn't do it. He would never break his promise to Rainer, no matter what Rainer might have done to him.

So Hans sat on the stool in his cell, alone and desolate. He felt sick, and he wished that he could go to bed and sleep. But when the time came, he didn't sleep well, and by morning he knew the illness was more than psychological. He had started with some uneasiness in his stomach that got worse all night until, by midmorning he was vomiting, aching, burning. He sat on his stool and rested his head on the table, and he longed to return to his bunk. What he knew was that he would receive no medication, no attention, no help. He longed for his mother. Always in his life, when he had been sick, it was she who knew what to do, she who would wash his face with a cool cloth. He remembered when he was little, the way she had held his forehead from behind, when he had bent to vomit, how willing she was to clean up after him, to sit up at night with him. But now, here in this jail, he could only kneel on the hard concrete, his face over a stained and stinking toilet, and wonder how many more years he would have to stay in this place.

# CHAPTER 14

When Gene came through the door, he smelled something acrid. He followed the smell to the kitchen, where he found Emily. She turned quickly when he entered the room, and Gene saw the look of frustration on her face. He also saw that the window was wide open, and even though cold air was rushing in, smoke was still lingering. "I was hoping you would be late," she said. She sounded upset, Gene thought, and her hair was disheveled, her face flushed.

"Sorry," he said, and he smiled. "Is that a burnt offering I smell?"

"It's the casserole I made on Sunday. I was heating it up and I fell asleep."

Gene laughed. "The Lord has seen fit to bless me," he said. "Sunday *and* Monday was enough for that stuff. I don't think I could have gotten it down a third day in a row." But Gene hadn't gotten the words out before he knew he had made a *major* mistake.

"*Fine!* I don't like eating the same thing three days in a row either. Just tell me what I'm supposed to cook on the budget you give me for groceries."

He tried to approach her, but she pushed his arms away and slipped past him. Then she walked out of the room. He followed after her and caught her in the hallway. Then he grabbed her shoulders and turned her around. "I'm sorry. I was just joking. I know it's hard to figure out good meals every day on the money we have."

"No, you don't. It's actually impossible. You give me *fifty* dollars a month. If my parents and your grandparents didn't invite us over to eat—and give us bread and things—we'd never get by."

"Do we need to budget a little more for food, then?"

"You said we don't *have* any more. Where's it going to come from?"

"Honey, we need to talk this over. But can we open a can of soup or something like that? I am hungry."

"I'm not. See what you can find." And she was gone.

Gene watched Emily disappear down the hallway and into their bedroom. He had never seen her quite this upset. He had the feeling there was more to this than burnt casserole.

The smell *was* disgusting, though. Gene went in and scraped most of the cremated noodles and hamburger into the garbage, and then he set the dish in the sink and ran some water into it. The room was cold, but he didn't think it wise to close things up quite yet, so he left his parka on and rummaged around in an almost empty cabinet. The only soup was a broth, and there weren't even any soda crackers. During the holidays Anna had stocked the kitchen up and then left most things behind for them, but not much was left now, well over a month later. He found the end of a block of cheddar cheese in the refrigerator. He cut the dried edges away and salvaged a few slices, which he set between a couple of thick slices of Grandma's homemade bread. Then he got out the waffle iron he and Emily had received as a wedding present. Anna had made waffles with it when she was home; Emily had never used it. But then, there was never time in the morning with both of them running off to the university.

Gene reversed the plates on the waffle iron so the smooth sides faced each other, and then he plugged it in to heat. He buttered the cheese sandwich on one side, set it on the iron, closed it, and then went back for the broth, which he opened. By then Emily had returned. "I'm sorry," she said. "Did you find something?"

"I'm making a grilled cheese sandwich. I'll split it with you. And I found this chicken broth."

"Oh, yuck. No. I'm not hungry."

"You may not be hungry, but that son of mine is down there saying, 'Come on, Mom, I need some supper.'"

She took that more seriously than he had expected. "I'll have a little of the broth," she said. She walked to the cabinet and got out a couple of bowls, which she brought to Gene. "There's something I need to talk to you about." She turned and walked away from him.

"Honey, I didn't realize how hard it was to feed us on that budget. We can come up with a little more."

Emily got some soup spoons from a drawer, and with her back still turned, said, "I made a decision today." Her eyes were still red from crying, but more than that, she looked dejected, and Gene heard something ominous in her tone.

She turned and faced him. "I dropped out of school. I'll get part of my tuition back. That will help. I'm also going to start working more hours. That should take some pressure off."

Gene was stunned. She had never talked about quitting school. "You've already done it?" he asked.

"Yes. Today was the last day to drop, and I talked to Mrs. Allen, in the Audio-Visual office. She said she could use me a lot more, if I wanted the work. I don't have to be a student to work there. I tried to call you, down at the dealership, but you were with a customer and time was running out. So I had to make a decision."

"But Emily, you know exactly what I would have said. I know how much you wanted to finish this year."

"But I didn't know how hard it would be."

Gene told himself to be careful, to be understanding, but he felt himself getting angry. Why would she do something so impulsive? "Maybe we get some tuition back," he said, "but we lose the rest." He was trying to control his voice, but the words had come out stiff, harsher than he had intended.

"I know that, Gene." He heard the anger in her voice again. "It's not like I haven't thought this through."

Gene lifted the lid on the waffle iron enough to peek in, then decided the sandwich could cook a little longer. He stepped to the stove and stirred the broth, and all the while he felt the tension—a mood he had never experienced with Emily, at least not to this degree.

"Gene, you don't know what I've been going through lately. I try to study while you're at work, but I can't get through a single chapter without falling asleep. Today I got back a paper I wrote for Beckman's class. I just hadn't put the time into it that I needed to. He gave me a C minus, which was a gift, but then he wrote this little note about the paper not being the quality 'he had come to expect' from me. It just about killed me."

"Honey, I can understand that. But I don't see why you dropped all your classes. You could have dropped one, maybe, or you could have accepted the fact that your grades wouldn't be quite as high as usual this term. That wouldn't—"

"Would you accept that? No way. You care more about grades than anyone else I know."

What was that all about? He heard the emotion, but he didn't understand the accusation. He took a breath and told himself to think for a few seconds before he responded. So he checked his sandwich again and then got a plate. He nudged the sandwich off the waffle iron and onto the plate before he said, "I wish you had at least left a message for me to call you, or maybe called back a few minutes later. It seems like it's the kind of thing we should have discussed."

"I knew that's what you'd say. I've been waiting all day for this little speech." She sat down at the table.

Gene was trying to pour the broth directly from the saucepan into a bowl and was making a mess. He set the pan down, took another breath, and then turned around. "Emily, I like you. I was under the impression that you liked me."

"If you like me, don't start in on me."

"Is that what I'm doing?"

Emily bent forward and rested her forehead on her arms. She didn't say anything. He thought she was trying to control her own anger, but for the life of him, he couldn't think why she was so mad.

She still had her head down when she said, "In my home, my dad made *all* the decisions. Mom tiptoed around him like he was the king of the house, and she was his vassal. I'm not going to live that way."

"Emily, I'm sorry, but I don't recall—even *once*—trying to be your boss. I'm not that way, and you know it. What we're talking about here is *you* making a decision on your own, not me. I wouldn't have told you what to do, and you know it. I just think we should talk things over when they're important."

She sat up straight. "Come on, Gene. Tell the truth. You *would* have told me not to drop out. You know you would. That's why I was glad I couldn't reach you. I knew it was what I had to do, so I did it. I was sure I'd have to go through this little interrogation afterward, but I didn't care."

"Interrogation? All I asked you—"

"Gene, you think I did the wrong thing. It's in your voice. It's in everything you've said. You sound so much like my father, it's scary. He always had this way of sounding reasonable, and he always claimed to have my best interest in mind, but he also made my decisions—unless I found a way to sneak around him. I don't want to do that now. I'm not going to be like my mother."

Gene felt as though he had been blasted with a shotgun. Where was all this stuff coming from? He came to the table and sat down—without the food. "Em, we need to start over. I don't think I'm quite clear what we're talking about. Have you felt like I'm trying to be the boss around here?"

"In some ways, yes."

"Okay. I didn't know that. Tell me what I've been doing wrong."

"Don't do that, Gene."

"Don't do what?"

"Make me look like the bad guy. I hear that, 'I'm so understanding and willing to listen' tone in your voice."

"Well, I'll follow your example then. I'll try to sound hostile. Will that be better?"

"Shut up."

He thought of a couple of comebacks but decided not to use them. He had never in his life heard his parents talk to each other this way, and he had a feeling that once this stuff started, it might never stop. At the same time, he knew better than to reach for her hand or tell her he loved her. So he said nothing. He sat and waited. He hoped that she would calm down, and then they could talk.

But Emily still sounded angry when she said, "Gene, where did this budget of ours come from? Who decided that we only have fifty dollars a month for food?"

"Well . . . I did figure it out. But I showed it to you and we talked about it. I thought it was okay with you."

"We didn't talk about it, Gene. And I didn't have any idea how expensive food was."

"Once you saw fifty bucks wasn't enough, why didn't you say something?"

"Because you never stop talking about how tight our money is, and how careful we have to be. We couldn't have ice cream on the way home from the movies last week. And you made me feel like some *profligate* for suggesting such a thing."

"Honey, I'm sorry. I didn't know I made you feel that way. Movies cost so much now, and I just thought that—"

"That we could come home and pop some popcorn—which by the way, you never would have let me buy. It was some your parents left."

"*Let* you? When have we ever talked about anything like that?"

"We walk down the aisle at the grocery store and you compare every price. I've almost quit drinking milk because you fuss so much about the cost."

This all sounded a little too accurate. Gene thought of the cereal Emily had wanted to buy. He had found some puffed rice—which he hated—that was much cheaper. "Okay. I see what you're saying. It's just that I haven't wanted to work any more hours because it's hard enough to get my study hours in as it is. I keep thinking it's only a few months and then we won't be under quite so many constraints."

"No. It'll be lovely. I'll be home alone with a baby while you go off to the army."

"Emily, let's talk about one thing at a time. I don't have any choice about that. The night we got engaged, I told you what I was going to have to do. You said it was all right. You wanted to get married anyway. Are you taking all that back now?"

"Gene, I'm so sick of you saying things like that. You *do* have choices. You just see things your own way, and you won't allow for any other possibility."

"Are you talking about trying to get in the Reserves? Do we have to hash all that out again?"

Emily stood up. Her chair fell over backward and struck the floor with a crack. "No. You're right. We don't have to *hash* anything over. You just *decide* for us and I'll be a nice little Mormon wife. I know exactly how that goes."

She headed for the door, but Gene was up quickly. He crossed in front of her, and when she tried to push past him, he took hold of her arm.

"Let go of me, Gene," she shouted in his face.

"Okay. Okay." He dropped his hand. "But please don't go. I didn't realize that we had these problems. But I'm listening. I see what you're saying about the budget. We need to work that out. I can see where I've been wrong."

"Do you know how furious you're making me, Gene? Just leave me alone. I will not be treated like I'm some hysterical *girl* and you're the good and wise *man*. You're trying to *manage* me, Gene, and I won't sit still for it." She pushed by him, and this time he didn't try to stop her. He thought she was heading for their bedroom again, but he heard the front door open and then slam shut. He couldn't stand that. He didn't know where she was going. Was she leaving him? So he ran after her. When he reached the front porch, she was getting into their car. He ran to the car, yelling, "Don't. Don't. We can talk. Please."

She had apparently grabbed her purse from the hall tree near the front door, and it was that purse that kept her from getting away. She was still looking for her keys when he reached her door. She slammed the lock down, so he raced to the other side. She was reaching to lock that side when he grabbed the handle and popped the door open. "Please don't leave, Em. Please. I love you. I know we can talk this out." He jumped into the car with her.

"Gene, don't be so dramatic. I'm just going for a ride."

"But I can't stand to wait for you when I don't know where you're going or how long you'll be gone. I've never been so scared in my life."

"There's nothing to be scared of. I'm just very, very mad. I don't get that way often, but when I do, you might as well learn right now to leave me alone until I'm finished. So hop out and I'll be back in an hour, no longer. How's that? Go in and eat your cold cheese sandwich."

"No."

"No, what?"

"Just let me go with you. I'll give you some time, and then we'll talk."

"Gene, give me one hour. Please."

He sat for a long time, not wanting to do it, but finally he opened the door and got out. He heard her say, "Thanks." Then she started the engine and backed out of the driveway. But she backed up way too fast, and that scared him. She still wasn't under control, and it worried him to think what could happen to her.

He walked back into the house, reheated the broth, and then ate the sandwich cold. But he wasn't hungry, and he couldn't stand the broth. Still, he kept what was left in the pan—placed a lid on it and set in the refrigerator. And as he did, he wondered about himself. He had never thought that he was a tightwad, and he hadn't noticed that he was making Emily's decisions either. But he knew he couldn't just think up a bunch of answers to her accusations. He had to take a hard look at himself and decide where she might be right.

He went out to the living room, sat where he could see the driveway, and he waited. Defensive thoughts kept jumping to mind. But he knew he had to look at all this from Emily's point of view. She had been sick all fall, and she was still tired much of the time. He could see how school must have been a strain and why she would want to escape that pressure. He also knew that money had worried him almost constantly. No wonder it worried her when he made such a fuss about an ice cream cone. What he wasn't sure about was her accusation that he was stubborn, that he would make up his mind and then refuse to back down. He couldn't really remember doing that.

Time passed slowly, and he glanced at the grandfather clock in the hallway at least once a minute. The ticking was something he had stopped noticing long ago, but he heard it tonight, and he heard the chimes that told him she had been gone fifteen minutes and then half an hour. But at forty-two minutes, not an hour, he saw headlights turn into the driveway, saw the car come to a slow stop in front of the garage. He offered a prayer—not the first one since she had left. "Help me to listen. Help me to change if I have to," he said. "Please, help her to love me."

She came in the front door quietly and started down the hallway toward their bedroom. "I'm in here," Gene said.

She stopped and looked at him. "I'm sorry," she said.

"I'm sorry too. We need to talk."

"Not tonight. I can't think straight, and I'm dead tired. In the morning, I won't be like this."

"But I have to leave early, Em. And I won't sleep at all if we don't get some of these things settled."

"They're settled. And I love you. I just work things up more than I need to. That was a tantrum. I didn't make a whole lot of sense."

"Please, sit down for just a minute. I don't want you to take anything back. You need to tell me what you're feeling—and not wake up in the morning and say there's no problem."

She walked into the living room and sat down as far from him as she could get, in a chair across the room. There was light from the hallway, but none in the room. Gene couldn't really see her face. "Some of what I've been thinking may not be right," she said. "That's why I shouldn't have let it all pour out like that."

"But tell me what it is."

"Well . . . for one thing, like I said, I think you do have choices. Your parents almost begged you to take some of their money while they were here, and you wouldn't do it. I know what you feel, that you want to handle things without their help. But it's hard to listen to you turn down the check your dad wanted to write, and then tell me that we don't have enough money to buy the makeup I've always used."

Gene cringed a little. He had told her that. "I see what you mean," he said. "My problem is, we're already living in their house, without paying rent, and Uncle Wally pays me more than I'm really worth. It just seems like we're getting so many advantages most students don't have. I want to prove to myself that I can manage, at least to some degree, on my own."

"I notice you say, *I* can manage? Not *we?*"

"Okay. Good point. That *is* what I said. What do you feel *we* ought to do?"

"I've done it. I quit school—which I wasn't doing well at anyway—and I'm going to work more. Now we can afford an ice cream cone once a month."

"You know, I'm thinking about something that's actually pretty surprising to me. My dad was always in charge of the money in my family, and even though he had plenty, he was always careful with it. And when I look where that came from, it came from his dad, who was the same way. I didn't know I was trying to be 'in charge.' But I guess that's what I was doing. Maybe that's what really bothered me when you told me you quit school—without talking to me first. That probably seemed like a challenge to my *authority*."

"Why do you say it that way? Probably? Don't you know?"

"No. I'm really not sure. It hasn't seemed that way until right now."

"Well, I don't know. But I shouldn't have quit like that. It was my little protest. I've been looking for a fight lately. The more I read, the more I recognize how much men are in charge of *everything*."

"I'm not your 'boss,' Em. And I don't want to be. In the temple, the sealer said that we were equal partners. That's how I need to think about it. That's how I thought I *did* think about it."

"I understand that you don't want to take a lot of money from your parents, but your mom said, 'Think of it as a loan, if you want to,' and without conferring with me at all, you turned her down. I knew right then that our tuition checks had pretty much cleared out our bank account, and I just wanted you to take a few hundred dollars—as a loan, if that's what you wanted to call it."

"Why didn't you say anything?"

"Because it's *your* parents' money, I guess. Or maybe just because you were so sure of yourself. It's like this thing with you going into the army. You have your idea what's right, and you won't allow for any other view."

"Could you feel okay about it if my dad pulled some strings and got me into a Reserve unit at this point?"

"I could feel *wonderful* about it. This is a bad war, Gene. No one ought to go over there and die while we're trying to figure out how to end the thing."

Gene had thought the same thing lately. But for him, it didn't change his decision. "Emily, I have to be a man of honor, or how can I even respect myself?"

"When you get to Vietnam, write home to me and the baby. Tell me how wonderful it is to be *honorable*."

"What do you want me to do?"

"Nothing."

"No. Tell me."

"Gene, I can't change who you are. I don't want to. I know you can't ask your dad to keep you out of Vietnam. But don't ask me to change who I am either. Every day of my life I know that our time is running out, and even if they don't send you to Vietnam, you'll be gone from home."

"If I'm not in the war, maybe you can join me somewhere, after basic training."

"I know. And I know that plenty of others are doing that. But I hate this war. It's not just that's it's killing people who shouldn't be dying; it's destroying the people who do live through it. I see guys on campus now, in their wheelchairs and walking on wooden legs. In the psychology department, I always hear what the war is doing to families. Men come home so messed up they can't function. They get hooked on drugs and alcohol. They have night sweats and bad dreams. You can't believe how many of them beat up on their wives and kids. It's like an epidemic."

"My dad said guys came home from World War II messed up too, but they did a better job of coming back from it, not spending their lives whining about all their bad breaks."

"If I shut my eyes right now, I would think your grandpa is sitting there, instead of you."

"No. His voice is deeper."

"His thoughts aren't."

Gene laughed. "You psychology majors are all a bunch of bleeding hearts. Grandpa taught me that, too."

"I'm not a psych major—not anymore."

"And you're feeling what you gave up today, aren't you?"

"Yes. It *was* impulsive. I did act like a *girl*. I should have talked to you first. But I wasn't doing well, and that's one of my problems. I can't stand not to excel. That's something else my dad expected of me."

"I'm sorry. I promise you that you'll get your chance to go back."

"Maybe. Maybe not. Not for a long time. And now I'm going to admit something so awful, I hate myself for feeling it. But I want you to know."

"What?" He got up and came to her, knelt in front of the chair she was sitting in, and took hold of her hands.

"I resent our baby. I try not to, but I do. I didn't really understand what it meant to have a baby. For a man, it means a few adjustments. For a woman, it means putting 'self' on hold. It means that another life is more important than your own."

"But—"

"Don't get me wrong. It's all right. It's what my mother did. It's what mothers have been doing forever. But no matter how much I should have known it, I didn't. I'm the one who's been whining all winter—not to you, but inside. I want to finish my degree. I'd like to have a career. I want to go on being Emily, but instead I'm going to be 'Mom.' My whole day, every day, is going to be devoted to a baby, to cleaning house, to making meals—and all the things that fascinate me are going to be things I don't have time for."

"Not forever, Em."

"Maybe not. I don't know. But right now, it feels like forever." She kneeled and bent forward as best she could, and Gene reached his arms around her. Finally, she cried.

Gene felt his love seem to deepen again, maybe for the sacrifice he had never understood until this moment, but mostly because she had told him, honestly, what she was feeling.

She cried for a long time. But when she wiped away her tears, she told him, "Okay, I'm finished. Everything I've told you is wrong, and I know it. There is nothing I can do in this life that will be more important than to raise our children. I should thank the Lord every day that I could get pregnant. I know women who can't, and I know how they feel about that. I'm a very, very selfish person and it's time for me to grow up."

"Honey, we're both trying to grow up—together. I had no idea I was trying to rule the roost. I'm going to do something about that—so you keep reminding me. I'm also going to help with the baby. In fact, I'll tell you what." He hesitated and moved her away from him a little so he could see her face. "We'll take turns. I'll get pregnant next time."

"You're not as funny as you think you are," she said, but she was smiling. And then she kissed him. Gene felt as though he had come back to life.

# CHAPTER 15

Weeks had passed. Hans didn't know how many. What he did know was that he had been close to death for a time, and during his illness, he had lost track of time. When he had first become sick, he had vomited for several days. Then after, he hadn't been able to eat. He had forced himself to drink water, however, and he thought that was probably the reason he had lived. At some point, in the depths of his weakness and despair, he had thought he might welcome death. But it was the thought of his parents and his sister that had kept him fighting. He kept thinking of the sorrow his death would bring them. And then one night, perhaps in delirium, he dreamed that he was sitting in front of a large congregation of Saints, looking out at the people. He was wearing a suit, and he felt confident, satisfied, loved. His dreams had been chaotic during his illness, full of jumbled images, but this moment for some reason had jolted him. He had awakened, stayed awake for a time, and in the morning he had remembered the satisfaction and happiness he had felt. At the time, he had still been too weak and tired to make much of the experience, but as he had gradually recovered, he came to think of the dream as a promise, as a little glimpse of the future, and he felt a powerful need to live up to it.

Hans had lost a great deal of weight. There was nothing left of him, it seemed. He could feel his own skeleton: his ribs, his bulging joints. He was trying to eat now, and he walked as much as he could, back and forth in the cell, but he had little energy. Once a week he was taken from his cell and allowed to shower, but what he longed for was a real bed, a warm, comfortable room, and some food that wasn't revolting. He wanted to go home, wanted his mother to look after him for a time, and then he wanted to start over, to rebuild himself. He tried, every day, to think of his favorite scriptures and remember the sermons he had composed. But it was nearly impossible to concentrate or to find the consolation he had found before. The weakness in his body also seemed to rob the power from his spirit, and the cold in his cell was such a constant preoccupation that he struggled to think of much of anything else. He didn't know whether the cell was colder than before. Maybe it only seemed so. But he also thought it possible that Felscher had arranged to stop the heat in the building from reaching him.

Hans didn't expect to see Felscher again. The man was waiting for him to break. Maybe Hans *was* broken. He liked to think that he wouldn't reveal names if he had known any, as he had always told Felscher, but he wasn't sure he could have held out at this point. He was only sure he wouldn't say anything about Rainer. Maybe Rainer had pretended to be a friend only to betray him, but it didn't matter. Even if that were true, he wouldn't match one wrong with another. He wouldn't break that promise. He hadn't spent all this time with the scriptures, measuring the worth of a life, only to throw over everything now. He would eat what he could, keep exercising, and get his strength back. Then he would hold on. Maybe Felscher would be the one to give up. Maybe he would send Hans back to a work camp, with better food, and the time would pass more quickly. Something good would happen if Hans held on; he was almost sure of it. He felt he had that promise now.

Finally, one afternoon, a guard appeared at his cell, just as in the past. "Come with me," he said, and Hans followed, walking as best he could. As he entered Felscher's office, he tried to stand straight and look sure of himself. Felscher looked up from his desk. "My goodness," he said. "I heard that you'd had influenza, but I didn't expect you to look like this."

"I'm all right now," Hans said. "And I have nothing to tell you." He wanted that over. He had thought, on the way to the office, that he might be coy for a time, and perhaps receive a meal, but he doubted he could eat much of it, and more than anything, he didn't want to bargain with this man.

"Didn't you receive any medical treatment?" Felscher asked.

"Nothing. You know I didn't. And when I begged for another blanket, I was told that there weren't enough, that they couldn't spare one for me."

"I believe you have three blankets. Most prisoners have only two."

"But my cell is freezing. I can't stay warm."

"That's terrible. I'm going to have a talk with those people down there. I hate to have your parents see you like this."

Hans stared at Felscher, who was smiling. Was the man toying with him again?

"Yes. I have your parents here. And your sister. She's such a pretty girl. They all want to see you."

"Here? Here at the prison?"

"Yes. I'll bring them into this room, and I'll give you an hour with them." He stood up. "I can't tell you how much this means to your mother. She was crying just now, so happy to know that she was about to see you. Your sister . . . Inga . . . isn't that her name?"

"Yes."

"She was holding your mother's hand, like an angel, telling her not to cry. I see why you love your family so much. You do want to see them, don't you?"

But now Hans understood. "What do I have to do?" he asked.

Felscher came around his desk. He put one hand on Hans's shoulder. "You know what you have to do, Hans. Simply verify what Rainer Kuntze already reported. I've told you, the information isn't important. We already have his full statement—a series of them actually. But if I can't show my superiors that you are cooperating, how can I explain that I allowed your parents to visit?"

"*Herr* Felscher, there's no logic in that. You claim that Rainer did what you wanted him to do. What difference would it make whether I tell you that it's true?"

Felscher dropped his hand from Hans's shoulder. "All right. That's a fair point. I understand your asking. What we would like to know is whether he held anything back. If you tell us what you told him and that fits with what he reported, you're helping him."

"No. You want to know that I told him things he didn't report. The only thing you do is look for ways to ruin people's lives. You *help* no one."

"I help the good citizens of this country, young man. And I do that by stopping those who work against our state. If you don't grasp that soon, you're going to regret your intransigence. I've offered you a chance to see your parents. You should thank me for that."

"Don't pretend to be my friend. This is only cruelty. My family isn't even here."

Felscher leaned forward and stared into Hans's face. "Oh, they're here. But you may not see them." His jowls shook as he shook his head. "It's time for you to decide." He walked back around his desk and dropped into his chair.

Hans took a seat too, but only because he couldn't hold himself up any longer. This was the hardest blow yet. He had allowed himself to believe, for a few seconds, that he would actually see them.

"I'm going to ask you a question, and all you have to do is answer 'yes.' If you do, you will see your parents, and I will get you as many blankets as you need. I will also see to it that you receive some meat and vegetables."

"No."

"Just let me ask the question. Did you tell Rainer about your involvement with the escape?"

"No."

"You must have mentioned your friend Berndt and how he died. It would have been a natural thing to do. Rainer claims that you told him—

and described your involvement. Simply say, 'Yes, that's true. I did tell him that much,' and I'll bring your parents in right now."

Hans had expected to say no, but he found himself hesitating. How could he be this close to his mother and father and not see them for a moment? He had wanted a priesthood blessing for such a long time, and his father was possibly waiting close by. How could he turn that down? It really did sound as though Rainer had crossed him, so what difference did it make?

"No," he said, suddenly, almost against his own will. And then he tried not to think. It would do him no good to keep considering, or especially, to regret.

Felscher didn't speak, not for a long time. But Hans was struggling. He didn't want to cry in front of the man. His answer had cost more than he had expected. He thought of going back to the cell and wasn't sure he could stand it. But he struggled to his feet. He told himself he might as well not prolong this pain. "I'll go back now," he said.

"Hans, I have to say, you're the strongest young man I've ever known. I wish more of our Free German Youth were as noble as you are. I wouldn't worry about the future of our country, were it so."

Hans felt the change in Felscher. This didn't sound like his usual manipulations.

"You've beaten me at my own game, Hans, and I like you for it."

Hans wouldn't look at him. He couldn't take any more emotion. He just wanted to be left alone now.

"Sit down. I'll bring them in." Felscher walked past Hans and opened the door. He spoke to someone outside, and then he stepped out and shut the door behind him.

Hans wondered now. Maybe this *was* one more ploy, after all. But it hadn't seemed so. He turned the chair so he could see the door, and then he sat and waited, hardly able to breathe. Nothing could be more cruel now than to come back without them.

A minute passed, and then two, and Hans didn't hear anything. Then he saw the doorknob turn, and he feared the worst. The door opened, but Hans saw only Felscher. Hans felt the last of his strength seep away. He clung to the chair, just to stay upright. But then Felscher walked back outside, and Hans's mother appeared at the door. Hans felt the sudden energy in his body. He stood and she came to him. "Mama," he said.

"Oh, Hans, what have they done to you?" she said, and she took him in her arms.

Hans was sobbing too hard to tell her. He was looking at his father over his mother's shoulder, and at Inga, who now came to him too and wrapped her arms around him and his mother, both. "We've missed you so much, Hans," she said, and she broke down.

Hans pulled away enough to reach for his father, who stepped closer and reached around the others. All four stood like that for some time, clinging to each other and crying. When they finally separated, his father wanted to know, "Don't they feed you, Hans?"

"Not well, Papa. But I've been sick."

"Don't they give you medical treatment?"

"They didn't, Papa. They wouldn't give me anything, not even an extra blanket."

"This is wrong. How can they do such a thing?"

"Don't say any more. They're listening—probably recording what we say."

"I don't care." Peter raised his voice. "I want it recorded. If this is what we can expect from our socialist state, our future is bleak, for certain."

Katrina had hold of Hans again. She kept running her hand over his hair, the way he remembered her doing when he was little. It was almost too much for Hans to accept—all this warmth after so much cold. "Sit down. Please," he said. "I want to look at you, and talk. I've wanted this for so long."

"You sit down. You don't look well," Katrina said.

There were wooden folding chairs in the corner of the office. Peter helped Hans open them, and they all sat down, Katrina and Inga on either side of Hans, and Peter in front of him. "Inga, you've grown up so much," Hans said. "You're beautiful. You'll be fifteen soon, won't you?"

She nodded. "In two more months." But she looked solemn. "When can you come home, Hans?" she asked.

"I don't know. It could be a year and a half—or even longer."

"Longer? Why longer?" Katrina asked. She was sitting next to him, holding his hand.

"They don't have to let prisoners out when their terms are up, not if they think they are unreformed. Or they can accuse a man of something new—like withholding information."

"What information, Hans? What could they expect you to know?"

But Peter was now saying, "Maybe we've said enough. Let's talk about other things."

"Tell me about home," Hans said. "Tell me about all the people in the branch."

There was not so much to tell as Hans had thought. In his own mind, it seemed as though he had been in prison most of his life, but for most of the Saints in Schwerin, little had changed. Old Sister Rittenbacher had died, to no one's surprise, and Sister Mayer, who hardly seemed old enough to Hans, had married.

"We wrote you about all these things," Mama said. "Aren't you receiving our letters?"

"Some have come. Not all, it appears. I don't know why. Did you receive the message I wrote for the branch?"

"No. We haven't had a letter for a long time, not since you first came here to Berlin from the work camp."

That idea was crushing to Hans. It was Felscher again, he was sure. At times the man was cruel merely for the sake of cruelty, it seemed. "I know what I wrote. I'll tell it to you. And you remember it as best you can. Then tell it to the members."

"Yes, yes. We can do that," Katrina said.

"Is it wise?" Peter asked. "Will this make things worse for you?"

"No. There is no worse." Hans shut his eyes and tried to remember the words he had memorized. "Dear Brothers and Sisters," he said, "I greet you as Joseph Smith greeted the early Saints from his jail cell. I tell you, as he did, that I still trust in the Lord. I have my friends, as Joseph did—you, my brothers and sisters. I am not alone, so long as I have you to believe in me. Sometimes I think of Job, who suffered as much as anyone except for Christ himself. When he was in a state of despair, he had to listen to the accusations of his friends. This makes me wonder what you think of me. I did help Brother Kerner, and all the days of my life I will wish that I hadn't. I thought I was being a friend when I drove him to Berlin, but—"

"Don't speak of this, Hans," Peter said. "It can't be good for you."

"It doesn't matter. They know. I've admitted all this." He shut his eyes again and searched for the words. "I thought I was being a friend when I drove him to Berlin, but I should have convinced him not to go. I will always wish I had done so, and I will always hope that Brother and Sister Kerner will forgive me. What I feel from them, and you, however, is love, and in this lonely place, it sustains me.

"In our church, we are well aware of the crucifixion, but it is the resurrection we proclaim with joy. We know that our Redeemer lives, and that even though worms destroy our bodies, we shall see the Savior in our flesh. We know that justice will be done, and the righteous who are held in bondage will be made free. We know that those who oppress will not, in the end, be victorious. The history of our people is a history of sorrow and trial, but it is also a story of triumph, and so shall we all triumph, if we hold to the truth.

"Forgive me, dear friends, and please stand with me. I look forward to the day when I can be with you."

Katrina slid her chair closer and slipped her arm around Hans's shoulders. He loved to feel her touch, but he was already realizing how hard it would be to let his family go, once the hour was gone. "Hans, no one holds anything against you," Katrina said. "The Kerners understand. They tried themselves to convince Berndt not to try something like that, but it was the only thing he ever thought of."

"I'll remember the message," Peter said. "I'll tell the members."

And then they talked again about home, the harsh weather lately, things that didn't seem to matter to Hans, but words to share for the lack of any others. There were other things he wanted to tell them, but when he tried, he found that he couldn't. He wanted to express the darkness he felt, down in his cell, and tell them how close he had been to letting death take him—how thinking of them had saved him. He wanted to talk to them about the long, hollow hours and the never-ending process of thought he tried to control, but he hardly knew how to explain it, and more than anything, he didn't want them to fear too much for him.

"Is it all right, here in the jail?" Inga asked. "I know you were sick, but do you have friends? Aren't there days that are not so bad?"

Hans couldn't tell her that he was all alone where he was. He knew that it would hurt her too much, so he merely said, "I had a Bible, but it was taken away from me. But when I had it, I read for hours every day, and now I can remember the stories and parables and all the things Christ taught the people. I tell the stories in my mind, and I think about their meaning."

"I've read the Book of Mormon since you've been gone, Hans. All the way through."

"That's good. I should have done that at your age. It would have saved me from some of the silly things I did when I was still in school. But I have so much more faith now, Inga. It can't be all bad, to be here, if my belief has been made so much stronger."

It was something good to send home with her, and with his parents, but he needed more strength for the future, and so he asked, "Before *Herr* Felscher comes back, Papa, can you give me a blessing?"

"Yes. It's what I hoped you would want."

So he stood, and he walked behind Hans, waited silently for a time, and then placed his hands on his head. Hans shut his eyes and felt the touch on his hair, and suddenly, it was though he were home. Papa blessed him with strength to survive and power to remember what he had learned here in this prison. "I love you, Hans," he said in the end. "You are my son—my strong, honorable son, and I thank God for sending you to me and your mother. We have tried to give you strength, but now, you are teaching us. You have gone beyond us in faith and in courage. You have deepened your love of God, and we feel in you now the power of your conviction. We know you have heavy days ahead, but I bless you with the will and the energy to resist despair. The day will come when the strength you have learned here will be a strength to many who have not suffered as you have suffered. So thank the Lord for this blessing, hateful as it is, and know that God is with you in your loneliness, in your sickness, in your darkest hours. Call upon him at all times, and know that your family, your friends, are praying too. The day will come, a bright day, when we shall all be together, and just as the Lord promises life after death, I promise you a life after this trying time. You will lead, and you will *know*, and others will be able to take strength from you. We are all in prison, son, all of us, but walls will fall someday, and we will dwell together with our Father in Heaven."

It was a time to cry again, but Hans felt as though he could now survive. He felt transformed, as though nutrition had come through the blessing, bodily strength to match the spiritual change. He got up and embraced his father, then held him for a very long time.

It was not long after that that Felscher came back. He was quiet, and he said in a kindly voice, "It was a great pleasure to meet all of you. You have a fine son." Then he looked at Hans. "Stay here for now. I wish to speak to you again."

Felscher allowed time for a final embrace from each of the family before he led them out the door. In only a minute or so, however, he returned. Hans was putting the folding chairs away when Felscher came in. "You didn't have to do that," he said. He took the last chair from Hans and placed it against the others, and then he moved Hans's chair closer to the desk again. He motioned for Hans to sit down and walked back to his own chair. "You knew that we were listening, and yet, you said all sorts of things you shouldn't. So did your father. If I were to have your conversation transcribed, what do you think my people would conclude from his comment about walls coming down—and all this religious expression?"

"It doesn't matter."

"You haven't been changed by prison, Hans. You are only more committed to your religion."

"There's no law against religion. It's what you always tell me."

"Be serious, Hans. You know what you need to do. You need to tell me anything you know about Rainer—or anyone else. And then you need to claim that you love our government and will always be true to it."

"I've told you, I won't ever oppose the government."

"No, but you'll pray for walls to fall. You'll look to Salt Lake City for your loyalty, not to the leaders of this nation."

Hans didn't deny that.

"I don't understand, Hans. You're an intelligent young man, a good young man. If you could commit to the socialist cause, you could be a leader of the people. Instead, you waste all your energies on Bible stories and rituals. Do you really believe your father has the power to put his hands upon you and bless you?"

"Yes. I do. Can't you see it in me? I'm stronger than I was when they got here."

Felscher nodded. "Yes, of course. It's religious fervor—easily explained from a psychological point of view."

But Hans was amazed by the change in Felscher. He lacked his usual irony. He seemed to have given up.

Felscher looked past Hans, toward the wall. He stayed that way for a surprisingly long time, as though he had no idea what to do next. "I'll tell you something, Hans," he finally said. "When your father performed this ritual . . . I don't mind admitting that it was an emotional experience for me. It was impressive, what you share with your father. I have children, but they don't feel this kind of affection for me. I could never share such an hour with them as you shared with your family. That's a fine thing, and even if it's based on myth, I'm certain that it's pleasing and satisfying. I think I understand a little better now why religion persists in spite of all that science tells us."

"Were you religious as a young man, *Herr* Felscher?" Never before had Hans asked him a question about himself.

"In a superficial way. My parents took me to church services. We said prayers there, and we did the kneeling and the singing. But it meant nothing to me. I have never prayed in my life—I mean, personally."

"Perhaps you should try it. Perhaps your children should. Maybe you could discover the same things my family has."

Felscher laughed. "What's this, a missionary effort? You won't find fertile ground here, my friend."

"Maybe not. But I do say it as a friend."

But that was going too far. Felscher seemed to catch himself. He sat up a little more straight. "Let me propose something to you, Stoltz," he said. "It may surprise you."

"What's that?"

"There are people in the West—religious groups and even the West

German government, who bargain with us for the release of political prisoners. My government sometimes allows certain prisoners to leave the country and go to the West. I know you have relatives in America. I suppose you could emigrate there if some arrangement of this sort were worked out."

Hans was suddenly frightened. Maybe a new game had begun. He could say the wrong thing. "I don't think so, *Herr* Felscher. I wouldn't want to leave my family."

"You would rather stay in prison and wait?"

"How soon would I be released?"

"It's hard to say. We usually hold people at least half their term before we make such an arrangement. You are very close to that point now. We would also have to be certain that you had told us anything of use. So that could play a role in this."

"I'm not saying anything. I've told you all there is to say."

"Yes. Yes, I know. But I could file such a report. I could say that I am now convinced that you knew no one involved in the escape, other than Kerner. I suppose I wouldn't have to say anything about the other matter, with Kuntze."

"Why would you do that?"

He smiled a little. "I can't break you. I told you that. And . . . there may be other reasons. For one thing, our country needs cash—foreign currency—so it's a practical matter to release some who have no desire to be here. We free ourselves of the cost of holding them in prison, or dealing with their dissidence, when released. What's the point of having people here who will never contribute to our goals?"

"I plan to be a good citizen, *Herr* Felscher. You need not think of me as a dissident."

"In all honesty, I don't. I'm only saying, that's the rationale. That's why we sometimes do these things. And I would like you to have another chance for a future. You know that you have little hope for one here."

It was what Hans had once dreamed about: the chance to be free of all this control, all the antagonism toward his religion. He could go to Utah, where his relatives would welcome him. He spoke some English, and he could improve quickly, once there. There would be someone there for him to marry, perhaps, and he could finish his education. He felt the old excitement. But as he did, he thought of his father's hands on his head, blessing him to return from prison to lead. Could he have meant somewhere else, not here in the GDR? Hans didn't think so. "I want to stay in this country," Hans said, and he meant it.

"Maybe, at this moment. But think about it. Your parents would be happy for you, I would think."

It did seem possible.

Later that night, when Hans lay upon his bunk in the dark, he wondered. Maybe Felscher's offer could shorten this hell, and maybe he could serve the Church in America as well as he could here. He knew it was something he needed to consider carefully.

But he felt better tonight. He could still feel his mother's arms around his shoulders, his father's hands on his head, his sister's soft kiss as she had left him. And Felscher had had another blanket sent. He was warmer than he had been in months.

# CHAPTER 16

Diane didn't live all that far from the Institute of Religion, where the married-student ward met, but tonight she drove to Relief Society. It was March, and still cold in the evenings, and that was part of the reason Diane took the car, but even more, she was afraid to walk through the University District after dark. The university seemed almost a war zone these days, and the violence sometimes spilled off the campus. Greg came home all the time now with stories about crazy things going on: everything from peaceful marches and demonstrations to skirmishes with the police—even rocks and bottles being thrown. The school year had started with someone setting the Navy ROTC building on fire, and all through the fall, along with the SDS antiwar rallies, the Black Student Union had been protesting the treatment of blacks by Seattle Police. There had also been a "love-in" on the Ave—an attempt to calm things down—but it had turned into a wild, all-night party with lots of drugs. Greg had seen fistfights between radicals and conservative students, and he had seen a bunch of hippies strip down one day, completely naked, and then go splashing and romping in Frosh Pond. Some of it was just wildness, but some of the protests had turned ugly, too. Recently, the news had been full of stories about a group of SDS members physically removing a recruiter for United Fruit, a company they accused of taking advantage of South Americans, from the Loew building. The SDS leadership had been disciplined by the university, and in response, just a couple of days before, there had been an enormous demonstration in the quad. The student paper said that ten thousand students had been there, but Greg, who had gone to see what was happening, said most of the students were just curious about what was going on, not really supporting SDS. All Diane knew was that the whole atmosphere was frightening and seemed to get worse all the time. She wasn't sure how she felt about Vietnam, but Greg kept telling her the war was justified, and whether it was or not, she saw no excuse for people being so hateful and violent.

Still, Diane had changed a few of her opinions over the past few months. Working around women who had been "around the block" a whole lot more than she had was rather shocking at first, but she had come to like those women. Even though they said things that embarrassed her, she still liked their good humor, their openness, and above all their kindness. They treated her like a little sister. She knew they were baffled by her innocence, but they were protective of her. Diane had come away from Utah with a belief that "the world" was evil, and that Mormons were not "of the world." But her friends were forcing her to see that things weren't that simple. Cherie—who was the most blatant about saying things that made Diane blush—was actually very caring, the one most likely to cover Diane's department for her so she could take a break. However scary big-city life was at times, Diane thought she understood some things she hadn't before, and she knew she would be more open in the future to people with different backgrounds from her own.

The women at the store also made her think about things she had never worried much about before. Shelly was concerned about the environment, and she was outraged by an oil spill near Santa Barbara, California. She was opposed to off-shore drilling, and adamant that Americans were wasteful and unconcerned about protecting "planet earth," as she called it. Diane had never really thought about such things, but much of what Shelly said rang true to her. When Diane brought up the oil spill with Greg, he said, "Hey, accidents are going to happen, but we've got to have the oil." Diane didn't know enough to argue with him, but she was starting to see him as insensitive to a lot of issues that deserved more careful attention.

There was actually one more reason she wouldn't have walked to the Institute that night. She wasn't feeling her best, and she knew why. She was certain that she was pregnant. She hadn't told Greg yet, and she felt guilty about that, but it also bothered her a little that he hadn't noticed on his own. Of course, she had misled him, so she knew she shouldn't blame him, but she still thought he should have been in tune enough to perceive, if nothing else, her bouts with nausea. What she wasn't quite sure about was why she hadn't told him. She was not sorry to be pregnant; it was exactly what she had wanted. But it was a big change in her life, and she found herself wanting to wait just a little before she accepted all the implications.

The "Spiritual Living" lesson that night at Relief Society was taught by Mary Innis, a woman Diane considered a powerhouse. She was older than most, and she had finished her master's degree in child psychology before she and her husband, Preston, had married. Brother Innis was almost finished with his Ph.D. in Chinese and had been in grad school for something like six years. Mary knew everything, it seemed, including the scriptures, and she had strong opinions on lots of subjects. She was faithful and spiritual but surprisingly frank about beliefs that sometimes seemed unorthodox to Diane. Still, she had become another sort of big sister to Diane, and for some reason she seemed to seek Diane out at church and take time to find out how she was doing. Diane's visiting teachers were also becoming friends, but Diane was especially pleased that someone so intelligent, so impressive as Mary, would think Diane worth knowing.

Most of the women in the married-student ward cared about being smart and well-informed. Diane never went to Relief Society without feeling that she was a child by comparison, that she knew almost nothing. She had continued to read in the mornings before she left for work, but even though she had found some novels she liked, she still paid attention to little more than plot. When she tried to study the scriptures, she picked up some ideas from notes she had written in the margins during her religion classes, but often the notes seemed cryptic, and she couldn't put the whole idea together. Diane had always told herself that her mother was smart but not as spiritual as she needed to be. What she had liked to believe about herself was that she was more devoted to the Church than her mom, maybe even more spiritual, but when she listened to someone like Mary, she realized that being strict about religion was not exactly the same thing as being spiritual. Her own faith felt shallow by comparison.

The lesson that night was on Christ's parable of the virgins. Mary asked what the oil in the lamps was and, more specifically, how one could gain a supply of it. She also wanted to know how the sisters could pass the supply on to their children. Most of the women seemed to agree that the oil was the spiritual light that a person needed to survive such challenging times. Some expressed their worries about feeling the Spirit while surrounded by kids and diapers and noise, and there was discussion about letting little children feel a mother's testimony.

The discussion worried Diane. Some of the women seemed to need this time to unload their frustrations. They talked about the meaninglessness they felt at times, just getting through another day, and they described their constant crankiness from being up at night with their babies. Diane noticed that the ones with the "easy answers" were mostly the younger ones with one baby, or none. The ones with two or three were looking for a chance to get some things off their chests.

Somewhere along the way, the discussion crossed over, as it often seemed to do, to the question that obviously plagued these women most. Connie Morgan—from Oregon, by way of BYU—raised her hand and said, "I just feel like I need a little time for myself each day. I need to read, or listen to some music, or go for a walk, and my husband doesn't understand that. I know how hard he works in school, but he seems to think that's our only priority right now. If I say one word that sounds like a complaint to him, he's always ready to remind me of his mother who raised seven kids and loved every minute of it."

All the women laughed, but Diane glanced back to see that Connie wasn't laughing. She was a pretty girl, with permed hair, light brown, and cute oval-shaped glasses, but she looked tired tonight, her eyes indicating that she was even more frustrated than she had admitted.

Someone in the back said, "I think we all have the same mother-in-law. And her goal in life is to make us look bad."

"So Connie, what are you saying?" Mary asked. "That it's hard to fill your lamp while you're raising children?" Mary was a tall woman with strong hips that weren't hidden quite enough in the corduroy jumper she was wearing. She had that look of someone who could walk across the plains with a two-year-old slung over one hip, but there was also a softness in her face, in her hazel eyes, and in the gentle way she smiled. She wasn't pretty, not so that anyone would have taken a second look to notice, but she was so intense and sure of herself that her presence made her seem attractive.

"Yes. I guess I am saying that," Connie said. "I know I'm not supposed to admit such a thing, but I had a bad day today."

What followed was a story about a grouchy four-year-old who hadn't taken his nap, and a screaming, teething baby. And that brought on more stories and even more complaints about husbands who didn't understand. Diane said nothing, but she found herself wondering about her dream. She had always imagined herself with babies, then with beautiful little children, and with a loving husband. She had known, of course, that reality was never quite so ideal, but she had never let reality sink in very deep. These women were in the middle of the experience, and they were understanding of each other, supportive, not only interested in expressing their frustrations but, in the end, concluding that they could meet the challenge. Diane was sure that most of the women came out of the discussion bolstered, ready to go back to the work, and even a little more forgiving of their husbands, since the discussion had gradually turned to the challenges graduate and professional students also had to face.

But Diane felt mostly deflated. She wondered about the days ahead of her. Her vision of marriage had always started with a pretty little house framed by a bright blue sky. At the end of a day, the handsome husband returned from work, and the family sat together at dinner and talked about the day. That image had changed to an apartment, long gray days, and an abiding worry that Greg was even less understanding than the husbands she had just heard about. Sister Innis had concluded her lesson by saying, "Sisters, raising children is the most important job we do in this life. But it's *also* the most important job our husbands do, and sometimes we may have to remind them of that." Diane was certain that Greg would agree. In fact, if he had attended the meeting, he would have been the first to raise his hand and express his own insights, his own support. But Diane had gradually developed an opinion of Greg that she still hoped was wrong: he seemed to be better at talking than doing. Maybe that was true of everyone, but when Diane looked ahead these days, life had begun to look frightening, and it had never felt that way before. Since Christmas, and her time with Mom and Grandma, Diane had vowed to talk more openly with Greg—but she hadn't done it. And even worse, she knew that she didn't dare say certain things to Greg. It was never a good idea to upset him. When she did, it was usually she who ended up apologizing or making amends, and nothing really changed.

After the lesson, Diane decided to leave quickly. She wasn't in the mood to chat with anyone. She was almost to the door when Mary said, "Diane, wait a sec." Mary was putting her books and papers away, so Diane walked back to her. "Are you okay?" Mary asked. "You seemed awfully quiet tonight."

"It wasn't a subject I know much about . . . yet," Diane said. She almost hoped that Mary would guess what the 'yet' meant.

"I know. I didn't mean for the lesson to go quite the direction it did—you know, so much about raising kids. I guess that's what's on most of our minds right now."

"It's good for me to hear."

"Diane, if you ever want to talk, or if you just get lonely, give me a call. I love to hear an adult voice somewhere in the course of a day, and I know you spend a lot of time alone."

"You sound like you're worried about me."

"No. I just . . . well, actually, maybe I am. I remember what a hard adjustment I went through when I first moved up here. I didn't know anyone, and Preston was gone all the time. I can see something in your eyes tonight. You look lonely."

Diane didn't say anything, couldn't, but she was looking at Mary through tears now.

"To you, I probably seem like 'the older generation,' so maybe I'm not the right one to talk to, but—"

"No. I'd love it if we could talk sometime." But now Diane was spilling some of those tears and trying very hard not to.

Mary hugged Diane for a moment, then held her by the shoulders and looked into her face. "Maybe this will seem a ridiculous thing to say," she said, "but the first time I saw you, I thought, this girl is very young and very beautiful, and she's going to need a friend. I've always felt sorry for beautiful women. I think they have some things to deal with that almost no one understands." Diane was stunned. No one had ever understood that part of her, not even her mother. "I'm so old and battered, I'm probably the last person you would think of as a soul mate, but I'm very good at friendship. It's my only talent."

"Thank you," Diane said again. "I . . ." She stepped back a little. She worried that people were looking at her, wondering why she was crying.

"Maybe we could get together some time," Mary said. "I could leave the kids with Preston some evening, and we could just take the time to get better acquainted."

"I would *really* like that, Mary. Greg stays late with a study group some nights. That might be a good time to get together." She quickly whisked the tears off her face, still embarrassed that she had let her emotions get away from her.

"Okay. Call me when you see a good time. But if you just want to talk on the phone for a while—tomorrow, or anytime—don't be afraid to call."

"All right. But I'm okay. It's not anything serious. I just have some things on my mind tonight."

"I understand. We all have our days."

But Diane could see in Mary's face that she was still worried for her, and that touched her again, so she hurried away. In the car, on the way home, she finally allowed herself to cry. She knew it was something she had to get over with. She drove for a time, first to cry, and then so she wouldn't arrive home with red eyes. She drove to Queen Ann Hill, then looped back toward her apartment. She wanted to resolve some issues, but her thoughts were much too jumbled. She did manage to admit her real reason for not telling Greg that she was pregnant. She knew that the minute she told him, he would say that he wanted her to quit work. She had felt it lately, that he didn't want her at the store, that he didn't like some of the stories she told about the other women. Lately, he had started asking, too, whether men ever made passes at her. She understood his concerns about the atmosphere at work, but she wondered whether that was his actual worry. The conditions at the law school were not so wholesome either, and he never worried about any negative influence on himself. What she suspected was that her job gave her a measure of freedom, and that Greg was uneasy about that.

But wasn't she thinking the worst about Greg? Mary had said in her lesson that night that women had to be careful about building up resentment against their husbands. They needed to talk things out, not let things simmer. The problem wasn't just her work; it was the whole way she and Greg related to one another. Diane needed to act like an adult if she wanted Greg to respect her. She needed to tell him that she was pregnant, and then she needed to explain, very simply, that she wanted to keep working for a while. She needn't be frightened to do that.

But Greg was deep into his books when she got home. It wasn't a good time. And the next morning, he was in a hurry. She called that morning to make an appointment with an OB-GYN who came highly recommended. When she found she couldn't get in for more than a week, she found herself relieved. She would wait a few more days before she said anything to Greg. But she kept putting the discussion off and finally ended up telling him the night before the appointment.

"Really? You think you're pregnant?" he responded, and he grabbed her in his arms. "Honey, that is *so* exciting." He kissed her, and then he shot his fist into the air. "I'm a *father*. That is so cool."

"It's not 100 percent sure. I've got to see the doctor tomorrow morning at 9:00. Can you go with me?"

"*Tomorrow* morning? Oh, honey, that's really bad. I was going to go over some cases before my eleven o'clock class."

"Can't you do that tonight, or maybe early in the morning, before we go over?"

"Sure. But then I won't get my other reading done. I feel like I'm in water up to my chin and about to go under. Could you go by yourself and then call me at school?"

"Yes. That's exactly what I can do. And to tell the truth, that's exactly what I *expected* to do."

"Ooh. Wait. Honey, just a minute." Diane was heading for the bedroom. "Is this like one of those things a guy is really *supposed* to do? I guess I don't know."

She spun around. "Let's see. Think about it for, say, five seconds, and see whether you can get an answer."

"Okay. I'll get after the books right now and try to get everything done. But even if I don't, I'll go. And honey, I really am excited about this." He walked to her and kissed her again.

Suddenly Diane was ashamed of herself. She had taken a stand and he had capitulated before she could walk five steps. Maybe she just hadn't stood up to him often enough. She needed to make her wishes clear in the first place, not resort to sarcasm and pressure. She really did tend to think the worst of him. It was time she stopped doing that.

On the way to the doctor's office the next day, Diane decided it was a good time to bring up the other topic—or at least she would if she could bring the conversation around to the right point without seeming obvious. Greg was talking about the baby, wondering aloud what sex it would be, and what life would be like with a little one around. He really was excited. "I'm going to try hard not to be gone so much," he told Diane. "I know I always say that, but I'll be in my second year when the baby comes, and from what I hear, the pressure lets up. The last year is supposed to be the easiest—unless I should happen to end up editor of law review. That's not likely to happen, but if I *were* chosen, I almost *couldn't* pass up that opportunity."

"Greg, you won't be home. You know you won't. If nothing else, you'll be with your study group."

"Not as much. Really. But that group has saved me a lot of times. They're almost all smarter than I am, and they give me insights that I would miss. I think I write better than they do, and that's the only reason I end up with better grades. It kind of bugs them, too." He laughed.

"Even Sondra Gould?"

"What do you mean?"

"Is she smarter?"

"Oh, yeah. She's probably the smartest person in our class. And her grades *are* better than mine. I doubt they'd choose a woman for editor, but she probably deserves the job."

"She's pretty, too. What a combination."

"She's not bad looking—until *you* come into the same room. Then she looks like a rag mop, by comparison."

"I'd trade to be her."

"Don't say that. You underrate yourself. I married you before you got a chance to come into your own. But you'll do some great things in your life."

That seemed as good an opening as Diane was going to get, so she took the chance to say, "I've decided that I'm going to keep working at the store for now. There's no reason not to, and I think it's a good experience for me. I'm learning a lot."

"Are you sure? Because a lot of stuff you tell me about that place bothers me. We can manage fine without the little bit they pay you down there."

They were pulling into the parking lot of the clinic where the doctor's office was, but Diane could see that they were early. Greg turned the engine off, but before he could open the door, she said, "I like getting out of the apartment. It's good for me. And I'm learning about the retail business, firsthand. I'm thinking I'd like to get a business degree some day. Maybe that's what I should have majored in before. I could manage your office once our kids are older."

"Yeah. Maybe." He seemed to consider the idea. "But I'm not sure there's anything more to learn from this little job you have. If you quit, you could take an Institute class from Jeff Holland next term, and then just do a lot of reading. I think you would grow more from that than you ever would from selling clothes."

"Greg, I'll go crazy if I sit at home all day. I'll put on a million pounds too."

"Hey, it's up to you. But once the baby comes, you'll never get a chance like that again."

"I get enough reading time with you gone so much. And right at first, babies sleep a lot. That'll be another time when I can read."

"Will they even want you down there, once you can't wear those cute little dresses they like to show off?"

"Greg, I won't be showing for a long time. I'll quit before we leave for Utah for the summer."

"Well . . . it's up to you. But I do think we need to talk some more about this." He opened the car door.

"I don't see that there's anything more to talk about," Diane said to his back as he slid from the car. "I told you, I'll quit when we leave for the summer."

He came around the car for her, but she opened the door herself. She wanted him to say that he agreed, but he didn't say a word. She decided she wouldn't push the matter for the moment. She had told him her plans, and at least he wasn't arguing. "What if I'm not even pregnant?" she said instead. "I'm sure going to feel stupid."

But she wasn't worried about that, and Dr. Stanley verified her suspicion. He was a middle-aged man, but he was wearing the long sideburns so many young guys liked these days, and he had a mustache that bent around the ends of his mouth. Diane thought he looked silly. "Good news," he told her. "Or at least I think it is. You're definitely pregnant."

Greg was sitting next to Diane. He wrapped his arm around her shoulders and pulled her close. "It's *very* good news. We plan to make up for all these 'Population Zero' maniacs who aren't having babies anymore."

Dr. Stanley didn't smile, and Diane wondered what he thought. Lots of people had strong opinions about that issue these days, and Greg never seemed to recognize that. He also made fun of the liberals at the law school who were vowing to have vasectomies after one or two children.

Diane listened closely to all the doctor's instructions. She was surprised that the official pronouncement that she was pregnant had affected her more than she thought it would. By the time she got to the car, she couldn't fight back the tears. "It's so amazing to think about, Greg. We're going to be parents. I still feel like a kid myself."

"You are a kid. We both are. But we're sure going to have to grow up now."

"It's going to be good for us, Greg. I think it's going to pull us closer together."

"Don't you think we're close now?" He started the car.

"Sure we are. But this will give our lives so much more focus. We'll have a child to look after and teach. All my life I've been saying that more than anything I want to be a mom, but now that it's happening, it's not just some fairy tale. I've got to get ready."

"You'll be great. You'll be a perfect mother. And what a *terrific* baby we're going to have. This could be the greatest kid who ever lived."

"Come on, Greg. Don't talk like that. It sounds too cocky. I just want our baby to be healthy and strong and love his Heavenly Father."

"Hey, I'm just kidding. That's what I want too."

Diane sat back and shut her eyes. She was trying to think what life would be like when she had a baby to hold, to take care of. She wanted to read some books on child raising. Greg always made fun of books like that, but how could it hurt to learn from an expert?

"Di, I do think we need to give a little more thought to your working. The things you've just said make me feel all the more that way. It's a sacred thing to have a baby, and this might be the perfect time to get prepared in every way."

"I don't need twenty-four hours a day, Greg. Those hours—"

"I know. You told me how you feel about that. But could we do this? Could we go home and have a prayer about it? And pray every day for a while until we're sure we have an answer?"

"Greg, I don't see why I can't make the decision myself. It affects me, not you."

"So you don't need the Lord's guidance? Is that what you're saying?"

"Don't do that to me, Greg. There's nothing wrong with thinking things through, making a decision, and then asking the Lord if it's the right one. In the Doctrine and Covenants, that's what it says we *should* do."

"That's all I'm talking about. Let's think it through some more, and let's pray for inspiration."

"You just want me to quit, and you won't let up until you get what you want."

She saw his hands grip the steering wheel, tight, but he didn't speak, and she didn't want to look at him. She had never said anything quite like that to him, but she felt it had to be said. "Well," he finally said, "it's nice to know how you feel about me. I had no idea that I was such a bad guy."

"Don't."

"Don't what? The last I heard, couples were supposed to work things out together. But you do what you want. I don't want to be accused of *running your life* for you."

In a way, that was a bit of a victory, but she knew it was temporary, and she also knew that she hated the feeling she had created, and so she said, "I'm sorry, Greg. I don't mean it like that. We do have to work things out together."

He didn't say anything for a long time again. She wondered what he was thinking. But when he finally spoke, he sounded more subdued. "Di, I don't know what's happening to us. I never thought we would talk to each other this way. There for a minute you sounded like you don't even like me."

"I'm sorry. Maybe I'm too emotional right now."

"I was thinking that too. But it's okay. We're okay. We just have to take good care of each other. I know I've been gone way too much, and I'm going to do better."

"That would mean so much to me, Greg."

"What worries me is that when I do get home, sometimes lately, it doesn't even seem like you're happy to have me there."

"That's not true."

"It sure seems that way. Especially when we . . . you know . . . go to bed."

"Greg, I've been so tired lately, and we never get to bed until so late."

"I know. But you can sleep as late as you want. I'm the one who has to get up."

"I get up at the same time, Greg. I make breakfast for you."

"I'll tell you what. You sleep in, and I'll make breakfast for myself. Just try to be a little more awake at night."

It was the same complaint, the one he had been making almost since their honeymoon. What was it he expected of her? "Greg, I'm sorry. I guess I'm not very good at those things," she said. "I'm not sure what to do about it."

"Don't say that, honey. You're the most beautiful woman I've ever seen. I'm just lucky that I do have you to come home to."

But Diane felt so inadequate, so unsatisfactory. She had always known that guys liked to look at her. It had never occurred to her that she wouldn't be able to make a man happy. This was the perfect time to ask for specifics, to have the discussion she feared so much. But she couldn't do it. Maybe she was afraid of the answers he might give, or afraid of getting into another argument. She rode in silence the rest of the way home, and when they reached their apartment, she gave him the only concession she could think of. "Greg, I've been thinking about it. I guess I will quit working. That way, maybe I won't be so tired."

"No, no. Don't do that. I'm sorry I made such a big deal about it."

But the next day, at work, she gave her two-week notice. She hated to think of the lonely days ahead, and she doubted it would change anything between her and Greg, but she didn't know what else to do.

# CHAPTER 17

Kathy knocked, heard some movement inside Professor Jennings's office, then saw the delight in his face when he opened the door. She liked his smile and the way his face, childlike, revealed his emotions. "Hello, young lady," he said. "May I help you in any way?"

"I just brought your book back."

"You didn't need to do that. I was in no hurry." He turned and waved at the mess in his office, books stacked everywhere. "It'll just get lost in here."

Kathy was embarrassed. She knew she hadn't needed to bring the book by. She had only done it because she wanted to see him. "When you get time someday, I'd like to talk to you about it," she said.

"Come on in. I've got class in half an hour, and I still have a couple of things I have to do. But I have something I want to ask you. We'll talk about the book later."

That was fine with Kathy. The book was a collection of Albert Camus's stories and essays. Earlier, she had read *The Stranger* with great interest, but this collection—which Gary had told her she "just had to read"—hadn't engaged her in the same way. Camus started with the assumption that the world was meaningless, and that wasn't something she found easy to accept. She simply hadn't been raised to think that way. She understood the essentials of existentialism, but the books Gary told her to read all seemed much the same. The authors, in her mind, were self-absorbed. She found herself thinking about the things her father and grandfather had said—that their thinking represented the "philosophies of men." She had kept her promise to her grandfather; she had prayed often since the day they had talked. She couldn't say she was getting specific answers, but she had gone back to reading the scriptures, which she had stopped doing in the fall, and as she read, she responded to the kindness of Christ, the humility. What he said reached her in a way that Sartre or Camus never did. Maybe she was only finding comfort in the familiar language and ideas—the Primary and Sunday School lessons of her childhood—but her reaction seemed nothing to discount.

At the same time, she liked Gary Jennings better than the books he gave her. She enjoyed his love of ideas, his openness to the world, and she was flattered by his obvious interest in her. He was still careful not to be overly personal, but he sometimes said little things that were clearly flirtatious. He thought she was pretty—she knew that—and she was always amazed when someone perceived her that way. Even more, she enjoyed being around him. His interests were so exciting to him, his moods so intense, and he seemed to know something about *everything*. He was as knowledgeable about horse training or fine chocolate as he was about group behavior—his specialty—or the history of philosophy, which he sometimes taught.

Kathy had grown up in a family of men who knew how to do things. They could make a business work, fix a leaking faucet, or conduct a meeting. What she wasn't used to was a man who knew how to talk about his inner self. Uncle Richard was a professor and clearly liked to think about things, but he said little of himself, and Uncle Alex could have talked with Gary about almost anything social or political, but she had never really known much about his inner life. Grandma always said that the men who had come home from the war had closed off parts of themselves. They dealt with the world and could be strong and good, but they held back the things that plagued them. "I can still see it in them sometimes," she had told Kathy. "Your father experienced things that deepened him and made him the gentle man he is—the same with Richard and Alex—but they refuse to unburden themselves. It's like a weight they carry around; it builds their own muscles, but they never ask anyone to share the load."

Kathy wasn't sure about that. She was not aware of any sort of pain, any horror, in the back of her father's mind. In fact, his approach to life seemed simple. Issues tended to be black and white for him, and truth was easily defined. He was certainly gentle in his approach to her, but she always wondered whether he merely knew no other way to deal with someone like her, so quick to explode. Gary, on the other hand, was willing to take her ideas seriously, whether he agreed or disagreed, and he was patient when she was too much like her father and grandfather, too quick to make blanket statements. He was softening her, broadening her understanding and perceptions. Maybe, finally, she was becoming someone people could disagree with without receiving a sermon.

What she couldn't figure out was who she was now. Every month or two she seemed to start over on herself. Now she was praying again, perhaps even believing, and at the same time she was drawn to this man who didn't believe in God. What would Grandpa think of her if he knew some of the ideas she was at least willing to try on for size?

"This weather is really getting to me," Gary said. He swung his hand in the direction of the window. "I'm like a three-year-old. Every spring is a surprise to me. It's like I forget that all this happened last year and the year before that."

The trees were budding out now, still the color of brass, and the early flowers were blooming: tulips and daffodils and hyacinths. "I'm sort of the same way," Kathy said. "I never feel like studying when the air turns so nice."

"Okay. You just said the right thing. All morning I've been thinking about something—something entirely *un*-academic. I want to take this weekend off and drive up to Vermont. But I don't want to go alone. Why don't you go with me?" He grinned and pointed a finger at her. "Wait. Don't answer, and don't get that troubled look on your face. I'm not trying to steal your innocence. This would all be very proper. Separate rooms, no hanky-panky."

Kathy laughed, but she was actually frightened, and she wasn't sure why. "I don't believe students are supposed to take weekend trips with professors—even in separate rooms."

"Of course they are. Haven't you ever heard of field trips? I'm sure we can find a field out there somewhere. We could even go romping in it, like young lambs."

"Sounds like a really bad movie."

"No, no. It'll be like that Liza Minelli movie, *The Sterile Cuckoo*. We can sing 'Come Saturday Morning' together. I love that song."

"I think there *was* some hanky-panky in that show."

"Yes, but it was all *her* idea. And that's how this will be."

Kathy wondered what that meant. Was he hoping for her to make the first advances? "Couldn't you get in trouble with the college?"

"Uuuhhhh . . . maybe. But we'd be discreet. I wouldn't come calling for you at your house. We could meet somewhere and then slip out of town."

Kathy was searching for an excuse, but the one that came to mind seemed far-fetched, even to her. Janet Stowe had asked Kathy if she wanted to go shopping in New York, and Kathy had turned her down. But now she found herself saying, "Some of my friends asked me to go to New York with them this weekend. I told them I would."

"You could cancel, couldn't you?"

"It wouldn't be fair. We're going to share costs at the hotel."

"I'm offering a better deal. I'll pay."

"I can't cancel out this late."

"Kathy, I'm sorry. I've scared you to death. I can hear it in your voice, and I can see how stiff you're sitting there. I never should have asked."

"No. Really. It doesn't bother me a bit—you know, that you asked."

"Okay, then. I won't ask again, but think about it. Maybe we could go some other time this spring. I've loved our talks, but I want to know you better. I think you know that."

She nodded. She wanted to know him better, too, and yet she couldn't bring herself to say that. What she did say was, "I guess we'll both be running off to the Peace Corps. It's hard to say when we'll see each other again—once I graduate."

Both had received acceptances from the Peace Corps. Kathy would be going to the Philippines and Gary to Nigeria. Gary smiled, softly, and she could see that she had saddened him. "Maybe we could ask them for a change of assignment, and they would send us to the same place."

"I doubt they'd do that."

"I don't know. This organization is more open-minded than most."

She wondered. Maybe that would actually be an answer for her. If they could be away from this campus, where they weren't always professor and student, maybe she could get to know him in some other ways. She wondered how he would do in the practical world where he might have to plant rice or help build a house. But there seemed no chance for them to "date."

"I guess we can write to each other," she said, and that was her way of saying, "Please don't write to the Peace Corps." But once again, she wasn't sure why. She seemed to have a million hang-ups.

"Well . . . anyway . . . think about a little trip. We could even do it right after graduation, when the college would have nothing to say about it."

She thought of her parents coming for graduation. She had tried to imagine, many times, their meeting Gary. She couldn't picture the four of them sitting down together, chatting about this and that, enjoying each other. She lived in dual worlds—each one so foreign to the other that a merger seemed impossible.

"Will you think about it?"

"Sure."

She got up. She felt her stiffness, and it embarrassed her. She could see that it embarrassed him, too. But once she was outside, she realized she had another problem. She didn't want him to see her, accidentally, this weekend—if he didn't take the trip to Vermont on his own. She could stay in her room, but she hated to do that, and even more, she was uncomfortable with her lie. Another hang-up. As the day passed, she realized what she wanted to do. She didn't care about shopping, but she had been in Massachusetts for four years, and she had rarely been to New York. She decided she wanted to go.

Janet was almost floored when Kathy told her that night that she did want to make the trip, and by then Kathy was actually rather excited. She was weary of her own seriousness, stressed by those divided worlds she lived in, and it sounded fun to leap to a third one, where she could enjoy a few days of guaranteed silliness. As it turned out, Janet had almost resolved to cancel the trip. Becky had been the only one willing to go, and typically, when Becky got to New York she spent too much time at home and left Janet on her own. But now, with Kathy going, Trisha agreed to complete the "old foursome" from their freshman year, and the trip was on.

The drive to New York turned out to be the most enjoyable thing Kathy had done in a long time. Janet was her usual wild self, and that kept everything light. The girls drank sodas and stopped way too often at gas stations, since someone always had to go to the restroom. Each time they stopped they bought junk food—or more sodas—to justify their request for the station key. So the trip took much longer than necessary, but the talk never ended and never touched on anything that mattered. Kathy was relieved to be with these friends without saying a word about Vietnam or any of the other old issues that had sometimes split them apart. She had a strange sense that she was discovering how to be young just when it was almost too late. She didn't picture the Peace Corps as a lot of fun, and once she graduated, that was the next stop.

They checked into an old, rather frumpy hotel with tiny rooms, but the four wanted to stay together, so they ordered two roll-away beds to go with the two single beds in a room that was more suited for one. They didn't try to open those beds for the moment, however. The day—Friday—had been slipping by, and Janet wanted to make it to Bloomingdale's while there were still "a few hours to shop."

Kathy actually ended up buying more things than she had thought she would. She told herself that she was thinking of her Peace Corps needs, but along with some sturdy shoes and a practical jacket, she bought a white satin blouse that she had absolutely no need for now that she didn't go to church, and a necklace she spotted on a street vendor's table. The young guy who was selling the stuff said he made it all himself, and the metal was "high quality" silver. She doubted that a little, but she liked the emerald stones, and she liked the maker.

Janet loved shopping, but she loved eating even more, and she lasted only three hours or so before she said she couldn't last another hour without a pastrami sandwich from the Carnegie Deli. So the girls stashed their packages in the already overcrowded hotel room and walked up Seventh Avenue to the Carnegie—just around the corner from Carnegie Hall. They split two of the giant sandwiches so they could "save room for cheesecake."

They had had to wait to be seated for a while, and had ended up sharing a table with some tourists—two couples from Indiana. The place was noisy and full of smoke, but it felt like New York, and Janet, as usual, created her own fun. She told the people from Indiana that she was pretty sure the guy in the corner, at the back of the room, was Henny Youngman. Kathy knew it wasn't him, but Janet loved a good rumor more than anything as dull as truth, and so she kept saying, "I'm pretty sure it is. I need to get a better look." She would twist around and stare, and soon people at other tables were looking too. Kathy couldn't stop laughing.

Eventually, over cheesecake, and the other end of the table empty for the moment, Becky was the one to say, "Can you believe this has happened? We were all freshmen the other day, and now we're two months from graduating. I wish school didn't have to end. I don't want to leave Smith."

"I don't want to get a *job*," Janet said. "I'd go to grad school if my grades weren't so bad."

It was strange to think about. Kathy looked at her three friends and wondered how she had let these years slide away. She wanted more time with them now, and yet, during her first couple of years, she had sometimes hated them.

"Have we changed?" Janet asked.

All three laughed, and Trisha said what Kathy was thinking. "*You* haven't."

"I know. I'm a perpetual teenager. I'm going to be one of those old ladies who's really embarrassing to her grandkids because she's always trying to be cool. But I don't care. When I'm eighty years old, I'm going to wear hippie beads and chartreuse pants, with four-inch spikes. You know—just make a complete fool of myself."

"And have a very good time doing it," Kathy said.

"Oh, listen to this," Janet said. "Little miss 'save the world' is now extolling the pleasures of a 'good time.' Four years ago we vowed to change you, and we've never even made a dent in your armor."

"I've changed," Kathy said.

"You dropped out of SDS, maybe, but you're still the same Kathy."

"It wasn't interesting for you to be in SDS anymore after the whole campus turned radical," Trisha said. "You have to go your own way."

"No. That's not true," Kathy said. "I've been looking around for 'my way' for four years—longer than that—and I still haven't found it. I think I've been walking in a circle."

Becky, always the quiet one, finally said, "But it's the searching that's the consistent part of you. The rest of us didn't even know what the questions were when we started college. You've been asking them since you were in high school—probably before that."

"Maybe. But I had a lot of answers at one time. I'm not so sure of myself anymore." Kathy looked up to see that a waitress was leading a couple with a son, maybe ten or so, to their table. She wasn't sure she wanted her friends to talk about her in front of other people.

Becky seemed to know that. She leaned forward and spoke softly. "But you still believe in your causes. Isn't that what the Peace Corps is all about?"

"I guess. But I feel like I've been fighting with a peashooter and taking on a cannon. Nothing I've done has made much difference. So I tell myself that maybe in the Peace Corps I can make a *small* difference—instead of always worrying about big differences."

"I respect you," Trisha said. "You're the most altruistic person I've ever met."

"No. You're making me sound better than I am."

"That's right. She is," Janet said. "You used to tell us we were idiots. I don't think the fact that you were right excuses you at all."

The girls all laughed, but Kathy said, "You're not idiots, Janet. You never were. I just didn't know how to grant anyone a different point of view."

"I'll tell you the real truth, Kathy," Janet said. "You're genuine, and you're good. I don't think I've ever known anyone who tries so hard to do the right thing. I know your idea of right and wrong has been changing, but you can't help being good. It's just who you are."

Kathy could hardly believe this assessment of her, but the other girls were nodding. "I think," Kathy said, after a moment, "that striving to do the right thing is part of what I grew up with—part of my family and part of my church. But I can be really self-righteous too. That's what I regret, and that's what I'm trying to get past. I guess that's why I'm searching hard for a larger perspective on life."

"Maybe. But Kathy, you're a Mormon right down to your bones. I know you've stopped going over to Amherst to church, but you're just as much a Mormon as you ever were. I remember that first day we met you and you told us you wouldn't go to a party and drink. I thought that wouldn't last long, but no matter how much you think you've changed, alcohol never touches your lips, and you couldn't use bad language if you tried. You'll never sleep around, either. All that stuff your family taught you is just in you, forever."

"If I were you, I'd embrace it," Trisha said. "I'd never *heard* of Mormons when you showed up out here. But now, when I find out someone's in your church, I think, 'She must be a good person. She's probably like Kathy.'"

Kathy thought of saying, "We're not all alike, Trisha," but something stopped her. Maybe it was the instruction she had received all her life to look for "missionary opportunities," or maybe she was just too embarrassed to keep the subject going. So she said instead, "You know, I think that *is* Henny Youngman." Everyone laughed.

The girls returned to Northampton on Sunday in a car so packed that they hardly had room for themselves. Kathy hadn't bought as many things as the others, but she had bought way too much, and she wondered about her budget for the month. Still, she felt happier than she had in a long time, and she told herself that maybe she had added one more piece in her never-ending attempt to put her puzzle together. She needed to laugh more, not spend every day analyzing what she believed. And she was interested in the perception she had created in her friends. She wasn't nearly as good as they thought she was. She understood her own rectitude, her tendency to live by rules, but she wondered whether Janet, in fact, wasn't more genuinely good. She was the one who accepted life, accepted people, and enjoyed connecting to them. Kathy even went to Janet's room and told her that, and Janet actually cried.

What Kathy didn't do was go by to see Gary Jennings. She wanted to. She missed him, but she didn't want to reply to his request. She hoped he wouldn't ask again.

She was coming out of the library later that week, however, and she happened to meet up with him. They stood outside on the sidewalk for a few minutes and chatted about her trip to New York. Kathy was relieved she didn't have to make anything up. They also talked about Gary's busy week at school. "It's good I didn't run off last weekend," he said. "I got a stack of papers read, and if I hadn't, I'd be in big trouble now."

"You're a responsible man, that's all," Kathy said. "I always appreciated how fast you got our papers back. Some of these professors, by the time you get the thing back, you can't remember that you wrote it."

"My problem is, I'm compulsive. I always want to take it easy, but if I have something I need to do I can't leave it alone."

"I have some of that in me too," Kathy said.

"I know. I've noticed. We're really alike in a lot of ways."

There was nothing dangerous in those words, but there was much more affection in the tone than Kathy wanted. "Speaking of which," she said, "I checked out these books because I've got to start reading for a paper I have due next week. I'd better go get started on it."

"All right. But I can't stand not asking—even though I promised not to. Have you thought at all about my proposal to go away together for a weekend?"

He pulled his tie loose and unbuttoned his collar, almost as though he thought he might have to wait for an answer—or enter into a discussion about it. Kathy had told herself what she had to say, but it was harder to do than she had expected. "Gary, I just don't think we should do that. I'm not comfortable with the idea."

"What idea?"

"I'm a student, and you're—"

"Tell the truth. You think it's improper. It's your upbringing. A nice Mormon girl doesn't go off to a hotel with a man she's not married to. The fact is, you know what I *really* have in mind."

"*Is* that what you have in mind?"

"Of course it is. But I told you, it could be as pure as you would like it to be. For now, I just want to get a lot better acquainted."

"We can do that without going to a hotel," she said quietly, since other students were walking by. She realized, too, that she was blushing.

Gary laughed. "Kathy, you're so funny to me. You can talk, in the abstract, about any idea, but when you have to make a decision, you revert to these Victorian rules you've been trained in."

"Then maybe that's who I am."

"Maybe. But you can't really discover your own truths when your whole ancestry is hanging over your shoulder, saying, 'Nice girls do this. They *don't* do that.'"

Kathy thought of her grandfather, thought of what he had said about living up to her heritage. When Gary spun the idea the other way, those pioneers did seem a weight on her shoulders. But she knew she wasn't ready to throw them off quite yet either. "Gary, when I was home, I told my parents I was going to break with our church. I made my official announcement, and I thought it was over. But my grandfather talked to me about that." She was tempted to tell the whole thing, about the voice he had heard in his head, telling him where she was. But Gary would have laughed at that, and maybe she would too, if she said it out loud. So she merely said, "He asked me not to make my decision yet. He asked me to keep praying. I believed in prayer for a long time, and I'm trying right now to see whether it's not something I still believe in. I'm reading the Book of Mormon again, too—some parts where Christ speaks to the people—and I love the way I feel when I listen to what he says."

"I know what you mean. I wish everyone would live by Jesus' teachings.

But don't let your grandpa pile up a load of guilt on you. You can believe in those teachings, and you can believe in contemplation, without accepting petitionary prayer. That kind of prayer is like a good-luck charm. You know, 'Hey, God, I want this. And send me some of that.'"

But that bothered her. She took Gary on with her eyes. "No. We may ask for the Lord's blessings, but it's also about gratefulness. It's acknowledging the source."

"Well, good. Next time you're talking to him, thank him for disease and famine and mental defects. If everything comes from God, we owe him. I'm just not sure what we owe him."

"Part of living on this planet is dealing with the hardships. A lot of people who've gone through hard challenges do thank God."

He didn't respond immediately. Kathy listened to a cardinal singing in a nearby tree, the sound coming from way up high. She would always associate the song of cardinals with living in the East, being away from home. It crossed her mind that she might, from now on, always associate the sound with this moment. She could hear in Gary's voice, and even in her own, that their friendship, or whatever it was they shared, was changing.

He waited until she looked at him before he said, "Is that what you believe?"

"It's what I've been taught and . . ." She hesitated. She wasn't going to do that. "It does ring true to me," she said.

"I guess you can take the girl out of Utah, but you can't take Utah out of the girl."

"Gary, I don't know that yet. But I promised I wouldn't throw all my heritage away until I had tried one more time. I wish you could have heard Grandpa Thomas. He asked me to look into his eyes, and then he testified to me. He told me what he *knew*, and I believed him."

"Oh, come on, Kathy. There are old fellows in every religion who *know* the truth. We need a little less *knowing* and a lot more listening to each other. Every culture has its—"

"Gary, I've heard you say all that before. I know how you look at things. But let me sort this out for myself."

"You're not sorting, *Sister* Thomas. You're running back to a safe place. And to me, it's tragic. You have a good mind, but you're scared to think where it might take you if you listen to your real feelings."

Kathy glanced down at the sidewalk. She thought of that day she had walked out of Highland High and had seen her grandfather drive up. "My grandfather thinks it's more important to hear God's voice than to hear my own. And if there is a God, that's true."

"Yes. If there is. But do you really think God is a man up in the sky listening to billions of requests and sending down answers when he happens to feel like it?"

The idea did seem ridiculous when he said it that way. But who had sent her grandfather to her when she had needed him? And why had she *known* the truth, at least for the moment, when he had testified? It was easy to make fun of belief, and commit to nothing, but Kathy didn't want to miss the voice if it really was speaking to her.

"I've got to go," Kathy said.

"Hey, I'm not trying to beat up on you. A lot of people find comfort in belief, and who am I to say there's anything wrong with that. I just—"

"I really do have to go." She turned to leave.

"Kathy, I'm sorry. We'll get together. I won't push you again. But we need to talk a lot more about all these things. Okay?"

"I'm not sure," Kathy said. She was still drawn to him no matter how divided he made her feel, but she wasn't sure that anything would come of their talks. He had his mind made up, and she still didn't.

# CHAPTER 18

Diane had awakened to a dreary April morning, but it was almost noon now, and the fog had burned off. The color of the sky was beyond blue, almost purple, and wrinkled leaves were emerging from the red-brown buds on a willow tree just outside the kitchen window. Diane had cleaned up the breakfast dishes and vacuumed a little, even dusted, though she saw no evidence that she needed to. She had never been so neat in her life, but she liked to be up and about for a while in the mornings. If she tried to read too early, she fell asleep before she got through more than a few pages. For a couple of hours now, however, she had been pushing ahead in her latest project: to read something by Dickens, since she had hated his books so much in high school. Her mom had suggested she read *Bleak House* since, she said, it was a commentary on the British judicial system. The title sounded dreadful to Diane, but she was actually quite involved now, even though Dickens moved his plots along much too slowly for her taste.

The time since Diane had quit working had been difficult. Even though Greg told her not to, she got up early and prepared him a "real" breakfast: eggs or waffles, or both, and usually bacon. She hadn't been terribly sick with her pregnancy, but the smell of bacon made her queasy every time she cooked it, and she hated the way the smell lingered in the apartment. But Greg loved bacon, and she was trying hard to do her part to make things work. She had felt too much tension lately, and it was devastating to her. Greg was often grouchy, and even though he apologized, and sometimes brought home flowers at the end of the day or took her out for a "romantic" dinner, he remained moody, and there were times when he hardly seemed to like her. He always said he was happy about the baby, but he was annoyed by Diane's sleepiness. "If you insist on getting up early with me, why don't you go back to bed after I leave in the morning?" he would ask her. "Or why not take a nap in the afternoon? We hardly have any time for each other anymore."

But she did take naps during the day, and she was still tired, especially when he studied late. And what irritated her was that he didn't actually show any interest in spending time with her, not to talk or share his day. What he wanted was for her to be wide awake when they went to bed. Some days he hardly spoke to her except to tell her how great the demands were on him, and how much he needed to study, but then, magically, he wanted her to be affectionate and loving, on his schedule. He was also meeting with his study group almost as often as ever. Diane's days were especially long and lonely when he did that.

Today, as Diane tried to read, her mind kept drifting back to what had happened the night before. For the first time ever, Greg had shouted at her. "Do you think I like to study this much? I'd love to sit around here all day reading novels and getting fat."

"You're the one who told me to quit working," she had answered, not loudly, but bitterly. "You said I *ought* to do more reading."

"I thought you'd read something worthwhile."

"I'm reading *classics*, not romance novels. What do you want me to read?"

"Something that will expand your *mind* a little. Why don't you read some of your old textbooks that you never *cracked* while you were in college?"

Diane had cried, and he had apologized, and then he had wanted to make up the way he always wanted to make up. But for once, Diane had said no. This morning, at breakfast, he had hardly spoken to her, and he had left even earlier than usual. So Diane was worried. She told herself that she had to try harder to be the kind of wife he needed. She didn't blame him for being short with her lately; she had done very little to make him happy. And she *was* getting fat. Her obstetrician had told her to expect to put on thirty pounds or so during her pregnancy, that it was actually healthy to do that. She had hardly thought it possible, since she had never really struggled with her weight, but she had been hungrier than usual, and even though she didn't feel much like eating in the mornings, she made up for it with snacks during those long afternoons and evenings.

So today she had made up her mind to eat very little and to take a long walk in the afternoon, then to stop in a bookstore to see what kinds of books, other than novels, she might choose to read. Greg actually knew that she didn't have any of her old textbooks with her in Seattle, but she did wonder whether she couldn't read up on some subjects she hadn't taken seriously when she was at BYU. Or maybe she ought to try to understand more about the law. One thing Diane worried a great deal about was the way Greg talked about Sondra Gould. "She's got a great legal mind," he liked to say. "She remembers *everything*, and she can analyze too. Over and over, she helps me see the implications of a case."

Diane knew she couldn't compete with that, but she thought it might be good if she understood a little more about the legal system. She figured there must be books on the basic concepts and some of the language Greg was learning. Maybe then she could at least respond intelligently when Greg tried to tell her what he was studying in his classes.

Diane walked across the canal bridge to the University Arboretum, and then, for more than an hour, followed some of the trails. Afterward, she hiked back to the U-District. She was feeling a little tired but much enlivened by the cool air and the pumping of her heart. Later in the spring, when the rhododendrons were in bloom, she wanted to make that same walk often. Her pregnancy wasn't showing yet, and when she checked herself out in storefront windows, she didn't think she looked all that bad. She knew she had gained a few pounds, and that the baby, so far, had little to do with that, but Greg had made it sound as though she were getting chubby.

What she also noticed was that she got plenty of attention. She was wearing a button-down collar shirt and white pants, and the guys looking her over were mostly "freaks," so maybe they were only thinking she was some sort of throwback. But she still liked to turn heads, and she wasn't sure why. What was the point of being pretty if her husband wasn't satisfied with her?

During her walk she had resolved to be happier that night and to show Greg more affection. The walk had been the right thing, and now she was going to find a good book or two. She had been putting too much of the blame for her problems on Greg; she hadn't tried hard enough to think of *his* needs. She knew she could be more loving if she tried. She walked into the big University Bookstore and looked around, tried to think where she could find books about the law. She wandered the aisles for a while, seeing nothing of the sort she wanted, and, honestly, seeing little that looked interesting. She tried to think of some subjects she might like to study. History didn't interest her, and many of the books sounded too academic: social issues, politics, science.

She was walking slowly between a couple of bookshelves, glancing at titles that seemed mostly about business, when a young man with black plastic glasses and long sideburns approached her. "I've noticed you wandering around like you're not sure where to look. Can I help you find something?"

She saw that look—the one she had known all her life. He was smiling more than seemed necessary, and his eyes were drifting over her. "Yes, maybe you could," she said. "My husband is—"

"You're *married?*"

She held up her ring finger. "Yes, I am."

"Whoa! Is that a diamond or a pound of glass?"

"My husband told me it was real. But what do I know?"

She was angry with herself immediately. She had used that coyness—her little "airhead" act—almost as a reflex.

"How old are you—if you don't mind my asking. I thought you were a freshman, or maybe even a high school girl."

"I'm older than you think, but that doesn't matter. My husband is a law student, and I'm looking for a book that might help me understand basic principles of the law . . . or . . . something like that."

The young man grinned at her. "Trying to keep up with him, are you?"

"No. I just—"

"I've got a feeling he didn't marry you because of your 'common interests.'"

But that angered Diane. How could she ever escape her image? "Look, do you have a book like that or don't you?"

"Sorry, sorry. You girls are getting so *sensitive* these days. I'll see what I've got on the history of jurisprudence, or 'how to speak mumbo-jumbo.' But I'll have to ask. That's not something I know anything about. I'm an art history major myself." He walked away, laughing.

Diane was rather proud that she had put him in his place. It was about time she stopped letting guys toy with her that way. She walked in the direction the sales clerk had walked and saw a shelf of self-help books. It had crossed her mind that she might want to buy a book that talked about sex—maybe some advice for newlyweds. She had heard about books like that, had even seen some in bookstores, but she certainly wasn't going to ask this guy to help her find one. In a couple of minutes he returned and led her to another shelf. "Look through this section right here," he said. "My boss says that there are some books that help people understand legal documents and that sort of thing. I think that might be what you're look-ing for."

"Yes. That does sound good. I'll see what I can find."

But he didn't leave. He stood next to her and scanned the book spines. He finally pulled a paperback down: *What's Your Lawyer Talking*

*About?* was the title. He handed it to her and she read the blurb on the back. "Yes, this looks interesting. I'll just see what else is here." She wanted him to leave.

"Okay. Hey, and if that husband of yours spends too many hours in the library, just drop by here and chat with me—any time you want." She turned a look of disdain in his direction, and he laughed. "Hey, just kidding. Who wants an art history major when you've got yourself a big-shot lawyer?"

"Thanks for your help," she said. She tried not to smile—but failed. He was a cute boy in a nerdy sort of way.

She looked through the other books on the shelf and found nothing better, but then she strolled back to the self-help books. Some were on babies and marriage, and she spotted a title on sex. She didn't want to be looking at books like that and have that same guy come by to offer more help, so she kept watching for him, but she found a surprising number of books of the sort she had in mind. The titles, however, were embarrassing. They were all about finding heightened pleasure, or providing it, and the thought of walking to the counter with a book like that was humiliating. She thought she might go to a library some time and maybe read some things there—without checking them out. As she continued to look about, however, she saw a book she had heard people mention. It was called *The Feminine Mystique.* Kathy Thomas had told her, some years before, that she ought to read it, and yet, it didn't sound like a Kathy sort of title. Diane had always thought of it as a book about being feminine and alluring. If Kathy would recommend it, though, it had to be something Diane could take to the counter without appearing silly, so she decided to buy it and the law book, but not get anything else for the present. She still had her own money from her last paycheck, but she wasn't sure how long that would hold out. Once that money was gone, she would have to start accounting to Greg for everything she spent.

She walked home, made a little snack out of celery and just a bit of cheese spread, and then showered. Greg had warned her that he might be quite late that night, so she would eat something more, later on. But regardless of what Greg had said, she knew she needed to watch herself now, early in her pregnancy, so she wouldn't balloon so big that she would look terrible after the baby came. She had known women who had never gotten their figures back after having their first babies. She absolutely wasn't going to be like that.

She sat down, still quite excited to learn something about the law, and then to tell Greg what she was reading. Maybe, after she had studied this first book, she could get his suggestions for other things to read. She might even try to read some of his basic textbooks. But she hadn't gotten far into this little paperback before she was suffering from a serious loss of interest. The subject was mostly the language of contracts and what to look for when buying a house or entering into a business partnership. She understood what she read; she just couldn't think how it would help her talk to Greg. He sometimes tried to explain to her the interesting questions that came up in his classes, and she understood as long as he explained in normal English, but he would usually resort to terms she didn't know and ones that, frankly, he had trouble explaining. She wasn't sure she was finding anything in this book that would help.

She did read about the word "tort," however—a term he had once tried to explain to her. She felt as though she understood the concept better now, and it would be something she could tell him. Then she could keep working her way through the chapters, and maybe ask him what other terms she ought to know.

For now, however, she set the book down and picked up *The Feminine Mystique*. Two hours later, she had hardly moved. When she finally did set it down, after having read the preface and the first two chapters, she didn't know whether she was frightened or angry or, at least in part, persuaded. She almost wished she hadn't read the ideas, and yet she was sure she couldn't simply brush them aside and forget them. She remembered now that someone in a class at BYU, or maybe in her student ward, had used the book to illustrate the evil way some women were starting to talk about their lives—dishonoring the role of being a mother and housewife. But she didn't exactly see that in the book. What she heard were women expressing their disappointment, talking about the "problem without a name"—the meaninglessness they were finding in their lives.

Maybe these women were just whiners—spoiled women who had things too easy. She probably shouldn't finish the book. It was the sort of thinking that was turning the world upside down and ruining attitudes about the most sacred experiences in life. Women were trying too hard to compete with men, and that was leading to the problems that were showing up in families.

But she couldn't stop thinking about the "mystique" that Betty Friedan talked about. Diane had always felt that she had to live up to an image, an idea of femininity that—now that she thought about it—was the product of men's fantasies. Boys grew up believing they had to be strong and smart and successful. Girls learned that they had to be pretty, were better off to hide their intelligence, and should measure their own worth by the number of men who desired them. The strange thing was, Diane hadn't been taught that in her own family. Her mother had been the model of a woman who loved to learn, who didn't think life was all about hairstyles, makeup, and fancy wardrobes. So where had Diane learned to care so very much about all those things?

But that wasn't Diane's greatest concern. What she wondered now was whether her own choices had led her to a life that would never be satisfying. If she expected all her sense of worth to come from Greg's accomplishments, would she eventually feel swallowed up in him? She wouldn't always be pretty.

Diane decided to call Mary Innis, just to see whether she had read the book and what she might say about it. She had talked to Mary a few times on the phone, but they had still not gotten together, the way they had planned. The fact was, Diane had feared talking openly to Mary. She wanted a friend, but she didn't dare tell anyone the things she was worried about. They were mostly things she didn't think she ought to be feeling. She certainly didn't want to tell Mary that the book, in some ways, made sense to her. But Mary didn't answer the phone, and Diane was left feeling almost frighteningly alone. She decided to call her mother, but she knew better than to call before five o'clock. Greg didn't like her to call her parents very often, even though it seemed to her that he called his own family more than she did. She knew that if he got a bill for a call before five—when the long distance rates went down—he would certainly have something to say about that. But that troubled her. Betty Friedan described that very kind of thing: men who treated women as though they were children; men who made the rules in their homes and expected compliance. Why had she been reading a book about law terms? Would Greg be pleased about that or make a joke of it? Would he only compare her to Sondra? Why did he like the fact that Sondra was bright, and then not really expect the same of Diane? Diane had the disturbing feeling that she had spent her life working herself into a corner, creating an image that was now dictating not only who she was in others' minds but also who she would always be.

She called her mother at one minute past five. It was an hour earlier in Utah, and she wasn't certain that her mother would be home, but it was Bobbi who answered the phone. "Diane, it's so good to hear your voice," she said. "How are you doing?"

"Fine. Really fine."

"And you're still not sick?"

"Not much. Only, you know, when I smell certain things or . . ." But her mind wasn't on the conversation.

She didn't finish, and Bobbi waited for a moment before she said, "Well, that's good. Is everything all right?" And this was a different question. She had apparently heard something in Diane's voice.

"I just wanted to ask you something."

"Sure."

"Have you ever read *The Feminine Mystique?*"

"Yes."

"What did you think of it?"

"Why?"

"I started to read it this afternoon. I was just wondering what you think of some of the things it says."

"Tell me first, what do you think?"

Diane wasn't sure. "I only read the first part," she said, "but it seems like some of it is right. I'm not really sure, though. It's sort of against the Church, isn't it?"

"What do you mean, 'against the Church'?"

"I don't know. Moms are supposed to stay home. We're always told that."

"Stay home our whole lives?"

"I don't know. You've worked some. Do you think that's all right?"

"You tell me. Did it bother you when I worked?"

"Sometimes."

"Did it hurt you?"

"I don't know."

"I never worked when you and Maggy were little. But I taught some classes when Ricky was fairly young. I've done a lot of soul-searching about that. It was something I really wanted to do at the time, but I've never been certain it was a good thing."

"You weren't gone all day, Mom. I don't think it caused us any problems. I used to get mad about it—but I was pretty selfish at that age."

"So what do you think is right? No work? Part-time work? Work only if you absolutely have to? Or what?"

"Mom, I told you, I don't know. I don't *want* to work. I don't *want* a career. But the writer, Betty Friedan—"

"It's pronounced Free-dan."

"She says that women who are home aren't happy. They want to develop their talents and do things in the world, but they don't, and they get sick of changing diapers and scrubbing floors. Do you think that's true?"

"Diane, there's no question that raising kids and keeping house is hard work. And there's no question that a lot of bright young women are feeling now that there should be more to their lives than that. But that doesn't mean you will feel that way."

"Mom, I've always wanted to be a mother. I think it's the most important job you can have in this life. It's creating an eternal family. How could I use my mind and my skills better than that?"

"I agree. I like to read, and I like to teach, so I've done some of that, but honey, I've always known those things were secondary. I'm just lucky I married your father. Men need to be loving, nurturing fathers, like Richard, and create some space in their wives' lives so they can do some things they love to do while they're also raising their kids."

"Mom, I have a feeling child-raising will be entirely up to me. Greg says he wants to help, but I don't think he will."

Diane waited for a long time but heard nothing on the other end of the line. That worried her. Finally, Bobbi asked, "So what are you going to do about it?"

"That's what I'm asking you. What *can* I do about it?"

"Stand up for yourself."

"Mom, you know me. You know how I am."

"You're kind and loving, and you'll be a wonderful mother. But if you let your husband *dictate* your relationship, you'll have no one but yourself to blame."

"Greg's just so busy right now, Mom. He probably doesn't have any choice about being gone so much."

"He has a choice, Diane. We always have choices."

"Does Dad decide everything about your money?"

"You know he doesn't. We talk about everything."

"Does Dad expect you to . . . I don't know how to say it . . . always be wide awake at night, and . . ."

"Say it."

"I can't, Mom. I just can't say certain things to you."

"Diane, you are beautiful. You've always been beautiful. But if that's the only reason Greg married you, he's got to start discovering what else you are. And he can't discover that unless you show him."

"I don't even know what that means." Diane had begun to cry. Finally she said what she had been thinking all day. "He's in love with my body, Mom, and I'm going to lose that. How am I ever going to keep him?"

"Oh, Diane."

"I know what you're thinking. You always thought I shouldn't marry him."

"That's not what I'm thinking. I'm thinking that you're being forced to grow up now, and that's okay. But you have to do it. You've got to tell him what you just told me, and then you've got to talk a lot of things out. Quote him some Betty Friedan. He won't like it, but if he loves you, he'll have to think about it, and you two will have to decide what a celestial relationship between a man and a woman really is."

Diane clung to the phone and tried to think what she could say to her mother so that *she* would understand. Greg would be mad that she had even bought the book, and he would be furious to hear some of the things that were in it. How could she talk to him about that? She couldn't even keep this phone call going much longer or Greg would be talking about the money she had spent. And so Diane said, "Okay. I do need to think all this through."

"Yes. But above all, you two have got to *talk*."

"Okay."

And after Diane first put the phone down, she told herself she would do it this time. But as she tried to imagine what she would say, she began to lose courage. She sat in the kitchen, at the table, and she tried to get herself under control, to stop crying, and then she went back to what she had concluded that morning. She had to do her part of marriage better, and then he would want to do his part. She needed to fix something special for dinner, and then, later that night, she needed to please him, make him really happy with her. Once things were going a little better, and he was feeling good about her, it would be time to raise some questions—about raising children *together*, and about sharing in decisions. But for now, she didn't want to cause any more fights.

# CHAPTER 19

Gene was vaguely aware that Emily had gotten out of bed a couple of times during the night, but there was nothing unusual in that. He was drifting, experiencing an odd series of half-awake dreams, when he realized that the hand shaking his shoulder was real. "Gene," he heard. "Gene."

"Yeah?" he said, but he was still trying to pull himself out of his dream.

"I think the baby's coming."

"What?"

"I'm having pains. Hard ones."

Gene opened his eyes. She had been having contractions for quite some time, and twice before she had told him she thought they were the "real thing" this time. "How often?" he asked. The doctor had told them to call him and then head to the hospital when the pains were coming in five-minute intervals. He raised up on his elbow and looked toward Emily. In the dim light he could see that she was lying on her back. Her rounded middle was making a shape like a watermelon under the blankets.

"They're not real regular yet. But they aren't going away either. I've been having them for a couple of hours."

"Do they hurt?" He sat up.

"Yes. But I want them to come. I want the baby out of there."

She had been saying that for a month or so now. He wondered if this could be more wishful thinking. "What time is it?"

"Almost six. I didn't want to wake you *too* early."

Gene remembered that this was supposed to be his big study day. Finals would start tomorrow. "Let me get my watch. Let's time the next few pains." He got up and flipped the light on, squinted as his eyes adjusted, and then found his watch on the nightstand. He put his glasses on and sat down on the bed. "Tell me when the next one starts, and when it stops."

"Don't act like that, okay?"

"What?" He twisted around to look at her.

"Aren't you excited?"

"Sure. But this happened before."

"No, it didn't. Not like this. This time it's really . . . oh, oh, oh."

He turned and crawled onto the bed, then placed the palm of his hand on the mound that had once been her abdomen. He could feel the hardness. "Are you okay?" he asked.

She was straining, breathing in grunts. She didn't bother to answer. It seemed to Gene a long time before she said, "Okay. It's going away."

"Okay. Let's see how long until the next one."

"Gene, get dressed. And help me get ready. That one was *very* hard."

"All right. But tell me when you feel the next one coming on." He tried to think what to wear. Maybe he shouldn't go to the hospital in his jeans, but that's what he would wear if he was going to spend the day in the library. And what about his studies? He really did need to put in some hours today. He pulled off his old green pajamas, tossed them onto the bed, and then went to his closet and found some khaki slacks, which he stepped into. He tried to think what sort of shirt he should wear. "I could be a father before this day is over," he thought, and the idea was strangely surprising. Hadn't he known that since last summer? But this was for real. This was the beginning of the change they had been talking about all winter. The new life. He wanted to see the baby, see what it looked like.

"What about your finals?" Emily asked.

"What about them?"

"You've been saying that you hoped the baby didn't come until after finals."

"Talk to the baby. Tell him to wait a few more days. He'll listen to reason, won't he?"

"*She* might. But are you really upset, if it comes today?"

"No. It's okay. I'll study while you do labor. Or I'll study all night. I'll figure something out."

"Are you mad at me?"

Gene still hadn't decided on a shirt. He couldn't think. He turned around now, still holding his pants around his waist with one hand. "Mad at you? Are you kidding? This is cool, Em. Really cool. It's the most exciting thing that's happened. We're going to be 'Mom and Dad.'"

"I love you, Gene. Will you help me today, even if you need to study?"

"Yes. I'll do whatever—"

But she was saying "Oh, oh" again.

Gene grabbed for his watch. He jumped onto the bed. Emily grabbed his hand and squeezed it until it hurt, but he didn't pull away. He was still adding up the minutes. "Honey, that's only four and a half minutes. What are you doing?"

She was letting out a long breath at the moment. But then she said, "I'm having a baby. We'd better call Dr. Richards and head for the hospital."

"It won't come on the way, will it?"

"No, no. It's my first one. They don't come that fast. But I think we'd better get over there. Help me up."

He hopped off the bed, zipped up his pants, and then hurried around the bed. He took both her hands and helped her to her feet, and then he leaned over her big stomach and took her in his arms. "I'm sorry you have to go through this," he said. "Thank you."

"It's too early for thanks," she said. Then she laughed. "And too late to say you're sorry."

❧

It turned out to be a long day. The pains came fast and hard for a while, but then slowed, and for a time it seemed as though Emily might be sent home. But the doctor said that everything was ready, and after he broke Emily's water, the pains picked up again. Still, it was almost five o'clock in the afternoon before she was dilated enough to move into the delivery room. Gene had spent the entire day with Emily, talking to her, timing the labor pains, letting her grip his hand. But he felt useless, and at times Emily seemed distant, as though she were passing through an experience he would never understand. He sensed that she was calling on a special reserve of strength. A spirit was coming into the world, and that was beautiful to think about. But the pain was real. All the probing and coaching, the panting and groaning, and eventually, the grunts and the blood—all of it was a little too stark for Gene. There were times when he wanted to go hide somewhere and not be one of these modern fathers who took part in the whole thing.

The doctor had given Emily a caudal block to control the pain, but it never had seemed to work right. She still had lots of pain, especially in her back. The final effort was enormous, exhausting to Emily, and frightening to Gene. He wanted this baby, but he didn't want it to be so excruciating to his wife. He felt almost desperate to help, and couldn't. But he was watching in a mirror over the doctor's shoulder when a head appeared, red, with dark, wet hair. The doctor got close then, so Gene couldn't see. He said that he was turning the baby's shoulders. But he stepped back then, waited, and with the next contraction, a sloppy little blob of flesh slipped loose. In the doctor's hands it transformed into a little human, screeching, upside down.

"It's a boy," one of the nurses said. "You have a fine, big boy."

"Is he okay?" Emily asked.

"He has all his fingers and toes," the doctor said. "He's a strong little tike, too. We'll run some tests, but I'd say you have a healthy baby."

The nurse took the baby in a towel, but after cleaning him off a little, she reached up and laid him across Emily's chest. He was still whimpering, looking like a little old man, all red and wrinkled. His head was distorted, cone-shaped on top.

Emily took the baby's tiny hand in hers. "I'm glad you finally got here, little one," she said. "You'll like the world once you get to know it better." She had begun to cry.

The nurse took the baby away then, and Gene bent over Emily and held her in his arms. "Thank you," he said. "Thank you, Em. I love you so much."

"You got the boy you wanted," she said.

"I'm sorry. I should have let you choose. Next time we can have a girl."

"Don't talk to me about next time right now." She sounded groggy, but she was laughing.

"So is it official? Are we going to name him Daniel?" Gene asked.

"Yes. I think he looks like a Danny boy."

"Don't call him that. I don't want a Danny Thomas. I want him to know he's like Daniel Jones—the missionary who brought the Thomases into the Church."

"He's still a little Danny."

Gene smiled. He liked to think of that. "Hey, Danny, throw me the ball," he called to the baby, who was now across the room. "Yeah, it sounds good."

She smiled and nodded, looking pleased. He could tell she was tired, but she looked heavenly, too, as though she had just come back from a visit to the other side. He kissed her, and then hugged her again.

Another nurse talked to Emily about what had to be done next, and Gene realized that some of the worst wasn't over. He didn't want to be there when they sewed her up, and so he walked to where the nurse was cleaning the baby. He watched, wondered at the detail of a newborn. Everything was there, in miniature, even tiny fingernails and toenails. He had seen new babies before, or at least he thought he had, but he was amazed to watch that lump that had been in Emily's middle turn into a person.

When the nurse was finished, she wrapped the baby tightly in a blanket, and then she handed him to Gene. Daniel's face was serene now, and Gene watched him for a time, but then the baby's eyelids raised, and Gene saw dark eyes looking back at him. He wasn't prepared for the reaction he felt—so suddenly. He loved this little boy, and the love had come instantly. He had known that a baby would change his life. What he hadn't known was that he would feel so transformed—a new person, immediately. "My son," he said, and he began to sob.

❧

Gene stayed at the hospital and sat next to Emily that first night—with the plan that he would study. But he couldn't concentrate on his books. He fell asleep eventually, but even if he hadn't, he doubted he would have prepared any better. Still, he crammed from about seven until nine, and then he took his first final and didn't do very well. He would pass the test; he wasn't worried about that. But Gene didn't like to do things half-baked. He wanted an A on every test he ever took. Fortunately, he had only one test that first day, but he had two coming up the following day, and he vowed to be ready. But he stayed much too long at the hospital that afternoon, and then, when he went home to study, he couldn't stand being away. He ended up running back to see Emily and to gaze at his boy. He couldn't get enough of that. Every move of the baby's face seemed important in some way he couldn't comprehend. This was a living person, moving his arms, opening and closing his fists, occasionally opening his eyes. His first yawn was almost more than Gene could believe. How did he know how to do that? Gene could tell the boy was smart—and *much* better looking than most newborns. There was no question in his mind that Daniel was going to achieve something wonderful in his life.

Gene got through finals, somehow, and then told himself it didn't matter whether his GPA dropped just a little this final term. What was on his mind was something much more important. His graduation ceremony wasn't until June, but when he didn't register for classes spring quarter, his draft board would get notice. That meant his student deferment was gone. He didn't know how long before he would be drafted, but he knew the notice would be coming, and he would have to leave this little boy behind. The government had announced that a lottery system would be instituted next year, but that didn't help him now. He had known all this for a long time, of course, and yet it seemed now that he had never known it.

On the first day the baby came home, Gene changed a really disgusting diaper, but he was proud of himself that he could do it. He wanted this; he wanted to be involved. He wanted to be close to his son, always. In only a week Daniel grew, changed immensely. How could Gene leave and miss *years* of his life?

Gene had always supported the war, but he was having his doubts now. There seemed no end to it, and no clear objective. Nixon had promised a secret plan to bring the troops home, but the secret seemed the same old thing: more bombs that didn't change anything. Gene knew he would be fighting a war that his country had already given up on. Ho Chi Minh was not going to bargain for peace; he didn't have to. America was wearing out, and North Vietnam had millions of young men they could keep infiltrating to the south, young men who served willingly, fanatically. They died by the hundreds of thousands, and still, they never stopped coming. So how could a war like that end? All the talk was of gradually turning the fighting over to the South, with the first withdrawal of 25,000 troops in June, but there seemed so little will in the South Vietnamese, and the corruption in the government was shocking to read about.

Buddhist monks in the south were pouring gasoline over themselves, lighting themselves on fire, in a cry for peace, and most of the world blamed America for the war, not the Communists. Everything seemed turned on its head. Hadn't the U.S. gotten involved as a self-sacrifice? Wasn't the U.S. there to help the country avoid the horrors of Communism? Why was it the South Vietnamese didn't seem to be as worried about that as we were?

Gene had been telling himself for such a long time that he wasn't trying to avoid the war. He was merely getting his education first. But the truth was, he had always hoped the war would end before he graduated. Now he had to face reality.

Daniel filled up both Gene's and Emily's lives. Gene wasn't quite as quick as Emily to jump out of bed when the baby cried at night, but when he heard her get up, he usually got up too, and he and Emily both worried about everything they were doing. Emily's mom had stayed with them for a week, and then Anna had flown out and helped for another week. But now, Mom had returned to Virginia, and Gene and Emily were on their own. Emily was tired but doing all right, and Gene was working full-time at the dealership but running home for a while in the afternoon so Emily could get a nap. All that was working okay, but he kept asking himself how she could handle things all by herself.

Gene hadn't begun to look for a long-term job, what with the draft hanging over his head. Uncle Wally had talked to him about taking a permanent role in the family businesses. Wally had said he could begin at the parts plant and learn the ropes for a while, and perhaps take that operation over at some point. Gene wasn't excited about the prospect, and he wondered whether any of his cousins might not want the opportunity, so he decided to stick with the dealership for the present and then think about the parts plant when he got out of the army.

Waiting for induction was nightmarish, however, and Gene found himself a little more anxious each day. One night, about a month after the baby was born, Emily had gotten out of bed to nurse him, but when she put him down, Daniel had begun to cry. Gene got up and asked what was happening. "Try to burp him. I couldn't get anything up, and you always know how."

"I usually get about a half-pint of puke up. That's what I get."

"Maybe you pound him too hard."

Gene thought that might be true. But he took the baby from Emily now, held him high on his shoulder, and began to pat him. The baby grunted each time, as though the pats were still a little hard, but at least he stopped crying.

"Emily," Gene said. "I'm thinking I'll go down to the draft board tomorrow and just ask them what's going on."

"I wouldn't. All you'll do is force them to make a decision about your status. Maybe you'll slip through the cracks if you don't say anything."

"I can't deal with things that way." He was swaying back and forth, patting steadily, even jiggling up and down, but nothing was happening.

"Maybe they'll give you a father's deferment now."

"They're not supposed to. The new law is, you can't switch from a student deferment to a 4-A."

"I know that. But what if they have plenty of single guys? Why would they want to pull in fathers if they don't have to?"

"In Utah, there are a lot of other guys just like me, Em. We go on missions and go to college, and that gives us deferments for six years, at least. When we finally get out of college, I'm sure they're waiting for us."

"Gene, you can't go now. You know that, don't you?"

What could he say to that? He knew what she meant, but he also knew he wouldn't have a choice. So he didn't answer. What he did get, however, was a resounding burp from the baby. After that, he gave Daniel a pacifier, then held him in his arms and rocked him. The baby was soon breathing steadily, but Gene kept rocking, thinking. Was there anything he could do at this point? He wondered whether he could ask his father to help in some way, but he felt guilty even considering the idea. Why shouldn't a congressman's son have to play by the same rules everyone else did?

"I just want to know what's going to happen," he told Emily.

"Gene, don't go ask them. Please don't."

"But that doesn't make any sense, Em. They're going to do whatever they want to do. I need to have some idea what I can expect."

"Don't talk to me about *making sense*. If anyone had any sense, we wouldn't be sending young fathers to the other side of the world to solve some problem we don't even understand. The only reason anyone can give me for staying in Vietnam now is that we went there in the first place. That kind of thinking is *full* of sense. *Nonsense.*"

"Not really," Gene whispered, not wanting to startle the baby with his voice. "We made a commitment. And just because we don't like the price of that commitment, that doesn't mean that we break it."

"Come on, Gene. All you're saying is that we're killing and getting killed for no reason, and we have to keep it up because it's such an honorable thing to do. I'm with Kathy. We should have elected Eugene McCarthy. He would have had us out of there by now."

"Maybe. Maybe not. He kept talking about a peace treaty and a coalition government in the south. But the south won't accept that, and the Communists won't negotiate. And you know what will happen if we just pull out. First there will be a bloodbath in South Vietnam, and then the Communists will overrun Laos and Cambodia."

"You still want to be a hero, Gene. I know you do. It's one more item on your list of things to do before you can tell yourself you're as good as your dad. Sports star. Student body president. 'A' student in college. War hero."

"Emily, that's not true." She was sitting in a chair by the baby's crib. Gene walked over and put the baby down, and then Emily got up and covered him. They waited for a moment to see whether he would stay asleep. Gene listened to the whisper of his breath for a time, and then he turned to Emily and took her in his arms. "I did have a list once. And one of the items on it was to be the AP while I was on my mission. When it didn't come, I learned a lot about myself. And the main thing was, I'm not much of a leader. I'm not my dad, and I never will be. But I can live with that."

"You don't know anything about yourself, Gene." She pulled herself away from him and walked around the bed to her side. "I listen to the things people say to you. They *expect* you to be like him. They think that you *are* like him. You deny it. You tell people what you just told me, that you can't live up to him and don't want to, but it hurts you to say it, and it hurts you even more to think it."

"Emily, I don't want to go into the army. I don't want to go to Vietnam. And if I do go, I assure you I won't try to be a hero. But I see no way out of this."

"Don't tell me. Tell Danny. Can't you at least call your dad and see what he could do? He probably knows someone on the draft board."

"Emily, there are a lot of things I *could* do. I could, for example, hold up a bank so we could provide for the baby a little more nicely. But you'd say that was wrong. Well, to me, it's just as wrong to sneak out of serving in the army and to let other guys do it."

"I know that speech, Gene. I've heard it before. I'll have your father give it one last time at your funeral."

"Come on, Emily. Don't be so dramatic. Chances are, even if I go into the army, I won't actually see action. It's a fairly small percentage who go over there and end up on the front lines."

"Not if you're drafted. Not if you go into the infantry."

"They might give me a specialty—you know, ordering and shipping and stuff. I'm a business major; they might want to use some of the things I've been learning."

"So that's it. You're going in?"

"No. I'm not *going* in. I'm being drafted."

Emily didn't respond, but he could see her well enough to watch her curl up on the bed without pulling up the covers. And he could hear her begin to cry. He walked around the bed and tucked her in. Then he sat down by her and ran his hand over her hair. "I can't help it, Em," he whispered, but she didn't respond. She cried for a long time, and when she finally stopped, he could hear her begin to breathe steadily, the way the baby had done.

Gene kissed her hair, and then he walked back to the crib. He stood where he could hear both Emily and Daniel breathe—in slightly different rhythms. The whole world seemed only those two, only their breathing, and he couldn't imagine a world of men, in a barracks or a jungle in Vietnam. He told himself that some things were so terrible they just couldn't happen. In the morning, at the draft board, some secretary would look at him and say, "Actually, we re-classified you with a father's deferment. Congratulations on your new baby."

He could see the woman in his mind and hear her voice, and the little vision seemed plausible for the moment. Maybe God was telling him that he was released from this obligation, that this cup would pass, and he could stay with his family.

But in the morning, he went to the Selective Service Office, and that was not the news he got. So he made a decision, and then he came home before he went to work. Emily was sitting on the couch, holding the baby. "He cries every time I put him down," she said. "He wants me to hold him all the time."

Gene sat down next to her. "He's just like me," he said, and he tried to smile.

"I don't know how to do this, Gene. I thought I would be a good mother, but I feel like I'm doing everything wrong."

Emily had been talking this way for a couple of weeks. Gene's mom had told him about the "postpartum blues," one more female mystery to

Gene. He wondered now whether he shouldn't have put his decision off a little. "You're a wonderful mother, Emily. I'm amazed at all the stuff you know how to do."

"What did they tell you, Gene?"

"Well, it's not good. They told me I would definitely be drafted but that it might be two or three months before it happened. I thought about that, and I just couldn't see what good it would do to sit around and wait. The thing I want to do is get it over with."

"What are you talking about? What did you do?"

"I asked them to move me up on their list and send out my notice as soon as possible."

"Gene, no. You can't be serious."

"Honey, I did. I think it's best. I might as well get out of here, so I can start the clock running. If I have to be away from you and Danny, I'd rather do it now, at a time he won't remember."

"And what am I supposed to do?"

"I'll still have a little time, a couple of weeks or so."

She was staring at him, the color all gone from her face. "Why didn't you go into the Navy? That's safer. Don't go into the *infantry*."

"Honey, if I go into one of the other services, I have to stay in longer. And with officer's training, it's the same thing—three years. This way, in two years it will all be over with. After basic training maybe you can be with me for a while. And if I don't get shipped to Vietnam, we might be able to be together most of the time."

"Why didn't you come home and talk to me first? Didn't you want my opinion?"

Gene knew this question would be coming. "Emily, there's nothing more to say. We've talked about this over and over. I can't avoid it, so I might as well get going now."

"When I dropped out of school, you gave me a big speech about how we had to talk everything over. But I guess that only applies to me."

Gene didn't know how to answer that. He leaned forward, put his elbows on his knees, and looked at the floor.

She didn't say anything, but he could feel that she was looking at him. Finally, he looked back at her. She stared into his eyes for a few seconds, and then tears began to drip onto her cheeks. She bent forward and held the baby closer.

"I'm sorry," was all that Gene could think to say.

# CHAPTER 20

For three months Hans had seen no one except for the men who delivered his meals. In some ways the days were less difficult now. Time moved slowly when he expected something to happen, when he hoped for some change. But now, as day after day had passed and he hadn't heard from Felscher, his senses seemed to dull. It was May now, 1969, and the last time Hans had seen Felscher, the man had claimed that an arrangement might be possible, that Hans might be allowed to leave the country. But nothing had come of that. Perhaps that had only been a ploy to get Hans to say that he *wanted* to leave. Felscher could use that as one more piece of evidence that Hans was a dissident. For a few days back in February, Hans had tried to think what he might do if the opportunity came, but since then he had put it down as another false hope.

Hans kept up his exercise as best he could, and he ate the food no matter how much he hated it. He also tried his best to recall scriptures he liked and the sermons he had composed, but his mind was losing its sharpness. He prayed more, but he didn't ask for much. Mostly, he asked for strength to keep surviving, and blessings for his family. He didn't ask to be released from prison and didn't ask for happiness. He liked to think he was passing through a kind of cleansing process, something like sanctification, and it would end only when the Lord knew he had learned what he was supposed to learn. The only problem was, as much as he wanted to believe that he was growing, Hans wouldn't be able to measure his progress until his life involved choices.

At times he experienced insights or moments of intense spirituality, as though he were being lifted outside himself, able to see beyond common realities to the larger meaning of existence. But there were also days when his lethargy deepened, and he couldn't concentrate. He would sleep most of the day, seated on his stool, draped over his little table. But then he wouldn't sleep well at night. Odd dreams would plague him, and night fears. It was as though Satan himself joined him in the room and tried to pull him away from the spirit and resolve he felt when he was at his best.

Then one morning, after breakfast, the cell block doors opened, and one of the guards walked to his cell. "Letters," he said, and he pushed them through the slot in the door and walked away. Hans hadn't had a letter from his parents since they had visited him in February. He was startled by the joy he felt, by the vitality that came back to him. He sat on his stool and looked at the envelopes. Two were from his parents, and one was from Elli. The postmark on Elli's letter showed that she had written it before Christmas, more than six months ago. He wanted to be angry that prison officials would play such games with him, but he was accustomed to it now and didn't really expect anything else. What he didn't understand was why some letters reached him, even if very late, and others never did. His family had also sent packages—which they had mentioned in letters—but he had never received one. Was all this merely to harass him, to demonstrate the power the system could wield? He wondered why *these* letters had come. And why now?

He opened the first of the letters from his parents, written just after their visit. It contained two fairly short notes, one from his mother and one from his father. One small section of his father's had been cut away, apparently with a razor blade, but most of the letter was intact. There was little news but much love. Mama and Papa both spoke of their joy in seeing him, of their hope for his future. The second letter was more recent, and it did have a bit of news from the branch at home. Mostly, Hans savored the sight of their handwriting, the tone of what they said to him. He felt how much they loved and missed him. They tried to encourage him, even though they had no idea what his true tests were. All of it helped; all of it provided him with a taste of life outside this cell. Sometimes, in this enclosure, he began to wonder whether life continued as he remembered it, whether people got up in the morning and ate a nice breakfast, whether they walked outside into the air, heard the sounds of life, rode a streetcar to work and listened to the clacking and the screech of the wheels against the tracks. He sometimes tried to imagine all those things, all the little parts of life that had seemed so ordinary when they occurred every day, and yet were so distant here in this prison.

He read the letters over again, holding them at an angle that picked up light from the muted window glass. Then he took Elli's letter out. Nothing was censored, but there was little she could say that would need to be kept from him. The letter read:

> Dear Hans:
>
> I hope you will forgive me for not writing more often, but I am never sure whether you receive my letters. I got a letter from you a long time ago, but none since, so I'm not certain that you want to hear from me, or whether you want to write. I do want to wish you much happiness for Christmas, and yet I know, these cannot be the best of days for you. Perhaps to think of Christ is a help, however. Perhaps, for now, it is the one thing that might give you hope. Christ's love has become, for me, my greatest joy in life.
>
> You will be interested to know that your friend still visits us often. I will soon be eighteen, and he admits to me that he likes to think of our having a future together. He is almost finished with his university training, and before too much longer, he may be in a position to marry. I am too young for that, and I can tell you, I'm not entirely certain how I feel about him. He's a good friend, and he makes me laugh, but I'm not sure how serious he is about the things that matter most to me. He

takes part now, and he told me about the day you and he talked about his grandmother, and how much he would like to believe that he will see her again. But I wonder whether he could ever commit to things that are so foreign to him. What I fear is that he's mostly interested in me, and not so much in the things I care about.

Hans, I wonder what you think about all this. Do you have any advice for me? Is there anything you would like to say to me about the future? I know how you thought when you were here, and I always regret that I was so young and silly then. I do hope that I will know you again someday, and then, maybe you will have a better opinion of me.

I feel satisfied with my work position at this point. I like the people in the office, and I have learned a good deal. But I think you know, my goal is to have a family and raise children who care about things that are truly important. I'm not so brilliant as you and your friend, and never hoped to study at a university, but I do have many things that interest me, and I want to share them with my children. So I hope to find someone who wants the same things.

She spoke then of things in Magdeburg, the weather in December, the news of some of the members, but nothing else that was personal. Still, Hans had understood what she was trying to say so very carefully. She clearly didn't want to mention the Church directly, but he was happy that she hadn't hesitated to mention her love of Jesus Christ. She was growing up, he could tell, and perhaps, if Rainer was serious, maybe he would join the Church and give her what she wanted. But Hans doubted that, and as he read the letter a second time, he was even more certain that she wanted Hans to return and show some interest in her. She didn't have a lot of options to find a husband in the Church, and clearly she saw

Hans as a possibility. She still cared for him—he could see that in her choice of words—and yet, she seemed afraid to say too much. After all, he had shown no interest in her when he had lived in Magdeburg.

Hans also wondered about Rainer. If he had been the one who had reported on Hans, what had been his motivation? Had he intended to get Hans put away so he could have his chance with Elli? And now, was he only feigning interest in the Church? Or was Felscher's scenario the correct one? Maybe Rainer hadn't reported on Hans at first but had only done so after being pressured by the Stasi. Perhaps, to prove himself to the Stasi, he was watching the Church and reporting back to agents, and it was Elli he had no genuine interest in.

But Hans didn't believe that. He believed that Rainer was his friend, and the Stasi had asked Felscher to induce Hans into giving testimony against Rainer. They needed information against Rainer only if Rainer was denying that Hans had said anything. So what was he supposed to wish for? That Rainer was his friend but that Elli didn't love him? That she would wait for Hans? It was difficult not to wish for that. She was a pretty girl, probably turning into a beautiful woman like her mother, and she was good. She cared about the right things. If he could leave the prison and get some decent work, maybe they could make a life together. But how much did she care about Rainer? What would happen if he joined the Church one of these days? Or maybe, by now, he had joined. Maybe they were engaged, or even married.

Still, for an hour or more, Hans let himself imagine the possibilities. He read the letter over and over, and between readings, he pictured a life with her. He saw her at the breakfast table, the way his family had always sat together in the mornings, and he saw her at home, in a little apartment, when he returned from work at night. He remembered those deep dimples he loved so much. He and she could only hope for a simple life, maybe even sparse, but they would sit in church together on Sundays, their little children by their sides, or maybe eventually, he would look down from the stand, the way his father had, and smile at his little family. He remembered the dream that he still felt God had sent to him, and he wondered if it would be possible that he could serve in a branch and bless the Saints with what he had learned in prison. It was all he would ever ask, if he could have that much.

But his fantasy gradually gave way to reality. The fact was, whatever work he received would pay very little, and he would be watched all his life. He would receive no chance for advancement, and his work in the Church would be viewed with further suspicion. If both he and his wife always worked, they would survive, but Rainer could offer her so much more. If he joined the Church and left the Communist Party, he would limit his future, but he wouldn't be a former prisoner and a dissident. He could give Elli a better life. If Hans wrote to her and encouraged her to wait for him, she might be willing to do that, but how could he ask such a thing in good conscience? What would he say? Could he tell her, "I want you to share with me a life of meager living, with little hope for change—both for you and our children"? Maybe he should say, instead, "Rainer is a good man. If he will make the commitment you speak of, he could be a wonderful husband for you. If not, think of attending youth conference again this year. It was at a youth conference that my friend Greta found her husband."

Hans fought against his emotions. He didn't want to feel too much of this. He didn't want to dwell on the loss of Greta. That, too, had been for the best, as it had turned out. He had known for a long time that he might not ever have the chance to marry. It was best to think that way. It was best to expect the worst. He almost wished these letters hadn't come. The numbness he had been feeling was so much easier.

∽✧∽

The following day, a guard came to Hans's cell again. He was carrying clothing with him, the civilian clothing Hans had been wearing the day he entered prison. "Put these on and then follow me," the guard said. Hans was astounded. He had no idea what this meant, but nothing terrified him more than hope, and these clothes tempted him to think that something was about to change. He thought of the letters the day before, and now this. It was almost certainly another way for Felscher to manipulate his feelings, and then to make demands.

But he followed orders and put on the clothes—a shirt and slacks and jacket. They draped over the remains of his body like the clothing on a scarecrow. He followed the man to Felscher's office and then sat in the familiar chair alone. He told himself over and over not to expect anything, but he couldn't sit still. His emotions had returned; his blood was pumping.

"So, my friend," Felscher said when he entered the office, "I have good news for you. It's something I've been working on for some time." He shook Hans's hand and then sat down behind his desk. "I'm sorry I haven't contacted you for such a long time, but it's not good to build up a man's hope and then destroy it."

"No, it isn't," Hans said.

Felscher laughed at the sarcasm. "It's what you think I'm doing now. But I'm not." He smiled and leaned back in his chair. "Hans, I like you. And I no longer believe that you have any information to give me. It took me a long time to come to that conclusion. I'm not certain that you told everything you knew about Rainer Kuntze, but that isn't so important. I suppose I respect you for holding to your principles."

This was a game. Hans was being set up again. He said nothing and waited for the next step in the logic.

"You'll be walking outside in a few minutes, so shade your eyes as you go out. You aren't used to bright sunlight." Felscher grinned, stretching his thick lips much wider than usual.

Hans almost asked where he was going, but he told himself not to play into the man's hands.

"You'll be driven to a jail on Magdalene Street, and there you will meet with a man named Wolfgang Vogel. Perhaps you have heard of him?"

"No."

"He's an attorney. He works with representatives from the West. I'll only tell you that for now. He'll explain the rest."

Hans took a breath, but he didn't nod, didn't speak.

"This is a great opportunity for you, Hans. Don't turn it down."

Felscher stood up, and Hans took that as a signal that he should stand too, but he was even more certain now that he was being played for a fool. He would be offered things, maybe even the chance to leave the country, but only if he provided information. The promises could also be a lie. The talk of people getting out, taken to the West—all the things Felscher had told him the last time they had met—were probably a planned part of the deceit. The whole idea had been to plant hope, dangle it before him while he waited for months to think about it, and then to expect cooperation. But it didn't mean that Felscher would keep his end of the bargain. It all came down to the same old impasse. Hans didn't know anything about the others involved in the escape plot, and he wasn't going to report on Rainer.

But Hans's hands were twitching, and he felt a new liveliness in his body. Felscher took him out to the guard, and the guard walked him outside. "Good luck," Felscher told him quietly, and he shook his hand.

Hans's reaction was surprising. He almost believed the man in spite of what he kept telling himself. "Thank you," he said as he turned away.

It was summer now, early June, and warm. Felscher was right; the sun did hurt his eyes. He squinted and looked down, let his eyes adjust for a few seconds, and then he shaded them as he looked around. He heard the noise of the city: traffic, voices. The smell of a linden tree nearby was overpowering, as though sap were dripping from the branches. The sound of a bee, as it whizzed past him, was almost shocking. Somewhere in the distance, he heard that streetcar he had imagined, rattling, screeching. If nothing else good happened today, at least he had these things to remember.

A Barkass van pulled up, and the guard motioned for Hans to get in. What surprised him was that he was allowed to sit on a bench in the back, not in an enclosure. The route of travel took him deeper into the city. Hans saw a thousand things he had almost forgotten. He watched men at a construction site, working in the sun, sweating, calling back and forth to each other. The scene was all so full of life that it made Hans wonder how such things could ever have seemed ordinary to him. He saw children at a school, out playing on a slab of concrete. Some of the boys were kicking a soccer ball. He saw a boy of twelve or so, in his school uniform, receive a pass, cradle it against his instep, and then dribble forward. He faked a pass, then drove hard past another boy, leaving him standing. It was a fine piece of work, something else to savor. Farther down the street, he saw an older man sweeping the gutter. The man stopped to rest but couldn't stand quite straight. He took off his battered cap, then wiped his forehead with his sleeve. Hans told himself that this might be the sort of work he would do someday, but after these months in jail he would always remind himself to take joy in being outside with the noise and heat, and with other people.

When the van reached the jail, Hans was led inside, and again he was directed to an office where he sat alone for a time. He had had his ride, and maybe he would be taking one back, or maybe he would be kept here for a time. Whatever happened, he told himself not to break, not to be manipulated, and to be thankful for what he had already seen and heard today.

The man who entered the office looked to be in his forties. He was rather stout, balding, and wore dark, plastic-framed glasses. "*Guten Tag*, Stoltz," he said. "Have you been told what's happening?"

"No."

"There are Westerners willing to pay the GDR a fee for the release of political prisoners. Perhaps you have heard of this."

"Yes."

"In your case, an American congressman—your uncle, I understand—has worked through certain religious groups in West Germany. He's negotiated for your release and has paid the price. In a little while—" he looked at his watch "—I will drive you to a checkpoint here in Berlin, and the guards will step aside and let us cross into West Germany. Officials from their government—and from the American consulate—will take care of you from there. Tomorrow morning, I think it is, you will be flown to New York, and from there to Salt Lake City. Your uncle and aunt will sponsor you, and you will have work with the congressman's brother. You will have the opportunity to become a naturalized citizen." He hesitated, smiled, and then asked, "So what do you think of this?"

Hans could feel his heart drumming in his ears, but he was frightened. "What do I have to say?" he asked.

"Nothing. No more interrogations. You are in my hands now, and we will wait here until we receive word from the guards at the checkpoint, and then we will get in my car and drive you away from all you've been going through."

Hans tried to think. Was all this as simple as Vogel was making it sound? Wasn't it too good to be true?

"I know you don't trust me or anyone else right now. I've learned that about the prisoners I work with. But I assure you that what I have told you is the entire story. There's nothing more to it. You are being released from prison, and by tomorrow night you will be in America, starting a new life."

It was what Hans had once dreamed of. Everything sounded exciting—but frightening too.

"So what do you say? If you agree to leave under these conditions, I need to have you sign some papers."

Hans almost said yes, but he was hesitating, and he wasn't sure why. He needed to think. "Could you give me a minute?" he asked. "I wasn't ready for this."

"Certainly. In fact, I need to leave you here for an hour or so while I take care of some details. So sit here and think it all over. But no one has ever turned me down." Vogel smiled, creasing his rounded cheeks. "Just ask yourself, do you want freedom or do you want to go back to prison? It's not such a difficult question." And then he left.

Hans tried to think what he was scared of. He was almost certain this was real. Vogel seemed to know what he was talking about. And the part about his uncle being a congressman was a convincing detail. Maybe it was the idea of so much change that was unnerving. He would have to learn English, to live in a world he didn't know. But he would have a job. And once his English was better, he could go to a university. There weren't any restrictions about that in America. And there were Mormons everywhere in Salt Lake City. He could find a wife, raise a family, live better than he ever could here.

But he knew the other reality. "I'll never see my family again," he said out loud.

That was the problem, the fear that was running through him. He could probably give up everything else easily enough. He didn't need the *Stasi* looking over his shoulder the rest of his life, and he didn't need all the prejudice against his religious beliefs. He loved Schwerin, the lake and the mountains and all the beauty of the place, but he didn't love the GDR. Still, how could he leave and know every day of his life that his parents and Inga were here, living with all the difficulties he had run from? He had told himself when he was young that every child left home sooner or later, that he could stay in touch. His father had left his own parents in America and come back here to marry his mother. Papa had managed the break.

But his father hadn't known it was forever, and he had been returning home, to all he knew. This was all the other way around. How could Hans know whether he would like a new country?

Another thought kept bubbling up, pressing to be noticed. What about Elli? Should he consider her as a factor in all this? He didn't think so. If he stayed, he couldn't have her, so why not leave and simplify her decision? But she had been in his mind so much these past twenty-four hours, and try as he might, he couldn't help thinking that somehow he and she could figure something out. He knew he shouldn't ask her to sacrifice so much, but she seemed interested, and maybe she understood what the dangers were.

All the same, it would be a huge mistake to let Elli be the deciding factor. This was a great opportunity. Any fool could see that. But an image from the night before, and from his dream, did strike him. It was the picture of himself sitting in church, looking down at his little family, knowing that he was serving and raising up believing children, here in the GDR. Who needed him in Salt Lake City? Would the Church do all right without him there? And what about the Church here? Could he make a difference? Maybe he could.

It was such a jumble. He changed his mind, over and over. As soon as he would decide one way, he would regret the loss. No matter what he did, he might be sorry forever. At one point he decided firmly that he would stay and remain with his family. But then he thought of Vogel's words. Did he want to leave for America, or did he want to go back to prison? The thought of returning to his cell now, after this chance to leave, was too much for him. He couldn't do that. He had to sign these papers. He had to choose freedom. Who wouldn't choose freedom over more months in prison and a lifetime of oppression? He didn't sign the papers, but he had his answer. His parents would understand his leaving. They might even be relieved to know he had a better future. They would miss him, but they would take joy in the successes he could relate in his letters. And maybe someday things would change in the GDR, and there would be opportunities for someone like him to visit. Maybe foreign travel would be allowed for citizens of East Germany, and he could pay to fly them to America. Later in their lives, they might want to emigrate; the government didn't mind getting rid of pensioners.

Hans prayed. He explained to the Lord what he had decided and detailed all his reasons. And as he did, each point seemed justifiable, right. He was sure he had his answer. But in the end, he told the Lord, "If I'm not supposed to go, tell me. Please tell me now."

He sat and listened, but he felt nothing. He decided to rely on the rightness he had felt as he prayed.

When Vogel returned, he asked, "So, did you sign the papers?"

"No. Not yet. But I will. I want to go."

"Go ahead, then. Sign in the places I've marked. You have to agree not to return, and not to oppose the GDR or speak out against it in any way."

"That's all right. I wouldn't want to do that."

"Good. Then sign at each mark." Vogel handed him a pen.

Hans pulled the papers closer and held the pen ready, but then he heard a voice. It was only himself, his own words inside his head, but they came without warning, and they were clear and firm: "No, Hans. They need you."

He didn't understand his own words, his own thought—or whether the thought had come from outside himself. Who was "they"? His parents? The Church? But it was only a thought, not something to base his decision on. So he set the pen to the paper. But he heard it again. "They need you."

He pushed the papers back. "I can't do it," he said. "Someone here needs me."

"Who needs you?"

"I'm not certain."

"Excuse me?"

"I can't explain it to you *Herr* Vogel, but I can't go."

"You *want* to go back to Hohenschönhausen?"

"No." The image of the cell came to mind again, and the churning in his head started all over.

"Don't be rash, Hans. Think very carefully. If you turn this opportunity down, I can't guarantee that I can put this agreement back together again later. I could always try, but one never knows about these things."

Hans was tempted to ask for another hour to think, but he knew better than to rely on logic. The voice in his head had been more than an impulse. He had asked the Lord to tell him if he shouldn't go—and the words had come on their own. He would go back to the prison, and he would make the best of things. It was what God apparently wanted him to do.

But it would be easier if he were absolutely certain. If only the voice had come from outside himself, had burst through the ceiling, not merely sounded inside his head. What if he regretted this later? In fact, he was almost sure he would regret it the moment his cell door closed. But he didn't know any other way to decide.

The ride back to the prison was unthinkably painful—worse than his first entrance into the prison system. He tried to look at the world, take something of it back with him to his cell, but he wasn't seeing with the same eyes now.

At the prison, the guard took him to Felscher's office, not to his cell, and there, Felscher was waiting. "What are you thinking, Hans?" he asked. "Vogel just telephoned me. He said it's not too late. He can still get you out this afternoon. You must go with him."

Hans shook his head.

"But why?"

"I can't leave my family," he said, even though he wasn't entirely sure that was the reason.

"Do you have any idea what your life is going to be like once you get out of prison?"

"I think I do."

"I doubt it. You're not a person anymore. You are an enemy of the state, and you always will be."

"I'm *not* an enemy. You know that."

"It's a category, Hans, not a reality. You will be treated in certain ways because you have a label. Don't try to deceive yourself. You won't receive forgiveness. No matter how long you show your loyalty, you will never be trusted."

"I have to stay."

"I'll let you telephone your parents. You can talk to them and receive their blessing."

"No. They'll tell me to go. I know that. But I can't."

"But you said you were staying for your parents."

Hans didn't know what else to say, and so he told the truth. "I prayed. And I believe that God answered my prayer. He wants me to stay here."

Felscher stared at Hans, his eyes wide, his mouth open. And then he cursed. "You fool," he said. "You're an intelligent young man, but your mind is warped by all this religious fervor you've been taught."

"No. When I receive an answer, I have to listen."

"Don't tell me that. Tell me that you love your country, and because of that you want to stay. I'll put that in your report, and then I'll try to help you. I can't do much, but it's far better for you that way. If I say you claim to hear the voice of God, this will be something government officials will ridicule, and the *Stasi* will hold it against you."

"I can't help that."

"Fine. I can't help you if you won't help yourself. Go to your cell and sit there for another year and a half. Have a good time."

Hans stood and Felscher opened the door. Then Hans followed the guard to the cell. The sound of the door closing was like a blow to the back of his head, and the dim little room felt like a grave. He looked around at the ugly walls, the toilet in the corner, the bunk on the wall. He had tried to prepare himself for this moment all the way from Magdelene Street, but the reality was worse than he had imagined. What if the voice he had heard was nothing—maybe a whim, an instinctive reaction to his fears?

Hans needed to know. He knelt and asked to hear the voice again, or at least to receive a confirmation in his mind or his chest that he had done the right thing. Somewhere in the cell block he could hear water dripping. But he heard nothing else.

# CHAPTER 21

"Get off the bus, you *maggots!*" Gene couldn't help smiling. He had heard about this stuff from guys who had already been through basic training. Two muscular soldiers in khaki shirts and buzz-cut hair were working their way up the aisle of the bus, which was full of new recruits, and they were screaming as if they were deranged. "Get it going, maggots. Get it going." When the recruits didn't move fast enough for them, they started grabbing them, pulling them out of their seats and then pushing them toward the door.

Gene waited his turn, and then he hurried off the bus, where several more drill instructors were waiting. "Fall in, you maggots," they were shouting. "Line up right here. Come to attention."

A friend of Gene's had taught him the correct "attention" position. He snapped to, with his chest thrust forward, stomach in, chin back, arms bent just a little, his thumb and index finger touching. He figured he would impress these trainers and not have to take a lot of guff. What surprised him was how cool the air was. It was early evening now, in May, and the air at Fort Ord, California, was coming off the ocean. The damp wind cut through his jacket. He was amazed that all these drill sergeants were out here in short sleeves, seeming not to notice the cold.

The drill sergeants were running back and forth screaming into the faces of the recruits, telling them what a waste of government money they were, how stupid they were, what *maggots* they were. And always with the worst kind of profanity, even vulgarity. Gene's friends had told him not to let that stuff bother him, just to act as though he didn't hear it.

It took a remarkably long time to get thirty guys lined up in formation and standing at attention correctly. By the time that happened, Gene was shivering from the cold, and he hoped he could get to his barracks as soon as possible. "What do you mean showing up here looking like that?" a tall drill instructor shouted at a young guy next to Gene. Most of these kids were eighteen. Some had signed up because they were about to be drafted anyway, but a lot of them were draftees, and they looked like most young guys: long hair, mustaches, long sideburns. About a third of the recruits were black, and most of them were wearing "Afros"—big globes of "natural" hair. Some of the men had on bell-bottoms and wild, psychedelic shirts—stuff that Gene knew these DIs, as they were called, would absolutely hate. Gene was wearing some fairly new Levi's and a button-down-collar shirt, and he had already had his hair trimmed quite short, since he knew it would be shaved off before long anyway.

"Did you hear me? I asked you a question? What kind of a *girl* are you? What's that hair doing all down your back? What kind of *fancy pants* you got on, boy? This is a *man's* army. Don't you know that?"

"Yes, sir."

Suddenly the DI's nose was not an inch from the recruit's face. "What do you think you're doing?" he bellowed. "I told you, absolutely no talking when you're at attention. And don't you call me 'sir,' maggot. I ain't no officer."

"Yes, sir. Or—"

Suddenly two more DIs were on the guy, all three screaming at the same time. "No talking. Absolutely no talking. Can't you hear good? Don't you listen to orders, you piece of scum?"

This time the kid knew enough not to answer. But Gene was having a hard time not laughing. It was all such a setup: ask a guy a question and then yell at him for answering. It was just the kind of stuff he had been warned to expect.

"Hey, cutie pie, what are you smiling about?"

And now the DIs moved to Gene. They crowded around him from three sides and began to look him over. Gene didn't move. "Look at this worm," one of them said. "What kind of a pretty boy have we got here?"

"Look at that *golden* hair and them *big blue* eyes. We got us a *ladies' man* here—every girl's dream boat. And he knows it, too. Check out that cocky look on his face."

"We're going to wipe that look away."

"That's right." One of the men cursed, then used a coarse term to suggest that Gene was homosexual. "This maggot is *ours*. We're going to make a man out of this sweet little thing."

"Get down, right now. I want to see twenty-five push-ups."

Gene dropped immediately, but when he did, he caught a barrage of abuse. "Hey, Goldilocks, you're at attention. What do you think you're doing? Stand up."

Gene jumped back up.

"All right, now. Hit it for twenty-five."

Gene hesitated, not sure what to do. "Drill Sergeant, may I have permission to do twenty-five push-ups?" he finally asked.

"Shut up, maggot. Now you're *talking* in the ranks. You're going on report. You're first up for KP duty, Little Miss Button-down. You're in a heap of trouble, and you just got off the bus."

But another DI was screaming, "At ease, scum. Now let's see those push-ups."

Gene assumed the at-ease position, with his hands behind his back. Then he dropped to the ground. He was ready for these guys. He had had his draft notice for three weeks, and he had spent every day running and working out. He knew that boot camp was tough, and he didn't want to come in weak and out of shape. He did the push-ups with a straight back, and he took them all the way down. He pumped them out fast, too—twenty-five without a moment's hesitation, and then he popped back to his feet and stood at attention.

"Oh, what have we got here?" one of the sergeants said. "Goldilocks thinks she's a atha-lete. We'll find out about that, won't we?" The others poured it on, continued to call him names, some more vulgar than others, and all of them were shouting, "I want this guy. He's mine."

But Gene was satisfied. He had taken their abuse, which he knew was coming sooner or later, and he surely must have impressed them with those push-ups. The other recruits may have been younger than he was, but most of them smoked, and very few of them looked as if they had played sports. He figured he'd do well in boot camp and impress these instructors, whether they ever admitted it or not.

What followed was even more demeaning. After the recruits listened to a harangue about their worthlessness, and about the demands and expectations during training, they were told to turn over all their civilian possessions. They had to strip naked, and their clothes, wallets, pictures—everything but eyeglasses—were bagged up and taken away. Then they were led into an old building where they were required to take an antiseptic shower that was supposed to rid them of parasites. The rest of the evening was spent standing in one line after another as they were handed their government-issue fatigues, boots, and equipment. None of the clothing seemed to fit, but it was easier for the men to accept what they were given than go back in line for another size. When they were finally dressed, and getting very tired, they were told to strip again for a search, "just to make sure you maggots haven't brought any dope in with you." There was no logic to the procedure, of course, and Gene was already growing tired of it. The thought of being treated this way for eight weeks was depressing.

Eventually, the recruits were ushered into barracks and assigned bunks. Gene could hardly believe the old facilities they were using: World War II barracks with cracks around the windows that let the air blow through. The place had been painted time and again until the paint, in clumps on the window frames, looked half an inch thick. The wooden floors were clean, but they were worn down in the walking areas like the sandstone steps in old castles Gene had seen in Germany. At the foot of each bed was a footlocker, with a wall locker alongside. Gene had heard how orderly he had to be about setting out his possessions and how carefully he would have to make his bed. He had practiced a little at that too, and he figured he could handle it better than some of the sloppy-looking guys who were piling onto their beds now, grumbling and cussing about all they had just been put through.

"Those guys are nuts," the guy in the next bunk was saying. "What do they think they're trying to do?"

Gene had his footlocker open and was trying to decide how to arrange his clothes. The men had been told already that they were not allowed to sleep in anything but their khaki skivvies and undershirt. He wondered whether the thin blanket he had been issued would be warm enough. He looked up at the man who had spoken. He was a black guy who looked a little older than some of the kids—maybe twenty or so. "The whole idea is to take everything away from us, make us feel worthless, and then build us back up. I don't know if I agree with that, but it's what the military has been doing for a long time."

"If one of those guys calls me 'boy' one more time, he may start wishing he was in Nam, facing the enemy. I ain't gonna take that."

"Don't react. It's what they want."

"Maybe so. But some of that stuff is going too far."

Gene stood up. He reached his hand out. "My name's Gene Thomas," he said. He thought about saying he was from Salt Lake, but he hesitated. Most people thought "Mormon" when they thought of Utah, and these days that was awkward when it came to blacks. The fact that the Church didn't give the priesthood to blacks was a big issue. Some of the black student unions on various college campuses had begun to protest their sports teams playing against BYU.

"My name's Willard Biggs. Some people want to call me Willy, but I don't much like that. I'm from L.A. now, but I grew up in South Carolina. Where you from?"

Gene had no choice but to tell him now. "Utah. Salt Lake City."

"You're a college guy, aren't you?"

"I was. I just graduated from the University of Utah."

"I see that ring on your finger too."

"Yeah, I'm married. I have a new little baby boy. He's just over a month old. It was a hard time to leave."

"I know what you mean. I got a couple of years of college behind me too, but I ran out of money and took a semester off. They jumped right on me. I'm not married, but I got me a woman who says she's going to wait for me. I didn't like what those sergeants were saying about our girls already being with someone else tonight. They don't need to talk like that."

"That's just more of the same kind of trash. I've got friends who've been through this, and they say the only way to get by is to let everything run right off your back. The DIs want to see if a recruit can take pressure and not fall apart, so they think up every way they can to make your life miserable. I can tell you one thing right now. It may be close to midnight, but they'll be in here at five—or earlier—yelling and screaming and calling us names again."

"I heard they shave our heads in the morning, and then make us run until we puke our guts up."

"Actually, I don't think that happens for a couple more days. We've got to take all those tests they were talking about, and then they move us into Headquarters Company, wherever that is. At that point, look out."

Willard was a big man—maybe six-two or so and built like a barrel—but there was a gentle quality in his voice and eyes. He didn't seem the sort to be a warrior. He seemed cut out to be a chaplain or maybe a medic. "Are you a Mormon?" he asked.

"Yes."

"Have you been on one of those missions they go on?"

"Yes. I was in Germany."

"You okay about bunking next to me?"

"Sure I am." But Gene stammered. He wasn't sure what to say. "I know what you might have heard. But we're not prejudiced. Or, I mean, maybe some are—like any other white people—but it's not part of our religion, the way some people think."

"I thought it was."

"It's true about blacks not receiving the priesthood, but it's not because we believe . . . I mean, we don't consider blacks inferior or anything like that."

Willard smiled, knowingly, and Gene felt his embarrassment deepen. "We're not inferior, but we can't have your priesthood the same as other men? Do you want to tell me how that works?"

"I don't know exactly. Some say we ought to change it, and maybe we will someday, but we believe God has to make any changes . . . you know, through our prophet."

Willard's smile got bigger. "Well, I'm glad to know it's God's fault and not yours."

Gene had no idea what to say.

"Look, that don't matter to me. I got no plans to be a Mormon preacher anyway. All my life I've seen stuff like that. White people always have some explanation why it's bad for us to drink the same water or sit next to them on a bus. I figure that stuff is going away, a little at a time, and it won't do me any good, personally, to try to fix it myself. The main thing for me is to look a man in the eye, no matter what color he is, and say, 'I'm a man and you're a man.' If that man will look back at me the same way, and we can work alongside each other, then that's all I worry about. You seem like a good man, and I know I am, so let's just leave it like that."

"That's good. I noticed you earlier, and I told myself I wanted to get to know you. I had a feeling I would like you."

"All right. But don't start in on me. I'm not about to join no Mormon Church. A couple of your missionaries knocked on my door one time. I let them in, and then I thought I'd never get them out the door again." He laughed, his voice suddenly louder.

Gene laughed too. "Well, I won't bother you about that—not if you don't want me to."

"Fair enough." They shook hands again.

⌀

The next four days turned out to be full of written tests and vaccinations, and then basic training began for real. The first two or three weeks were vicious for most of the recruits, and they were tough for Gene, too, but not exactly in the same way. He could handle the long forced marches, the double-time runs, and he could do the push-ups. But the abuse he received for doing well was sometimes so constant and intense that it was all he could do not to blow up and knock a drill instructor on his back. Most of the men lost their names in the first few days of training. Everyone got his own nickname from the DIs, and the names were always designed to debase a guy. They called Willard "Shoeshine," and he denounced them every night when he got back to the barracks, but he didn't explode. Gene remained "Goldilocks," even though his hair was gone, or "pretty boy," or "college boy," or some variation on those ideas. But it was his ability to learn what they taught—whether field-stripping a weapon, marksmanship, or map reading—that seemed to bother them most. He picked things up quickly and easily, and apparently that bothered them. They seemed to think he hadn't been brought down as low as they wanted him. A sergeant named Draper was by far the worst. He was a little man with the dark shadow of a beard, even early in the morning. He had learned, somewhere along the way, that Gene was a Mormon, and he didn't like that. He told Gene that his sister had married a Mormon, and he hated the guy. "He thinks he's better than other people—just like you," he told Gene one day. "It's guys like you—guys who think they got everythin' figured out—you the first ones, when a firefight starts, to curl up on the ground and cry fo' your mama."

That's what he told Gene privately. In front of the recruits he didn't say anything about religion, but he never stopped telling Gene he was going to be a coward in battle—although he had more colorful, more obscene ways of expressing his opinion. Gene told himself he didn't care what the guy said, but it wasn't easy to be put down in front of a group of men. The fact was that Gene did wonder sometimes how he would feel if he had to go into the jungles of Vietnam. He had heard stories about snipers and booby traps and the torture that prisoners took. He didn't like to think about any of that, but he also didn't want to believe that he would have any more trouble than these other guys dealing with fear.

It was during his fourth week at Fort Ord that Gene got called before his commanding officer. He was told during a training class to report immediately to the orderly building, which housed the CO's office. Gene had no idea what that was about, but it worried him, so he double-timed to get there. A sergeant told him to sit down, but then, in only a couple of minutes, he was invited in before Captain Pearson. Gene stepped into the office, saluted, and barked, "Private Thomas reporting, sir."

The captain threw off a weak salute and then said, "At ease, Thomas."

Gene widened his stance and locked his hands behind his back, but he was tense. He had no idea what the captain wanted.

"I'm hearing some good reports on you, Thomas. You came here in good condition. You're smart. You have some leadership ability, and you're a college grad. Why haven't you applied for Officers Candidate School?"

Gene didn't want to say the wrong thing. He thought for a moment and then answered, "Sir, I'm satisfied to be an enlisted man."

"We need men like you to lead out. How would you feel if I recommended you for OCS now?"

"No, thank you, sir."

For the first time Pearson took a long look at Gene, and Gene tried to match his gaze. Pearson was starched and straight, a man of thirty or so. He seemed hardened, with leathery skin and creases that made the corners of his mouth droop. His office was full of the smell of cigar smoke. "I just honored you by inviting you to serve as an officer in the United States Army, and that's all you can say, 'No, thanks'?"

"Sir, as I said, I'm happy to serve as an enlisted man. I want to do my part, but I have no interest in becoming an officer."

"What you want is to be out in two years."

"Yes, sir. That's true. I'm married. I have a little son back home. I want to do my part and then get back to my wife and son."

"If you wanted to do your part, why didn't you sign up instead of waiting to be drafted?"

"I wanted to finish college first, sir."

"And hope the war was over by then. Right?"

"I didn't know whether it would be or not, sir."

"But now, since you got drafted, all you want to do is get in and get out. It never crosses your mind that maybe you have a duty to help your country win this war."

"Sir, I do want to serve my country. I'll serve as best I can."

"But on your own terms. Two years, max."

Gene didn't respond.

Pearson stood up. "Get out of here, Thomas. I can't stand to look at you anymore. You're what's wrong with this country."

"Yes, sir."

Gene saluted and left the room, but he felt sick. He had been called a coward for four weeks by men who were trying to harass him, but now he had been denounced by a man who really meant it. All the way back to his training class he wondered at himself. His father had served for something like four years. He had gone behind enemy lines. He had put his life on the line for his country, and Captain Pearson was right: Gene wasn't willing to do that. He wondered at himself, even thought of going back to tell Pearson he had changed his mind, but every time he got that far in his thinking, he remembered Emily home with the baby.

The fact was, five minutes never passed without Gene wondering how Emily and Danny were doing. Emily's letters were upbeat. She was trying to be brave about all this. For now, she had moved home so she would have her mother's help, but she was hoping to join Gene somewhere, if she could. In almost every letter she would tell Gene something new that Danny had done, and Gene felt the loss—a moment he had missed and could never get back. And yet soldiers had been making that same sacrifice forever. Why should he be any different? He wasn't a coward, and he was willing to serve where he was called. Soldiers stayed in Vietnam only a year, whether they stayed in the service two years or three, but he didn't want the extra time just to be trained as an officer. What was wrong with a man choosing to go in as an infantryman and pull the worst duty of all? Why couldn't Pearson respect that?

Gene never knew whether Pearson told the drill instructors that he had turned down the offer for an OCS recommendation, but they seemed to turn up the heat on Gene, singled him out for exceptional abuse. He got extra KP time because his "gig line"—the line formed by a man's shirt front and his pants zipper—wasn't straight. He was put on report for being "out of uniform" because he hadn't put his poncho on when it was raining. But in fact, it was the same drizzle that often fell at Fort Ord, and he hadn't seen anyone else wearing a poncho. What Gene told himself was that he would hang on. In four more weeks he could get away from these sadistic DIs. He would simply count the days down, show no hint of weakness, and not let anyone get to him.

Gene found himself spending more time with Willard than anyone else during the minimal free time the recruits had. He and Willard were older than most, and in one sense their backgrounds were similar. Willard was a religious man who had gone to church all his life, sung in church choirs, and even done some preaching. The recruits received no leave, no weekend passes, so there was no drinking or carousing, but most of the guys talked of little else. They made lewd comments about their past triumphs, and about the conquests they planned, and they made drunkenness seem almost the only joy in life. Willard said he drank a beer from time to time, but his parents had taught him never to get drunk, and above all to avoid the "whoredoms" that so many soldiers indulged in. "My girl, she's as sweet as a plum, and they ain't no way I'm going back to her, telling about all the wrong things I've done. I just hope no one else comes along and takes her away from me."

Gene told Willard all about his wife and his little son, and they talked about their schooling, the sports they had played, and their families. Gene had known a few black people in his life, but he had never really had a close friend who was black. He was rather surprised to realize how close his thoughts and feelings were to Willard's.

One aspect of boot camp was a lot tougher for Willard than it was for Gene. Willard was a big man, and the forced marches in heavy packs, and especially the long runs, were almost too much for him. Gene usually managed to stay close to Willard and talk him through, but one day, climbing a steep hill, just as Gene reached a ridge, he reached back and grabbed Willard's hand and helped him make the last couple of steps over the top. Draper saw that and shouted at Gene, "What are you doing, Goldilocks—holding hands with that boy?" And then he threw out some of his usual insults about Gene not being a man.

Gene paid no attention, but at the end of the run, when everyone was bent and sucking for breath, Draper approached Gene. "You let Shoeshine climb his own mountains," he said in his raspy voice. Gene was still leaning over. "You come to attention when I talk to you, Maggot," Draper barked.

Gene raised up, came to attention, but he stared at Draper and challenged him with his eyes.

"You want trouble from me, Thomas? Is that what you're looking for?"

Gene took a breath, but he didn't say anything.

"I'll give you all the trouble you want, college boy. Tomorrow, we take that same run, but this time you're going to do it with a pack on your back, and you're going to carry a rifle."

Gene continued to stare at the man, but now he was trying not to show his feelings. Still, his anger hadn't diminished, and clearly, Draper could see it.

"What do you say about that, Goldilocks?"

"Yes, Drill Sergeant."

Draper stepped closer, and he laughed in Gene's face, his breath full of tobacco. "You're mine, sweetheart. I own you. Don't you forget it."

"Yes, Drill Sergeant." But Gene was outraged, and Draper surely heard that in his voice.

Recruits were not usually ordered to take long runs two days in a row, but run they did, and Draper carried out his threat. Gene had to run with his pack and his rifle, but he was determined not to let that break him. He ran at the front of his unit all the way. He lost some ground on the hard climb, and he thought he would pass out before he reached the ridge, but he used the downhill to catch up, even to move back to the front, and he finished his run that way. Then, with his lungs searing and his legs ready to go out from under him, he stood tall and stared at Draper again. You don't own *me*, he tried to tell Draper with his eyes.

That night Gene was in pain. He sat on his bunk across from Willard, and the two talked about the glorious day when they would finish basic training. Willard was rubbing his feet and wishing for a pair of boots that weren't a full size too small. Gene happened to glance toward the barracks door just as Sergeant Draper and another DI—Sergeant Godek—burst in. "Atten-*hut!*" Gene bellowed, and all the recruits leaped to their feet and snapped to attention at the foot of their bunks.

The two DIs walked through the barracks. They checked footlockers, inspected the soldiers themselves, and ranted at the "maggots" who didn't have their belongings in proper order. But Gene wasn't worried. He had learned to keep everything in place, and he was one of the best at making a tight bed. He stood at attention while Draper and Godek went through his footlocker, and he waited for them to voice some of their usual insults. But suddenly Draper stood and held something out toward Gene. "Hey, what's this?" he shouted.

Staying at attention, Gene let his eyes drift to Draper's hand. He couldn't believe what he saw. Draper was holding a cigarette, Gene thought at first, but then he realized it was rolled and pointed: a marijuana joint. He had actually never seen one, except in movies. "Drill Sergeant Draper, that's not mine," Gene said.

"What are you talking about, Pretty Boy? I just pulled it out of your footlocker."

"It's not mine, Drill Sergeant."

"So what are you saying, that I'm a liar?"

"No, Drill Sergeant. But I don't smoke that stuff."

"Oh, you don't, don't you? Well, I'll tell you what, you can have that conversation while you're serving your time. You're going to end up in Leavenworth."

Gene felt the fear. He didn't know what Draper was up to, but he knew he could be in big trouble, and he had no idea what to do. "Maybe someone put it in there, Drill Sergeant Draper, but it's not mine."

"Come with me," Draper said. "We're going to get an MP. We're not talking about demerits this time, Sweet Pea. This is the real thing. You play up like you're so all-fired straight, but this time you broke the law, and you have to pay for that." He grabbed Gene by the arm and walked with him a few steps.

"Wait a minute," Willard suddenly called out.

The two sergeants stopped and spun around.

"That ain't right, Drill Sergeant," Willard said, but his voice sounded tense. "Thomas don't smoke. Someone must have put that joint in his footlocker."

The barracks was silent. Draper merely stared at Willard for a time. "Shoeshine, you're on the edge. You shut your mouth right now or you're going to be talking to an MP yourself."

"I ain't causing no trouble, Drill Sergeant. All I'm saying is, I know Thomas, and he don't smoke. He wouldn't be hiding no joint."

"What are you *saying*, boy? That *I* put it there?"

"No, Drill Sergeant."

"Of course you are. You're insubordinate, maggot. You just bought yourself more trouble than you know what to do with. You fall in with Goldilocks, and the two of you follow me."

Draper walked from the barracks; Gene and Willard followed, and Godek stayed behind both of them. They walked across the compound to another wood frame building and into Draper's little office. Gene and Willard entered and stood at attention, and Draper ranted for a time, then let Godek have a turn. For a time, Gene thought maybe this was all a show, just something to scare Gene and break his spirit. But then Draper told Godek, "Let's get an MP up here. We've got paperwork to do to get these boys locked up."

Godek took a step toward the door, but as he did, Willard said, "Drill Sergeant, do we get a phone call?"

"What?"

Willard was looking at Gene by then, not Draper, and he sounded almost desperate when he said, "Thomas, call your dad."

Draper was in Willard's face, instantly, screaming, "You're at attention, Shoeshine." And then he spun toward Gene. "That sounds about right, Goldilocks. That's exactly what a sweet young thing like you will want to do. Call your daddy, and don't forget to cry. But it's time you learned; no one can hold your hand this time. You've got to be a man."

Gene held his position. He *was* frightened, but he didn't want to let Draper see that. He was trying to think what he ought to do.

"Drill Sergeant, you need to know," Willard said, "Thomas's father is a congressman."

Gene saw the doubt come into Draper's eyes, saw him glance quickly at Godek. "Don't try nothing like that on me, Shoeshine," he said, but his confidence was gone. He looked back at Gene. "Is that right, Thomas? Is your old man a congressman?"

"Yes, Drill Sergeant." Gene hadn't wanted to play this card, but now that it had been played for him, he could see the effect it was having. So he took advantage. "I've been wanting to ask him what he thinks about a drill instructor who calls a black man 'Shoeshine' and 'boy.' Knowing him, I don't think he would like that."

Draper seemed to be shrinking. His shoulders had lost their stiffness; his face looked soft as clay.

"Drill Sergeant," Gene said, "I didn't put that joint in my footlocker. I have no idea how it got there. And Biggs was just standing up for me. We don't want any trouble."

Gene had said all this still at attention, but Draper didn't seem to notice. He stood for a time as though trying to think what his next step should be. "Well, now, Thomas, it sounds like you're finally taking the right tone of voice. You can be a good soldier if you do some work on that attitude of yours."

"Yes, Drill Sergeant. That's what I'm trying to do."

No one moved for a moment, and then it was Godek who said, "You know what I think, Sergeant Draper. I think someone planted that joint in Thomas's footlocker—some guy who don't like him because he's such a good soldier."

"It could be," Draper said. "I think maybe that's right." He looked at Willard. In a voice so weak it hardly seemed Draper's, he added, "It ain't right, whoever planted that joint. We're going to keep looking into this." He hesitated and then added, "Thomas, why don't you and Biggs return to your barracks. We got a hard day ahead of us tomorrow."

"Yes, Drill Sergeant," Gene and Willard said at the same time, and they were almost all the way across the compound before they finally allowed themselves to laugh.

But the laughter didn't last long. The resentment both men felt ran too deep. As Gene lay on his bunk that night, still too upset to sleep, he thought about what might have happened, had his father not been who he was. He hated the idea that he couldn't fend for himself, that the rules had changed for him because of his father. He was a man, a soldier, and he could do what he had to do. The fact was, his dad could probably keep him out of harm's way, keep him in a rear echelon position, even if he did get shipped to Vietnam, but Gene wasn't going to use his name ever again. His father had done what he had to do in Europe, back in World War II, and Gene could do the same. He had no desire to kill, and the training he had received had only convinced him all the more that he had no real stomach for it. But if he had to fight, he would fight with valor. He would never curl up and cry, the way Draper had said he would.

Saying that to himself made him feel better. But he wondered about his motivation. He knew what Emily would say—that he was still trying to be as great a man as his father. He knew he had promised her that he wouldn't take chances, that he wouldn't try to be a hero, but all these weeks of being called a coward had been tough to take. If he ended up in battle, he didn't plan to be foolhardy, but he knew he had to leave the army someday, still respecting himself. He thought again of the things

Captain Pearson had accused him of. Maybe Gene did want to do his service in two years, but when he received his honorable discharge, he wanted to write a letter to Pearson and tell him, "No one fought harder than I did."

# CHAPTER 22

K athy was coming out of a class when she noticed a rally going on near the student center. She decided to walk over and hear what was being said. She had once been considered a little too intense because she was involved in the antiwar movement; now, Smith was becoming more involved all the time. Antiwar rallies were happening on campus, not just at Amherst or the University of Massachusetts. Smith also had its own chapter of SDS. Some of the women in the group had come to Kathy and asked her to help get the chapter started, but she had refused. "I'm just as opposed to the war as I ever was," she had told them, "but I don't like what SDS has become. Too many members have no problem with the idea of blowing up buildings."

"What's a building?" one of them had asked her. "It's wood and brick. In Vietnam we're taking lives, every day."

Kathy had nodded. "I understand that. But it's still using bombs against bombs, and I don't think that's the answer." All across the country, demonstrations were now turning violent. ROTC buildings, administration buildings, and recruiting centers were being bombed. Kathy felt awful about that. She felt responsible that the organization she had been so much a part of was carrying out a lot of these attacks.

"We *heard* that you had lost your nerve," one of the women had told Kathy.

Kathy hadn't answered that, but she said, "We all have to decide what we can live with. I'd be happy to help, though, if you've got a peaceful march going, or maybe a teach-in."

But the women had left, and she knew they wouldn't call on her. It was strange to be the "older woman" now, the one with the experience, but especially strange to be accused, in effect, of not being radical enough for this new wave of activists. Three years earlier Kathy had been something of a social outcast because she had stood at the student center handing out antiwar leaflets. These women, now, were dressed up like guerrilla fighters, in khaki and camouflage. Lots of students were going to classes in worn-out jeans, Levi jackets, and peace beads. They talked constantly of ridding themselves of their middle-class trappings. More and more, Kathy was hearing Betty Friedan and Gloria Steinem, both former Smith students, quoted on campus. College women were no longer "girls," and they weren't going to adorn themselves for men. For too long women had been nothing but sex objects, they were saying—Barbie dolls, wanted for their bodies and not for their minds. No longer were they going to hide their intelligence to satisfy a male-dominant society.

Kathy didn't really disagree with any of that, but she was bothered by the hostility in the tone and the hatred of men that she heard sometimes. It was all quite similar to what many blacks were feeling: a powerful resentment toward whites. What Kathy dreamed of was a world with less hatred, not some place where the oppressed tried to turn the tables on the oppressors. She had never used much makeup, but she felt no need to abandon it altogether, and she had returned to her impulse to look neat without trying to look either sexy or sexless. What she found in herself was a loss of anger. She had been so angry for so long, and it had never resulted in anything positive that she could identify. Now that the campus—the world, it seemed—was turning to anger, she was already weary of it. She had heard a lot of talk lately that the Peace Corps was just one more veiled attempt at American imperialism, a way of trying to make other countries "more like us," but Kathy didn't see it that way. She wanted to escape the debate, the anger, all the accusing, and go someplace where she could offer her help to a village or a family or a single person.

Still, she walked to the rally, stood and listened. The atmosphere was reminiscent of what she had experienced at UMass when she was younger. Certain things had changed, however. The crowd was already large, several hundred there and more students gathering, and they all seemed to support what was being said. They shouted out their agreement. The language of the speakers was more hostile, more angry, full of profanity, and the antigovernment accusations received the strongest responses. Nixon was already as much the target of attack as Johnson had been before the end of his term.

Kathy stood close to the front of the crowd, off to one side. The organizers had set up a microphone with a large amplifier. The speakers were using a small wooden platform that elevated them a couple of feet higher than the crowd. A young woman Kathy knew—Susan Halpert—took the microphone. "Last fall Richard Nixon promised that he had a secret plan to end the war," she shouted. "We now know what the plan was. Bomb Vietnam into the Dark Ages. Destroy a country in order to save it. It's really just the same old thing we saw from Lyndon Johnson."

"Right on!" someone shouted, and the crowd joined in.

"I am *ashamed* of my country," Susan shouted. "I'm *disgusted* with America. I'm *sickened* when I learn that our all-American boys interrogate Vietcong soldiers by threatening to push them from the door of a helicopter—and then carry out the threat. Or shoot civilians—men and women and children—on the off chance that they *may* be enemies. What's gone wrong with us when our freckle-faced American boys are over there stabbing babies and—"

Suddenly Kathy was shouting, without expecting to. "Come on, Susan. That's not fair."

Susan spun toward her, and an amazing silence fell over the crowd. "What?"

"Don't blame it on the soldiers. They got drafted, and they—"

"That's right. They did. But they didn't have to go, did they? The heroic guys are refusing to go, burning their draft cards, even leaving the country if they have to."

The crowd roared, and Kathy realized this was not a time to introduce reason and moderation into the discussion. She was about to walk away when Susan said, "I'm not blaming the war on the soldiers, but I'm shocked by how many of those guys get to the war and *embrace* it. They accept the values of a sick nation. They kill with joy. They fly high over a beautiful, green country and drop their Agent Orange, their napalm, their immense bombs, and they fly back to their bases, throw back a few beers, and have a good night's sleep. Then, in the morning, they get up again to destroy more villages, more forests, more civilians."

Susan was staring at Kathy. She hesitated, waited. Kathy said, softly, "It's not that simple. Most of them don't kill with joy, and a lot of guys come home hurt inside by what they've had to do." She was thinking of T. D., the young man she had spoken with in Fulton, New York, the summer before.

Few had heard what Kathy said, but Susan shouted, "Kathy, here, who dropped out of SDS because she didn't have the courage of her convictions, is feeling sorry for the boys who have to kill. And I couldn't agree more. But I hope she'll forgive me if I'm just a little more concerned about the ones *getting* killed."

This invoked another loud cheer. "Our boys are getting killed too," Kathy said, but no one heard her. She walked away. She didn't need to be portrayed as someone who didn't care about the Vietnamese. She had championed their cause long before anyone else in this entire crowd. But she also worried about the effect an ambiguous war had on every soldier. It had been hard enough for her father and uncles to fight Hitler and the Axis powers, but the young boys going now were, in most cases, not much more than eighteen, and they had to fight a war that most Americans now agreed had begun as a mistake.

Kathy walked back to her house and hid away in her room. The only trouble was, at dinner that night, a sophomore girl named Wendy Searle, couldn't resist saying, "Hey, Kathy, I don't think I'd try to take on Susan Halpert again. She *trounced* you."

Wendy was an intense, outspoken young woman from California. She had arrived at Smith the year before as something of a Barbie herself, but she had found the movement, and now she was wearing the costume. Kathy was almost at the opposite end of a long table, and Wendy had spoken loudly enough to be heard throughout the room. Kathy was well aware that Julie Nixon was in the room, and students were usually careful not to be too outspoken against her father when she was around. That was part of the reason—but only part—that Kathy decided not to get into a debate.

But Wendy wasn't finished. "I know that a lot of our soldiers don't want to be in Vietnam. But when I watch the news and see what they're willing to do, I have no pity for them. They get over there and they buy into the whole thing. Search and destroy. Burn villages. Whatever they're asked to do."

The room had gotten quiet, probably for Julie's sake. She didn't fit in at the house all that well, but she was a nice person, and most of the students tried to make her feel comfortable. Kathy waited, hoping that conversations would pick up again, but she didn't hear so much as the click of utensils. Everyone was waiting. Finally Kathy said, quietly, "Nations win wars, I guess. But I don't think soldiers ever do. They pay a price the rest of their lives for what they see and what they have to do."

"I don't think a lot of these redneck soldiers we've got over there will ever give the war a second thought," Wendy said.

And someone at another table said, "Most of our guys are so stoned they won't even remember the war."

This caused a few laughs.

"I met a guy last summer," Kathy said, "when I was campaigning. I wish all of you could have talked to him. The war had torn up his body.

He'd lost both his legs, and he had a terrible scar on his face. From his point of view, he had only done what his country asked of him—and for his effort, he had lost virtually everything that mattered to him. Then he came home and was treated like an enemy by a lot of people. To me, he was a victim of the war as much as anyone."

Kathy saw some of the women at the table nod, and she felt in the quiet an acceptance of what she had said.

"He should have refused to go," Wendy said, but the words sounded harsh now.

A woman sitting close to Wendy said, "My brother's over there. He hates it. He's got about two months to go, and every time he writes, he tells us how many days are left. He only wants one thing, and that's to come home."

Kathy looked at Wendy, but she was eating now, unwilling to look at anyone. What Kathy felt was that their little disagreement was like the war: no winner, two losers.

∽⧫∾

Two weeks later was graduation weekend. Kathy's parents were coming to Northampton for the first time. They arrived Friday evening and, as arranged, stayed with LaRue. Saturday was "Ivy Day," when the graduating seniors, all dressed in white, were led by alumnae through the campus. The students stopped to plant ivy, which symbolized the continued connection of graduates to the college. That evening was "Illumination Night," when the campus was lighted by colored lanterns and students and parents gathered for entertainment and conversation. Dad said he wanted to take Kathy and LaRue out to dinner before the evening's activities. That was fine with Kathy, and in fact, the opportunity she was looking for. She wanted to introduce her parents to Gary and felt that it might be easiest if LaRue were there too, just to help with the conversation. So she asked whether she could invite "Professor Jennings."

Wally seemed hesitant, but Lorraine said, "Please do. We'd like to meet him."

Kathy and Gary had continued to see each other, and talk, all spring, and he had stopped trying to talk her out of her continued commitment to prayer. "It's probably something you need to do," he kept telling her. "It's all part of a process you have to go through." But clearly, he was confident about how that process would end. Sometimes that annoyed Kathy, and other times she was glad she had him around to help her keep her search honest. If she ever went back to the Church, she wanted to do it because she really believed, not because she was too frightened to make the break. And if she didn't go back, Gary still seemed an option in her life. However annoying he could be at times, she loved the way he looked at her, and she admired his rigor in addressing the same questions she was dealing with.

Gary accepted the invitation, and all in all, things didn't go badly at dinner. LaRue carried much of the conversation, and she and Gary had plenty in common. But Kathy felt awkward when, shortly after the entrées had arrived, Professor Jennings broke a silence by saying, "So, Mr. Thomas, I understand you run a car dealership in Salt Lake City. Is that right?"

Wally seemed to hear what Kathy had heard. Somehow, after all the talk about finals and campus life, and now, going off to the Peace Corps, Gary's tone seemed patronizing. "Yes. That's one of our businesses," Dad said. "We also own a parts plant. We make parts for washing machines and various other products."

"So did your congressman brother run off and stick you with the whole operation?"

"Not really. He had been on his own for quite a few years. He operated a construction and land development company before he ran for office."

Jennings laughed. "If there's one person I trust less than a politician, it's a guy who tells me he 'develops land.' Every time someone starts *developing* land, the trees and grass disappear and a house or a high-rise gets built."

This was clearly meant to be a joke, and Kathy made a point of laughing, just to make sure her dad knew. But Wally hesitated for a moment, and then he said, "So where do you live, Professor Jennings. On the land? Or did someone build a house for you?"

Gary laughed again, but the awkwardness at the table was uncomfortable until Lorraine said, "You ought to get to know Alex, Professor Jennings. I've never known anyone who cares more about doing the right thing—whether it's taking care of the land or looking out for the poor. You two would have a lot in common."

"Uncle Alex still believes in the Peace Corps," Kathy said, "even though Nixon obviously has his doubts about it."

Gary nodded and then couldn't seem to resist one more jab. "I'm always amazed at how many wealthy politicians say they care about the poor. Maybe, if they really mean it, they should share some of their wealth."

Kathy glanced toward her father, scared that he would say, "Maybe they think people ought to work for their money," or some such thing, but again, Mom, in a careful but kindly voice, said, "Alex does share what he has. He's not really what I would call rich, but he could have been very well off if he had chosen to hoard his money. He and Wally, along with the rest of the family, have set up a foundation, and they do a lot of good. Alex could certainly be making a lot more right now if he hadn't chosen to run for office."

Kathy knew what Gary thought about that. She had heard him say politicians were mostly wealthy people who weren't quite satisfied. They wanted power to go with their wealth. But he didn't say that now, and Kathy thought it was because he had heard the kindness in Mom's voice.

Instead, he said, sounding repentant, "I'm sure he *is* a good man. Kathy has always spoken very highly of him."

"She speaks highly of you, too," Lorraine said. "She tells us that she's learned an awful lot from you."

"Oh, thanks. I'll tell you, she was as good a student as I've had here. She's very bright, and she *cares*. I guess the acorn doesn't fall very far from the tree." He was looking at Lorraine, not Wally.

After dinner, Gary thanked Wally and Lorraine and then went his own way. LaRue begged off too, but Kathy and her parents walked to campus and spent some time at the "Illumination Night" party. Afterward, Kathy walked with them to LaRue's house, but she didn't stay long. She needed to pack and wouldn't have much time the next day. She also wanted to have time to talk to some of her friends before everyone began heading in different directions. When she got back to the house, however, she was surprised to find Gary waiting in the common room downstairs. "Oh, hi," he said, obviously feeling out of place. "Do you have just a minute? I wanted to talk to you."

"Sure," Kathy said.

He gestured toward the door, and they walked outside. He waited until they were away from other students and walking along the Elm Street sidewalk before he said, "I never expected to be put in my place by a car salesman and his wife, but I think that's what happened." Kathy stopped, instantly angry. He took another step and turned back. "No, no. Don't take it that way. I was just joking. I liked your parents. They're impressive people. Very nice people. I expected much worse."

"Why?"

"I don't know. I always see two sides to you, and I associate your parents with the side that resists me. So they've been the enemy, in my mind. But I have to say, I understand better now how you became the person you are. They're actually a big part of what's best about you."

Kathy liked the words well enough, but she was still annoyed with something in the tone she was hearing. At dinner, especially at first, he had seemed too full himself, as though he thought he was impressing this "car salesman" by showing off some of his brilliance. He had talked with LaRue about his love of Shakespeare, quoted lines from *King Lear* at some length, and then bridged somehow to his decision to leave teaching for a time to "serve" in Nigeria. He had seemed to Kathy rather calculating in his language by implying a comparison to missionary work. Through all that, he had hardly spoken to Kathy's parents, as though he assumed they would know nothing of Shakespeare, or even the Peace Corps. LaRue had been much more down-to-earth, as she always was, joking about a bad performance of *Merchant of Venice* on campus recently, and kidding Gary about going out "into the bush" with all these young people who would consider him an old man.

The contrast had been revealing to Kathy. Hearing the two together, she had liked LaRue better. She had never realized, quite so forcefully, how much Gary thrived on an audience, and how he played to his young students. But he couldn't use that style with LaRue. Even more surprising for Kathy was discovering that she also liked her mother better too. Her graciousness, which had sometimes bothered Kathy in the past, had seemed genuine, and she really had managed to win Gary over, even disagree with him without sounding defensive. Gary had seemed pompous, by comparison, and his condescension toward her dad's business had struck Kathy as essentially mean-spirited.

"Gary, my father may sell cars, among other things, but I don't think you have any idea what sort of person he is. He may be conservative about some things, and I disagree with him on lots of issues, but he's no simpleton. He thinks about things; he cares about things; and he puts in more time 'volunteering' every week of his life than most people do in a year. A lot of his church work is similar to what you want to do in the Peace Corps. He's always counseling families or finding help for people who are going through hard times. In our church, if a guy is out of work or gets hurt or sick, there's no way his family will go hungry. My dad is one of the people who sees to that. A lot of what we do in our church is the stuff you think is so important. We look out for each other."

She wasn't finished, but he took the chance to say, "Wow. I've opened up a bees' nest here. I was making a joke about your dad being a 'car salesman.' You know that."

"Sure I do. But it's *your* kind of joke—one that puts someone else down. My dad wouldn't do that to you."

"Oh, come on. He thinks I'm the devil himself. You told me how afraid he is of what I might *teach* you. He was polite to me tonight, but I know what he would say if we had really taken the gloves off."

Professor Jennings had a point. But not *the* point. A couple of students were approaching, on the sidewalk, so Kathy moved over and let them go by, and then she began to walk, slowly, and Gary walked beside her. "That's true. If you two were to sit down and talk about existentialism, he would tell you exactly what he thinks of such 'godless philosophies,' as he would call them. But he would listen to you and respect you, probably would even like you, in spite of himself—just because he likes people. But you would be sarcastic and condescending with him. You'd make fun of his ideas every chance you got. And when the talk was over, he would remember you as a person, and you would walk away only thinking of his words."

"Well, then, tell me this. If he would be so generous with me, why aren't you? You seem to be choosing to think the very worst of me."

"I know. You're right about that. And I've always been that way. I argue about ideas and I forget about people. I've known that for a long time now. It's what I want to change."

He was the one who stopped this time. He waited until Kathy looked at him. "I came over to tell you three things, Kathy, but I've handled this so badly, I'm sure you won't listen to any of them."

"What three things?"

"Well, all right. I'll try." He stuck his hands into his pockets and smiled, but sadly. "First was to say that I liked your parents, especially your mother, and I can see why your Mormon background has taught you to be the good person you are."

"Thank you."

"Well, yeah. But I already messed that up." He shrugged. "The second was to say that now that you're graduating, I'd like to figure out a way to spend some time with you before we both take off for our training."

"I'm going home the day after tomorrow."

"I know. I was thinking I could make a trip out to Utah. I'm not sure how we could work that out, but I'd like to see you 'at home.'"

Kathy didn't say anything, but she couldn't see that happening.

"The third was that I don't want our relationship to end here. I want to keep in touch while we're gone, and I want to see what might happen between us, once we're back from our assignments."

"That's so far off right now."

"I know. But our lives are on hold for two years anyway. It would be nice to think we could get to know each other for real after we get back. I don't think I'm quite so bad as you're thinking I am right now."

Kathy looked at him, his face mostly in shadow, but his manner like a high school boy's, innocent and a little scared, as though he were asking her to the prom. It was a nice side of him, and disarming, but still she said, "Gary, I don't think we could be happy together. I like a lot of things about you, and I'm impressed that you're willing to give up so much to go into the Peace Corps, but I'm still praying, every day, and I don't know how to define what I get from it, but it's something I don't think I'll ever give up."

"Why would you have to give it up?"

"Gary, you know what I'm talking about. We're just too deeply different."

He stood for a time, his hands still in his pockets, and he nodded.

"Maybe so. I suspect that in ten years you'll be your mother. You'll be liv-ing in Salt Lake, raising lots of kids and doing your church work."

"Would that be so awful?"

"No. It's fine, if that's what you want. But you've spent most of this year telling me that all that was behind you, and I don't think it is."

"I know what you really think—that I'm losing my nerve. That's what the SDS crowd thinks of me too."

"I suppose I do think something like that. But I don't know. Maybe, in the moment of truth, you're choosing to retreat to your roots, and maybe that will make you happy. It's not easy to live with the idea of meaning-lessness. Most people, in the end, invent some way to explain away what terrifies them."

Kathy knew this was actually an insult, given his point of view, but she felt the kindness in his voice. What he was doing, she understood, was giving up on her, turning her loose. Her response was to wonder about herself. Maybe she *was* getting scared. Maybe she *was* retreating to safety rather than daring to break with her family. But capitulating to Gary's confidence, Gary's interpretation of the world, was also a way of running from her own confusion. Sooner or later, she really did have to make a decision for herself. "Well, anyway," she said, "I'm not sure what's going to happen to me in the next two years. I'll probably be in some totally new place by then. But right now, I can't see the two of us together."

"You may be right. But I do want you to know that I'm *very* attracted to you. I love to be around you. I love your concern about truth and life. Most people play a role. They pretend to be what they think they ought to be. But you're the genuine article—a truly good person. You just haven't found a comfortable place to express your goodness. I think you will, though. And I'd like to imagine that maybe it could be with me."

It was what her friends had told her, too—that she was good—and yet, it wasn't something Kathy believed about herself. "It's strange you say that," Kathy said. "When my mom was talking tonight, I thought, 'My mom is such a good person. I'm nothing like her.'"

"Then you don't know yourself, Kathy." He leaned forward slowly and waited, as if for permission, then kissed her lightly on the lips. The act seemed natural to Kathy—right. "Congratulations on your graduation," he said. "And have a very nice life. If, in two years, you think you want to get to know me better, let me know. In fact, I'll probably get in touch, and ask again where you are in that regard."

She put her arms around his neck, hugged him, and then said, "Thanks. I needed someone this year, and you helped me sort out a lot of things."

He wrapped his arms around her, held her, and then walked her slowly back to the house, neither one of them saying a word.

After the commencement ceremony on Sunday, and before a reception that would follow at Baldwin House, Kathy pulled LaRue aside and said, "I almost wish I could do these four years over, and this next time get it right. If I did, I'd not only study more; I'd spend more time with you. I thought I would, but life always seemed too busy."

"You were in your larva stage. You needed some cocoon time."

"Then why didn't I turn into a butterfly?"

"I've been wondering that about myself for a long time. Maybe we have to finish mortality before we earn our wings."

"You've *always* been a butterfly to me, LaRue."

"Thanks." She hugged Kathy, held her for a long time, but when she stepped back, she said, "I'm turning forty this fall. I have the feeling that I'm heading for some sort of crisis. I need people to tell me I'm okay."

"If you had your life to do over again, would you do anything differently?"

LaRue leaned against a big sycamore tree, smiling a little but looking thoughtful. She was wearing a pretty, emerald-colored dress, which looked striking against her dark hair. Kathy was reminded again how beautiful

LaRue was. Kathy had always seen her as the woman in the family who had broken the mold enough to be herself, and yet, in her own way, tragic. Kathy tried to tell herself that life didn't have to include marriage, but the idea of being married, having a family, had always seemed basic, essential.

"I wish some things had turned out differently," LaRue said, "but I'm not sure which of my decisions I would change. I love what I do. I just wish there had been someone for me. I didn't mean to scare off suitors. I really didn't. But I separated myself from . . . well, from Utah, in the first place, which played a role in all this. And I became *different*, without exactly meaning to. I think I liked that for a long time. Now I can't do anything about it. And I still scare men off."

"Men don't want women to be intelligent."

"Kathy, I'm tired of some of the excuses I've used all my life. That's true of some men, I'm sure, but it isn't the main problem. I think the big thing was, I wanted my own life, and I wasn't willing to adjust my priorities to fit with someone else's. I've known Mormon men who seemed to be interested, but I think they saw how uncompromising I was. Maybe it would have taken only one situation—just the right one—for me to decide I was willing to make that compromise. It just never happened. Some of these things don't seem to be about choice. They just turn out the way they turn out."

"You still might marry."

"I know. And I'm more willing now to make those adjustments. But my chance to have a child is running out fast, and I feel sad about that. It's a lost opportunity, and I can see that some of my choices led to that loss." She made a little motion with her hands, with her palms turned up. "But it's too late to change that now. I'm not going to dwell on the past." Then she smiled more brightly. "Here's the more important question. What are *you* going to do with your life? You started with some of the same choices. Are you going to do anything to avoid my mistakes?"

"I do want to get married, LaRue, but if I don't, it wouldn't be the worst thing that could happen. I see a lot of bad marriages, and I wouldn't want that. I don't think I'm going to be an easy person to live with."

"This choice to go into the Peace Corps is the kind of thing that could have a big effect. Once you reach a 'certain age,' men start looking at the younger girls. In our culture, age twenty-four is getting past your prime, and that's how old you'll be by then."

"Maybe so. But I'm not ready to *be* married. I'm still trying to figure too many things out."

"Let me give you one piece of advice."

"Okay."

"Go back to church."

"Let's see. I think Grandma and Grandpa, Mom and Dad, all my uncles and aunts, my cousins, and almost everyone else I know have already mentioned that as a good idea."

"Forget about them. Listen to me. I'm the living cautionary tale in the family."

"Go back to church so I can get married? How can I go back and marry a member if I end up unable to commit to the Church?"

"Kathy, you *are* a Mormon."

"That's what my friends told me. And that's what Gary said last night. He told me I'm my mother and I just don't know it."

"At last he's right. I thought it would never happen." LaRue laughed. But then she added, "Kathy, for a couple of years now, you've been telling me that you don't fit in, that you go to church and feel uncomfortable because people have different opinions. You make it sound like the Church is driving you away. But it's the other way around. You're the one separating yourself. I struggled for a long time, feeling so different from other members and being single, being a professor—all kinds of things that didn't fit the mold. But I didn't leave. And somehow, I've managed to fit in. I've had to rub away some of my rough edges, and other people have had to expand their idea of what a Mormon is supposed to be, but I have a place in my ward and in the overall Church. We don't all have to be alike, and we don't have to agree about everything. What we have to do is accept Christ and not fight against the things that are essential to his teachings. The rest has turned out not to matter nearly as much as I thought it did when I was your age."

"But, LaRue, everyone thinks alike in the Church."

"No. That's not true. I've heard you say that for a long time now—and I used to say it—but it's just not true. For one thing, Mormons are careful around each other. They watch what they say, not wanting to seem unorthodox. But all you have to do is express an offbeat opinion about politics or some such thing, and you find out you're not the only one who feels that way. People come up to me after a Sunday School class, or after Relief Society, and they say to me, 'I've thought that for a long time, but I didn't dare say it.'"

"But that's one of the things I don't like. Why can't they just say what they think?"

"I don't know. We could talk about that for a long time, and I think I could even make a case that it's not very important. But the point is, you need to decide who you are, not what you think. And those are different things. If you believe in Christ and want to follow him, all the little nuances of *opinion* about this world don't really matter much."

"I've kept my promise to Grandpa Thomas, LaRue. I'm still praying, and it's been good for me. I like the idea of being closer to God, and sometimes I've felt that. I like unburdening some of my fears and worries and imagining that he really is listening. But I'm not sure I trust some of my emotions. Maybe I want to believe—just to make everything easier."

"Read Alma 32 one more time. Faith starts with tasting just a bit of the Spirit—of God's love—and realizing that you want more. If you pray, and it feels right, that's what you're tasting. *Experiment* with God's word. Show a little faith and see what happens next."

"I don't know whether I'll be able to go to church while I'm in the Philippines."

"There's more to coming back to the Church than being able to attend. But find the Church if you can. You need to *know* people, know the goodness of the Saints. You need to be part of a ward. You worry way too much about what people *say*. You always have."

"But so many opinions drive me crazy."

"I know all about that. But don't wait until you're forty to work this out. Go back to who you are, and let some good things happen to you."

Kathy actually wanted to do that. It sounded so simple, so much easier than what she had been doing these past few years. But she admitted the truth. "I just don't know if I can, LaRue. The only thing I know is that I have to make up my own mind. So many people are telling me what I ought to do, but I have to do this for myself."

"I know. I only offer it as advice—because I love you."

"Thanks."

Kathy took LaRue in her arms again. "I'm going to miss you so much. I hope we won't end up in different places all our lives."

"I think we're both going home, gradually. So we'll end up in the same place."

Kathy had begun to cry—partly because she hoped LaRue was right but mostly because she feared that she wasn't.

# CHAPTER 23

Diane and Greg were on a ferry crossing the Strait of Georgia to Vancouver Island. Their car was parked below, but they had chosen to sit out in the air on the main deck. It was June now, and the school year had just ended. In a few days the two would be driving home to Utah, where Greg would clerk in his father's law office in Salt Lake all summer. Diane had expected to head for Utah the day after finals ended, but Greg had surprised her by announcing that they needed a vacation—a little time together away from the pressure of school. He had made a reservation for three nights in a hotel in Victoria. They had driven north to British Columbia, spent a night in Vancouver, and then caught the ferry the next morning.

Diane was beginning to feel chilled, but she was worried about motion sickness and thought she might be wise to keep the cool wind in her face. She was more than five months along in her pregnancy now, and she had suffered very little morning sickness, but she was wary of the motion of the sea. She also liked the way Greg was holding her. He had gone into the enclosed part of the ferry, found a blanket, and brought it out to her, and then he had wrapped her up and pulled her into his arms. He had even given her his flat-top rain hat that he often wore around Seattle. She knew it looked silly on her, but she didn't care. She loved to have Greg pay so much attention to her.

"This is so great," Greg told Diane. "It's so nice not to have to study for a while. I don't have to do one thing but enjoy myself—and enjoy being with you."

Diane nestled closer to him and said, "I love you, Greg. I'm so glad we could do this."

"I think the worst is over, Di. I really do. I made it through the first year of law school. It's a great feeling just to know I survived."

"You didn't just survive. You *distinguished* yourself. I'm so proud of you for making law review."

"Well, to some degree. I actually wanted to be number one in my class, and I didn't accomplish that. But I think when these grades come out, I'll at least be in the top ten. And I'm not giving up. By graduation, I could still make it to number one."

"You'll *never* stop pushing, will you?" But Diane sensed immediately that she had said the wrong thing. This was no time to chide him for his devotion to school.

Greg let some time pass before he said, "I'll always work hard, Diane. You know that. But I was gone too many evenings this first year. I've promised you I won't spend so much time with my study group next year, and I mean it. I know that when the baby comes, you're going to need me. Next year I have to do the impossible: be the husband and father I should be, and still do my best as a student. But I'm going to put first things first. You're first, and the baby will be a close second."

Diane liked Greg's words, wanted to swallow them whole, but it was hard not to listen to a voice in her head that was saying, "That's what you've told me before." She wanted this closeness, though; she didn't want to argue, didn't want to upset him. And so she said, "Greg, I understand what you're going through. You're trying to start a great career, and you're doing that for me and our children, not just for you. I'm not frail. I can do my share. I'd like to have you home more, but I've whined too much about that. I'm going to try not to do that next year. I'll have the baby to fill up my life."

"I'm so lucky I married you," Greg said.

"I hope you still feel that way, honey. I'm so fat and ugly right now.

Every time I look at myself in the mirror, I can only think how awful it must be to have to look at me."

"What are you talking about? You're prettier than ever. You've got that glow of motherhood on you, like an aura."

Diane wondered. Her face looked so puffy now, and her slimness—her tiny waist, even the trimness of her legs and arms—all of that was gone. She worried that her shape was gone forever. She told herself that she would exercise hard and watch everything she ate, once this pregnancy ended. She would get her "self" back as quickly as possible. But she saw so many other girls who never again looked as good once they had had their first babies.

In spite of what she had been telling Greg, she also wondered about being alone with a baby all day. She wanted to use part of her time improving her mind, but she had given up reading her book on law terms. When she had tried to discuss the concepts with Greg, he had told her that the explanations in the book were simplistic and misleading. To illustrate, he would describe the complexities of a particular case, but she would usually end up saying something that would either make him laugh or begin to sound impatient. So she had let that go. She had gone back to reading novels and gradually found herself picking up best-sellers and romances. They killed her time, much like the afternoon soap operas she watched, but they didn't deepen her. What she was beginning to feel was that she was as shallow as some of the women Betty Friedan described in *The Feminine Mystique*. She had actually finished reading the book, but then she had put it away and never told Greg that she had bought it. She decided that Friedan's attitude only discouraged a woman from enjoying motherhood, and Diane's great hope now was that being a mother would be as fulfilling as she had always hoped it would be.

One thing Diane had been consistent about was studying her scriptures. She had finished the Book of Mormon and had read the Gospels and Acts, in the New Testament. She was now working on the epistles.

She knew that she didn't understand with the depth of her religion professors at BYU, but she felt good about her effort. This baby inside her, kicking now, was a frightening responsibility. It would need a mother, not a cover girl. She listened carefully as she read about the people Christ respected: the humble, the meek, those willing to sacrifice even when they didn't have much to give. She wondered at herself, at who she was. She had talked a great deal about spirituality at BYU, but it had all seemed an abstraction—something she connected with a certain style or demeanor. She had always thought of plain girls as somehow more spiritual, as though it were something a girl had to develop if she didn't have much of anything else going for her. But now she needed to help a child understand what mattered in life. What if her baby turned out to be a pretty little girl? How could she teach her that her beauty wasn't as important as a lot of other things? It was strange to think that those were the things her mother had tried to teach Diane, and Diane had often seen those admonitions as insults.

Diane wanted her children to feel her spirituality, to love God, and to love things of importance. She didn't want them to be vain and proud. But that thought led to a painful realization: Diane had always suspected her own superiority to other girls. After all, didn't everyone want to look nice, and hadn't she always looked the best? God loved humble people, and she had never been humble. Yet, as she had clung to pride in her appearance, she had also heard those nagging voices, especially her mother's reminders, that seemed to say, Diane, that's all you are, and that's not enough. She had long feared this day. Now she had to be something more—a mother, a contributor in her ward, a person of substance. In spite of that realization, all she could find to do that she truly liked was reading escape novels and watching television. She had actually bought a one-volume history of the world, simply because she knew that she had never taken any care in her study of history, and she often heard references to people or events she wouldn't be able to explain to her child. But the book usually put her to sleep, or even when it didn't, piled up information that by the next day she had already forgotten.

So Diane was scared. She wasn't sure Greg loved her as much as she had always dreamed her husband would, and she wasn't sure she was prepared to be a mother. She wasn't even sure she was the sort of person Christ loved. She knew he was supposed to love all his children, but surely he was disappointed with many, and right now, she suspected she was one of those.

Still, she felt she had to be attractive, at least to Greg. Her looks had always meant so much to her, and try as she might, she couldn't seem to put that need aside. She pressed her face against Greg's chest and wrapped her arms around him. "Don't tell me that I glow," she said. "That sounds like something you tell a grandma."

"You're the most beautiful girl I've ever seen, Di. You always will be."

"But I'm not—" She stopped herself. There were other things she wanted him to say, but it was childish to manipulate him into saying them. She needed to earn them. She told herself, once again, that after this trip, she was going to spend more time improving herself. She had already made up her mind that she would get some guidance from her parents this summer and spend her time on things more worthwhile. Diane would be home with her mother part of the summer and in Greg's home the rest of the time. If she wasn't careful, she could get caught up in the shopping and social life her mother-in-law loved. She vowed not to do that. She wanted to spend more time reading—studying—than she ever had in her life.

"You're not just pretty, Diane. You're righteous, and you're strong, and you're going to be a great mother."

She wasn't sure she believed that, but at least he was saying nice things and trying to be close to her, so she squeezed him and she hoped. She had always dreamed of a great marriage, and this last year she had sometimes feared what was happening to her and Greg. But now she had him gripped in her two arms, and he was holding her fast too. She was afraid to break the spell even though she was so cold she really wanted to go inside.

∽᳕∾

That evening was perfect. Greg had made reservations at the Empress Hotel, the finest, most elegant hotel in Victoria. They ate a beautiful dinner in the hotel, and then they walked along the waterfront and past the fine old buildings in the neighborhood. Greg was so gentle and loving with her that she felt almost as though they were on another honeymoon—even in her maternity dress. It was pretty in its way—lavender, with a white lace collar—but it hung over her like a tent, even though she wasn't really all that big yet, and she knew she was anything but graceful when she walked.

They picked up information from the hotel concierge and learned that a person really couldn't leave the island without seeing the Butchart Gardens. Greg seemed somewhat less than excited, and Diane wondered about so much walking, but they felt they should at least see what the place was all about. As it turned out, however, when they reached the gardens in the morning, they soon understood why people came so far to visit. It was not one garden, but several of different kinds, covering an area of more than fifty acres. The rhododendrons and azaleas were still in bloom, and the rich reds and purples were the prettiest they had seen, even after watching what spring had produced in Seattle. Diane was surprised to see Greg reading all the signs that labeled the plants and flowers, and studying the map to make sure they hadn't missed any of the trails or paths.

But finally, Diane's feet were aching so badly she said, "Could we sit down for just a few minutes?"

"Oh, sure," Greg said. "I'm forgetting. You must be really tired."

Diane sat down on a bench on the edge of the rose garden. Most of the roses were not yet in bloom, so it wasn't the prettiest of the areas they had seen, but the patterns, even of the greenery, were impressive. So Diane sat and gazed about, feeling that she had never seen so much beauty concentrated in one place. She glanced at Greg, about to tell him just that, when she saw that he was noticing another kind of beauty. There were two girls, maybe college age, bending to smell one of the bright orange roses that had come into bloom. One of the girls wasn't being as careful with her draping neckline as she might have been. "Greg!" Diane said.

"What?"

"I saw what you were looking at."

He laughed. "Just the roses in bloom," he said.

"Yeah, right."

The girl was pretty, Diane thought. She had long, dark hair, and she was wearing a yellow shirt, with a very short, tan skirt. She had athletic-looking legs, like a tennis player's, and plenty of the "blossom" that Greg had been noticing. She was probably Diane's age, or even older, but Diane suddenly felt matronly compared to her. She thought of the stretchy maternity pants she was wearing. She had been pulling at them all morning, but they didn't want to stay up. Her top was paisley, practical, and made her middle look bigger than it was.

Diane looked at Greg again. His eyes had wandered back to the girl. Diane understood that his eyes hadn't been able to resist that first look. She sometimes looked at guys the same way. But she watched now as he continued to track her as she walked amid the roses. "Had enough yet?" Diane asked.

"Enough of what?" he asked, and this time he sounded irritated.

"Of that yellow rose."

"Come on, Diane. I always watch people."

"Some more than others."

"A married guy can still notice a pretty girl."

"Is that what you were doing—noticing her? Or was a little fantasy running through your mind?"

"Hey, that's not fair. Don't do that."

"I haven't seen you look at me that way in the last few weeks." Diane knew she was making a big mistake, but she couldn't seem to resist. She was sometimes shocked by how powerful her emotions were these days.

"Are you ready to walk some more?" he said.

"I think maybe I'd better be."

"We haven't seen the sunken gardens yet. Let's go over that way."

He was clearly pointing in the opposite direction that the girls were heading, and that was good, but Diane still felt the anger or sadness—or whatever it was that was going on inside her. She knew, however, that it was important not to say anything else. Greg was walking faster than he had all day, and he wasn't commenting, wasn't stopping to read any signs. But once on the path that rimmed the sunken gardens, he did begin to talk again. They both commented on the display of color in the various types of flowers.

Diane was already sorry she had made such a big thing of Greg looking at the girl. She held his hand now, leaned in close to him when he stopped, all to show him that she wasn't mad. What she didn't feel, however, was much affection in return. He still seemed rather formal with her, as though he were harboring some resentment. And so she whispered to him, "I'm sorry, honey. She was pretty. Any guy would look. Nothing wrong with that."

But he didn't answer. He walked on and then stopped at another lookout point. He studied his map for a moment. "It says that everything in here thrives in shade."

"I think this is the prettiest area yet. Don't you?" Diane asked.

"Yeah. I think so."

They walked some more, and even though Diane's legs were aching and her feet felt swollen in her Keds, she didn't complain. She waited until Greg finally said, "Are there any other areas you wanted to see?"

"No. I think we've seen it all. I'd just like to come back here about three times, at different times of the year."

"Yeah. That would be nice."

But she wondered what he was really thinking. Was he thinking that he had married too soon, too young? Was he wishing that he were free to keep shopping around?

They walked toward the main entrance gates of the garden. Just outside, Diane saw the two girls again, standing in line in front of a little concession stand. Greg hadn't seemed to notice them yet, but they were certainly looking at Greg. The girl in the yellow said something to the other one, and they both laughed. What was that about? Greg was good-looking, and she could imagine that the girl might have said, "There's that cute guy again." But why had they laughed? Had she made a joke out of Diane? "The poor guy got her pregnant and had to marry her"—maybe something like that.

"Do you want to get something to drink?" Greg asked.

He pointed toward the line where the girls were standing, but Diane was almost sure he still hadn't seen them. It wasn't important anyway, she told herself. "Sure," she said.

So they stepped up to the end of the line. There were two older couples standing in line, talking in a little cluster. The four were in between the girls and Greg and Diane. Diane kept glancing, and she saw, finally, that he had noticed. But when he did, he looked away immediately. She smiled. This whole thing was a silly little comedy. Greg was *hers*, after all. What was she fussing about?

Neither said anything until the girls had their drinks, had turned, and were walking past Greg. But Diane was shocked when she heard Greg say, "Hey, do you two go to the U-Dub?"

Diane could see what Greg had noticed. One of the girls, the one with lighter hair, was wearing a gray T-shirt with a little University of Washington symbol on the front.

The girls stopped and smiled. "Yes. How did you know?"

Before Greg could answer, the girl in yellow said, "I think he was checking out your chest, Lisa."

She flashed a bright, sexy smile and stared directly into his eyes, almost as if she wanted to say, "I don't care that you're holding hands with your pregnant wife. I'm going to flirt with you if I want to."

Greg laughed, stammered a little, and then said, "I just noticed the UW symbol."

"So are you a student there too?" the girl in yellow asked.

"Yeah. I'm at the law school. Just finished my first year." It seemed time to say, My name is Greg and this is my wife, Diane. But he didn't. "What are you studying?"

"Who knows? I'm very interested in the Greek Alphabet, I know that."

"So you like the frat boys, do you?"

The other girl, Lisa, answered, "Vanessa likes all the guys. She specializes in the football team."

"That's not true," Vanessa said, tossing her dark hair back with a flip of her head. "I'd rather meet some of the guys in the law school. Maybe you could fix me up."

"Hey, that wouldn't be a problem. I know some guys who would certainly be interested."

"Really? Any who'll be millionaires in the next few years?"

"Sure. Just give me your phone number and I'll see what I can do."

But Vanessa looked over at Diane, as though she had decided her game had gone far enough. "Be careful," she said. "I think your husband is trying to get my phone number." And then, finally, without the playfulness, she asked, "When's your baby due?"

"October."

"You look so beautiful. Lisa and I were talking over there about how pretty you are. Your husband's a lucky guy." But she couldn't resist a last glance at him, with some of that flirtatiousness in her smile. "See you on campus sometime," she said. And the girls walked away.

Greg was quick to say, "You can tell she has no morals. I'll bet she does *specialize* in the football team."

"Why did you stop them?"

"What do you mean? I just saw that U-Dub shirt and thought I'd say hello. I do stuff like that all the time."

"But they're a couple of college girls, Greg. Would you start talking to them if I weren't around?"

The older couples had their drinks now, and Greg stepped up to the window. "What do you want, Diane?" he asked.

"Nothing." She walked a few steps away.

In just a few moments, however, Greg came to her, carrying two cups. "Is Sprite all right?" he asked, clearly trying to sound as though nothing had happened.

She took the drink, but she didn't answer.

"Honey, what's all this about? I might talk to them if you weren't around. I talk to students every day, at school."

"Greg, she was flirting with you and you know it. And she was doing it right in front of me. How could you ask for her phone number?"

"Diane, she was joking and so was I. I wouldn't line her up with any of my friends. Some of the guys might want a one-night stand with her, but she's not the kind of—"

"What about you?"

"What?"

"You didn't have to say anything to them. You knew it bothered me when I saw you checking them out."

"Diane, you've got a problem. I think you have a dirty mind. Or maybe right now you're just jealous of anyone who doesn't have a big belly. But to tell you the truth, I'm getting sick of all this kind of stuff. I've always thought I was a pretty good husband, but now, if I talk to a female, that means I want to step out on you."

"I'm sorry. I didn't mean that. But how do you think I felt, the way she was looking at you, tossing her hair back, making little *overtures* about wanting to meet a law student."

Greg rolled his eyes. He took a drink of his Sprite, and then he stood for a moment, looking disgusted. "I don't know what's happening to you, Diane," he said. "That girl was very nice to you. She told you how pretty you are, but you don't even notice that. Do you really think I'm going to look for her on campus? Do you think I would mess around with some other woman?"

Diane knew what she had done now, and she felt his power as he leaned over her, felt the logic of what he was saying, but at the same time, she heard a distaste for her in his voice—a tone she heard rather often lately. She didn't want to cry, and she didn't want to fight. Above all, she didn't want to ruin their vacation. She wished she had never said anything. "I'm sorry, Greg. It just seemed so . . . inappropriate."

"Well, I'm very sorry then. From now on, I'll sit gazing at only you, all day, every day. I'll tell you a hundred times an hour that you're the only pretty woman in the world—because you love to hear that so much. And if a girl ever says hello to me, I'll tell her she has no business making such a blatant pass."

"Greg, I only—"

"Just give me a list. Write it all down—all the reasons I'm not what you wanted in a husband. I'll fix myself just as fast as I can. I'm sorry I'm such a huge disappointment to you."

"You're not, Greg. Really. I'm sorry." But now she *was* crying. "I don't mean that. I just . . . never mind. I'm too emotional right now. I'm the one who's wrong."

He turned and started walking toward the parking lot. Diane

followed. "Greg, please. I'm sorry," she said twice, then three times, before they reached the car. But at the car, he said nothing. He merely opened the door for her, let her in, and then drove much too fast from the parking lot.

They had driven halfway back to Victoria when Diane apologized again, and finally he said that he was sorry too. "It's just not easy to be accused that way, when I don't think I was doing anything wrong," he told her.

"I know. I don't know why I made such a big thing of it. That girl was flirting, and it made me mad, but I shouldn't have taken it out on you."

"Hey, I'm the one who got all upset. You know me and my temper. I'm sorry."

Diane was relieved, but now there was quiet in the car, and she realized that she had lost this one—as she always did when she tried to take Greg on. The fact was, she still felt that what he had done was inappropriate, but as usual, she was the one who had to apologize. She resented that more than she wanted to, but there seemed nothing more important now than to patch things up. Marriage was all about give and take, and sometimes she probably had to apologize when she didn't really mean it, and maybe sometimes she had to go a little more than halfway to end a fight. She could do that. Greg was a wonderful guy, hardworking, smart— all the things she had always wanted—and she couldn't let her own bad temper ruin everything. Back at the hotel, he began to kiss her before she felt all that much like kissing him, but it was best to show him affection now. It was always the thing that made him feel better about her. She knew that she didn't look like that girl in the short skirt, but she should be thankful that he still found her desirable.

❧

When Greg and Diane arrived at their apartment, back in Seattle, it was still not dark, but it was getting rather late, with the June light lingering. Greg told Diane to take the elevator to their second-floor apartment and he would bring in their luggage. "I know you're tired," he said, and she was touched by his thoughtfulness. But she also felt just a hint of accusation in his voice.

She walked inside and opened the mailbox, which was crammed rather full. Most everything looked like junk mail, but on the elevator she began to sort through the letters, and she came to a large, linen envelope that clearly held a wedding invitation. She glanced at the return address, in Walnut Grove, California, and wondered who was getting married. She waited until she reached the apartment and then tore open the envelope. She read the fancy script, but she didn't recognized the name of the bride or her parents. Then she saw the name of the groom: Kent Wade.

She quickly sat down at the kitchen table. She had no idea why she felt so out of breath. It was good that Kent had found someone to marry. He was having a reception in California and another in Virginia, she noticed, and she was impressed by the quality of the invitation, with the engraved lettering. But she tried not to think of anything else. As she began to tuck the invitation back into the envelope, she noticed a little note inside. She pulled the slip of paper out and recognized the handwriting. "Dear Diane," the note said, "When I left on my mission, I couldn't have imagined that things would work out this way, and especially that I would be so happy about it. I know you have a wonderful marriage and that Greg is a great guy. I think you chose the man who was exactly right for you. Now I've found the right girl for me. Carla and I were meant for each other. So everything worked out well, and I want you to know how happy I am. Have a wonderful life. I hope the four of us can be good friends. Love, Kent."

Diane knew immediately that she didn't want to show the note to Greg, and yet she had no idea why. What she did know was that she needed to hide the invitation before Greg reached the apartment, at least for tonight. She hurried to the kitchen cabinet and tucked it, with the envelope, under some dish towels. Then she went back to the table and continued to sort through the mail. But already she was asking herself what she was doing. Was this at all the same as what Greg had done, when he had talked to those girls? It didn't seem so, and yet the two acts somehow connected in her mind. What was it that she wanted to hide?

Greg came in with the suitcases and then went back for some other things. While he was gone, Diane pulled the invitation out and thought of putting it back on the pile of mail, perhaps without the note, or putting that out too and not mentioning it until Greg said something—as though it hadn't been particularly significant to her. But she couldn't do that. She took the invitation instead to the bathroom and this time tucked it between some towels in her linen closet. She knew why she had chosen that spot, but she hardly wanted to admit it to herself.

All the same, once she and Greg had finally gone to bed that night, rather late, Diane—even though she was tired—waited until Greg was breathing deeply, obviously asleep, and then she got up and went to the bathroom. She got the invitation out again, studied it over, and thought of how it might have read had things turned out differently. And then she read the note again. She knew she was wrong, but she needed to do this. She didn't care so much about the words, but she loved to see the handwriting and hear Kent's voice in her mind. She savored the sound, even took some pleasure in the sweet pain, and then she sat down on the edge of the tub. She covered her face with her hands and she cried—sobbed right out loud. She just had to let herself feel the grief—or whatever it was—once in her life, and then she would let it go. She didn't worry about the noise she was making. She knew that Greg wouldn't hear her.

# CHAPTER 24

Kathy was lying on her bunk, flat on her back. She wanted to curl up and pull the blanket close around her, but she couldn't. Both her shoulders hurt too much. She had just received her second series of shots for typhoid, tetanus, and cholera, and right now she felt as though she had contracted all three. But the worst for her was knowing that in an hour she had an appointment with the psychiatrist who interviewed each of the Peace Corps candidates several times during their training. "If they deselect me after giving me all these shots," Kathy told Betty, her roommate, "I'm going to sue somebody."

"I was thinking more along the lines of murder," Betty answered. And she didn't laugh.

Betty Morgan was normally an outgoing girl, and talkative, but her body had reacted even more severely than Kathy's to the shots. She had been nauseated all day, and her arm, near the shoulder, was swollen like half an apple. She was a strong-looking girl with a thick waist and big legs. She hardly seemed the type to be knocked so low by just three little injections.

Kathy was still thinking about her interview with the psychiatrist. All kinds of rumors were going around about these visits. The Peace Corps didn't want to send people who would crack under pressure or not be able to adjust to foreign cultures. So the idea was to assess everyone, psychologically, and try to predict which of the trainees was likely to fail. In every group, some were being washed out. Administrators of the program, however, had not wanted to use the word *fail* and had come up with the term *deselect*. The word was a joke to the trainees, but it was also the source of a great deal of stress. Who wanted to be sent home because some interviewer considered you a likely basket case?

"What kinds of things is that psychiatrist going to ask me?" Kathy asked.

"I'm not supposed to tell you what he asked me, and from what I hear, he doesn't ask the same stuff all the time anyway."

"I know. But did he give you any trick questions, or—"

"He asked me whether I thought my body was beautiful. What am I supposed to say to that? If I say yes, he's thinking, 'You gotta be kidding. You're thirty pounds overweight.' And if I say no, he's thinking, 'This girl has some real hang-ups about her appearance.'"

"So what did you say?"

"It probably wasn't a good answer. In fact, I know it wasn't."

"What did you tell him?"

Betty laughed quietly, and then she said, "I told him that God had made all bodies, so they were all beautiful. But all in all, I wished that I looked a little more like Gina Lollobrigida."

"Did he laugh?"

"No. He wanted to know all about that—what it was that made me wish for someone else's body, and what it was I liked about hers. I told the guy, if he didn't know the answer to that one, he ought to go to the movies a little more often. He didn't laugh at that, either."

All this wasn't helping Kathy. She didn't want to face this guy, not feeling the way she did, and at the same time, she almost wished that she would wash out. She had been living for almost a month now at a little training center, just outside Hilo, on the big island of Hawaii. The main building of the center had once been a hospital with some nurse's dorms around it. The only trouble was, the place had been empty for quite some time, and it was falling apart. The Peace Corps had made some repairs, but it was anything but a pleasant place, with its mildewed showers and chipped paint. Still, that's not what bothered Kathy. Her trainers liked to say that this was the nicest facility the volunteers would live in for the next two years, and that was frightening. When she had first received her assignment to the Philippines, she had pictured a little grass shack to live in—and had found the idea exciting. But now she was hearing more about insects, about snakes, about water that had to be boiled, and she feared that she couldn't handle all the changes that were coming.

Still, when the time came, she dragged herself over to the main building and waited outside the psychiatrist's door. She rather expected him to have a German accent and wear a little goatee, but actually he looked rather ordinary, if a bit scholarly, with his thick glasses and thinning hair. He asked Kathy to come in, and then he took a seat in an upholstered chair, directly across from Kathy, who sat down in a matching one. "Kathleen Thomas, is it?" he asked, looking down at a sheet of paper on a clipboard.

"Yes. Most people call me Kathy."

He nodded and studied the paper for a time. Then, without looking at her, he said, "So tell me, Kathleen, why did you apply for the Peace Corps?"

Kathy had thought about this. She had expected the question, and she didn't want to sound naive or overly idealistic. "I feel that it's an excellent program," she said. "I like helping people, and I think I will also learn a great deal from the experience."

"What, for instance? What do you expect to learn?" He still wasn't looking at her. He was holding a pen, but he showed no sign that he had any plan to write anything down.

"I want to understand other cultures, meet people with backgrounds different from my own, and learn more about how people in the Philippines think about life."

"You've had things pretty much the way you've wanted all your life, haven't you?" He finally glanced up.

Kathy uncrossed her legs and smoothed out her skirt, but she was reminded of the tenderness of her shoulders when she did. She had heard something accusative in his voice, and she knew it was important not to react to that. "I've been blessed to have a nice home and family. But I've worked hard too."

"Worked hard? I don't see anything about hard work on your sheet."

"I got very good grades in high school, and I—"

"When have you ever *worked*?"

"I worked every summer during high school and college—first, at an ice cream store; later, at a car dealership, where I did secretarial work; and I worked for a professor at Smith College, doing—"

"Isn't Smith a finishing school for rich girls?"

She could see what he was up to. He wanted to see whether she would get angry or defensive. She wasn't going to let him get to her that way. "Some of the girls are well off—not all of them."

"But you are."

"My father runs a business, but no, I wouldn't say that we're rich."

"What do you think the people in the barrios of the Philippines would think if they saw your house, the cars you must have driven, the food on your table."

"I suppose almost all Americans would look rich by those standards."

"How would you know? Have you ever seen how the other half lives—even in the States?"

"Actually, I have. I spent some time in Mississippi. I was involved in the Civil Rights movement, and I helped out during Freedom Summer, clear back when I was in high school."

"I'm beginning to get the picture. You're a wealthy young woman who feels guilty. You have to go out and do some good in the world, to salve your conscience. Then you can retreat to your castle, marry some other blue blood, and tell all the girls in your bridge club how much you sacrificed to help those poor, unfortunate Filipino people. They'll all want to look at your snapshots, and I'm sure they'll think you quite the adventurer."

The man—who had never bothered to tell her his name—had finally struck a nerve. Kathy had been asking herself these same questions lately. The Peace Corps had been such an obvious choice for her when she had applied, but the training had raised lots of questions. What were these things she was going to teach the people of the Philippines? What did she know that they didn't know? What could she do that they couldn't do?

But she didn't want to say any of that to this psychiatrist. She was feeling a deep tiredness, probably from the shots, and a weariness of mind, not only from the questions he was asking but all the questions she had been asking herself. She just wanted to answer as simply as she could and then be allowed to leave. "My motives aren't complicated," she said. "If I can be of help to someone, I want to find a way. I don't have a camera with me. I don't play bridge—and I don't plan to start playing. I don't fit your stereotype at all."

He studied her closely now, watched her so long that she was the one who finally looked away. "How do you feel about Vietnam?" he asked.

The question caught her off guard. She answered without considering what he might think of her. "I think it's an immoral war," she said. "We have no right to dictate to other countries what form of government they ought to have. Thousands of people are dying in a war that never should have been fought."

"Do you plan to tell that to the people of the Philippines?"

"I'm not going there to talk politics. You asked me my opinion, and I simply—"

"What did you think of the moon landing?"

"It was exciting."

"Wasn't it a waste of money? Shouldn't we be worrying more about feeding the hungry?"

This was a little eerie. Had he been listening in on her private conversations? Just a few days before, on Sunday morning, July 20, 1969, the trainees had gathered around an old TV, with terrible reception, and they had watched Walter Cronkite—and listened to the astronauts—as the lunar module from *Apollo 11* had descended toward the moon. The last few seconds had been wild, with fuel running out and flying debris obscuring the surface, but then, after a quiet moment, a voice had sounded: "Houston, Tranquility Base here. The Eagle has landed." Kathy had cried right along with Walter Cronkite.

Later that afternoon, the volunteers had gathered again, and they had seen the fuzzy image of Neil Armstrong descending the steps from the module and then saying, "That's one small step for man, one giant leap for mankind." Kathy had cried again. It was unthinkable. A man was actually on the moon. It was something out of science fiction.

But later that evening, after watching the astronauts on the surface of the moon, she talked with some of the others, and she wondered out loud why humans couldn't make up their minds that no one in the world needed to go hungry. There was enough food if it could just get to the right places. But was she that predictable? Could this psychiatrist guess her opinions just from knowing her profile?

"A couple of years ago I had decided that the space program was a waste of money," she said. "But I don't know. On Sunday, I felt good about what we had done. It's like we announced to the world that humans—especially Americans—can do almost anything if we make up our minds and refuse to fail. That gives me hope that we will do something about poverty."

"What if the Peace Corps asks you not to express your opinion about Vietnam? Or about American superiority—which I hear implied in that remark? Will you agree to do that?"

He obviously knew about her campus activism. But how did he know? "I told you, I don't plan to talk politics."

Kathy saw no reaction. But he did move on. He asked about her education, her family, asked what talents she had to offer, and he managed to make her feel that a newly graduated liberal arts student actually had little to give. But still, she kept control and didn't make any big mistakes. And then he asked about her religion. "Mormons are known for their missionary efforts," he said. "Do you plan to use the Peace Corps to further that work?"

"If I had meant to do that I would have served as a missionary for my church."

"Why didn't you?"

The fact was, that possibility didn't seem so entirely remote as it once had. Kathy had felt somewhat better about the Church lately, had felt good about her prayers, and about the promise she had made to her grandfather. During the time she had been home that summer, she had gone to church, and at certain moments, she had loved what she felt there. She was surprised by how much she liked the women in Relief Society, for whom commitment was as natural as their heartbeat. She only wished they wouldn't try to explain what they believed. Kathy had always been skeptical about easy answers, but Gary Jennings had taught her a language of skepticism, and it came to mind whether she wanted to hear it or not. But she wasn't going to talk about any of that with this man either.

"There are many ways to serve people," she said. "A lot of the trainees are religious people. Our beliefs inspire us toward doing good things with our lives, but we don't see missionary work as the only service we can do."

"Do you plan to have sex while you're a Peace Corps Volunteer?"

"No. I don't."

"Many of the volunteers do. Some of the volunteers develop romances with other volunteers. Sometimes they meet native people they like. It's a very common thing. And two years is a long time for young people to go without sex."

She wasn't going to get into all this. She had seen some of the things going on around the dorms. Maybe it was true that quite a few of the

trainees were religious, but a fair number of the guys seemed mostly moti-
vated to avoid the draft, and quite a few had lived a "hippy" sort of
lifestyle. Volunteers were expected to be clean-cut Americans during their
service, and drugs were certainly forbidden, but it was obvious that many
were radicals at heart. One of the trainees had made overtures to her,
leaving no room for interpretation as to what he desired. She had tried
not to seem a fanatic as she set him straight about his hopes, but she knew
that people were talking. She was already seen as "the Mormon"—the one
who didn't fit in, as usual.

"I have standards for my behavior," she said, softly. "I plan to hold to
those, and—"

"And look down your nose at anyone with other beliefs. Mormons are
known for that."

She smiled. "I don't know how many Mormons you know," she said.
"But stereotypes are just that. I certainly don't believe everything I hear
about psychiatrists, even though you're trying your best to change my
mind."

He smiled. He actually smiled. Kathy wasn't sure whether that was a
good sign, but the interview ended soon after that, and she was able to
return to her bunk, take two aspirin, and listen to Betty moan.

∽⁄∾

Two weeks later, Kathy learned that she had not been "selected
out"—another Peace Corps term—nor had Betty, and that they were
heading for the Waipio Valley, in a remote area of the island. A village
had been built there—one designed to look like the country barrios they
would probably live in. All her life she had heard her father talk about his
years in the Philippines, both the fun of his military years, and in less
detail, about the challenges of his POW years. She knew about tropical
temperatures, the rainy seasons, nipa huts—and so many other things.
She had been excited about going to the Philippines for that very reason.

It would give her something to share with her dad, and in a way, a chance to give something back to people who had treated him so well. What she wasn't quite prepared for was the beauty of this place. She hoped that the Philippines would be as lovely. It was all like a paradise, with waterfalls and pools and a rich growth of palms and flowering trees.

But it was a paradise with challenges. And the first was simply to hike down an extremely steep hill into the valley while carrying a big pack. Kathy was embarrassed to realize how much harder the hike was for her than the others. She was built like a giraffe, not a mountain goat, and she wasn't strong. She had never given the idea much thought, but she had done little in her life to develop muscle. The hike was not actually long, but she was tired when she reached the village. She was shown where to place her few belongings, inside one of the huts on stilts, with palm fronds for a roof, but she was anything but pleased when she saw that her "bed" was merely a mat on the floor. She had been told that she would have a western-style bed and stove and refrigerator in the Philippines, but apparently, the idea of this training facility was to teach the trainees how native people lived.

She didn't admit it to anyone, but she struggled with the food. She liked the rice, but she stared at the octopus and really wondered whether she could eat it. And the *patis* sauce smelled disgusting. Still, she ate everything on her plate. She disliked the *patis* as much as she had expected, but the octopus wasn't bad, once she accepted the rubbery texture. The taro root wasn't difficult to eat, but it seemed to have no flavor at all.

She hardly slept at all that first night on the thin mat, and the next morning she was roused from bed early. All day the trainees received information about the life they could expect. She heard more about hookworms and parasites than she had wanted to know, and exploring the jungle around the village led to mosquito bites all up and down her arms and legs.

Along with Tagalog language lessons, and health and personal care lectures, the trainees put in a certain amount of village work each day. Kathy had to feed pigs and chickens, and one day she was required to try her hand at plowing a portion of a small field, walking along behind a carabao—an animal that looked like a water buffalo and apparently was related. She was by far the worst of the trainees, her arms and back not strong enough to hold the plow straight as the carabao dragged the plow through the soil. She got thrown off her feet a couple of times, and her furrow was so crooked that Rex, one of the trainers, had to do her section over. The other new recruits laughed and kept calling out teasing insults. Kathy laughed at herself, too, but she was worried. She wouldn't be plowing fields in the Philippines, but she wondered what kind of work she might have to do, and how well she could handle it. Maybe the psychiatrist had been right. Maybe she had had things too easy all her life.

One project was to build a little walking bridge over the stream that ran through the bottom of the valley. There were ten trainees headed for the Philippines, six of them women. The ten were provided lumber and some crude tools but no instructions. They were to plan the bridge and construct it with nothing more than their own ingenuity to guide them.

Eight of the ten gathered at the stream early one morning. The other two, both men, were scheduled for their interviews. A fellow named Austin Kerr showed everyone the plans he had come up with. Fortunately, he had graduated in engineering, and he knew more about building than the rest of the group put together. Betty was a strong woman, but she had majored in elementary education, as had two of the other girls, Raelynn Barber and Penny Putnam. Charlotte Oborn—a pretty girl who looked very young for her age—was a nurse, and the other, DeAnn James, had been an art major. Austin's partner, George Owens, was likely to be of little help. He had majored in history, minored in philosophy, and competed for his University of Maryland College Bowl team. He knew everything. He just didn't know how to *do* much of anything. He had plowed a better furrow than Kathy, however, so she still suspected that she would be the least helpful on the building crew.

But Austin had a good plan, and he got right to work. He got people sawing posts, and once he had enough, he told Kathy to stand in the water and hold one up. That she could do.

"It's more important to find a good base for these posts than it is to make the bridge symmetric," Austin told the others. He trudged into the water and felt around in the bottom of the stream with his Keds. He located good spots, then set the posts and asked George and Kathy and two of the other girls to hold them in place. Then he began to make measurements for the planks that would form the bridge. "Keep the posts as plumb as you can," he kept saying. "We have no level."

Kathy didn't know exactly what "plumb" meant, but she wasn't going to ask and give everyone another chance to laugh at her.

"Kathy," Betty finally said, "keep it straight up and down."

Kathy realized what "plumb" was, but her job was suddenly harder. The shallow water had seemed quite pleasant at first, but it was becoming cold the longer she stood in it, especially around the calves of her legs. But she tried to stand straight and keep from fidgeting about, and she tried to hold the post straight in front of her while Austin measured.

She was doing fine until she spotted the big sow that usually wandered the village. It was waddling down the path toward the water. She knew the thing was curious, always sniffing and digging about. What she didn't expect was for it to walk into the water and check out the building operation. Kathy hated the smell of the pig and its mud-caked hide. When it approached her, however, she tried not to move. "Scat," she said. "Get away."

Betty was laughing by then. "Scat? You tell a pig to 'scat'?"

"What would you tell it?" But now it was nestling up against her leg, pushing her off balance. "Hey, stop that!" she shouted.

Everyone was laughing by then, and George said, "What is this, a love affair? I think that pig has a thing for you."

"It's a girl pig," Charlotte said.

"Hey, tell the pig, not me," George said, and even Kathy laughed.

Betty walked into the water. "Come on, old girl, out of there," she said, and she bent low to give the sow a push. But when she did, she slipped and dropped to her knees. The pig grunted and then sidestepped, driving Kathy's legs out from under her. She went down, over the top of the pig, but that scared the pig. It jumped ahead and rolled Kathy onto Betty, who had been trying to get up. As Betty straightened, shedding Kathy, Kathy dropped on her back into the water, with the post on top of her. She was laughing and gasping and trying to roll the post off her, and at the same time trying to keep her nose above water. Austin jumped in rather quickly and moved the post.

Kathy got up then, soaked of course, and feeling incredibly stupid. The sow had bumbled out of the water and was heading up the trail as fast as her legs would carry her. "Love hurts sometimes," Penny called toward the pig.

"The course of true love never did run straight," George said.

And Raelynn said the obvious: "No, but that pig is running pretty straight."

Kathy knew that her only hope to salvage a little respect was to take all this in good humor. "She didn't even get to know me," she said, "and she's already gone. She's just like all the *guys* I've ever dated."

All the laughter actually made her feel a little more connected to the group than usual, but as the attention returned to the bridge, Austin said, "I'll tell you what, Kathy. Why don't you let Betty hold that post, and you can help me measure. You *can* hold one end of a measuring tape, can't you?"

Dear Betty had to add, "I don't know, Austin. Do you have any lighter work she could do?"

Kathy took the teasing, even joked about it herself, but that night, as she lay on her mat, she wondered what she was doing. Peace Corps volunteers were supposed to be ingenious. They were supposed to go into a neighborhood or village and see what was needed, then figure out solutions to the problems. "Betty," she said, "are you asleep?"

"Are you kidding? Whoever said it's quiet in the great out-of-doors must have never been there. The noises in this place drive me crazy."

Kathy had wondered about some of the sounds too, and she had seen the gecko lizards all around the hut. She worried every night that one would run across her face. Everyone said they were harmless, but the idea of them being inside the hut was repulsive. She waited a moment, and then she asked the question that was on her mind: "Do you think I can do this?"

"Do what?"

"Be a volunteer? I'm thinking they'll deselect me after we finish here. Or if they don't, maybe I should quit."

"Funny. I've been thinking the same thing," Betty said.

"*You?* You don't have trouble doing anything."

"This isn't what it's going to be like, Kathy. This is a test of willpower. It's just a way to find out whether we can take it. But when we get to the Philippines, we'll be teaching. When I did my student teaching, I didn't do very well. I sort of ran away to the Peace Corps. It never even occurred to me that I'd end up a teacher."

"I hear that a lot of us will only be assigned as aides. How tough can that be?"

"Rex told me they're trying to get away from that. The volunteers have been complaining that they don't have meaningful jobs in the Philippines, so they're cutting back on the number, and they're starting new projects in food production and things like that. But people like us, we might get our own classrooms."

Kathy had been hearing the same thing. That idea frightened her, too. "Betty, I've never taught. I have a B.A.—no teaching degree. I don't know how I ever got this far."

"Sure you do. You're smart. You're easy to talk to. You'll be a natural teacher."

"I don't know anything about disciplining kids or planning lessons."

"Rex said the kids in the Philippines are really polite."

"Then what are you worried about?" Kathy asked.

There was silence for a long time. Kathy could hear the sounds of birds outside, or maybe insects, and the constant rustling of the palm fronds. It was all so strange and discomfiting. She often longed to go home but never so much as at night when she had to lie on this mat, roll around trying to find a comfortable position, and listen to the strange sounds.

"Kathy," Betty finally said, "I never expect to do well. I got through my college classes by working my head off, but professors always treated me like a big old pet—someone they liked, but not someone they expected to accomplish anything. It sounded cool to tell my friends I was going into the Peace Corps, but the truth is, I was afraid to stay home and try to be a teacher, and I didn't want to admit to myself that no guy is ever going to want to marry me. What I really want is to have a life like my mother's, and it's not going to happen. All these women's lib ladies make such a big deal out of having a career and doing all these exciting things, but all I can think is that I have no idea what I'm going to do with my life. I'll probably spend all of it alone."

"Wow. Betty, I thought I was the only one who felt that way."

"You? You've got to be kidding. You've probably got ten guys waiting for you to get back."

"Betty, I've never had a real boyfriend in my life. I met a guy just before I went off to college, and I really liked him, but I scared him off. I'm always spouting my opinions, sounding like I think I know everything. He got sick of me, and after a while, when I'd come home from college, he wouldn't even bother to call."

"Where is he now?"

"He was a missionary for our church, but he got back last fall. I've heard he's going to the University of Utah, but that's about all I know. He's probably engaged by now, or at least going with someone. While I'm over here, there's no question he'll get married. He's this really cute guy, and gentle and caring and smart. He's every girl's dream, really, but we just disagreed about too many things. It seemed more important then than it does now."

"Well, you're ahead of me. I had some *buddies* in high school, but the only dance I ever went to was girls' choice. I asked him, but he never asked me to anything, not even a movie."

"I had a few dates in high school," Kathy said, "and I've had a few guys take an interest—guys who had things in mind that I didn't, if you know what I mean—but I feel the same way. I'm probably always going to be alone. And now, I'm not sure what I'm doing here. I'm tempted to quit, and yet I don't want to be deselected—just because the idea of it annoys me. So I'll probably do this job for two years and wish the whole time I could go home."

"That's what I'm starting to think."

They lay silent for a long time. Kathy tried to think of something else to say—some way to cheer herself up, and Betty with her. But she couldn't think of anything, and eventually she could hear Betty's heavy breathing—a kind of snore—and knew she had drifted off. But Kathy didn't sleep, not for a long time. She thought about Marshall, about the night she had left for college and he had kissed her for the first time. And before that, their first date—the night he had taken her up to Alta just to look at the stars. She had the feeling that she had made a lot of bad choices in her life, and maybe the worst had been not working harder to keep that relationship alive.

But she also couldn't think what to do now, so she went to sleep on her mat, and the next morning she continued with her training. And when the training period ended, she received word that she hadn't washed out, that she was heading for the Philippines, and so was Betty. Kathy suspected that she had made a huge mistake, one more time in her life, but she just couldn't stand the idea of quitting. She did decide, however, that it wouldn't hurt to write to Marshall. She at least wanted him to know that she had changed in some ways. She wasn't sure why that made a difference to her now, but it did.

# CHAPTER 25

G ene was on an airplane, flying home. After basic training, he
had attended a week of jump training at Fort Benning, Georgia.
It was something he had requested from the beginning. He
wanted to be in an airborne unit, like his father, even though parachut-
ing was almost a thing of the past in the modern army. After he made his
jumps, and passed the course, he was sent to AIT—Advanced Individual
Training—in radio operation at Fort Gordon, also in Georgia. He and
Emily had talked of her joining him for those extra weeks of training, but
when the time came, the expense was just too great for her to relocate for
the couple of months he would be there. They decided she would join
him if he got a longer assignment at a base in the United States. But he
had known all along that wasn't likely to happen. He now had a thirty-
day leave to be with Emily and little Daniel, and that's all he wanted to
think about, but the reality was, he had received his orders to "The
Republic of South Vietnam" and would soon be on his way to the war. It
was October now, and it pained him to think of missing Thanksgiving and
Christmas at home, about missing his son's first birthday, his first steps.

Gene had picked up enough horror stories about what to expect in
Vietnam that he felt uneasy every time he pictured himself there. He had
begun to hope that he would be assigned to some post far from the action,
perhaps *receiving* radio communications rather than being out in the jungle
calling in reports and requesting artillery or air support. But the chances
were, he would serve with an infantry unit in the middle of the action,
which was frightening on so many levels. As he sat in the airplane, he
looked out the window at the broken clouds and the farmland below, but

nothing seemed real to him. He had thirty days to enjoy, and then he would leave everything behind.

The world had never seemed more confusing to Gene. He was conscious, on the airplane, of his uniform, his short hair. He noticed people glancing toward him as though they were embarrassed for him. As he had boarded, two young women in peasant dresses had given him a disgusted look. In August, in upstate New York, close to the little town of Woodstock, there had been a gigantic "happening." He had watched scenes on television news of crazy, hippy types—tens of thousands of them—cavorting in the mud and rain. The whole thing was all about drugs, rock and roll, and what was called "free love," which really meant promiscuity. But he had seen interviews with the young people there, and they had talked about freedom, and about "the revolution." Half of them looked stoned, and all of them looked filthy and unkempt to Gene, and yet he was the one getting strange glances from the passengers. During his AIT, he had had a chance to get off base and see the movie *Easy Rider*, which, as far as he could tell, had no point to make except that drugs and alcohol were great, and that "straight" people were full of hatred for the ones who knew how to enjoy life. Had it really come to that?

So many things shocked him these days. That summer Ted Kennedy had been returning from a party on the little island of Chappaquiddick and had driven off a bridge. A young woman in his car—not his wife—had drowned, and he hadn't reported it until the next day. It all looked incriminating—wrong—and yet Kennedy was spinning a web of words, not owning up to his responsibility. Later in the summer, a strange cult had been uncovered. A man named Charles Manson had induced his followers to commit heinous murders. He had made drugs and immorality the center of a quasi-religious group that honored him almost as a god. Gene kept asking himself how much more the Lord could put up with. The world didn't seem capable of becoming much more wicked.

Emily and Danny were waiting at the airport. Gene hurried to them and grabbed them in his arms, then held them for a long time. But nothing felt quite right. It was as though he were going through the motions, acting a part. He wanted to feel this moment, take pleasure in it, but he was numb inside. And Emily seemed to know it. She stepped back, smiled at him, then kissed him gently. "Are you okay?" she asked.

"Sure."

"You look . . . far away."

"No. Not at all. It's just impossible to imagine that I'm with you again." He took Danny from her arms. Even though Gene had seen some pictures, he wouldn't have recognized the little guy. He was six months old. He looked like a little boy, not the infant he had held before he left. And Danny wasn't sure he liked Gene. He looked at him warily, seemed a little confused, and then stretched hard for his mother.

Emily took him back. "He just needs to get to know you again. I'm glad you'll have some time to be with him."

Maybe that was true, but then Gene would be gone again. How long could a six-month-old baby remember? "Honey, you look so good," he told Emily. He took her in his arms again.

"So do you. You've lost weight, haven't you?"

"A little." He felt conspicuous in his Class A uniform, but he had had no other choice. He had long since sent his civilian clothes home. He wondered whether they would fit now. His shoulders were bigger, and he had lost an inch or so around the waist.

Gene told himself to give way to this moment, drink it in, but something had left him. He felt as though he weren't the same person. Emily didn't know what had happened to him. He wasn't sure he could ever feel the way he once had. He missed himself: the young missionary who had returned from Germany emotionally attached to the Lord. He hadn't thought of himself that way at the time, but when he compared the memory to his present self, he felt the loss.

As Gene walked through the airport with Emily and then waited to pick up his duffel bag, he kept trying to think of things to say—things he had wanted to tell Emily all summer—but he ended up talking about the flight, the weather lately, things that didn't matter. When they reached the car, Emily gave him the keys, and he found it strange to drive again. He popped the clutch a little too fast and made a rather shaky start, and then he looked over and tried to smile, but Emily looked serious, and Danny was still staring at him.

"Tell me what's wrong, Gene," Emily said. "I feel kind of scared. I thought you'd be so happy to see me."

"I am. I am. I wish we could hide somewhere and just pull down all the shades. Or go somewhere and forget that anyone else exists."

"In your letters, you never seemed to be telling me everything. You kept saying you were okay, but you never really said what things were like."

"It's the army, Em. I don't know how to tell you what it's like. It's a different world. But it's not anything I want to talk about. Let's just enjoy this month."

"It's been such a hard time for me, Gene. I haven't wanted to make you worry, but it's just been so lonely, and so . . . empty."

"I'm sorry. I wish there was something I could do." He made a left turn onto the highway, heading east toward the city. The mountains were beautiful to him. He told himself he had to do better. He had to lift his own spirits and help Emily lift hers. "We're okay," he said. "Lots of people are going through this. We can handle it." But then he added, "Do we have to see anyone tonight, or can we just have some time alone?"

"Mom's taking Danny overnight. And your mom called and said we should go back to your house this month—so we can have some time alone. My house is just way too crowded."

"Good. That's what I thought we ought to do." But suddenly he was crying. It was more than he could imagine, to sleep in a bed, to hold

Emily, to be himself. What he wished was that he could stay here, be with his wife, his son, and never leave this valley again.

"It's okay, Gene. It's okay," Emily was saying, but she was crying too.

Gene looked at Danny, who looked frightened, and he realized he couldn't do this. He had to be a man. So he reached over, touched Emily's cheek with the backs of his fingers, then patted Danny on the head. "I know. We're fine. We'll be okay."

~∞~

The next couple of weeks passed quickly, although Gene hardly knew what he did to occupy his time. He spent lots of hours with Danny, and he visited his grandparents and spent some time with Joey, and he and Emily took long drives. The fall colors in the mountains were mostly gone, but the quaking aspen, up high, were brilliant yellow and even shades of orange. He liked to drive up Emigration Canyon, or Big Cottonwood, mostly to be with Emily, but also to remember. He felt a nostalgia these days that was like nothing he had ever experienced. He told himself over and over that the percentages were all on his side. Yes, soldiers were dying in Vietnam, but it was actually a small percentage of those who went. Even those who were wounded usually survived and made it back. But he still looked at the mountains, or out across the valley toward the lake, and he wondered. Would he see this place again? If he didn't get back, how would Emily get by? What would happen to his son? He never once admitted to Emily that he was thinking about that, and she didn't say it either, but they both knew they were considering the possibility, and it made their days together sweet and frightening, and sometimes tense. Some anger had built up in Gene this summer, and that was something new for him.

One night, when Danny wouldn't settle down for bed, Gene found himself surprisingly frustrated. "What in the world's wrong with him tonight?" he asked, his tone too harsh.

"There's nothing *wrong* with him, Gene," Emily said. "He's a *baby*."

"I know. But he's not usually like this."

"How can you say that? You don't know what he's like."

"Honey, I'm sorry. I just meant—"

"He's like this quite often. I have to put him down and let him cry. And I just hate it. Half the time I go pick him up, and that's supposed to be the worst thing you can do. I'm probably spoiling him rotten. But it's just so hard to make *all* the decisions by myself."

"I'm sorry."

He reached for her, but Emily turned and walked from the room. "You put him down tonight," she said.

So Gene held Danny, talked to him, and then gave him a bottle. But Danny woke up as Gene tried to put him down, and he put up a terrific fuss. "I'm sorry, Danny. It's bedtime," he said, but he wasn't sure what he should do. He had no experience with any of this, and he should have had half a year to learn. The frustration he felt with Danny, with the crying, was suddenly directed at the army, at the president, at everyone who thought up reasons to take fathers away from their children. He walked from the bedroom and shut the door. But Danny continued to scream. Gene sat in the living room and waited, but the sound went on and on. He only knew what Emily had said, that it wasn't good to go get him, that that would teach him that his crying would finally pay off. But the sound was breaking Gene's heart and splitting his head. He stood up, paced for a time, and finally couldn't stand it. He was feeling violent impulses, and he didn't want that. He went back to Danny and picked him up, took him back to the living room, where he gave him a pacifier, held him, and rocked him, and finally the little guy did give up and fall asleep.

After Gene put him down again, carefully, he walked to the bedroom. He found Emily curled up on the bed on top of the covers, asleep. He sat on a chair and took off his shoes. "Did he finally go to sleep?" he heard Emily ask.

"Yeah. But I did it wrong. I got him back up and rocked him."

"It's okay."

"I thought I wasn't supposed to do that."

"You're not. But it's okay. We'll ruin him together."

He went to the bed and lay next to her. He wrapped himself against her, tucked his legs in against hers, and held her around the waist. She snuggled closer to him, and she whispered, "I love you."

"I love you too," he said. And he knew that a month from now, two months, six months, this would be a moment that would come back to him. He clung to her and tried to let the joy sink in, but there was too much desperation in it. He was trying too hard. Nothing was as good as he wanted it to be right now.

༄

The last weekend that Gene would be in Salt Lake, his family flew home to see him and to say good-bye. They filled up the house, and that was a little difficult, but it was good to see everyone. Grandma Bea prepared a "Thanksgiving dinner" on Saturday, since Gene would be gone for the real Thanksgiving, and she invited all the family. It was a great afternoon: noisy, fun, full of talk and too much food, especially too much pie. But Kathy was in the Philippines and Diane in Seattle. Gene wished he had them to talk to. He did spend some time with Kurt, who was actually quite friendly. But there was still a flippancy about him that worried Gene. And he wondered where the boy was going when he left Grandma's and took off with some friends.

Danny hadn't had much of a nap that afternoon, so Gene and Emily put him down early and then went to bed themselves. Gene slept for a time and then awakened. It was something that had been happening to him lately. He would suddenly be wide awake, and tense, without anything specific on his mind—just some generalized nervousness. He had learned to get up, read a little, not force things, and then go back to bed when he felt sleepy again. But that was harder with his family home. So he lay in bed longer than usual before he finally got up. When he did, he grabbed his flannel robe off a chair, pulled it on, and then walked quietly out to the family room. He saw from down the hallway that a light was on, and then he saw his father, sitting in his chair with a floor lamp lighted. He was reading some papers.

"Dad," Gene said, "haven't you been to bed?"

"No. Not yet."

"What time is it?"

Alex looked at his watch. "Going on one. Kurt promised me he'd be in by 12:00."

"Are things still not going well?"

"I wish I knew for sure. He's still not doing much in school, but he hasn't been caught for doing anything wrong lately. The trouble is, I have a feeling he's just being more careful. I still don't trust him, and that's a terrible thing to say about your own son."

"Do you think he's doing drugs?"

"I guess I'd have to say yes. But I hope I'm wrong."

"Do you talk to him about it?"

"Yes. But he hates my monitoring him. I always know that bringing up the subject will start a fight, so I avoid doing it very often. I have no idea whether I'm doing the right thing."

Gene sat down on the couch. "I didn't know how hard it was to be a parent."

Alex laughed. "Oh, Gene, you haven't even begun. Babies still depend on you. They even like you."

"But if you make mistakes when they're really little, you can teach them the wrong things, and then have to live with the outcome."

"I suppose," Dad said. He stretched his legs out in front of him, leaned back, and shut his eyes. He was wearing some old tan slacks that were frayed at the cuffs. They were the slacks he always put on when he was around the house. "I'll tell you something, though. Spirits come to this world with a personality of their own. Sometimes you feel like you could do a terrible job with one kid and he would be fine anyway. And you can try your hardest with another one, and everything you do turns out to be wrong."

"My little Danny sure has a mind of his own. I worry about his stubbornness."

Dad laughed again. "Hey, you were like that. But raising you has been like teaching a fish to swim. You just always knew what you were supposed to do."

Gene thought about that. "I've always tried to be like you," he said. "Emily thinks it's a problem for me—that I'm always worried that I have to live up to what you've done."

"Oh, Gene." Dad's eyes came open. He sat up straight. "Don't do that. You're a better person than I am. Everybody gets caught up in trying to achieve something great, and in the long run, most of what humans think up to do isn't really all that crucial. It's not what you *do*; it's what you *are* that matters."

"But what you do comes out of who you are, don't you think?"

"To some degree. But too many people try to force it. They think life is all about building a résumé. A lot of big shots in this world are going to be very disappointed when they answer to the Lord. Some quiet little guy who's cared about his family, loved his wife, and served his fellowman is going to be the one God exalts."

Gene believed that. In fact, he had felt it more than ever lately. He would be satisfied right now if he could just live a quiet life, a good life. He let some time pass. He had wanted for a long time to ask his dad some questions.

It was his father who seemed to know. "Why are you up?" he asked.

"Sometimes lately, I can't sleep."

"I can imagine." He looked at Gene for a few seconds, appearing unsure, as though he were trying to make a decision. "I've been wanting to say something to you about the war," he finally said.

"Yeah. I was hoping you would."

"I guess I don't mean 'the war.' I just mean 'war.'"

Gene nodded. That's what he wanted to talk about too.

"First, I'd say this, Gene. If you get in the fight, play your role, carry out your assignment, but don't take extra chances. In the movies, that always looks great: Audie Murphy taking on the whole German army. But most of the time, guys who do that kind of stuff only get themselves killed, and the war goes on. You don't win a war with acts of daring. You win with good strategy and the right weaponry in the right place."

"Can we win, Dad?"

"Well . . . that's another question. I guess I'm really talking about winning battles. The fact is, in Vietnam, we win the battles, but we're not winning the war."

"Why not? Why don't we just open up and do what we have to do to get this thing over with?"

"Gene, it's all so complicated and political. But I think the simple answer is, the North has plenty of people, and their government sees them as expendable. We all hoped that when Ho Chi Minh died, that might make a difference, but clearly it hasn't. Their soldiers will never stop coming at us. We've tried to win this war with body count, by wearing them down, but we're the ones wearing down."

"Why can't we bomb Hanoi into submission?"

"Gene, we've dropped more bombs on Vietnam than we dropped in all of World War II, and we've hit Hanoi pretty hard at times. It just doesn't seem to make any difference. It's a thin line we're trying to walk. Do you wipe out a nation in order to establish the type of government we think is right for them? And then there's always China to worry about. Do we want to force this thing too hard and start World War III?"

"Can we turn the war over to South Vietnam, the way Nixon wants to do?"

"We have to. It's our only way out. But I don't see any sign that it's going to work. It's always been our war, not South Vietnam's, and that's the heart of the problem. Even with our weaponry, I don't think the South has enough will to hold out very long."

"So what will I be fighting for, Dad? I read in the paper that even Senator Moss has come out against the war now. When they had this last big demonstration, there were housewives and businessmen out there. The antiwar organizations are promising that *millions* of people are going to march in November. I'm going to a war that no one wants anymore. We're trying to shut it down—not win it."

"I know it sounds hollow to say that you're fighting in the name of 'honor,' but finally, it does come down to that. I don't see that we're going to accomplish what we set out to do—you know, stop the spread of Communism. But the only reason I know to stay over there right now is that we've made the South dependent on us, and if we walk out, the North will come in and kill everyone who cooperated with us."

"Aren't we just delaying the inevitable? That's what McCarthy was saying last year. I thought he was wrong back then, but now I'm not so sure."

"No. I'm not either. But it's one thing to say we have to end the war, and it's another to know exactly how to do it." Alex finally set his papers on the floor. He glanced at his watch. Gene knew he was worried about Kurt. "Gene," Alex said, "I don't know how to tell you what I want to say. You'll understand, once you've been over there for a while, but it might be impossible right now." He folded his arms across the faded red East High sweatshirt he was wearing. "Once the fighting starts, you don't think about what you're fighting for. You just fight to stay alive. And you fight for the guys right around you. So I guess I would say that war is war, whether there's a good reason to fight it or not. To some degree, you have to let your government make the political decisions, and you just have to think about carrying out your duty. Back here at home, that sounds contradictory, but in the middle of the battle, you'll do what you have to do because there's no other choice. There won't be any politics on your mind."

"But if I get shot up, I don't want to spend my life knowing that I sacrificed myself for nothing—or at least nothing I understand. What makes it worse, I'm not feeling very patriotic right now. The way the army treats draftees, the way our drill instructors treated us during basic, I'm feeling more anger and resentment than any sense of duty. We claim that we fight for freedom, but for the last five months I've had less freedom than a prisoner. I've been treated like a *maggot*. That's what they called us. And there's no justice in the army. They can do anything they want to you. I saw guys get beaten up by sergeants who were nothing more than masochists. The weaker a guy was, the more they dumped on him."

"Gene, I'm not sure I agree with them, but I know how military men think. They know that if a kid right out of school or college goes out to kill, he just can't do it unless he's been made over in some way. We always say we have to dehumanize the enemy; otherwise, nice kids won't kill. But I think basic training is just as much about dehumanizing our own soldiers so they won't respond the way they've been taught all their lives."

"Most guys came out of basic hating the army a lot more than they do any poor North Vietnamese soldier who probably had to go through the same stuff."

"I know. I do think we have to change that. But the only change that will ever really work is to stop waging wars. You can't raise a kid to love God and obey his commandments and then tell him to shoot his brother. Those two things never will fit together, and war is a sickening attempt to make it happen."

Gene grasped his hands together and looked at the floor. This whole situation was such a mess. "So I shouldn't try to be a hero. Is that your only advice?"

"It might be my only advice, but I've got some other things I want to say. I'm just not sure how to tell you." He rubbed his hands over his face. "In the last few months I've thought a thousand times that I'd like to make a few phone calls and see whether I couldn't get you assigned to some base far from Vietnam. I knew that wasn't right, of course, but I'll tell you, if I could go in your place, or I could find some way to end this war—or do almost anything to keep you out of it—I would. I'll spend my whole life wishing I had never seen the things I saw in Europe."

"You've been saying things like that all my life, Dad. But you don't explain. You've never told me, in any kind of detail, what you're talking about."

"I don't know how, Son. And maybe it doesn't matter. You'll know soon enough. But war is nothing like it's portrayed in the movies. It's not adventurous. It's not satisfying. It's exciting at times, of course. Fear is a powerful emotion, and some people get so they like that rush of adrenalin. I've even seen guys who get a taste for the blood—and that's understandable. When someone's trying to kill you, there's a momentary joy in getting him first. But after the battle, or especially after a war, you feel as though your spirit has been stained. You know you've done something no one ought to do. You've *been* someone no one ought to be. You think you've pushed it out of your head, but you go to bed at night, and your brain is too confused, too disgusted maybe. It sends the images back into your consciousness. And they never go away. Never. No matter how often I'm called a hero, what my heart tells me is that war is a sin, and I'm ashamed for the part I played in it."

"Dad, I already feel some of that—just from what we've been trained to do. And from the whole atmosphere in the army. I find myself feeling that religion is naive—a good thing, of course, but not something that explains the way one human being can treat another."

"But remember, God doesn't think up these wars. We do."

"Then why do we talk about war the way we do? My whole life, I've heard people say you were a great man because you're a war hero."

"You've never heard me say that."

"No. But we talk about war heroes like they're the people we should look up to more than anyone else. I grew up thinking World War II was really cool. I remember cheering when John Wayne would shoot the Germans. It never seemed to cross my mind that a German soldier was a human being."

"And then we sent you there on a mission."

"Yeah, but that was different. I knew there were real Germans—like Mom. I didn't connect them with the Germans in the movies. They were just these evil Nazis, and every time you killed one, that was one chalked up for our side."

"I know. It's the way we make war palatable. But Gene, I *do* honor the men who put their lives on the line in that war. We did need to stop Hitler. And I honor boys like you who are willing to serve their country. But every soldier knows the truth: we have to explain war, back home, in a way civilians can comprehend. So we use all these glorious terms to describe it. I think soldiers like to cling to that stuff too, because it explains, after the fact, what they did. But it doesn't change those deepest feelings that hide inside you. You do unthinkable acts in war, and you see a kind of mutilation that sickens your soul. There are smells and sounds and cries in war that are just too horrifying to live with, so your soul and your brain handle them any way they can. Part of that is a lifetime of telling yourself that it had to be done. The only trouble is, all that justification builds itself into reasons for the next war, and on we go. We think up another one."

Gene leaned forward and rested his face in his hands. He could feel the sickness in his stomach again, the dread and fear. Finally he said, "I'm sorry, Dad, but I don't see why you're telling me this. I'm scared to death already."

"I'm sorry. I shouldn't have said anything."

"Dad, give me something. I've got to get on a plane in a few days."

"I don't know what else to say." Gene heard his father's voice break, and he looked up. Tears were in his eyes. "I guess I want to inoculate you, prepare you in some way, so you won't go in as naive as I was. I find myself thinking, maybe if he knows, he can prepare himself a little. And I still say, don't try to be a hero."

"But after you had been over there a long time, and you had already seen what war was all about, you jumped into Germany, behind the lines. That's when you won those medals."

"I spoke German. Not many people did. They asked me to go, and I thought about saying no, but what could I do? Someone had to do it. But I wish I could trade in the medals they gave me—and have my memories erased."

"So how do I get through it, Dad?"

"For a while, after the war, I couldn't feel anything. It didn't matter what anyone else told me; I believed in my heart that God was ashamed of me for what I'd done. I don't want you to put that kind of load on your shoulders. Hold onto that good spirit you have. Remember that God loves you, and don't try to hide from him. That's the mistake I made for a while. I felt so evil and so full of hatred that I thought I shouldn't pray. If I had it to do over again, I'd do it the other way around. I'd tell the Lord what I felt. I'd tell him that I took no pleasure in killing his children—my brothers." Alex dropped his head to his chest, and Gene saw the tears begin to drip from his chin. When he finally looked up, he said, "But Son, God does love me. I know that now. And God's not a pacifist—not exactly. He understands what a mess some of his children make of this world. There are times when he approves of war; we know that from the scriptures."

"Dad, I don't know whether he approves of this war."

"I don't either. Maybe we could have found a better way. But we didn't, and that's not your fault. It's the legacy my generation passed to yours. I don't know anything else to tell you. Just cling to the Lord. Ask him to give you the strength you'll need."

Gene sat for a long time, trying to think what he wanted to do with what he had heard. And then he said, "Dad, some of the things you've said really scare me. But I do think, when I'm over there, it will help me just to know that you understand."

"I pray every night that you'll get an assignment that will keep you out of the fighting. If you can sit on some base and handle their radio operations, be thankful for the chance."

"And let someone else go to the front? You decided you couldn't do that."

"That was different, Gene. Not many guys knew German the way I did. But don't compare yourself to me. If the Lord chooses to protect you—and keep you in a safe place—accept the blessing. Please. Will you promise me you'll do that?"

Gene didn't answer. He wasn't sure he could make that promise. He remembered what he had told Captain Pearson. He had no desire to be a hero, but he had hated being called a coward. And Dad seemed to know what Gene was thinking. He didn't ask again.

Gene didn't think he could sleep, but he did want to go back to bed. He wanted to be next to Emily. "Dad, thanks," he said. "Right now, I almost wish we hadn't talked about some of these things. But I think, in the long run, it will help me. I am going to keep praying."

Alex stood up, and he took Gene into his arms. "If you'd like, I'll give you a blessing before you go," he said.

"Yeah, that's something I've been planning on."

"It's why we came home—more than any other reason."

"I know. I love you, Dad."

"I love you too, Son."

Gene stepped back, said goodnight, and then headed down the hall-way. He was almost to the bedroom when he heard the front door open. He stopped and listened. "Kurt, you told me you'd be home by twelve," he heard his dad say. And then he heard the excuse begin, a rather compli-cated explanation. Kurt always had one. Gene thought of his own son, thought of the father he wanted to be to him. He hoped the Lord would give him the chance.

❧

Three days later, Gene was at the airport again, dressed in his Class A's. And this time Emily was falling apart. They had left Danny home with Grandma, and the two had driven to the airport alone—after a dif-ficult farewell at home. But now he was clinging to Emily and she was sob-bing, actually losing the power in her knees, slipping down as he held her. But he was being called to board his plane. He finally had to let her go and make her stand on her own. As he walked toward the gate, and then out to the airplane, he wondered whether he would make it through the day, let alone the year.

But his dad had given him a blessing. He had told him that he would come home, that he would grow from his experience, that he had impor-tant things to do on this earth. When Gene sat down in the airplane, he tried to see Emily but couldn't, and so he shut his eyes and tried to remember exactly what his father had told him. He was going to cling to that.

# CHAPTER 26

D iane tiptoed from the bedroom and then turned and shut the door softly. Little Jennifer had been fussy all day and only wanted to sleep when her mother was holding her. It was late October now, and the baby was three weeks old. She was a dear little thing, but she had not been an easy baby so far. She seemed to spit up half of what Diane fed her—and yet she wanted to nurse all the time. Even after a shower, Diane felt as though she smelled like sour milk, and she wondered whether she would ever get another entire night of sleep. Worst for her, however, was that she had gained more weight than she should have while she was pregnant, and she wasn't losing it. She intended to exercise every day, but in spite of all Greg's promises, he was spending as much time at the law school as ever, and so she rarely got out of the house. Greg kept saying that his law review duties were keeping him busy. He would get on top of what he had to do, and then he would be home a lot more. But Diane no longer believed that. She told herself sometimes that she had a hardworking husband who would be successful and would always be gone a great deal. Lots of husbands were like that. But what she suspected, or at least feared, was that he didn't want to be home, didn't want to help with the baby, and didn't care for her as much as he once had. Diane's mother had come to Seattle when the baby was born, but she had only been able to stay for a week; since then, Diane had felt pretty much on her own.

Just as she closed the door, the phone began to ring. She hurried to the kitchen and picked up the receiver quickly to stop the sound, but then she walked with it, stretching out the long cord to the kitchen table, where she sat down before she said, "Hello."

"Hi. Diane?"

"Yes." She didn't know the voice. It was a man, a young man, but not Greg.

"This is Alan Dobbs." Alan was LDS and a student in Greg's class at the law school. Diane was about to say, "Greg isn't home yet," when Alan said. "There's something I want to talk to you about for just a minute, if that's okay."

"Sure." Alan was older than Greg. He had been out of school for a while before coming back to law school. He and his wife, Cindy, had three children, the oldest one only five. Diane often wondered how Cindy managed. But one thing she did know: Alan was a lot better about coming home.

"I want to tell you something that's kind of—I don't know—awkward, or delicate, or. . . . something like that. I don't want to feel like I'm telling tales, and I don't want to alarm you, but I just feel that if I don't say something, later on I might wish I had."

Diane had a terrible feeling strike her stomach. Her thought was, "I've been expecting this," even though she didn't know what Alan was about to say. But she didn't respond.

"I know you've mentioned to my wife that Greg spends a lot of time at the law school—that he's in a study group and works for law review and those kinds of things."

"Yes."

"Well, that's all true, of course. And he does really work hard. He's doing a lot better than I am. But it just seems like you ought to know that I'm not the only one who's noticed some things that seem sort of 'questionable,' I guess you would say."

Diane was admitting the truth to herself now. She did know what Alan was going to say.

"He does study a lot with that group, but he also spends quite a bit of time alone with Sondra Gould. They study, just the two of them, and they usually have lunch together, or they hang out in the lounge. It's not like they're doing anything immoral, but to me—and to some of the other students—it doesn't look good. It seems like it could lead to trouble, if you know what I mean, and it seemed like something you ought to know."

"Is there anything else?" She was angry—for the moment, angry with Alan for telling her—and, of course, angry with Greg. But mostly, she was angry with herself. She had known this, somehow, and she had tried to push the thoughts out of her head.

"Well, sort of. Sondra is not nearly as attractive as you are, but she's a flirt. I see her touching him more than it seems like she should. You know, just putting her hand on his arm, or leaning against him when she laughs—things like that. It seems to a lot of people that she's after him. That's mostly why I called. I don't think he's done anything wrong, but I feel like she has designs on him. She doesn't have our values, and I don't think she would care if she broke up a marriage. I mean, you know, he's good-looking and smart, and he comes from a family that—"

"I see what you're saying, Alan. But you're not aware that he's done anything wrong?"

"No. And Diane, I can hear in your voice that you're upset with me for tattling like this, but at the very least, it hurts Greg's reputation at the law school. I've heard people say, 'I thought he'd been a Mormon missionary.' You can tell they think he's doing more than just hanging around with her. I'm sure they're wrong, but it looks bad for him, and to tell you the truth, it looks bad for the Church. If you say anything to him, he'll know who told you, but I guess I don't care. I'd rather stick my nose in where it doesn't belong, if I can head something off."

"Yes. You mentioned that."

"Diane, I'm sorry. I really did think I was—"

"It's okay, Alan. It's good you called."

"It might be completely innocent and—"

"Thanks, Alan. I need to go. My baby is crying." She said good-bye, then got up from the table, walked back, and hung up the phone.

The truth was, Jennifer wasn't crying, but Diane almost wished she were. She was left standing in the kitchen with nothing to do but think. She was furious with Alan and knew she had no right to be. But she hated him for creating the fear that was growing quickly to a panic. What if her marriage ended in divorce? How could she face the failure and shame? What would people back home or at BYU think of her if she couldn't keep her man? She, of all people?

Her other reaction was hard to admit to herself. She knew she had to confront Greg, but she also knew how he would react, knew what an explosion could occur. She wondered how to do this right, so he would stop what he was doing but wouldn't end up *too* angry. There was something seething in him lately, waiting to react. He seemed capable of throwing over everything if she said the wrong thing.

The afternoon stretched out very long. Jennifer slept for more than an hour and was wide-eyed and alert when she woke up, but Diane was preoccupied, unable to play with her as she normally would have done. So she held Jennifer, rocked her in the rocking chair that had been Greg's Mother's Day gift to her, and she tried to think. She considered dozens of ways she could approach the subject. What she decided eventually, though, was that she wouldn't tell him what she knew. She would come at the subject more subtly than that. She would ask him about the atmosphere at the law school, whether the women ever flirted with him, and try to find out how he was thinking about all this. Maybe he would tell her about Sondra on his own, show that it was all very innocent, and then, on his own, conclude that he ought to stay away from her.

She made a special dinner, and she cleaned up the apartment. Then she put on some nice slacks and a pretty pink top. She also put on some lipstick and eyeliner, and she brushed her hair. She even put a Neil Diamond album on their portable stereo. But when the telephone rang again, this time it was Greg telling her he had to stick around "just a little late." And that was more than Diane could take.

"I think you need to come home," she said.

"I know you've probably fixed dinner already, but just make a plate, and I'll heat it back up when I get home."

"No, Greg. I need to talk to you. I need you to come home." She could imagine him with Sondra, and she wasn't going to sit there with the baby and wait while he laughed and flirted.

"What's up? Has Jennifer been—"

"Greg, listen to me. This is very important. I need you to come home."

"Okay. Give me maybe—"

"I want you to come right now."

"All right. All right." And now, for the first time, she could hear that he was put out, and she knew she had made a mistake. But she wasn't sorry. Maybe this had to happen.

Half an hour went by, longer than it would have taken him to get home if he had come directly, and then another fifteen minutes passed. By the time she heard his key in the apartment door, she was angry and scared and shaking. She took some long breaths and told herself to do this with control. But Jennifer had picked that moment to start to cry. Diane walked to her, picked her up, nestled her against herself, and then looked at Greg, who had shut the door behind him but was standing with his coat on, his briefcase still in his hand. "What's wrong?" he asked.

Diane had forgotten what she had planned to say first. She stood in front of him, holding the baby, and what came out of her mouth was, "I know what's going on between you and Sondra."

"Going on?" He stared at her for a moment, and then suddenly that big, charming smile broke across his face. "Is that what this is all about? There's nothing going on between Sondra and me. I can look you right in the eye and tell you that, categorically. I don't know what someone has told you, but you can stop worrying this instant." He walked toward her and reached out with both hands to grip her shoulders.

Diane stepped back. "You're not going to do that this time, Greg. I'm not saying that you're sleeping with her. I'm saying that sometimes when you tell me you're with your study group, you're lying. You're with her. And you have lunch with her and hang around the lounge with her, and she's *after* you."

"Hey, I'm flattered. I've never seen you this jealous before."

"Greg, I'm serious. This is nothing to laugh about."

"Well, I happen to think it is. And I know exactly what's happened. Alan Dobbs has gone home to his super-straight wife and told her a few things. She's overreacted and called you. And you've bought into their interpretation. The fact is, Sondra is smart, and it helps me to study with her—and others—but I don't have the slightest interest in her otherwise. She's outgoing and touchy, and friendly, and maybe to some people that's improper, but I've never said or done a single thing that's remotely wrong."

"People are talking—and not just Alan. They're wondering how a returned missionary can act the way you do. They think it's wrong for a married man to spend that much time with a single girl."

Greg shook his head, for the first time looking frustrated. He set down his briefcase and took off his wool-lined raincoat. He tossed it over the couch and then challenged Diane with his eyes. "Diane, I'm your husband. I married you in the temple for time and all eternity. I wouldn't think of breaking that promise in any way. I've done nothing wrong, and I think you ought to listen to me and not to a bunch of busybodies. That should be the end of this discussion."

"But it's not. I think you're playing with fire. Maybe you haven't done anything morally wrong, but getting that familiar with someone else isn't right. It could lead to terrible things."

"No. It couldn't. Because I take my vows seriously, and you ought to know that."

"I want you to stop spending so much time with her. I want you to come home. It's been very, very hard to be here all the time with the baby. You promise and promise that you won't be gone so many hours, but *those vows* don't mean anything to you."

"Let's see. I think this is where I came in. This, as I recall, is what I come home to every night. I try to get through one of the hardest times of my life, and the only thing I hear from you is how hard it is to be what you're supposed to be: a mom. I'm sorry, but I'm a little tired of hearing you cry about that. My mother raised a big family and actually seemed to take some joy and satisfaction in it. I guess that's too much for me to ask of you."

Diane was breathing hard now. She couldn't believe this. She gripped Jennifer a little tighter, took one more breath, and then said, as calmly as she could, "Greg, we sat in the Wilkinson Center one night and we talked about all this. You promised me that you would treat me like a queen, that you would—"

"Yes, your majesty, I did. But I thought you would show me a little consideration too. We talked about helping each other, being patient with each other, understanding one another's needs. But since I started law school, I only hear about *your* needs. Oh, how hard it is to be home with a baby. Oh, how hard it is to get up in the night. But I'll tell you what Queen Diane, I'd sure like to trade with you. Do you want to make that deal?" He grabbed his briefcase and walked into their bedroom. She waited, wondering what would happen next. Her anger was giving way to fright. She had handled this all wrong.

She heard the toilet flush and then heard him open the closet door in their bedroom. She walked to the bedroom, then stood in the doorway. "Greg, I'm sorry. I know this is a hard time for you, too. And I don't want to get in a big fight. But you do tell me over and over that you'll stay home more, and then you never do it. I miss you when you're gone all day *and* all evening. I love you."

He was sitting in a chair, bending down to unlace his shoes. He had thrown his dress shirt and tie on the bed and had pulled on a navy blue collarless knit shirt he often wore at home. He kicked off both his shoes and then stood and slipped off his pants. He tossed them onto the chair and then walked to the chest of drawers, where he pulled out a pair of jeans. He slipped them on, then buttoned the fly before he finally looked at her. "I'm not sure I'll ever satisfy you, Diane. Nothing is ever quite enough. It's not easy to be accused of things like this. I know I put in a lot of hours at school, and I keep trying to cut back on that, but I've never looked at another girl—not in the way you're talking about—and now I have to answer for that. If you think you didn't get what you bargained for, go ahead and file for divorce. I know some good lawyers; I'll suggest a few."

"Greg, I haven't said one word about divorce. Don't even bring that up. Can't we talk about this?"

"Of course we can. I'm wrong and you're right. I'll try to get home sooner at night. And I'll stop talking to Sondra—since it *looks* so terrible. Anything else?"

"Honey, don't. Can't you understand what I'm trying to say?"

"Oh, I understand. But now, do you want a list of ways I'd like you to change—as long as we're talking?"

"Yes. I would."

"Okay. I'd like, just once, to come home at night and *not* hear you tell me how hard your day was. I start to wonder whether you even love our daughter. I hear it every day: the baby cries; the baby spits up. But the last I heard, that's what babies do. Maybe . . . just maybe . . . *you're* the baby. Maybe your mother was right when she said you weren't old enough to get married."

"Greg, I'm sorry if I sound like that. I think it's hard to understand what it's like, if you—"

"A whole lot of women have done it before, Diane. Are you the first one to *suffer* quite so much?"

"I don't mean to . . ." But she couldn't think what to say.

"Number two on my list. Maybe . . . just maybe . . . a man likes to come home to a wife who *looks* like she's happy to see him. You're usually dressed like you don't care whether I see you or not. Then, when it's time to go to bed, you're *too tired* for *that*. So maybe you could explain to me why it is I should be so eager to run right home as quickly as I can. Is it for your wonderful cooking? Oh, well, maybe not. Is it to be loved and appreciated? Sorry, that would go beyond the call of duty. I seem to have learned about marriage from old-fashioned people who thought both partners tried to please each other."

Diane was devastated. Greg was right. She did complain too much. She did find it difficult to do things that millions and millions of women had been doing forever. And she looked terrible. She knew she did.

"Maybe I talk to other girls because they have something to talk about. Have you thought about that, Diane?" He stepped up closer to her, so his face was close to hers, but he spoke quietly. "Do you ever read a newspaper? Do you watch the news on television? When you've had some time to read, what did you do? You spent it reading *novels*. So how surprising is it that you don't *know* anything and don't seem to *care*?"

Diane was crying now—and certain he was right—but she said, "You knew who I was when you married me, Greg. I think the only thing you ever loved about me was that I was pretty. You talked me into quitting school before—"

His hand flashed out, grabbed her by the arm, hard, and he jerked her around so she was facing away from him. Then he pushed her forward, forced her in front of the mirror. "Take a look, Diane. If I married you because you were pretty, I sure got a bad deal. Look how fat you are now.

Look at your cheeks. I didn't think you would be the kind of woman who would let yourself go like that. We've been married *one* year, and you already look awful. What are you going to look like in *twenty* years? My mom didn't let that happen to her, and I just assumed you'd take the same kind of pride in yourself."

Diane was still holding the baby, and she was sobbing. "I'll try harder," she said. "I'm going to start exercising, and—"

He grabbed her again, pulled her around to face him, hurting her arm, squeezing it brutally. He shouted into her face, "Yes, and that's what you've been telling me every day for a month." He shoved her backward, hard against the mirror. The frame struck the small of her back. She bent forward in pain and grasped Jennifer too tight. "So don't tell me about breaking promises. I'll change my behavior when you do."

Jennifer had begun to scream, and Greg was striding from the bedroom, maybe heading for the front door. She didn't know. But Diane realized what had just happened. Greg had crossed a line. "No!" she shouted.

He spun around to face her again.

"You are not going to shove me around. You are not going to hurt me. And you will *not* talk to me that way. I *will* get a divorce."

Greg was the one taking long breaths now. But he seemed to be thinking things over, as though he wasn't quite sure what he would do next.

"I'm going home," she said. "I should have done that before this baby was born. I started to see who you really were even before we got married, and I was too stupid to admit it to myself. Everyone saw it but me." She caressed the baby, told her, "It's okay, honey. We'll be all right."

"I don't want a divorce," Greg said. "We do need to talk."

"You don't talk, Greg. You manipulate. And you're destroying me. You're right that I don't know enough, but you wanted me the way you *saw* me. And that's all you ever cared about. I'm going home, and I'm going to file for divorce. Jenny and I will be all right. Maybe I still have time to meet someone who will love me for who I am."

She walked to the closet, still holding the baby, who was calming gradually. She used her free hand to pull out her suitcase. "Please don't," Greg said. "I lost my temper. But I do love you. We can work this out."

She set the suitcase on the bed, and then she laid the baby down next to it, but Jennifer started to cry again, so Diane picked her back up. She was relieved, in a way, for the delay. Panic was setting in again. She didn't know how she was going to do this: how she could get to the airport, buy tickets, get to Utah. And an image was beginning to form itself in her mind: she saw herself at home, with a baby, and already a failed marriage in her past.

"Honey, listen," Greg said. "When I get mad, I just seem to lose it. I don't even make sense. I say things just because I know they will hurt."

"You can't take things back that easily, Greg. It doesn't work that way."

"I know. You're right. But I didn't really mean any of that stuff, and above all, I didn't mean to hurt you. I'm glad you aren't letting me get away with it. I can't ever do that again. If I do, you have every right to leave me. But give me a second chance this time."

"Everything you said was true," Diane said. "I'm not smart, like Sondra. I'm not as interesting to talk to. And I know I look awful."

"No, no. That's not true." He walked to her but didn't touch her. "You keep saying that you need to lose weight, and so I turned that against you—just because I was mad—but you're beautiful, Di. Honestly, you are."

"Don't do this, Greg. You just say whatever you think I want to hear. Maybe you did lose your temper, but it was obvious that you meant every word you said." But now Diane's anger was gone, and the hurt was hitting deep. She held Jennifer close, and she cried.

"Honey, listen. Of course you'll look better when you lose the weight you gained while you were pregnant, but it doesn't make sense for me to expect you to do that immediately. Those things take some time."

"It's hard to exercise when I'm alone with the baby all the time."

"I know it is. And it's easy to eat too much when you have so much time on your hands."

That was actually not true. Diane hadn't been eating much at all. In fact, she had worried that she wasn't providing the baby with enough nourishment. She wanted so desperately to look as good as she once had. "Greg, I know that's what you think—that I have all this time on my hands. But it's not that way. The baby keeps me busy a whole lot more than you think. And when she sleeps, I'm washing diapers, and I'm trying to clean up the house."

"Yeah, I'm sure that's true."

"Everything's suddenly true now. Anything I say you'll agree with. Just so I won't leave."

"No. It's not that. I just feel bad about what I said. I'm trying to be fair."

"Greg, I think you're worried how it would *look* if we broke up. You got it into your head, back in school, that I was a prize you had to win. Now you're not so sure you got what you wanted, but you don't want people to think you blew it. For you, life is all about winning victories and looking good. But I don't think you love me. I'm not sure you ever did."

"That's not true, Di." He looked at her longingly, and then tears began to drip onto his cheeks. "I'm not as good a person as I ought to be. And I am too competitive. I know all that. But you're so much more than a prize to me. You and Jennifer are my life. And I've been messing up, not being here with you enough. I think too much about school, and not enough about the things that really matter. But I do love you. I married you for eternity, and more than anything in this world, that's what I want."

Diane wanted to believe all this, but her instincts told her that he wouldn't change, that he would be nice to her for a few days and then the pattern would return. "You hurt me," she said. "You bruised my arm. You hurt my back. If I let you get away with that, I have no self-respect."

"I didn't realize. I'm sorry. I just wanted—"

"Greg, you grabbed my arm *hard*. You pushed me against the mirror. What do you mean, 'you didn't realize'?"

"Diane, I will *never* do anything like that again. That's an absolute promise."

"We made promises in the temple already, Greg. That should have been enough."

"I know. And I still can't believe I did that to you. I'm as surprised as you are. But it's good to learn, early in my life, that I have a temper that can get me in trouble. I'll be a lot faster about getting myself under control next time."

"Will you talk to the bishop about this?"

She saw a look of shock come into his face. "Honey, I don't think I need to do that. I mean, I grabbed you kind of hard, but—"

"Okay. Fine. I'll talk to him. I'll show him the bruise on my arm and on my back where I hit the mirror frame."

"No, you're right. I'll talk to him. I'll tell him what I did. But does that mean you're staying?"

It did mean that, of course. Diane had been realizing, gradually, that she didn't have the courage to leave. Questions had been jumping into her head. How would she live? What would it mean to Jennifer if she called this marriage off? What would life be like if she tried to make it on her own? But there was still the other matter. "What about Sondra?" Diane asked.

"There's nothing going on, Diane. I'll just stop hanging around with her. That won't be difficult at all. She's annoying in a lot of ways."

So Diane nodded, and that seemed the end. But she knew what she felt: that she had just lost again, that she really should have gotten on that airplane.

Greg put his arms around her, held her and the baby, and he told her how much he loved her, but at the moment, she wasn't certain that she loved him. When she went to bed that night, she stayed far away from him, knowing she didn't want his touch, and after he was asleep, breathing in his gravelly way, she found herself thinking, as she had so often lately, about Kent. She wondered what life with him would have been like. She was glad she had Jennifer, and she wanted to believe that nothing this bad would happen again, but she wondered about the choice she had made. She thought again of the things Greg had told her: how uninteresting she was, how lazy, how ugly. All of it felt true to her. And yet she was almost certain that Kent never would have made her feel that way.

# CHAPTER 27

Hans had had a long time—six months—to regret his decision to stay in the GDR, and sometimes he did feel regrets. But he didn't let himself dwell on such thoughts very long. He was certain that the Lord had given him his answer, and now he had to trust that he would someday understand. The problem was, after he had turned down the chance to be released, he had been returned to his cell, and he had faced weeks of nothingness. He had tried to remember the sermons he had once prepared, and even to create new ones. But all the months without the scriptures had created a distance, and he had found it increasingly difficult to remember what he had read. There was something so terribly dulling about the monotony of his life. It was easy to become lethargic, and in the worst moments, to give in to self-pity.

Then one day in September, without explanation, his Bible had been returned to him. Since then he had been sitting at his table most of the time, and he had started over, intent on reading the Bible cover to cover, studying it more closely than ever before. He was finding more significance in the Old Testament than he had recognized before. Many of the prophets had been rejected, cast away, much as he was. All this gave Hans new resolve, and he began to exercise more vigorously again. He had the feeling that his food was improving a little too, and it was certainly coming in larger portions. Hans wondered about all this, wondered whether Felscher was behind it, and if so, what he hoped to accomplish. But the important thing was, Hans was not breaking, and even though Felscher had told him he might be held for his entire three years, he had two years behind him now. If he could return to a work camp, he thought that might help a great deal, but he had his Bible, so he wasn't going to complain.

When Hans was finally summoned to Felscher's office in October, he wasn't sure what to hope for. He knew enough to steel himself for the worst. Felscher might still need Hans to say certain things before he could allow him back to a camp, and he was the sort of man who could always find another approach, another way to twist the knife.

"So, Hans, I'm happy to see you," Felscher said, seeming almost cheery. "Sit down."

Hans thought he understood now. The Bible had been a gift to soften Hans. The pressure would be subtle and gradual, but it was coming. "Thank you," Hans said, and he sat down as Felscher was motioning for him to do.

"I'm curious. Do you find yourself wishing now that you had taken the offer to leave?"

"Sometimes I think about it. But I still feel that I did the right thing."

"But it wasn't for the love of the GDR. You aren't going to claim that, are you?" He grinned. He seemed relaxed this morning, almost casual.

"This country is my home. I love Schwerin. And I love my parents and my sister. It was mostly for them that I wanted to stay."

"And for your church."

"Yes."

"It will always be a struggle, living here, and your church will struggle too. You could have had much more."

"I know. More of some things. But I'm satisfied."

"Hans, I want to know about that. I have no pen, no paper. I'm not writing any of this. I'm merely curious about you. I wonder what makes you the young man you are. What is it in this religion that inspires you?"

"I believe in Jesus Christ. I believe in what he taught. If we would all live by what he taught us, this world would be much better."

"What teachings do you mean? What, specifically, would make the world better?"

"Humility. Love. Too many people want power. They want to rule over others. Christ believed in peace and goodness, even turning the other cheek."

"So is that how you see our government—exercising power over its people?"

"Christ said that if a man was asked to go a mile, he should go two. If we would all live that way, doing what we can for each other, government wouldn't matter very much. That's all I'm saying."

"But it's socialists who want to share, to see to it that everyone prospers. It's the capitalists who believe in uncaring competition—some becoming rich and powerful, others left in poverty and want."

Hans knew what it took to *enforce* such "sharing" on people. And he knew that corruption seemed to come into any form of government. But he couldn't say any of that, not here. So he merely said, "Love comes from inside. Government can't demand it."

"But it can base its principles on fairness, not on greed. It sounds to me as though you believe more in our system than you do in all the hatred and racism and elitism of America. Maybe that's why you stayed."

Hans decided not to answer. He knew better than to describe the abuse of power he saw all around him. But he wondered what Felscher was fishing for. Did he want to write in a report that Hans had reformed and now believed in socialism? Or was he trying to document the opposite, that Hans put his religion above the state?

Felscher's chair creaked as he shifted his weight forward. He laced his thick fingers together. "Hans you're a better person than most—perhaps the best young man I've ever met. Why? How? What's in you that I don't discover in others?"

Hans wasn't sure he knew. "A lot of things have gone wrong in my life," he finally said. "I used to feel sorry for myself. But here in prison, I've had everything taken away, so I've had to ask myself what really mattered to me. I've spent my time reading the scriptures—when I've had them—and I've prayed. I feel like I've gotten closer to understanding myself, and understanding what I want out of life."

"Lots of people read the Bible. And they pray. But I can break them in no time. What's helped you stay so true to what you believe?"

"God can speak to us when we're ready to listen. It was your prison that got me ready."

Felscher shook his head. "None of this answers my question. I want to know who you are, and you won't tell me. Maybe you don't know."

Hans did want to answer. He tried to think what was getting him through all this. "*Herr* Felshcer," he said, "at certain times, when I try to do what's right, I feel something—it's just a sensation, a peaceful feeling—that verifies to me that there is a power outside myself. And when I feel that, I don't wonder what is true. At least for that moment, I *know* it. I don't feel it all the time, but I've felt it enough to know that God is real, and religion isn't just ritual."

"And you're telling me this is it, this sensation, that you rely upon?"

"Not just the sensation, but the knowledge that comes with it. Don't you know what's right sometimes even though you don't know how you know?"

Felscher sat for a long time, staring off toward the wall behind Hans. "Maybe," he finally said. "I'm not certain. But I do know this. I wish there were more people like you in this world, fewer like me. I wish I had your courage and trust. I wish I could go back a little and make some other choices. And I wish I had such a son as you."

Hans nodded, and so did Felscher, and it was clear that he couldn't talk. But when he could again, he said, "Hans, I have reported to my superiors that I am confident you've told me everything. And I've made a case that we need engineers desperately in this country. I actually tried to have you readmitted to a university, but I had little hope that could happen, and of course, I was right about that. Still, we need draftsmen. We need men who can work in engineering offices and do much the same work that fully educated engineers do. What I was able to gain for you—after making the case that you are a good socialist, in your way . . ." He stopped and smiled. " . . . is an opportunity to move out of the prison and into an apartment in Leipzig. You will, technically speaking, still be a prisoner of the state, and you will only be allowed to go back and forth from work to your apartment, or perhaps to a grocery store in your neighborhood—such things as that—but your rent will be paid, and you will have a job that will pay a minimal salary. At some point, if you prove yourself in this 'halfway' condition, you may be allowed your full freedom, and your salary will increase. It may be another year before that happens, but I suspect it won't."

Hans was breathing hard, overwhelmed by the idea of being out of this place.

"You cannot travel anywhere, but your family will be able to visit you at your apartment. Once you are moved to a regular position at your place of employment, you may live as anyone else does, but I doubt that your wages will ever amount to very much. I cannot say for certain that will always be the case, but it's what my superiors are saying now."

"Thank you. Thank you for the help."

"The real help I gave you was the opportunity to leave the country. I'm afraid that the condition of your life, here, will be very discouraging. I suspect that the *Stasi* is hoping that you will fail, that under the pressure you'll have to face you'll resort to trying another escape, and then they can tell themselves you're the menace to our country that they thought you were."

"I won't do that."

"No. But you might become embittered. I hope that in twenty or thirty years, you're the same man you are now. But I doubt very much that that can happen. You'll work hard all your life and receive so little compensation that your life will be difficult, and you will always be watched. The slightest mistake, and any improvement in your situation will be rescinded. That's all I have to offer you, but at least you'll be away from this dreadful place."

Hans smiled a little. "You must not have your recorder running," he said.

"Needless to say, I do not."

They both understood a great deal from that, but neither needed to say any more. They shook hands, and Hans felt some warmth from this man he had once thought so cold.

❧

On the following morning, Hans was driven in a van to Leipzig—a big city south of Berlin and very far from Schwerin. He was given his few belongings—the clothes he had worn the day he had entered the prison, and the suitcase he had been carrying that day—and he was handed the key to an apartment on the third floor of a rather dreary looking postwar, concrete apartment house. Then the van driver got back in the vehicle and drove away. Hans was outside, alone, and—at least in some ways—free. He walked up the stairs and opened the door. He found a tiny apartment, almost as confining as the cell he had lived in. There was a bed in the same room with a little stove and sink, a small table and one chair. But there was an actual bathroom with a rusty but functional toilet, and a bathtub. And in the main room there was a window—with clear glass. He unlocked it and discovered that it actually opened. He stood and looked outside for a time, and then he took out his Bible, along with the Book of Mormon that had been taken from him when he had first entered prison. He set them on the table. He looked around, then turned on an overhead light. The lamp was dim in the daylight, but it worked, and the room would surely be brighter than his prison cell.

This was all good. Very good. But there was something else he wanted to do. He walked back downstairs and out into the street. It was a busy, downtown street, and he loved the noise, the smell of exhaust, the movement of people and automobiles. He walked slowly down the sidewalk. He was aware that someone might be watching him, so he didn't wander, but he went to a grocery store and then waited in line to get into a butcher shop. He couldn't buy much, but he made a few purchases, including a bottle of milk and a dab of butter, both of which pleased him just to think about, and then he walked back outside, and he smelled the city again, listened to it, and watched all the colors and the life.

He walked until he found a little shop that sold stationery, and he bought a few sheets of paper, some envelopes, and a pencil. Then he returned to his apartment. He used part of the afternoon to write a letter to his parents, letting them know of his new circumstance and inviting them to visit him as soon as they possibly could. He wished so much that he had been sent somewhere close to home, but he wasn't going to think much about what he didn't have today; he was still overwhelmed by what he had.

He thought of writing Elli, but he decided he'd better not. Perhaps she was committed to Rainer now. Hans didn't want to get in the way of that. But even if that wasn't happening, he knew the obvious truth. It would be wrong to encourage her to think of him. If he could ever hope for marriage, it could only be after years of work, and after his conditions improved.

But he had known all that for a long time, and he didn't dwell on his future. He had learned not to do that. He was happy to fix himself a nice little meal, with an apple, a carrot, and some fresh cabbage, and he savored a bit of *wurst*, the first meat he had eaten in a long time. Afterward, he read his scriptures for a time—loved the chance to read the Book of Mormon—and then he stood at the window and watched the sun go down. He couldn't see the horizon from his window, but he saw the color of the sky, watched it change from blue to a pale green. And he watched a big cloud turn orange, then shade to dark red before it returned to gray. It was a wonderful thing to see, and he told himself that if he only had that every day, life couldn't be so awfully bad. He knew, in truth, that after a time, he would probably pay little attention, but he promised himself that he would try to remember what a gift it was to see the light.

༄

When Gene stepped to the door of the big cargo airplane, the humid heat struck him, frightened him. He had been told how humid it would be, and he had experienced some muggy days in Georgia that summer, but this was something new. This air seemed too wet to breathe, so hot he couldn't think of living in it. Would his barracks be air-conditioned? He knew the answer, but he couldn't think how he would be able to sleep. It would be like living underwater.

But he jumped down from the airplane and walked toward an old bus. The light around him, coming off the pavement—coming from everywhere, it seemed—almost blinded him. And now he was smelling something foreign, wet, rotten. He smelled diesel exhaust, but beyond that, there was an odor like a city dump, but riper, more rancid, putrefied. He told himself there must be some sort of compost heap or . . . he didn't know what . . . nearby. The whole country couldn't smell this way. He couldn't stand to live with a smell like that all the time.

A young lieutenant, looking tired, his fatigues wet from sweat at the neck and down his sides, greeted Gene and the other men from the airplane. "Welcome, soldiers," he said. "You're at Tan Son Nhut air base, not far from Saigon. Get on the bus. We'll be taking you to the Long Binh Replacement Center. You won't be there long—maybe a day or two, and then you'll get your unit assignment, and you'll be shipped out. Get all the sleep you can when you get to the barracks. You might pull guard duty tonight. If not, I'm sure you can sleep until tomorrow and still not feel caught up."

"Sir, is it always this hot?" one of the men asked.

The lieutenant didn't smile. He said, "This isn't the worst time of the year. The rainy season is almost over. May and June are hotter. Up north isn't quite so bad sometimes. Some of you might end up there."

"Yeah, but that's Indian country," another guy said.

The lieutenant looked at him for a moment, and then he said, with a hint of anger, "You guys think you know all about it, don't you? Just get on the bus." Except that he used the favorite army word as a modifier, even got it in twice.

The men worked their way toward the bus, stood in line, and then piled on. As Gene walked past the heavyset corporal who was driving, he heard the man mumble, "Don't stick your fingers through the wire." Gene didn't know what he meant. But when he took a seat, he noticed that the open window was covered with chicken wire. As the bus passed through a little street, just off the base, the kids, even adults, shouted at the soldiers on the bus, "Go home, GI," or used that same favorite army word. And then a rotten piece of fruit hit the bus close to Gene's screened window. He got the point.

"Aren't these the people we're fighting for?" the kid sitting next to Gene asked.

"I think we got off in the wrong Vietnam," Gene said, and he tried to laugh. But this wasn't funny to him. It had never occurred to him that the people in the south wouldn't think well of him. Some of the guys on the bus started yelling through the windows, calling the people "gooks." What a great start.

But all this seemed to fit with an article he had read in a *Time* magazine on the way over. The cover story had been a disturbing piece about an army lieutenant, William Calley, who had ordered his soldiers to massacre hundreds of Vietnamese civilians in the village of My Lai. What bothered Gene almost more than the incident itself was the speculation in the article that the war in Vietnam seemed to create an atmosphere where such atrocities were not uncommon. Some Vietnam vets were even saying that My Lai was only a large-scale example of similar crimes that were occurring constantly. It was hard enough for Gene to think about fighting a war most Americans didn't expect to win; how could he face the idea that at least in some cases, his fellow soldiers were acting like the bad guys?

The replacement center turned out to be a grim place: rows of rough-wood barracks, built on hot sand. But Gene was too tired to care. He hadn't been able to sleep in the uncomfortable seats on the airplane, and he had now been underway almost thirty-six hours. So as soon as he was assigned a barracks, he pulled off all the clothing he could. He had grown used to life in khaki underwear, but he still felt the loss, the sense that a sacred part of his life had been taken from him. Still, he didn't worry about that now. He dropped onto a cot and let himself drift away. He didn't know whether this day counted toward his 365, but he wanted to sleep for as long as possible, and maybe that would start his count the easy way.

He slept for a long time—the rest of the day and most of the night. But eventually he was working at it, trying to stay on the cot but becoming increasingly restless. His mind was playing tricks on him, mixing memories, thoughts of home with new images: the tin and cardboard shacks he had seen on the way here; children running naked; hostile faces. The heat had backed off in the night, but not enough, and the smell of body odor from all the men in the barracks only added to the corrupt, lingering stench from outside.

At some point Gene came wide awake, and the thought that opened his eyes was: I can't do this. I can't possibly live here for a year. I can't be away from Emily that long, from Danny. I can't take it. There's got to be some way out. But he knew he couldn't think that way. He had to take everything one day at a time, just handle what came.

And then he heard the war. In the distance was the sound of artillery or maybe bombs, bumping and rolling. How could that be happening so close to Saigon? He had heard gunfire at basic, but it had always been practice, just target shooting. Now people were probably dying out there, not very far away. It seemed, in his tired mind, that he had never known that, that he hadn't signed on for real shooting, for death. He couldn't believe how frightened he was. Was this the beginning of an attack—something like the Tet offensive, last year? He knew the North Vietnamese had actually reached Saigon back then, that some of the fighting had taken place right here at this base. He lay there and wondered, how soon would he be in the fight? Would he be able to act like a man? If he was this scared now, at a big base like this, how could he handle the jungle, if that's where he ended up?

But he was roused from his bunk early, not long after first light, and the sergeant who ordered him up seemed not to notice that any shooting was going on. Gene spent his day hurrying, only to stand in line and wait. He signed papers, was issued weapons, uniforms. And that afternoon, he got his assignment: Camp Eagle, in the north. Back in the states there was always talk about "hot spots" and "Indian Country," the places where the action was going on. He didn't know the name of this place, but he did see "Rangers" on the company he was joining—Lima Company, 75th Infantry—and he wasn't sure how that could happen. He thought that Rangers received special training. They were supposed to be tough guys, ready for anything, and he didn't think a guy coming out of radio school could get an assignment with men like that. But one of the men in the barracks told him, "I'll bet that means you'll stay on the base and receive radio communication. I doubt they're going to send you out in the field with a bunch of Rangers, not with the training you have."

Gene didn't know. What the guy said made sense, but if Gene had learned one thing about the army so far, it was that nothing ever made sense. Anything predictable was wrong; anything illogical was entirely to be expected. So he flew again the next day, and this time with deeper fear, and yet, with a flicker of hope. Maybe he would work in an office. Maybe it was air-conditioned. Maybe he wouldn't have to sleep in a tent or a hooch, and maybe he wouldn't have to go out into that dense jungle he could see down below.

He arrived at Camp Eagle, near Hue, and was picked up in a Jeep by a corporal whose answer to every question was "I got no idea" or "How would I know?" He seemed hostile, as though he hated Gene for no reason, and he cursed as though he were seething with some sort of chronic disgust. The corporal dropped Gene off in front of a "hooch"—a hut-like structure, halfway underground and completely surrounded with sandbags. "This is where you're assigned for now," he said. "There'll be an empty cot. Take that one."

So Gene descended into the hooch, down a few steps, into semidarkness. The heat was bad inside, but not unthinkable. That was the best, but Gene couldn't imagine living with the smell, the closeness, and with these men who looked at him warily. They said hello, said their names, shook hands, but he didn't like the look in their eyes. At Long Binh some of the men had had mustaches, even hair that seemed longer than regulations allowed, but these guys looked more like Marines, with "white sidewalls" high above their ears, and no facial hair. Four of the five guys in the tent were white, which seemed a higher percentage of whites than he had seen in Long Binh. Gene wondered why. He also wondered why the men looked dirty, as though their fatigues had, at some point, gotten too filthy ever to be clean again.

Gene tried to ask some questions, but he got the same kind of answers the corporal had given him. He did learn that Camp Eagle was a 101st Airborne camp, and that L Company had been transferred only recently from the 101st over to the Rangers. "We're Lurps," one of the guys told him, but Gene was embarrassed to ask what that was.

He had been in the hooch only half an hour or so when a sergeant first class walked in. "Thomas?" he said.

"Yes."

"Come with me. The CO wants to talk to you."

So Gene followed the sergeant to the commanding officer's head-quarters, glad for the chance to get an answer or two. He entered a another building that was lined all the way around with sandbags, and then the sergeant said, "Sit down. I'll tell Captain Battaglia you're here."

So Gene sat in another dark, humid room, and then, when called upon, walked into the office, snapped off a clean salute, and said, "Private Eugene Thomas, reporting for duty, sir." The officer looked up at him with a curious look on his face, as if to say, "What's all that about?"

He did wave a half-salute at Gene, and then he said, "Sit down, Private. I need to talk to you. We've got ourselves a bit of a situation here."

"Situation, sir?"

Battaglia was a handsome young man, dark-haired, with thick eye-brows and dark eyes. He seemed no older than twenty-four or so, Gene's age.

"We're a Lurp unit. Do you know what that is?"

"Not exactly. I've heard people mention the word."

"It used to be L-R-R-P. Now they just write it L-R-P. But it stands for Long Range Reconnaissance Patrol. We send out small patrols, usually six men. We insert into the jungle, look for Charlie, and then pull out in a few days. It's serious stuff. Dangerous stuff. We got you here because we saw your papers and noticed you were older than most, that you did well in basic, and above all, that you're a radioman. We're in bad need of guys with radio training."

Gene nodded, but he had lost his breath.

"Now that I have some detail on you, I'm thinking this is the wrong thing. We can't send just anybody out there. A guy who can't handle it can get a patrol killed off, quick. It's a volunteer kind of thing. You've got to be good to do the job, but you've got to be nuts to be willing. We put our butts on the line every time we go out there."

This was not what Gene wanted—and the last thing his father wanted him to do. Or his wife. Maybe he could say no.

"When we asked for you, we didn't know enough about you. I'm thinking I'd better get you shipped to another unit. You might have to sit around here a few days before I can get you transferred, but I guess that's not the worst thing that could happen to a guy."

"What do you mean, sir, you didn't know enough about me?"

"We didn't know that your old man was a congressman. We didn't know you were a college grad and a new father. And we sure didn't know you'd been a missionary."

Gene felt the insult. It was the same old thing. "I don't understand. What does that have to do with it?"

Captain Battaglia stared at his desk for a time. "The very fact you have to ask shows you just got here from 'the world.' You don't know how things go down over here." He was quiet again for a time. "Let me put it this way. We ain't short of radio operators because all the ones we had got old and decided to retire."

"They were killed?"

"Not always. Some were just shot up."

He stared at Gene and waited. Gene felt the fear, but he was also angry. "So you think a congressman's son can't handle something like that?"

"Maybe. Maybe not. But this is no work for a missionary."

"My dad was a missionary, and he was also a war hero. He was in the 101st Airborne. He received a battlefield commission, and he was dropped into Germany, behind the lines. He did reconnaissance for the men crossing the Rhine."

"Look, that all sounds dramatic. They should make a movie out of it. But Germany wasn't Vietnam. This is a different world. When you go out with us, you can't have anything else on your mind. Your patrol has to depend on you, absolutely. If you start worrying too much about getting back to that wife and little baby, you'll make a mistake. You don't just get yourself killed—a whole team can go down."

Gene hated the accusation, the implied assessment of him. He knew as he said the words that he was making a mistake, but he said all the same, "I can do what I'm asked to do. If you don't want me, that's up to you. But don't assume who I am, based on what you know."

The captain nodded, and then he stared at Gene for several seconds. He might have been smiling, ever so slightly. "All right," he finally said. "You're big enough to pack a radio, and if you're stupid enough to try this, we'll take you out a time or two—then decide if we want to keep you. But it's your call. If you've got any brains at all, just back away from us."

"Where would I go, if I turn you down?"

"Most likely out to the boonies somewhere. You'll hump the hills with an infantry unit."

"Is that any better?"

"I guess it depends on how you look at it. We've only got the *best* with us. Our men aren't sitting out there in the jungle smoking dope. We know what we're doing, and we do it well. Most infantry units are full of brainless kids, just counting their days. Some guys like to know they're fighting with the best men over here."

"But you say I'd have to be stupid to stay with you?"

"No. Not necessarily." Suddenly Battaglia grinned. "But it helps."

Gene couldn't think what to do. Either option sounded bad. But he kept thinking of his promise. This all sounded like hero stuff, and Dad had told him not to be a hero. "Could I possibly stay here but serve with the 101st?"

"Probably. In fact, that makes sense, since you've got jump training. And the Screaming Eagles are good soldiers. That's how I came up. Of course, those guys are working the same hills we are, and they stay out in the jungle a lot longer." He hesitated and then added, "But then, their casualty rate ain't as bad as ours, either."

Gene didn't know what to do. He had dreaded, as much as anything, living in the jungle. At least reconnaissance teams went out on short missions. "How often do Lurps go out? Do they—"

"Look, you obviously have some doubts. That tells me all I need to know. I'll have you transferred in a day or two. If I was you, I'd call your dad. Have him pull some strings and get you sent to some post far away from the action—someplace where you can get to church on Sunday." The captain stood up.

Gene stood too. "Sir, I haven't asked for any special favors. I never mention my father, and I'm surprised that's even in my file. I don't think he should come into this at all."

"So what are you telling me? You think you're a man?"

"Find out what I can do. I think I can handle it as well as anyone else. I was the best athlete in my high school. I was a quarterback, but I played defense too, and I played *tough*."

The captain laughed. "Well, Thomas, that's just the kind of stupid statement I've been waiting for. I'll give you a try."

Gene liked the way Battaglia was looking at him now. Maybe this was stupid, but Gene needed to respect himself. He couldn't stand the thought of ducking his head and asking for a softer job.

But by the time he got back to his hooch, the momentary pride had disappeared, and Gene began to think about the things Battaglia had said. He wondered why so many radio operators had gone down. And that brought him to the other question. What would Emily think of him if she had an idea what he had just done?

# CHAPTER 28

Kathy was on a bus—but not like any bus she had ever seen. It was rusty and noisy beyond belief, but it was the goat on board that had taken her by surprise. An old fellow had boarded at the last stop leading a gray goat—a mangy, smelly thing—and then he had walked down the aisle and chosen the seat across from Kathy. The goat was standing next to her now, eyeing her as though it wondered whether she might be edible. But all it really needed to do was look around a little. There was food everywhere. People were not only eating; they were passing their food around, sharing with each other. Kathy's first thought had been that she had gotten on a bus full of friends on a holiday. But people got off and on at the many stops, and the party continued, the new guests always welcome. She tried the food that people offered her—fish of some kind, and a rice cake—and didn't find the flavors all that much to her liking, but she claimed she did and received more.

People knew about the Peace Corps, and they recognized that she must be a volunteer. Some talked to her in English that she usually understood only about half of. She tried the bit of Tagalog she had learned, and they seemed to understand her about as well. But they were clearly happy to have her along; they even showed her a certain deference, which embarrassed her. Still, the welcome felt good, and the people seemed nice. She would merely have to get used to the atmosphere. She wasn't great at meeting people for the first time, and these people didn't mind staring at her, asking her surprisingly personal questions. One woman asked her whether she was married, and when she said no, simply asked, "Why?" It was hard to know how to answer. But worst was the way everyone talked about her, pointed to her. She heard the English word "tall" a couple of times, but mostly they pointed to her and spoke in dialect, and they stretched their arms as high as they could, clearly to indicate her enormous height. One man kept saying, "Stand up. Show the people how big you are."

Kathy laughed and tried to be good natured about all the attention, but she wasn't about to stand up. She wasn't, after all, the giant lady in a circus sideshow. She wondered whether she would cause so much attention her entire time in the Philippines.

Most of the people seemed clean and rather nicely dressed, the men in their white *barong* shirts, the women in white blouses and long, dark skirts, but the bus was steamy hot, and the smell of the food and the bodies was strong. After four years in western Massachusetts, she felt a little as though she had fallen through the earth and landed in a place that was turned upside down. *Everything* was different.

Kathy had flown from the Hilo airport three weeks before, had spent a nice little mini-vacation in Honolulu, and then had flown to the Philippines by way of Hong Kong. She had attended a couple more days of training in Manila and then had spent two weeks with two other volunteers, both teachers at a high school. She was now on her way to San Juan—a barrio just outside Manila—where she would teach high school English. She would have two classes of her own and would work as an aide to another teacher, Mrs. Sanchez, the rest of the day. What she had learned so far was actually rather discouraging. The volunteers she met seemed almost apologetic about the results of their service. When Sargent Shriver and other early Peace Corps leaders had tried to get things started here, the acceptance by a government accustomed to American involvement was immediate. But almost all the volunteers had been placed in an education system that turned out to have too many teachers. To avoid replacing regular teachers, and putting them out of work, most of the volunteers had become teachers' aides. These positions had come to be called "non-jobs" because the duties were so vague. Recently, more of the volunteers were taking on their own classes, but it was a good question as to whether they offered much of anything that local teachers couldn't have done as well.

One of the trainers in Manila, a fellow near the end of his two-year stint, had told the new volunteers, "You have to look for ways to contribute, and to tell the truth, a lot of times, what we do for these people seems negligible. It's more 'good neighbor' stuff than it is 'change the world' stuff, and I think most volunteers start out expecting to have more impact. But just remember, before you try to change what you see, learn from these people. A lot of the change comes to us, not to them, and that's not a bad thing. Maybe the most important thing we do here is learn to understand each other."

But that seemed a cop-out to Kathy. She had the impression that Filipinos were too easygoing, that they weren't trying to make things better for poor people—and she had already seen disgusting levels of poverty. She feared that Peace Corps Volunteers in the Philippines had taken on a little too much of the behavior of the natives. Some gave her the impression they were just putting in their time, rationalizing their own laziness. She hoped she could be a good teacher, and worried about that, but she had been taught in all her training that PCVs—Peace Corps Volunteers—had to perceive local needs and do something to improve the community. She had heard about amazing projects to clean up water supplies or upgrade farming techniques. She doubted that she could do anything quite so technical, but other volunteers had set up libraries or taught the people to practice better hygiene or better nutrition. In Hawaii her trainers had warned her about the challenges: the heat, the diseases, the mosquitoes, and above all the difficulty in changing the ingrained practices of a very poor people. But she had vowed that she wasn't going to get lazy or discouraged. She would leave her community a better place.

When the bus entered San Juan, she was rather shocked to see how different the town was from the training barrio in Waipio Valley. She saw some nipa huts on stilts with cooking areas underneath, but she also saw houses that looked more like "shelters" to her: little stucco or cinder-block buildings with tin roofs, or worse, shacks made of scrap lumber. Little alleys were full of rusted bicycles and old wooden boxes, piles of junk. The *Sari-sari* stores, which she recognized from her training village, weren't the neat little shops she expected but cubbyholes crammed with a mass of items for sale, all piled on top of each other. The kids in the street, many in shirts with no pants, looked like little urchins she had seen only in documentaries on educational television. The rainy season was ending now, she had been told, but mud was everywhere, clogging the streets and walkways. Certain low spots were a quagmire of standing water and deep mud. She saw a group of men sitting in a circle in front of a little store, or maybe it was a bar. They were drinking something—probably *tuba,* the alcoholic drink made from coconut juice that Kathy had been told about. But it was the middle of the day. Didn't they work? she wondered. If they didn't have jobs, why weren't they doing something to drain off some of that standing water, or to pave some of the muddy walkways? A person didn't have to look around much to see there was work to be done.

Kathy stepped off the bus and looked around for someone from the school, or from the Peace Corps, to greet her. But no one was there. What surprised her was the way the children came running from all directions. They kept calling out "*Mabuhay, mabuhay,*" and some were saying, "Hello. Good day. Good day." But they also laughed and pointed at her, stretched their arms high, and she realized again that they were astounded to see how tall she was. She patted some of the sweaty heads, said hello to everyone, but the truth was, she was a little frightened. The kids were bumping against her, jostling her, and most of them were caked with mud. She wasn't sure what she was supposed to do.

"School?" she asked. She had no confidence in trying Tagalog, since she hadn't understood much of what the kids had been saying.

The children knew the word "school," and they pointed up the street toward a little hill. She wondered why these kids weren't in school somewhere themselves. It was almost funny to think what her trainers had told her—that she would have to be in the community a while before she figured out where she could help. If kids were wandering around, not in school, she certainly didn't have to think too hard about what problem to deal with first. She also wondered what was causing the strange mixture of smells. Some of it seemed to be animal dung, but she had also seen a small boy urinating in the street, and in the middle of all these kids, she was picking up aromas from them that hardly seemed clean and healthy.

Kathy decided she might as well walk to the school. She tried to pick up her suitcase, but two of the bigger boys grabbed for it, and then, with good-natured smiles, decided to carry it together, one on each side. It was a big bag, very heavy, and it was all they could do to stagger ahead with it, but when she tried to take it from them, they waved her off. "We carry. We strong," they told her. She was glad to know they were learning English. She had been told that English was the language of the schools after third grade.

Kathy walked with the children, amid all the chatter, and still the laughter about her height, but some of the kids ran ahead. Kathy took her time, partly because she was sweating so badly her clothes were soaking through, and partly because she was trying to avoid the worst of the mud. Her shoes were a mess already. Halfway up the hill, she saw an *Americana* coming down the hill toward her.

The young woman waved and smiled. She was half a foot shorter than Kathy, and still taller than most Filipino women. She didn't hurry. In fact, she stopped and waited. But when Kathy reached her, she extended her hand. She was wearing one of the white blouses with pretty stitching that many of the native women wore. Her light hair, almost blonde, and her gray-blue eyes set her apart from everyone else. "My name's Martha

Sommers," she said. "Welcome." Kathy shook her hand. "Don't mind the kids. They get excited when a new volunteer arrives."

"They think I'm funny looking, don't they?"

"Well, sort of. They think you're *very* tall. But Alena here thinks you're pretty. That's what she kept saying." Martha pulled the little girl close to her and held her against her side. She said something in Tagalog, and Alena, looking embarrassed and shy now, nodded.

Kathy thought Alena was beautiful, with such big, dark eyes and short, boyish hair. "Nice to meet you, Alena," she said. The little girl put out her hand and let Kathy shake it, and then she laughed. Kathy wasn't sure why.

"I had no idea when your bus would get here," Martha said. "There's no real schedule. I'm glad the boys wanted to help you with your bag."

"Yes. They're very nice." But she was nervous about the muddy spot where they had set the suitcase. She hoped the water wouldn't soak through into her clothes.

"Out in these barrios, there aren't any taxis or jeepneys. Sometimes you can hire a little horse-drawn cart, but I haven't seen Ferdinand today. When it's muddy, it's probably just as fast to walk anyway."

"So the mud does dry up sometimes?"

Martha laughed. "Oh, yes. It won't be long until dust replaces the mud. You'll find yourself wondering whether you didn't like the mud better."

"Couldn't sidewalks be built?"

Martha laughed even harder. "Oh, Kathy, you're new here. We all start with the same questions. The best advice I can give you is not to worry too much about things that seem strange to you at first. After a while, you start to understand how things work—or actually, don't work."

Kathy was alarmed. This was more of what she had been hearing from other volunteers. They talked like some of the hippies she had known, as though it was fine to "just go with the flow." She definitely wasn't going to let herself slip into that kind of thinking. But she decided not to challenge Martha already, having just met her. She did need to watch and learn before she made up her mind about everything. She couldn't resist one more question, however. "Why aren't the kids in school?"

"Well, that's a little complicated. I'll just call it a day off. You'll see the older kids working on the school grounds. These younger ones are supposed to help, but they can't do all that much, so they wander off. Attendance at school is . . . I don't know what to call it. It's not exactly voluntary. Kids are supposed to go. But it's . . . I don't know."

"Haphazard?"

"Well, yeah. But that's such an American way of looking at it. You need to spend some time here before you start to make a lot of judgments. You're going to love the Filipino people, Kathy; I promise you that. Just give everything some time."

Kathy was still walking as carefully as she could, but she noticed that Martha was sloshing through the mud without worrying about her shoes. The ones she was wearing looked bulky, like hiking boots, and they were trashed. Kathy didn't like the idea, but she could see that it made sense. "How long have you been here, Martha?" she asked.

"I came last year. I've put in one year at the school already."

"Do you think I'll be here the whole time, both years?"

"It's hard to say. Usually, that's how it's done. But the Corps is cutting back the number of volunteers in the Philippines. They've decided there are too many of us. So they might be spreading us around a little thinner at some point."

"Why do I keep getting the feeling that the Peace Corps isn't accomplishing much in the Philippines?" Kathy asked.

Martha glanced over and smiled. She was not a pretty girl—not exactly—with rounded cheeks and a face too circular, too featureless, but she had a kindly smile and an endearing quality that Kathy liked already. Kathy had seen it in the tender way she had embraced little Alena, and she felt it now in the way she reached out and patted Kathy's arm. "For now, I just wouldn't make up your mind about *anything*," she said. "We all come with these notions about things, and all those expectations have to be adjusted, or discarded, and then you can start over. But every time I make up my mind that this whole thing is a waste of my time and Uncle Sam's money, something happens to make me think otherwise."

Kathy tried to accept that, but as she looked around, she wondered where she would live and what it would be like to be among these people for such a long time. The area was beautiful, in its way, with palm trees and flowers and so much green, but she was struggling with the smells, the suffocating air, and the grungy, broken-down look of things.

"What about the teaching? Is it satisfying?"

"Overall, yes. It will be especially nice this year. You and I are each going to have two classes of our own. Last year was frustrating. I was called an aide, but I didn't know what to do. I found some things, but a person could argue that I didn't have to be sent halfway around the world to do them."

"Is it a decent school?"

"Yes. I know San Juan looked rather dumpy where you got off, but that's the worst part of town. It's actually the *población*—what we would call the county seat—and that's why we have a high school. Kids come from the other barrios around here. The ones who go on to high school are smart, and they come from supportive families. But sometimes, the way schools are operated will baffle you. The school year starts at the end of the summer, but hardly anything happens at first. They keep transferring teachers around. Then they stop to fix up the grounds—because the district supervisor is coming for a visit—and there are a thousand interruptions and nothing runs on time, and . . . well, you'll see. But you know what? The kids do learn, and they know a lot of things you and I never will understand. So, yeah, it's not such a bad school."

But none of this sounded good to Kathy. She found herself wondering how she was going to live here. Two years was suddenly sounding like a very long time.

"Where are you from, Kathy?" Martha asked.

"I'm *from* Utah. But I've been at Smith College, in Massachusetts, the last four years."

"Not exactly the combination I'd expect. How did you happen to go there?"

"I have an aunt who teaches at Smith. That was what got me interested. But I also wanted to experience something new."

"I did something like that. I grew up in South Dakota, but I went to college at the University of Michigan."

"Did you like it there?"

Martha smiled again, with that mild manner. "It's such a big place, and I was from a small town. At first I thought I would drown in all the humanity. But I found a few friends, and that's all I needed. That's how it's been here, too. You latch onto the other volunteers, to some degree, but most of the enjoyment comes from the Filipino people. You'll like a lot of the teachers, and you'll fall in love with your students. They're just amazingly agreeable."

"Martha, I've never taught. I don't even have a teaching degree. I don't know what I'm doing."

Martha laughed. "We'll help you," she said. "We've been working on an English curriculum ever since the first volunteers came to this school. The kids speak enough English to understand you pretty well, and you'll understand them once you get used to their pronunciation."

"How important is it to learn Tagalog?"

"*Very*. They'll never really feel close to you until you learn the language. Try, right from the beginning. Say anything you know, even if it's just a greeting. They'll love you for that. And it's beautiful how they respond. The kids *want* to love you."

Kathy wondered about that. She wasn't one to be so personal, to touch children the way Martha had done.

"I hope someone warned you—our house isn't anything to get excited about."

Kathy hated to think what the place might be like. She pictured a bamboo nipa hut with no screens. But she saw the school first, and she was pleasantly surprised. The high school and elementary were side by side, actually in several nice-looking buildings. The kids followed Kathy and Martha past the school to the house, and Martha thanked them and laughed with them, hugged some of them again. The boys who had carried the suitcase stood in front of Kathy and smiled. "Should I pay them something?" Kathy asked Martha.

"Oh, no. Just thank them."

Kathy patted each boy on the shoulder and thanked them in Tagalog. The boys beamed.

"Oh, dear, I hate to tell you," Martha said, "but two little boys just fell in love. You're going to see a lot of those guys around here."

Kathy was pleased, but she turned her attention to the house. It was a little stucco place, the plaster broken away in patches, revealing concrete blocks, but when she stepped inside, she saw that the plaster had held up better there, and even though the ceilings were low and the rooms small, the windows were screened. The kitchen was rather neat and cozy, with a little wooden table, an electric stove, and a noisy but functioning refrigerator. Best of all, Kathy had a bedroom of her own.

"This isn't so bad," Kathy told Martha, after they had walked through it.

"I'm glad you think so. But there are some things that will take some getting used to. It looks like we have a shower, but at least for now, it's only what people call a 'dip and pour' arrangement. In other words, it's just cold water in a bucket, and you have to pump your own water out in back. You can heat the water on the stove. The only trouble is that we have to boil water for drinking, too, and the electricity goes out a lot. When the worst heat comes on, in the spring, there are brown-outs all the time. We actually have a system out back that pumps water to a barrel on the roof, and then the shower works by gravity. But the pump has gone out. I've been pleading for months to get it fixed, but no one ever gets around to it."

Kathy did lose a little of her enthusiasm for the place at that point.

"One other thing." Martha smiled, but she looked apologetic. "Sometimes, at night, you'll hear mice and rats scratching around. I've come face to face with a rat in our kitchen a couple of times. I don't want to get you upset, but you have to know, they're really big. A lot of people in the Philippines believe it's bad luck to kill rats, and needless to say, I don't go along with that, but if you poison them, they can die inside the walls, and then you end up with a smell that you can't believe. Sometimes I've set traps, but then you have to carry their bodies out. It's strange, but after a while, you just don't think too much about having them around."

"I think I'll set traps," Kathy said. She was feeling something in her knees: a weakness from the climb up the hill maybe, from the heat and the smells, or maybe it was from the picture in her mind of that huge rat. She had been wondering for a long time whether she was up to this, but the question had suddenly taken on a new seriousness.

"Kathy, I've hit you with a lot of stuff, all at once. I know how I felt about everything when I got here. But just take the days one at a time for a while. It's surprising how many things you get used to. The first time someone serves you dog meat, you think—"

"Dog meat?"

"Oh. I shouldn't have said that. You don't have to eat it. People understand that Americans don't eat things like that. I'm just saying that—"

"Let's just go back to the one-day-at-a-time thing. Don't tell me any more, okay?"

Martha laughed. "It's a deal. But honest, Kathy, you're going to be fine. I promise. I love this place. I really do."

Kathy believed her, and she liked the confidence in Martha's lovely smile, but Kathy also needed to be alone for a little while. She took her suitcase to her bedroom and started to unpack. Martha left her alone for quite some time, but then she took her to the school and introduced her to the teachers, the principal, and some of the students. After they returned, she cooked a tasty dinner of rice and fried fish and served delicious fresh mango for dessert. Then, after dinner, Martha tried to explain a little more about the operation of the school, but Kathy's mind wasn't on the conversation, and she was extremely tired. Martha was the one who told her she'd better try to get some sleep, even though the bedroom would be awfully hot for a few more hours.

Kathy's bed looked more like rattan lawn furniture than a bed, but she soon learned why. The lattice work allowed the air to pass through, as did the mat she slept on. Kathy realized that a mattress, by comparison, would be oppressively hot. She was also tired enough to fall asleep quickly—until the noises began. She heard screeches and chirps and rustling palm fronds, all in a blend louder than she ever could have imagined. She assumed she was only hearing birds and tried to think pleasant thoughts about that, but in the morning she learned that one of the sounds was from a big lizard. She immediately thought again of taking the bus back to Manila, and from there an airplane all the way home. But Martha told her that the lizards were harmless, and good luck. Kathy had almost bought that idea in Hawaii when the lizard was the size of the horned toads she had caught in Parley's Ravine when she was a little girl. But these were giants. She hadn't seen one, but she had heard the cry, and she now had Martha's detailed description to tuck away along with all the other images she was trying to get used to.

The work on the schoolyard continued for a few more days, and that at least gave Kathy a little time to settle in. But then school opened again, and the first couple of weeks were as difficult as anything Kathy had ever faced. She relied on Martha and the other teachers for a lesson plan, but she worried every night and spent countless hours preparing. Most of the kids could recite what she told them, but they couldn't really converse very well in English, and her Tagalog was hopeless. She didn't even try to use it, except to greet them or to thank them. The students were patient with her, and even acted as though they liked her, but she felt as though she were teaching through a screen. How could she work with people she couldn't understand and who couldn't understand her unless she limited her vocabulary to the simplest of terms? Another teacher usually stayed around to help her, but that meant Kathy was only a human record player, there to provide an example of American pronunciation. She read sentences, which the students repeated, but any genuine discussion had to be directed toward the "real" teacher. The rest of the day wasn't so frightening, but it was unbearably boring. Kathy didn't know what was expected of an "aide," and Mrs. Sanchez wouldn't give her anything to do. "Just listen for now," she would say. "Enjoy yourself. Get to know the students." But Kathy spent her time at the back of the class, feeling no connection to what was happening.

One day after school Martha asked, "Kathy, have you started your home visits yet?"

"No. I don't know what I'm supposed to do. What do you talk about?"

"It depends. Why don't you go with me now? I have to visit a family of one of our former students. He was in my class last year, and he was supposed to come back this fall, but he hasn't done it. I'm going to go see whether I can find out why."

Kathy knew she would be up late that night if she didn't start her preparations soon, but she also needed this experience, so she agreed to go along. The only problem was, the family lived in another *barrio,* a two-mile walk. There was a bus that made the trip, but Martha said it was usually easier to walk and then hail the bus if it happened to come by. As it turned out, they walked the whole distance along a rutted road that was beginning to turn hard under the baking sun, now that the rains were subsiding.

They arrived at a little, neat house in the village—a place much like San Juan but considerably smaller—and Martha knocked. A woman came to the door, nodded deferentially to Martha, almost a bow, and said in Tagalog, "Please come in." Kathy knew that much.

"Mrs. Vasquez, may we speak English?" Martha asked. "This is my friend Kathy. She's new with us—a new volunteer. She doesn't speak Tagalog very well yet."

"Yes, yes," the woman said. Kathy tried to think how old she must be. Something in her diminutive size made her seem young. Everyone seemed that way. And yet, there was a worn, thick quality in the skin around her eyes. She was wearing a simple dress, cotton, brick red with yellow flowers.

"How are you, Mrs. Vasquez?"

"Good. Very good." She motioned for Martha and Kathy to sit down at the kitchen table. They slid back chairs and sat, and then Mrs. Vasquez did too.

"And your husband? Is he well too?"

"Yes, yes."

"Tell me about Diego. What is he doing now?"

"Work. With his father."

"Then he's becoming a gardener?"

"Yes."

"Where does he work?"

"The rich people. Dey give him work. Like his father."

"Does he like this work?"

Mrs. Vasquez nodded. "It's good work," she said.

"But is it what he wants to do?"

She shrugged, looked away. "It's good work," she said again.

Kathy watched Martha, saw her look toward the living room. A little girl, maybe six or seven, was playing quietly on the floor. She had a little doll. She was putting a dress on it, straining to get an arm through the sleeve. "And your other children? Is everyone well?"

"Yes, yes."

Kathy was a little confused. Hadn't they come to convince the woman that her son ought to return to school?

"It's good to see the rains end."

"Yes."

"Mrs. Vasquez, would Diego like to come back to school?"

"Maybe. I don't know."

Martha slid her chair a little closer, and she touched the woman's hand. "He wants to be a teacher, Mrs. Vasquez. He would be a wonderful teacher."

The woman nodded again.

"Did he tell you he wanted to be a teacher?"

Again she nodded.

"He could help other children. He would be very happy. And teachers make good money."

"I tell him."

"You will? Will you tell him we want him to come back?"

"Yes."

"Should I talk to his father?"

"No. I tell him."

All was quiet. Kathy wondered what sort of strange game this was. Couldn't Martha come back and speak to the boy himself?

"He could still come to the high school," Martha said. "It's not too late."

"Yes. I know. I tell him."

But Kathy sensed that Mrs. Vasquez didn't mean it. Kathy couldn't resist saying, "Sometimes we have to do the thing we love. If we don't, we are never happy. If he wants to be a teacher, not a gardener, shouldn't he have his chance?"

"It's a good job."

"But he can help so many people as a teacher."

Mrs. Vasquez stared at Kathy for a time, looking mystified.

Martha finally said, "Will you tell him *for sure* that it's not too late? He can still come back."

"Yes. I tell him."

"Will you try to convince him?" Kathy asked. "It's terrible for him to miss his chance."

Again the mystified look. "It's a good job," she repeated.

"Very good, Mrs. Vasquez," Martha said. And then she talked about nothing at all, as far as Kathy was concerned. It was so frustrating to hear the woman say she would do something, and to know very well that she wouldn't. How could the Peace Corps ever raise people out of poverty if they didn't place more value on education? Here was a boy who had a chance to improve himself; Martha ought to take a stronger stand.

The conversation switched to Tagalog at some point and became warmer, richer in sound, and Kathy could see in Mrs. Vasquez's eyes how much she loved Martha. Kathy felt a little jealous of that, but when she and Martha finally left, Kathy couldn't wait to say, "She's not going to talk to him about coming back to school. Why didn't she just say so?"

"Filipinos don't do that," Martha said.

"Don't do what?"

"They don't disagree—especially not with us. We have very high station in this society. We're teachers. We're Americans."

"What does that have to do with it? Can't she be honest and just say, 'His father wants him to be a gardener'?"

"No. She really can't. She thinks that would be insulting to us. So she pretends to agree, just to be kind."

"Will she even talk to the boy about our visit?"

"I don't know. She might tell him we came. But she won't try to talk him into coming back to school—not if his father doesn't want him to."

"So how can you ever get through to these people if they won't tell you what they really think?"

"At the end, after we had talked for a time, in Tagalog, I told her that I admired her son and considered him very intelligent. I told her that he would make a wonderful teacher. She got tears in her eyes. Maybe you saw that. So I don't know. She might say something."

"But she probably won't. Right?"

"Yeah. I guess I'd say that."

"I don't know whether I can do this, Martha."

"Kathy, didn't you see how much love she had for us?"

"Not for me, she didn't. What difference does that make anyway? A boy who has the ability to go to college is going to do common labor all his life—and have nothing more to give his family than he got from his father. So what difference does it make whether she loves you or not?"

"It makes a big difference, Kathy. It's almost the only difference we do make."

The sentiment was beautiful, and Kathy respected Martha for her kindness, but there was no logic to what she was saying. The woman could love Martha forever, but if she wouldn't listen, wouldn't speak to her son, and would let him do the wrong thing—just because it was what his father wanted—why was the Peace Corps even here? Kathy felt she had to get an answer to that question, and soon. If she couldn't, she really did have to leave.

# CHAPTER 29

G ene hadn't expected to be sent out on a reconnaissance patrol so soon. He had trained hard for a week, working on patrol procedures, night defensive positions, equipment, hand signals, radio protocol, and dozens of other things, but he felt as though he had been trying to drink from a fire hose and would need at least another month to feel somewhat ready. All the same, the word came down on a Thursday morning that he would fill in as a replacement on a six-man team called "Spartan" that would insert at last light the following day.

Gene attended Captain Battaglia's mission briefing the following morning and then returned to his hooch. Staff sergeant Ben Caruthers, the team leader, came back with him. As Gene knelt on the floor and packed his rucksack, Caruthers advised him about what to take. Gene would be carrying a PRC-25 radio and his newly issued CAR-15 rifle, the carbine version of the M-16. But he also had his web gear to strap around his waist, made heavy with two canteens, plus bandoliers of ammunition and a pack full of C-rations and equipment: extra radio batteries, pen-gun flare, compass, poncho liner, and a number of other things. He had lost a little of his conditioning during the month he had been home, and carrying this much weight wasn't going to be easy, not on a mountainside and not in this heat. But that wasn't the biggest thing to worry about. He had heard lots of warnings these past few days about all the ways there were for a guy to get himself killed.

When Gene was packed, he tried everything on and Caruthers checked him out. But when he pulled his rucksack back off, the sergeant didn't leave. He stood in front of Gene, looking solid, with his feet set rather wide apart and his hands on his hips. "Now, listen," he said, "I know you don't feel ready to go out yet—and this *has* been too fast—but no one is ever ready for that first time out. The best training happens in the field. Just watch and learn, and follow *absolutely* what I tell you to do. I'm going to walk in the tail-gunner spot, and you'll be right in front of me so I've got your radio close. But that's also so I can look out for you."

Gene was glad for that. Caruthers was the kind of guy who inspired confidence. He sounded smart; he was built like an athlete; and he had a deep, strong voice. But he also had the look that Gene noticed in a lot of these experienced recon men. There was a seriousness behind their eyes, even some hint of evil—like a guy you didn't want to mess with.

"You won't catch me freelancing out there, Sergeant," Gene said.

"Watch Pop Winston. He'll be walking point, and he'll be carrying an M-60 machine gun. He's good. He did a full tour and then re-upped. He's survived more missions than any Lurp we've got now."

But that wasn't quite the whole story, and Gene knew it. Still, he tried not to sound concerned when he said, "Someone told me he's been wounded twice."

"That's right. But he doesn't want to get hit a third time. That's why he's careful. We call him Pop because he's like somebody's angry ol' man when he's out in the green. He sees *everything*. He knows exactly what's going on around him—both with his own men and with the enemy. But if you mess up, he'll come down on you hard."

"I thought he was a team leader." Gene knew a little about Pop, who bunked here in the same hooch. He was black, and he had grown up in Detroit. He was short, compact, and hard, and he had little to say. Everyone claimed he was a good guy, in his own quiet way, but he could be hard-nosed with his men.

"He usually does take his own teams out. We're lucky to have him as our ATL this time. He knows the jungle better than anyone."

Gene was starting to catch on to the language. "ATL" meant "assistant team leader." He wondered whether two such experienced leaders, both sergeants, were going out together this time because they were taking Gene, a new guy. The men in the unit had several names for green troops—all vulgar—but Gene thought he understood. When a single mistake could get a whole team killed, who wanted someone along who didn't know what he was doing?

But all the other guys on the Spartan team were experienced, and that gave Gene a sense that he would be well looked after. These teams always carried at least two radios in case one went bad—or got shot up. Rick Kovach, a big guy from Cleveland, would be humping the other one and walking "slack"—the second position, right behind the point man. A guy everyone called "Ears" Dearden would walk third. His actual name was Phil, and he did have big ears, but the men said he had better hearing than anyone they had ever been around. He had grown up hunting in the woods in Louisiana, and he had told Gene that these missions were a lot the same as hunting. "I'm just stalking gooks now, that's the only difference."

The other man on the team also had a lot of missions behind him. He was an eerie guy named Giles Melnick who looked like a boxer, with a flat nose and bumps over his eyes. He was from Nevada and claimed he had worked as a bouncer in Reno. He told Gene a story about peeking through some big leaves, shaped like elephant ears, and finding a North Vietnamese Army soldier looking him straight in the eyes, not two meters away. He laughed when he talked about the look on the NVA's face—just when the guy realized he was going to be blown away. The story had stuck in Gene's mind, had already turned into a symbol of what it was he hated to face: not just the fear of death, but the fear of killing.

"Here's the thing, Thomas," Sergeant Caruthers said. "We aren't going out there to get ourselves in a firefight. When that happens, something's gone wrong. This whole thing is about silence. We find Charlie, let the brass know where he is, and then we get out. So do whatever the rest of us do, and we'll be back here in three days having ourselves a beer."

Gene nodded. Some of the men knew he was a Mormon, but he hadn't said much about the way he lived.

"Most mistakes are made early. If the gooks see us insert, they try to get to us before we can move out. If we make that move too fast, before we know what's going on around us, we can foul up, but sticking around too long is the one sure way to get ourselves in a mess. So when we hit our landing zone, you have to be right with us. We've practiced enough this week to show you how that goes, but things can change fast, so watch me and be ready for anything."

"All right."

Caruthers smiled. "I'll tell you what, Thomas. It's kind of a high, and you can get hooked on it. As far as I'm concerned, we're the baddest guys over here. Even the gooks tell stories about the 'men with the black faces.' Intelligence guys hear stuff like that from NVA prisoners all the time. The reason Charlie comes looking for us so fast is that he knows we'll call fire down on him, or get him tore up with gunships. What we are is the guys who know the jungles as good as the gooks—maybe even better."

Caruthers left after that, but by then Gene had made up his mind. He would complete this mission, but then he would talk to Captain Battaglia about getting assigned to a regular unit. Gene just wasn't like these guys. He didn't know how to be "bad," and he certainly didn't need the image. He was never going to call any human being a "gook." As much as anything, he didn't want to go through any more days like this, so scared he could hardly breathe.

The hours passed slowly the rest of the day, and by the time the team walked to the helicopter pad, Gene couldn't stop his hands from shaking. And when his team had to wait for a few minutes, he felt his kneecaps jumping. As he approached the pad, he could see two big Cobra helicopters—gunships—waiting not far away, their rotors already turning. On the opposite side was a smaller helicopter without all the hardware. "That's our Loach," Melnick yelled to him over the sound of the two "slicks"—transport helicopters, one to carry the team, the other to serve as a decoy. "Loach" was the slang term for LOH, the light observation helicopter that Battaglia would ride. He would stay close in the beginning and wait for a situation report—called a "sitrep"—and if trouble came, he would direct the response from above.

The CO signaled with his thumb that the mission was a go, and Caruthers waved the team ahead. They jogged to the first slick and piled on through the side door, and then they sat on the floor. When the helicopter took off, it lifted twenty or thirty feet and then dropped its nose and angled away, fast. The motion made Gene's stomach roll. He had felt sick all day and hadn't been able to eat much. That worried him, since the men carried as little food as they could get by with, but for the moment he couldn't imagine getting very hungry.

Gene's fear that he might vomit passed in a few seconds, but he knew the real test was still coming. The mission was to take place a few kilometers beyond Nui Khe, in the mountains west of Camp Eagle. Gene knew that the two helicopters would leapfrog around, each making several false insertions. This was so the enemy would be unsure where the team had actually been dropped, so it made sense, but it was going to be a wild ride. Gene hoped he would have some time now to get his heart to stop pounding, but it wasn't long before the slick was cruising over dense green jungle and then skimming over the trees into a valley with steep inclines on both sides. Gene saw the other slick descend and hover, then lift again, the first fake insertion, and then his own slick slowed, dropped, and pulled back up. His stomach was in tangles again.

He kept taking long breaths, rode out another descent, and then saw a clearing not far from the Khe Dau River in the bottom of the canyon.

That was their landing zone—the "LZ." Gene recognized the site from photographs he and the other men had seen that morning. This time, as the slick descended, Caruthers got ready at the door. Gene forgot about his stomach, but he was shaking so badly he wondered whether he could get up. While the slick was still hovering, Caruthers waved the men off. Pop Winston was already on the skids, and he dropped from several feet in the air, and then everyone else was rolling off the same way. Gene was stiff with fear, but he moved to the door. When he felt Caruthers slap him on the back, he hurried a little too fast. Handling his rifle and balancing all the equipment on his back was tricky. He came off the skids on an angle and let go too soon. His right foot hit the ground first, and he slammed to the ground on his right shoulder. He didn't ask himself whether he was hurt; he merely scrambled to his feet and followed the other men, who were running for cover. Caruthers, by then, had caught up with him, but Gene outran the sergeant. He pushed his way into the dense vegetation, crouched next to them and froze in place. The "whomp, whomp" of the slick's rotors was disappearing, and gradually everything was quiet. Gene listened, and he looked around at the other team members. He had been watching these men with their black and green face-paint all along, but they looked fierce now, their eyes intense, motionless under the brims of their flat-topped jungle hats. In their camouflage, and in the semi-darkness, they seemed almost part of the vegetation around them, but their eyes were bright white, and they were concentrating, listening. Gene, was trying to do the same, but he hardly knew what to notice.

After three or four minutes, Gene realized that he had crouched in an awkward position, and on top of that, the shoulder he had banged was beginning to ache. So were his ribs. Still, he didn't dare move. No one had moved at all since they first ducked down. What he had been taught that week was that the first few minutes after insertion were the most dangerous. If Charlie had observed their drop, he would gather a unit and hurry to the LZ. NVA soldiers knew these jungles, knew the trails that they had cut themselves, and they could move quickly and quietly. Now was the time to detect them if they were out there. A last-light insertion offered very little room for error. Once dark fell, pulling out was much more difficult. For any insertion, "E and E"—escape and evasion—was always planned. That involved either a careful withdrawal to a planned LZ, or a headlong, wild run, with Charlie in full chase.

In these few days since Gene had arrived at Camp Eagle, he had heard dozens of stories about all the things that could go wrong, and the stories had always been to warn him of what not to do—or what to do when things turned bad—but the effect had been to fill his head with ugly possibilities. He heard palm fronds, distant and subtle, and he heard the click of some sort of insect. Mosquitoes were buzzing around him, but he was covered with repellent, and they didn't land. Gradually, he could see that the other men's faces were relaxing. Only Pop Winston looked as focused as ever.

Gene's muscles were aching, but he didn't move. Caruthers had told him that they would freeze this way for fifteen minutes. By the time the man finally spoke, however, Gene would have sworn that an hour had passed. The sergeant whispered to Gene that he needed the radio for a sitrep. Gene was relieved to move but terrified he would make too much noise, or that Caruthers would draw attention when he spoke on the radio. But Caruthers, in a low whisper, contacted TOC—the Tactical Operations Center—back at Camp Eagle, checked his coordinates, and verified on his map, from landmarks, that the team was in the right spot, and then he contacted Captain Battaglia in the Loach. "We've got a cold insertion here," he whispered, and that released the gunships to return to base. Then he made a third contact, with a firebase six kilometers north. Caruthers had not been happy that there was nothing closer to work with. If the men needed help fast, six "klicks" was more distance than he liked.

Once he was off the air, Caruthers got off his knees and sat down. "Okay," he whispered, "wait for the night sounds." Gene understood. It was one more thing he remembered from training. As night fell, the insects and nocturnal birds began to put up a clatter. If enemy soldiers were moving through the cover, the jungle remained quiet.

Time passed and the clatter came on, but the sounds were eerie. Gene had slept in the Utah mountains on Boy Scout campouts and knew something about the music of crickets and frogs, but everything here was exotic and frightening. After the hard run and the wait under the humid cover, he felt as though he were wrapped in a hot, wet towel. His "jungle utilities"—the fatigues the men wore—were soaked. That was bad enough, but the sounds were evil. He had heard stories about snakes and leeches, and he worried about those things, but this alien darkness that was coming down on him was worse than anything he had imagined. He didn't want to move, and he couldn't have seen far if he had looked around, but he wondered what was out there. Enemy soldiers could be crawling toward him, ready to strike from behind, or lurking, preparing to ambush the minute the men moved out.

The black gradually settled deeper, and Gene watched the faces disappear. He was amazed at their discipline, how silent the men were, how little they moved. They were more than trained; they were full of too much wise fear to get sloppy. But he had sensed something else over the past few days, and now it struck him more clearly. No one wanted to make a mistake and let the others down. These men had seen some of their friends ripped apart, and they didn't want to bring down that kind of hell on this team. He was surprised at how much he cared about the other guys already. He had sensed all day that they were concerned about keeping him alive, and he, above all else, didn't want to be the one who endangered them.

Another thought had been suggesting itself for a while now, and he finally gave it a little room in his consciousness. He pictured Emily putting Danny down for the night. It was some other time in Utah, even another day, but still, it seemed that night was coming on and his wife would be putting his son to bed. The thought came to him in a wave, like the nausea he had felt before. He didn't want to be here; he wanted to be with them. But Captain Battaglia had told him that a guy who was worried about his wife and kid could lose focus and mess up. Gene actually shook his head a little, told himself not to think about anything but what he was doing. He listened again, tried to get so he could hear what was normal so that he could recognize what wasn't, if the enemy did show up.

The night had taken over, but Gene's night vision seemed to kick in. Lurps liked to tell stories of special perceptions they developed from being in the jungle—the ability to smell the enemy, to pick up on the most subtle of sounds, and to see in the dark. Gene was surprised when he was able to see Caruthers wave his hand forward—or maybe he only heard it.

In any case, Pop had seen the signal too, and he got up slowly and carefully. The others followed, and they moved out in their assigned order. They crossed through the LZ and then headed downhill. The plan was to break through the low vegetation as silently as possible and move toward the river. They suspected a "high speed" trail—one that was well-used and free of growth—at the bottom of the valley, near the river. Most reconnaissance centered on these trails, since a team could observe them and learn about NVA or Vietcong movements, possible build-ups, or even imminent attacks. Lately, the NVA had been launching long-distance 122mm rocket attacks on Hue, Phu Bai, and even Camp Eagle. The Spartan team needed to see where the NVA was operating and then track down those rocket-launching sites so that bombers or artillery could knock them out. Sniffer sensors, which picked up human scent, had been indicating plenty of enemy troops in the area, but that didn't tell anyone where the camps were or where the launch sites might be located.

Gene knew the plan: move about twenty meters, then stop for five minutes to listen, then move another twenty meters. They would keep going that way until the team got well away from the LZ and closer to the suspected trail. What he hadn't been prepared for was the work of moving quietly in all this heat through heavy brush. The four guys ahead of him were doing more work than he was, but Gene could hardly believe the control of the other men, to move so slowly and not give in to the desire to speed ahead. Gene worried that the little noises they were making were attracting the enemy in around them. But each time they stopped and waited, he heard nothing that alarmed him, and he sensed plenty of confidence from Caruthers.

After the fifth move forward—what should have amounted to about 100 meters—Caruthers quietly moved past Gene and on up to the point. Then he turned and waved the men into some cover, off to the side. Gene could see in the dark, or hear, that the men were removing their rucksacks and releasing their web gear. When he tried to do the same, he was aware that he was making more noise. Pop stepped up to him and helped him get the heavy rucksack off, but he didn't say a word. What he did do was get hold of one of Gene's canteens, and he handed it to him. Then he helped him take off his web gear. Gene had heard so much about Pop's grumpiness, but this was an act of kindness that seemed monumental— although Gene hardly understood why. He was choking with thirst, but it wasn't just that. It was fatherly, this concern, and protective. Gene had made up his mind for certain now: this would be his only recon mission. He couldn't do this again. But he wasn't sorry, at the moment, that he had experienced this time with these men.

Caruthers had left the group, but Gene knew why. He had told the men at the briefing that after they had moved down into the valley he would go back and sanitize the trail, replacing leaves and sticks that the men might have moved. Gene had no idea how he could see enough to do that, but he trusted that he was good at it. The other men began to set up a night defensive position. They got out poncho liners to cover their faces from insects, they reapplied insect repellent, and then, once Caruthers had returned, they set out claymore mines. These were weapons that could be triggered from inside the perimeter and would explode into a savage half-circle of flying pellets. The mines were protection from NVA who might be creeping toward them, but once the claymores had been fired, that line of protection was gone, so the timing of their use was crucial.

Gene had learned to hold the claymores against his chest in the darkness, to find the curved side so the mine couldn't accidentally be set to fire the wrong way, but the experienced men took care of the job tonight. Caruthers had also told the men that they would all stay on alert until midnight, and then they would trade watches, each putting in an hour while the others slept. But the men had told Gene ahead of time, "Don't even worry about sleeping that first night. Just rest. Guys who've been in the boonies a long time learn how to sleep with one eye open, but you won't relax for a second on your first mission."

Gene had believed the men at the time, but now the thought of waiting all those hours until first light was almost more than he could stand. He sat like a statue and tried to concentrate on the sounds, but it was Emily who kept intruding into his awareness. She would be furious if she knew where he was. He thought of going to bed at home, in clean sheets, of hearing her breathe next to him, being able to throw back a blanket or pull one on, or move to a more comfortable position.

He eventually began to believe that Caruthers had changed his mind and decided to keep everyone up all night. How could it not yet be midnight? He stared into the darkness, trying to make out anything that might be out there, but when he did, he kept thinking he saw movement, and his fear kept him constantly on edge. He had been told not to focus on one spot, to watch with his peripheral vision and move his head back and forth. The eye seemed to see things that weren't there when it stayed fixed on one area. But he couldn't seem to stop himself from concentrating on the objects he could make out, and several times he almost warned the other men that something was out there.

Gene lay down when Caruthers finally whispered that it was time, and he wrapped his poncho liner around him and over his face. The air was still warm, and his fatigues hadn't dried at all. He told himself that he might be able to sleep after all, he was so exhausted, but he heard everything, even his own men making the slightest move, or breathing a little more heavily than seemed safe. He kept listening for the nocturnal life and actually took some comfort in the strange sounds, but each lull in the racket scared him, and when he tried to stare into the darkness, he thought at times that he could see things moving.

Gene was on second watch, and the time came as a relief. At least he could sit up and not pretend he was resting. But the one hour seemed like four, and then he lay down again, and by then, the other side of jungle life was showing itself. The cold was coming on, as it always did before morning. He had been told not to carry any more than he had to, and the poncho liner was the closest thing to a sleeping bag that they brought along, but now he needed warmth, and his wet fatigues were sending chills through him. He lay there and shook, and he waited for morning. What he felt was that he had aged a year in a single night. He understood why men went AWOL, just made up their minds they would rather face prison than life in the jungle. He had 352 days left, and he couldn't imagine how he could last the time out—not if he had to keep doing this.

And then he realized that someone was crawling toward him. He jerked, almost called out, but he heard someone—big Melnick—whisper, "Sergeant, I'm picking up some movement above us. And I think below us too."

Gene's legs locked, and his chest seemed to clutch against his lungs.

"All right," Caruthers whispered. "Everyone on alert. Keep your weapons ready. Let's get a bead on these guys."

Caruther's calm released Gene's chest. He took a breath. He sat up and put his rifle on his lap, as he had been taught to do.

But then Gene heard a voice—an actual whisper, outside the perimeter. He felt his throat choke, his heart begin to hammer. He wanted light. He wanted gunships and helicopters. He wanted out of there. Someone was coming through the jungle, in the night, looking for him.

"Radio," Caruthers whispered. He called the relay firebase, reported the movement, and asked them to let TOC know what was happening. In a couple of minutes, he had a response. Gunships and a slick would come in at first light to extract them. The mission was hopelessly compromised now. They had to get to the E and E landing zone, either that or find another place where the slick could get down.

As soon as Caruthers was off the radio, Pop whispered, "The gooks are making noise on purpose. That's not normal, what we're hearing." Gene had heard more voices. He could also hear a lot of movement in the underbrush, and he was almost sure it was getting closer.

"They want to run us out of here, into an ambush," Caruthers said. He had obviously reached the same conclusion that Pop had. "Let's sit tight and wait for first light. They know we inserted up above, but they don't know where we are now. If they did, they'd be coming in quiet."

Wait for the light. That was so easy to say. Gene couldn't understand how these guys could do that. He wanted to run, and do it right now. But he had heard a tone in the two sergeants' voices that kept him from busting out on his own. They were worried but not panicked. He tried to breathe in some of that assurance.

The dark kept hanging on, and the enemy voices gradually quieted. What did that mean? Were the NVA waiting now for first light themselves? Had they moved on? Maybe it was just a troop movement, and the soldiers had talked out loud because they had no idea the recon team was there. Gene wanted to raise all those questions, but the men on the team didn't talk. They listened, and they reapplied the "camo," as they called it, on their faces. It was hard to believe they could stay that calm. But as the light gradually came on, Gene watched the men. They weren't as tranquil as he thought. He saw how fixed their eyes were.

"Maybe they missed us," Caruthers finally whispered.

But Pop said, "They know we're here somewhere. When we didn't flush, they decided to sit tight."

"We've got to get to an LZ," Caruthers said, "and our E and E site is across the river. Let's move out, get to the river, call in the slick, and then cross. If we get movement close to us, we'll have to give up our noise discipline and make a run."

Pop nodded. "That's exactly right. I'm going to take it slow for now. We're not far above the river. If they've got an ambush waiting, it could be at the trail or at the river. When I signal for a stop, everyone get down until I check out the trail."

All the men were nodding, including Gene.

Pop got up and slipped on his gear while Caruthers and Dearden pulled in the claymores. When Pop moved out, he worked his way into lighter cover but moved with excruciating slowness. Gene could still hear his heart beating in his ears. He expected every moment to hear gunfire— or to see someone jump out at him.

They had moved maybe twenty meters, in four short moves, when Pop froze and held the palm of his hand back toward the team. Gene heard a whisper again, up the valley to the west. And then he heard a loud clack and his knees almost went out from under him. In a few seconds the same noise sounded from several different directions. "They're using bamboo," Pop whispered. "They're trying to drive us."

"Stay quiet for now," Caruthers said, but he waved his arm for Pop to move out. And then he stood behind Gene and used the radio in his rucksack. He told the captain that they were facing immediate contact and were heading for the E and E site.

Pop moved ahead, working a little faster now, and Gene assumed that this was the beginning of a break. The enemy sounds weren't that far away.

Gene glanced back to see Caruthers with his M-60 machine gun ready. He had turned around and was watching behind them, obviously expecting contact, or at least fearing it, and yet Pop was still moving care-fully. Then a voice cracked through the jungle. Charlie was calling out, and that had to mean that the team had been spotted.

"Go!" Caruthers hissed.

Pop spun around. "They're pushing us east. Don't go that way. Follow me to the river. Let's go!" He took off hard now, crashing down the hill through the brush. In only a few seconds, he crashed out of the cover and jumped. Gene soon reached the same spot and saw that Pop had jumped down onto the trail without checking for an ambush first. This was serious.

They all rushed across the trail and then crashed beyond it, back into deep bracken under the high jungle canopy. When Gene broke out of the cover into the river, behind the others, he was caught for a moment by a harder current than he expected, but he did what the others did. He held his rifle high and pushed through the knee-deep water.

He was almost to the other side when he heard everything seem to explode. He looked back to see Caruthers standing on the opposite bank of the river, swinging his M-60, rapid-firing into the jungle behind him. At the same time tracers were flying through the trees, and bullets were buzzing in all directions. "Go, go, go," Caruthers was screaming as he con-tinued to fire.

Gene's first instinct was to turn back to help Caruthers, but he heard the command, and his fear turned him into a sprinter. He caught up with the others and up ahead saw a burst of purple smoke. Pop was marking the LZ with a smoke grenade, and Gene could hear helicopters somewhere. He hoped the gunships were coming down on the enemy.

He glanced up as he reached the clearing, a narrow opening in the jungle that was the only possible LZ. He couldn't see the slick, but he could hear it, and then he saw one of the gunships flash over, and a sec-ond later, the roar of machine-gun fire. He saw the muzzle flashes for only a second, and then the Cobra was out of sight—but still no slick. He looked back through the cover they had just crashed through, and he saw Caruthers, running hard, one arm hanging down.

And now the slick was suddenly there, whomping its way down through the opening in the jungle canopy. When he looked up, he saw three holes appear in a string on the metal sides of the helicopter, almost magically. It took him a moment to realize what was happening, that the slick was taking small arms fire. Still, it kept coming down, and Pop was waving the men forward. Gene ran for the slick, but he glanced back, and just as he did, he saw Caruthers go down.

Gene didn't think. He simply ran for Caruthers. He got to him in a few steps, then opened up with his rifle. He saw muzzle flashes and swung his weapon toward them. But suddenly Pop was there, firing an M-60, slashing the vegetation into pieces. "Get him," he screamed.

Gene hoisted big Caruthers onto his shoulder, hardly feeling the weight. He ran hard, dumped his sergeant toward the men who were reaching for him. Then he clambered on himself. In another moment, Pop had jumped on behind him. Gene heard the crash of bullets striking the slick, but it was lifting fast, and then it dipped its nose and careened away. Suddenly they were in the sky, and the only sound was the chop of the rotors. But Caruthers had taken hits in his right arm and chest. There was lots of blood, and the sergeant's face was frighteningly pale. He began to cough, and Gene could hear the sucking sound from his lungs.

❧

The men worked on Ben Caruthers all the way back to Camp Eagle, and a medical team was waiting when the slick touched down. In a couple of minutes Caruthers was on a Medevac helicopter and gone. As the sound faded, the others on the team were left standing, looking at each other. A good many of the other Lurps, who had been tuned in to the radio chatter, had gathered with them, but no one said much for a time.

"He's going to make it," Melnick finally said. "Caruthers is tough."

Pop nodded, seeming to agree, but then he said, "But he won't be back here."

Gene was covered in Caruther's blood, and he was still shaking. His thoughts were racing, and the sudden change of reality—back to safety—was hard to accept. He couldn't get rid of the fear that fast. But he was trying not to show any of that. He looked from face to face and saw what the loss of Caruthers was costing these men. Gene had only an inkling of what they were feeling, but he knew that this kind of stuff was happening way too often lately. Six recon men had been killed in 1969, and more than twice that many had been wounded. At the same time, more missions were being scheduled all the time, and replacements were getting harder to recruit. What everyone knew, but never said directly, was that things were bad and getting worse.

Looking at these guys wasn't helping Gene; too much was already going on inside him. So he turned and walked away. He didn't know where he was going, but he needed to be alone, and he needed to pray.

He walked past the helicopter pad and on past a row of sandbagged hooches. When he came to the fence—the first rolls of wire that marked the camp perimeter—he stopped and looked toward the mountains. Emotion was trying to explode in his chest, but he was fighting against it. He asked the Lord to help Caruthers, and then he found himself apologizing to Emily, out loud, and in his own mind, that was part of his prayer.

Gene didn't want to be a hero. He didn't ever want to go back out to that jungle again. He had to talk to Battaglia about that. But he had no idea what to do right now. What was he supposed to do—go have breakfast? Sit down and chat with the men?

"How're you doing, Thomas?"

Gene turned to see Pop standing there, his hands and arms stained with blood, even splashes of red on his camouflaged face. Gene shrugged. "I don't know."

"It was a bad start. I'm sorry it went down that way."

Gene had no idea what to say. He had an impulse to scream, or to take off running. He had to release some of this emotion.

"You handled yourself very well, Thomas. You covered Caruthers when you had to. A man never knows what he'll do in a situation like that, not until it happens. I saw how scared you were—the same as the rest of us—but you went back into the face of all that fire."

Gene wasn't sure he remembered it that way. He remembered the fear that Pop was talking about, but he didn't remember going back. He had suddenly been there—that was all. He was not entirely sure that he had ever fired his weapon. "I don't think I can go again," he finally said.

"I think the same thing every time I come back."

"Then why didn't you go home when you had your chance?"

Pop looked at him for a long time before he said, "They're going to send someone out there, and I know how to do it."

Gene tried to think about that. It was almost what his father had said—why he had dropped behind the lines in World War II. He had been the best guy to do it. Not everyone could.

"Let's go get some breakfast," Pop said. "And you need to sleep if you can. You're a good man, Thomas. You probably saved Ben. The men are all saying they want you to stay with us."

Gene still couldn't think. He still felt as though he were breaking in half. He wasn't hungry, wasn't sure he ever would be again, but he walked with Pop to the mess hall.

# CHAPTER 30

Hans's one-room apartment was more than cramped, but Hans was thrilled. His parents and Inga had come on the train to visit for the weekend. They had brought bedding and slept on the floor—filling the entire room. They had spent Saturday with Hans, walking and talking, and then had gone to church on Sunday in the Leipzig Branch. Afterward, they had returned to the tiny apartment, and Katrina was now cooking. She had brought food in a suitcase—all she and Peter could afford for now. It would help Hans get by on his meager paycheck.

But today nothing seemed meager. The smell of roasted chicken, red cabbage, and baked bread mixed with the warm voices in Hans's room, and it all seemed too good to be true. Hans was sitting on his bed, with Inga next to him. His arm was around her, and she was leaning against his side. Mama, in her apron, was waiting on the chicken now, standing, turned away from the oven, and Papa was sitting in the only chair. They had talked about everything, it seemed, and yet Hans kept most of his prison experience to himself. He didn't want them to know what he had had to live through.

His mother seemed to understand, and she clearly sensed what he was feeling now. "Will it be worse for you when we go?" she asked.

They would leave on the train in a couple of hours, and he knew the room would seem hollow—too much like his old cell. But he told her, "It won't be so bad. You've made my little place smell like home. It will last for a time."

"Have they given you any idea how long you will have to stay here?"

Peter asked. "When do you think you might be able to take a trip to Schwerin?"

"They tell me nothing. I have no idea. It will be better when I can travel, but I may have to be in Leipzig for many years. Maybe always."

"Let's not speak of this," Katrina said. "Let's be thankful for what we have. Hans will prove himself. He'll do a good job. And they will trust him more and more. Every year things will get a little better."

"Something good is going to happen," Inga said. "God is going to bless Hans."

But Hans wasn't sure things would change very much. His job was rudimentary. He drafted simple plans, based on architects' guidelines. He saw no opportunity to advance. He could probably gain some modest pay raises, but no one in his office was paid very much. Some days he tried to imagine spending years, maybe his entire life in this same office, and then he thought of America and what he had turned down. He hadn't planned to tell his parents about that choice, but now, with the thought of their leaving soon, he needed some reassurance.

"There's something I haven't told you," Hans said. "Uncle Alex made arrangements to pay a price to get me out of the country. I was offered a chance to leave the GDR and emigrate to Salt Lake City. But I told the government no, that I didn't want to leave."

"But why?" Peter asked. He sounded not just surprised but disappointed.

Hans immediately wished that he hadn't said anything. He didn't want his parents to feel that he had sacrificed for them. "I almost took the offer," he said, "but then, just as I was about to sign the papers, I heard a voice in my head, saying that I shouldn't do it."

"Hans," Katrina said, "will they still let you go? I would miss you every day of my life, but things would be so much better for you over there. It would be such an opportunity for you."

"I know. But the voice said I was needed here. It was only me—my own voice—speaking in my head. But it was very clear, and it told me that I was needed."

"Yes. This is right," Peter said. "It's where you should be."

"But Peter," Katrina said. "In America he could study at a university. He could find a wife in the Church."

"If the voice came to him, it is right. The Church has to hold on in this land. God needs young men like Hans, who can lead."

"But if he hardly has enough to live on, how can he—"

"The Lord will bless him. Inga's right about that."

Katrina stood with her arms folded, and she looked down for a long time. Finally she said, "I want him here. I want grandchildren. I want to see him lead in the Church. But the government will make everything so difficult."

"I don't know how, but things will get better," Peter said.

"Peter, he tells me he doubts he can marry—that he'll never have enough money. How can that be good?"

"He'll marry."

No one spoke for a time after that. Hans liked his father's confidence. He wanted to believe that he was right, but he also shared his mother's fears.

"Do you hear anything from the young woman in Magdeburg?" Peter asked.

"No."

"Have you written to her?"

"No, Papa. It wouldn't be right. I can't offer her a decent life."

"Write to her."

"Papa, I've thought about this many times, but I would only be encouraging her interest, when I have nothing to offer."

"Write to her. And trust in the Lord. He told you to stay. He will bless you."

Hans had wanted so often to write, but he had told himself that it was wrong, that it wasn't fair to Elli. But now he said, "It's good, Papa. I will."

∽≫∾

Diane had never cooked a turkey, but she was actually quite excited to learn. She and Greg had decided not to drive all the way to Utah for Thanksgiving; they would be doing that for Christmas. So Diane had invited two other couples from their ward—couples who were also away from their families. She had prepared the stuffing the night before and then had gotten up at five in the morning to get the turkey started. She had planned to go back to bed for a while, but she found herself a little too nervous for that. There was so much to do, and before too much longer Jennifer would be up. So she mixed up her grandma's recipe for hot rolls, and while the dough was rising, peeled potatoes and yams. The other women were bringing salads and pies. Diane was relieved that she didn't have to try a pie quite yet, but she wanted the turkey to turn out perfectly and wanted the dressing to be something special. She had called her mother-in-law and gotten her recipe, since she knew Greg loved it so much. What she wanted was for Greg to be pleased with the whole meal. She wanted him, at the end of the day, to tell her that she had come a long way in her cooking. She had been telling herself lately that if she wanted Greg to make some changes, she had to do her part too. She had lost six pounds in the past four weeks, and she had done it mostly by the sheer force of willpower. He had been coming home earlier lately, as promised, but the sun went down so early this time of year that she hadn't gotten out to do much jogging or walking. Still, she sometimes took Jennifer for a walk in her stroller, and she was eating nothing but celery and carrot sticks for lunch each day.

When Jennifer woke up, Diane nursed her and played with her for a few minutes, and then she put her on the floor, on a blanket, and hoped that she would be content long enough for Diane to get a relish tray ready.

Before long, however, Jenny wanted more attention, and Diane found herself running back and forth, entertaining her with a rattle, then putting the rattle in her hand and rushing back to open a can of olives or peel a few carrots. It was almost nine before she heard Greg in the shower, and then he came out and turned on the Macy's Thanksgiving Day parade. But when she asked him to look after Jenny, he seemed happy to do so. He held her and talked to her, and made her smile. It was the kind of thing Greg was doing more lately. Diane felt that he was making a real effort to change his ways, and he assured her that he was having nothing—or very little—to do with Sondra. He had also met with the bishop, and although he didn't say what they had talked about, Diane had the feeling that Greg wanted to set things right.

"Do I need to help?" Greg asked after a time. "Set the table or anything?"

"For right now the best help in the world is to keep Jenny happy. She'll be going down for a nap before long, and then maybe you could help me put the leaf in the table."

"Is it going to be crazy around here today with four babies?"

"It could be. But the little babies aren't so bad. We'll have two two-year-olds, and that should give you a whole new outlook on what we've gotten ourselves into."

"Maybe they're Dallas Cowboys fans. We can let them watch the football game."

"Yeah, right. You daddies better not get so involved in football that you leave the kids *and* the dishes to us."

"No way. We're modern fathers. We'll probably do the dishes, take care of the kids, and watch the football game, all at the same time. Maybe you and Janet and Bridgette can take a little nap."

"Oh, brother. That'll be the day."

But Diane loved to hear Greg talk that way, even if he was only kidding. He had been so sweet to her since that day he had lost his temper. She was glad now that she hadn't left him.

"I had an interesting talk with Professor Wilson yesterday," Greg said. "He was telling me that some of these big Seattle firms like to hire the top students from the law school to clerk for them in the summer. He says it might be a mistake to head home to my dad's office this year. It might look better on my résumé to clerk for someone else—especially a big-name firm."

"What difference does it make, if you're going to go back and work for your dad anyway, once you're finished?"

"That's what I said, but he told me not to do that. He said I can always work for my dad, sooner or later, but if I put in a few years with a prestigious firm, I could widen my options. Dad does well, but if I want to build my name and be able to demand some big-time fees, I probably can't do that in Salt Lake, in a small firm."

Greg, at intervals, was saying "boo" to little Jenny, then laughing when she smiled. Diane waited for a time, enjoyed watching the two of them. "So are you thinking that's what you want to do? Stay here after you graduate?"

"Maybe. The thing I'd have to do is look at specific offers when the time came."

"You've always said you want to live in Utah."

"I do. Sometimes I think about politics as a possibility, and it's probably easier for a Mormon to run for office there than most places. But I think Utahns respect a guy who has gone out and done something important somewhere else—you know, has proven himself—and then comes back."

Diane walked into the living room. She lifted her apron and wiped her hands, which were wet from washing some of the pots and pans. She stood in front of Greg. He glanced up from the baby.

"We'll make the decision together, won't we?" she asked. She had been very careful with her voice. She didn't want to sound sarcastic or angry.

"Oh, sure. I'm sorry. I am making it sound like it's all up to me. Would you rather go back to Utah?"

"I don't know. Seattle's nice. I could live here. I'm just saying, I think we should decide together."

"Absolutely."

There was something Diane had been wanting to say to Greg, but she had put it off for a long time. The moment now seemed right. "Have you ever heard of Betty Friedan?"

"Of course."

"I read *The Feminine Mystique* quite a while ago. It sort of scared me, some of the things she says. But I was looking at it again this week. It's way too radical for me, but one of the things she says is that a lot of women are unhappy because they feel they have no control over their lives. They're just along for the ride. Men think as long as they give their wives enough money to run the household, what else do they need? But women lose their sense of self if they don't have any say in what happens to them."

"Sure. That makes sense."

Diane continued to watch Greg for any reaction. She wondered what he thought of her reading the book.

Greg looked back at Jennifer, then suddenly leaned forward and said "boo" again. Jennifer jumped a little, and then a look of delight came over her face. It was something she had only started to do, just lately.

"Where did you come up with a book like that?" Greg asked, seeming to work a little too hard to sound casual.

"I bought it at the University Bookstore, back when I was still working last spring."

"Why didn't you ever mention it?"

"I don't know. I guess I thought you wouldn't want me to read it."

"Hey, I'm not going to tell you what you can and can't read, but I do think we ought to discuss it. From what I've heard, the book is basically a bunch of anti-family garbage." Again, he surprised Jennifer with another "boo."

The tone of Greg's voice worried Diane just a little. She thought she heard a hint of tension, maybe even the beginning of anger. "I guess that's mostly what it is," she said. She knelt next to his knee, got her face close to Jennifer, and said her own "Boo!" "There's a lot of complaining by women who seem kind of spoiled to me. No matter how well-off they are, they say they aren't happy."

Greg seemed to like that. He smiled. "I'll tell you what. I'm going to make you *very* well-off. And I think you're going to be thrilled to death with the life you'll have. If I were you, I'd chuck that book in the garbage can. We don't need that kind of stuff in our house."

Diane wasn't sure. Was he *asking* her to throw it away? She wished now she hadn't been quite so quick to agree with him. So many things in the book actually made sense to her. But she rested her head against his knee, and he touched her hair, then stroked it. Diane loved the tenderness in his touch. She decided it might be wise to follow his advice and get rid of the book.

~⚬~

Kathy was having a difficult day. It was Thanksgiving in America even if it was Friday in the Philippines. She had thought about home all day. She would have given almost anything to be at Grandma's house. And the truth was, she would probably still quit the Peace Corps if she didn't have to feel ashamed about doing so. One thing she knew already was that she wasn't much of a teacher. Her students were painfully polite but mostly unresponsive. They repeated her language exercises, but when she tried to discuss the literature assignments with them, in English, they watched her curiously, as though they wondered what it was she was doing. They seemed to have no idea what she was talking about—and the problem ran deeper than the language. She would ask them why Juliet chose to kill herself, and the answers were disappointing. "She think Romeo dead," a student would say.

"Yes, but why kill herself? What did she feel?"

"Unhappy."

"But why so deeply unhappy that she didn't want to live?"

And then they would stare at her.

"She's very young—like you. Why do young people respond so strongly and emotionally?"

Silence.

Kathy didn't know the answer to the question either, or at least not any one answer. She wanted a discussion. At Smith, every woman in the class would have had something to say.

She talked to Martha, to the Filipino teachers. She prepared carefully every night. She tried to think of the right questions. She had to get them to look at more than mere plot. What good was it to teach young people to *pronounce* English? A literature teacher was supposed to raise awareness, teach people to think and to care. She had seen it done so well in college. If she spent two years in the Philippines and got no further with the students than this, she would go home feeling that her time was wasted.

Martha had invited two male Peace Corps Volunteers over to the house on Friday, after school. They taught in a neighboring barrio, and Kathy could tell that Martha had a thing for one of them—a fellow named Jeff Levenger. He was a tall, skinny guy, sort of minimally handsome and maximally fun. He had gone to the University of Alabama and spoke a charming southern dialect. He liked to play off his country-boy style, but he was intelligent and had a remarkable knowledge on a wide variety of subjects. He and his roommate, William Griggs, dropped by fairly often, especially on weekends. William was a kind of vanilla-flavored guy, not particularly interesting but polite, nice, quiet. He was from Massachusetts but had gone to college in New York, at Columbia. Kathy was sure he must be smart, but if so, he had an extraordinary capacity to hide it. He seemed to know the cliché to fit every situation.

The irony that Kathy was catching onto was that William was interested in Martha but never did very much to show it, and Martha was interested in Jeff and did *everything* to show it. Kathy was trying to remain an innocent bystander to this awkward triangle, but she had lately had some suspicion that Jeff wanted to raise the confusion to a rectangle by showing some interest in her.

In any case, Jeff and William had come over for Thanksgiving dinner, and Martha had gone all out to please them. She had figured out a way to get a turkey through some American military people she knew, and even though she replaced potatoes with rice, and taro root for yams, she had managed to come up with something that had at least the look of a Thanksgiving dinner. The poor turkey had suffered through many hours in a dysfunctional oven, was black in places and raw in the middle, but somewhere in the layers, Martha had found some white meat that tasted quite good.

After dinner, the guys stayed and helped with the dishes, and then sat down in the rattan chairs of the living room. They had brought some San Miguel beer—the ubiquitous brand found in the Philippines—and Jeff, after drinking a couple, had begun to spin tales of his youth. The alcohol had intensified his accent, along with his loquaciousness, but had diminished his charm just a bit.

"You gotta understan'," he told the others, "a southern boy knows right from wrong. He's taught it at his mama's knee. But there's not a one who doesn't consider every apple still hanging on a tree to be the legitimate property of any courageous young man who has the skill to climb a fence."

"It's not so different where I come from," Martha said.

"I see. Well now, that's good to know. I thought northerners had stricter rules about that sort of thing. In any case, you may not extend the same rights of possession to larger produce. Alabama boys consider the *punkin'*, in southern parlance, equally subject to such claims. And it was in that capacity, as a *punkin' claimer*, that I joined some of my esteemed companions—"

"Just say you were stealing pumpkins and get on with the story," William said.

But Martha said, "No, no. Tell it your own way."

Martha had had only one beer, but Kathy had to believe it had affected her judgment. Or maybe love was doing that. In any case, Kathy found her own mind wandering, trying to think what time it was in Utah. But then someone knocked. Kathy felt certain she was the most expendable in the foursome, so she got up and walked to the door. But when she opened it, she was surprised to find two of her students, girls, standing outside. They were still wearing their blue jumpers and white blouses, the school uniform. One of the girls—Isobel Lopez—was holding a paper bag, and the other, Mona Guevarra, was apparently assigned to do the talking. "We bring you diss from the class," she said. "For Tanksgibing."

Kathy was taken by surprise. She said, "Thank you," but she could think of nothing else to say.

"We know that you very sad now," Mona said. "You miss your mother and your father."

"Yes. Thank you," Kathy said again, "but it's nice to be here with you." She looked inside the bag. It was full of fruit: mangos and papaya.

"Miss Sanchez tell us you have Tanksgibing dinner. We bring you dessert. From whole class."

"It's so kind of you, girls. Come in, so Miss Sommers can thank you too."

"No, no. Diss for you. And we come to tell you, you are very good teacher. You very kind to us. We sorry we don't know answer to questions."

"Oh. It's all right." She stood for a moment. "I must ask the wrong questions."

"No. You teacher. You ask good questions. We make no good answers."

"I'm sorry. I don't mean to make you feel that way." Suddenly she did what was hardest for her to do. She reached for Mona, took her into her arms, and hugged her. "I'm so sorry," she said. "You're lovely students. You're so nice to me." And then she took Isobel in her arms and embraced her the same way. "You're such lovely young women, so beautiful."

"Thank you," they both told her, and she saw the change in their eyes.

When they left, she walked to her room, not back to the living room, and she sat on the bed and stared at the dingy white wall. She thought about her classes, what she had been doing. "I've been asking the wrong kinds of questions," she told herself. But it was another minute or so before she realized there was more to it than that. So she told herself the rest: "My whole life, I've been asking the wrong questions."

She thought about that for a long time, considered the way she had related to her family and her friends. She even reviewed the decisions she had made over the years. It was pointless to wish she could go back and change some things, but she did know something about her future. She was in the right place. She would stick out her time with the Peace Corps.

# Author's Note

I n 1967 my wife and I moved to Seattle, where I attended graduate school at the University of Washington. Kathy and I had been married less than a year when we set out from Ogden, Utah, in an old Mercury Comet packed with almost all of our belongings. The world was going crazy in those days, but Utah, to a large degree, had remained oblivious to the madness. On our first day in Seattle, we visited the campus and were impressed by its beauty, but we were also shocked by the hippies on the streets in the University District. In the five years that followed, I worked on my Ph.D. while the distracting chaos of the antiwar movement raged around me. I arrived on campus some mornings to learn that buildings had been bombed. I saw police pelted with rocks, and I saw students knocked over the head with nightsticks. I saw rallies and marches that involved thousands of protesters, mostly students. There was no walking into the union building without being handed several leaflets. It was an amazingly intense, emotional time, and every human value was up for question.

It was almost impossible not to change in some ways during that time. Kathy and I saw some of our values deepened, mainly because we had to defend our positions. But we also had to think about many beliefs that we had taken for granted, and we found ourselves adjusting our views on important topics. For one thing, we were forced to think about our relationship with each other. Activist women were speaking up, and we tried to answer their questions—not to satisfy them but to define our own beliefs about marriage. More important, *Kathy* was asking *me* questions, and some of my attitudes, inherited from previous generations, didn't hold

---

463 ———

up very well. President Gordon B. Hinckley often speaks today of married couples being "co-equal partners," but I don't remember anyone using that term in the fifties and sixties. What I remember is a series of decisions— or in some cases, gradually changed perspectives—that redefined the way we related to one another, treated one another, and respected one another. It's something I think we're both thankful for today.

If you wonder why "women's issues" come up so often in *How Many Roads?* it's because that's the way I remember the time: the questions were in the air, demanding answers. There were all sorts of "movements" back then, and many young people thought they had started a revolution, but much of the excess of the time has passed away. And yet, the most lasting change of the era may well be the redefined relationship of men and women. Some of that may be for evil as much as good, but young couples had to create their marriages in the context of all that change. What you see in Gene and Emily and Greg and Diane are two couples working out some of the issues my wife and I dealt with. Kathy Thomas is not married, but gradually she is thinking less about "revolution" and more about feminism. That was a common pattern of the time.

When I wrote about World War II, I had to research the time, talk to the people who remembered, and try to grasp what it was like for others who lived through that era. In this novel, however, the young characters are passing through the same process I was. Every young couple had to wonder whether Vietnam would pull the husband away, for instance, and couples had to take the wife's education into account much more than previous generations had done. There's a danger, of course, in relying too much on one's own memory. Some who lived through the same era at the same age may wonder what I'm talking about. They may not remember any such turmoil in their own experiences. But the questions were there, and changes have occurred, perhaps, in some cases, without much awareness of the process.

To keep these books from being too much about my recollection, I have continued to read widely about the late sixties and its topics. As always, let me mention a few books that have helped me. Since I was taking a character to Vietnam, I read a great deal about that complex and controversial war. A landmark book on Vietnam that is disturbingly candid and probing is *A Rumor of War*, by Philip Caputo (Henry Holt, 1977). *Fortunate Son*, the autobiography of Lewis B. Puller Jr. (Grove Weidenfeld, 1991), communicates both the tragedy for those who were wounded in Vietnam and also their will to survive. Another classic is *We Were Soldiers Once . . . And Young*, by Lt. General Harold B. Moore (HarperCollins, 1993). Mark Baker's *Nam: The Vietnam War in the Words of the Men and Women Who Fought There* (Cooper Square Press, 2001) is an upsetting book that demystifies war—particularly the Vietnam war— and does so in the profane parlance of the soldiers themselves. I hesitate to recommend the book because of its language and graphic portrayals, but it's a stunning antidote for the movies and novels that glorify and romanticize war. A more philosophical approach to the same issues is *War Is a Force that Gives Us Meaning*, by Chris Hedges (PublicAffairs, 2002).

Less philosophical and more particular were the books I read about Long-Range Reconnaissance Patrol units in Vietnam. (If you take more than one to a cashier, expect some strange looks, because many are paperbacks that look as though they are written for "wannabe" commandos. And let me warn you, virtually all books on Vietnam are full of bad language.) Gary Linderer has published several books about "Lurps": *The Eyes of the Eagle*; *Eyes Behind the Lines*; *Six Silent Men*; and *Phantom Warriors, Books 1 and 2* (all from the Ballantine Publishing Group). Another book that is accurate but not for the squeamish is *Death in the A Shau Valley*, by Larry Chambers (Ballantine, 1998). Equally intense is Cherokee Paul McDonald's *Into the Green: A Reconnaissance by Fire* (Penguin, 2001).

I also tried to learn all I could about the Philippines in the sixties, and about the Peace Corps work there. Stanley Karnow's *In Our Image: America's Empire in the Philippines* (Random House, 1989) gave me a long-term perspective on Philippine history. *The Peace Corps Experience: Challenge and Change, 1969–1976,* by P. David Searles (University of Kentucky Press, 1997) also centers particularly on the Peace Corps in the Philippines, and *One Grain of Sand: A Peace Corps/Philippine Experience* (Gasat Company, 1988) is a memoir by Steve M. Shaffer, a Peace Corps volunteer. Another charming memoir is *Ants Have No Taste,* by Juliet S. Blanchard (Vantage, 1980).

I have continued to study the German Democratic Republic, its politics and particularly its prison system. Some books that helped me on this volume were *Licensed to Spy: With the Top Secret Military Liaison Mission in East Germany,* by John A. Fahey (Naval Institute Press, 2002); *The Stasi: The East German Intelligence and Security Service,* by David Childs and Richard Popplewell (Washington Square, 1996); *Stasi: The Untold Story of the East German Secret Police,* by John O. Koehler (Westview press, 1999); and *A Guest of the State,* by John Van Altena Jr. (Henry Regnery Company, 1967).

Even though I lived in Seattle in the late sixties, I learned much and was reminded of specifics by reading Walt Crowley's *Rites of Passage: A Memoir of the Sixties in Seattle* (University of Washington Press, 1995). In studying the 1968 Eugene McCarthy campaign and the Democratic convention of that year, I read *The Selling of the President, 1968,* by Joe McGinniss (Trident, 1969); *The Year of the People,* by Eugene J. McCarthy (Doubleday, 1969); and *No One Was Killed,* by John Schultz (Big Table Publishing, 1969, reprinted in 1998).

I also wish to thank some friends who gave me great help by reading my manuscript and advising me. Mary Ellen Edmunds, well-known LDS speaker and writer, checked my facts on the Philippines in the late sixties and made some valuable suggestions. Richard Jeppesen, a Marine Corps officer and veteran of Vietnam, served as my "military expert," helping me make the boot camp and battle scenes more accurate. Several friends and family members once again gave me artistic and proofreading help: David and Shauna Weight; Pamela Russell; my sons, Tom and Rob; my daughter, Amy, and her husband, Brad Russell; and especially my wife, Kathy, who is always patient enough to read draft after draft (even though she's a very busy woman these days).

Let me explain one little matter, just in case you're wondering. The Institute Director at the University of Washington, when we first arrived there, really was "Brother Holland," as I call him in this book. Now we call him Elder. He has remained a wonderful friend, with his wife Patricia, and they are two of the people in this world I admire most.

Back in those Seattle years, Kathy and I became close friends with Jerry and Tina Adams, who were in our student ward. Jerry and I ended up finding jobs at the same university in Warrensburg, Missouri. Eventually we served in a bishopric together, and even though Kathy and I moved away from Missouri, we remained lifelong friends with Jerry and Tina. What we didn't expect was that "lifelong" would not be so long as we had anticipated. Jerry died this year, unexpectedly, at age sixty-three, and we miss him. I saw Jerry grow remarkably in his life. In his early sixties he became a patriarch and a sealer in the St. Louis Temple. I watched those callings refine his spirit, and my hope now is that during the balance of my life I can grow as much as he did in his. Tina told me that on the day of his death, she noticed my last book, *Troubled Waters*, on Jerry's desk, with a bookmark in it. I don't know why hearing that touched me so deeply, but it does seem to symbolize the connectedness that lasted so long in our lives. So I dedicate this book to his memory, and to our continued friendship with Tina. I don't know whether Jerry will ever get a chance to read this book—or finish the last one—nor do I think that's very important. I'm sure he has much more important things to do now. But this book, dedicated to him and Tina, is a way of thanking him, and thanking Tina, for shared lives and shared love.

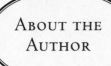

## ABOUT THE AUTHOR

**D**ean Hughes has published more than ninety books and numerous stories and poems for all ages—children, young adults, and adults.

Dr. Hughes received his B.A. from Weber State University in Ogden, Utah, and his M.A. and Ph.D. from the University of Washington. He has attended post-doctoral seminars at Stanford and Yale Universities and has taught English at Central Missouri State University and Brigham Young University.

He has also served in many callings, including that of a bishop, in The Church of Jesus Christ of Latter-day Saints. He and his wife, Kathleen Hurst Hughes, who has served in the Relief Society general presidency, have three children and nine grandchildren. They live in Midway, Utah.

If you liked this book, you'll love the *Children of the Promise* series by Dean Hughes!

What was life like during World War II? How did the war affect the lives of those who fought and those who kept the home fires burning? Find out in *Children of the Promise*, the carefully researched and beautifully written story of a family living through those turbulent years from 1939 to 1947. Meet the characters readers have come to love: Alex, who served a mission to Germany and returned to fight those among whom he had preached; Bobbi, a Navy nurse with a divided heart; Wally, a young rebel who finds his true path in the trials of a prisoner-of-war camp; and many others. *Children of the Promise* will touch your heart in an unforgettable way!

Volume 1: *Rumors of War*

Volume 2: *Since You Went Away*

Volume 3: *Far from Home*

Volume 4: *When We Meet Again*

Volume 5: *As Long as I Have You*